PRAISE FOR

D1409219

"*Original Syn* has one of the ....gs in modern
science fiction, with roots in real theories and ideas. Kander's
novel puts a bold new twist on the classic 'Romeo and Juliet'
story while also introducing a large variety of new characters
and concepts that keep the book feeling fresh and new."
— *Clarion-Ledger*

"A gripping story whose words pop off the page... humor,
love, masterful storytelling... Beth Kander paints a complex
picture of the human condition. *Original Syn* is a transfor-
mational piece of literature."
— Andrew Slack, Founder, The Harry Potter Alliance

"*Original Syn* is a heart-pounding book that will keep readers on their toes and turning the page."
— Mia Siegert, author of *Jerkbait*

"The novel's disparate worlds are revealed slowly, and the story is sophisticated enough to engage both adults and teens.
The book maintains a taut pace to the end, concluding with
a plot twist that turns the tables and stimulates interest in a
second volume, soon to come."
— *Foreword Review*

"*Original Syn* is the kind of book that stays with you long
after you've read its final pages; an unforgettable story that
pulls you in and takes you along for the ride."
— Francesca G. Varela, author of *Seas of Distant Stars*

BORN IN SYN

BORN IN SYN

BOOK TWO OF THE
ORIGINAL SYN TRILOGY

BETH KANDER

OWL HOUSE BOOKS

AN IMPRINT OF HOMEBOUND PUBLICATIONS

Quantity sales. Special discounts are available on quantity purchases by corporations, associations, bookstores, and others. For details, contact the publisher or visit wholesalers such as Ingram or Baker & Taylor.

All Rights Reserved
Published in 2019 by Owl House Books
Cover Design by Daniel Dauphin
Interior Design by Leslie M. Browning
ISBN 978-1-947003-50-7
First Edition Trade Paperback

Owl House Books is *an Imprint of Homebound Publications*
WWW.HOMEBOUNDPUBLICATIONS.COM

10 9 8 7 6 5 4 3 2 1

DEDICATION

This book is the second in a trilogy. It is something in-between. But it's in the middle moments that life tends to embed the most important stories of all. That's why this book is dedicated to the people who have shared liminal spaces with me. It is offered in gratitude to those who helped me get from where I was to where I needed to be, allowed me the privilege of standing alongside them at their own crossroads, and make every chapter more inspiring.

These stories are for you.

Especially you, Christy.

AS CAL CRAWLS through the window, he gives silent thanks for his abruptly miraculous circumstances. He feels as if he is in the midst of a prayer being answered. Everything about this moment feels surreal. Dreamlike. Too good to be true. Thus even in his heated exhilaration, his instincts warn him to be wary. His skin prickles slightly as a shadowy, foreboding question casts its looming pall over him:

How did I get here?

ANN ARBOR 1962 – 1963

CHAPTER 1: ERNEST

"**I**S TODAY THE DAY I GET TO MEET HIM, DADDY?"

"Hope so, buddy."

"Your eyes are saggy. Are you *exhausted?*"

"I'm tired, yes," said Ernest Fell. He wasn't in the habit of lying to his son, and the observant little boy would know if his father fibbed. And Ernest was, as a point of fact, exhausted.

The past week had been a blur of shuttling between home and hospital, dividing his time between the maternity ward where his wife Lila was recovering from a traumatic labor and the neonatal intensive care unit where his newborn son was breathing with assistance in a carefully monitored incubator.

Baby Nathan was born five days ago. Five weeks early.

"I want to meet my brother."

"I know, Howie. I know."

As he lowered himself to the floor to meet his son's eyes, Ernest's knees popped in a way they never had until he hit thirty. He held out his arms to his big-eyed toddler, and Howie crawled onto his father's lap, first nuzzling into his narrow chest, then sitting up and taking Ernest's tired and stubbly face into his chubby little hands.

"And I can see Mommy?"

"Yes, son," Ernest nodded, smiling at the feel of Howie's hands clasped on his cheeks, following the motion of his nod, up-down, up-down. "Yes. After we take a little nap."

"Ugh! I abhor naps!"

Despite his fatigue, Ernest chuckled. Howie was an early talker, deploying dozens of recognizable words before his first birthday and speaking in full sentences by sixteen months. The little sponge picked up vocabulary so rapidly, his parents could barely keep up with him. *Abhor* wasn't a word most two-and-a-half-year-olds used. But Howie wasn't most two-and-a-half-year-olds.

How is this kid mine?

Ernest taught English at the local community college. He was a lifelong reader and did his best to keep up with world affairs. But he wasn't a genius. Not like his son. Ernest frequently teased Lila about sleeping with Einstein the Milkman. But Howie looked just like Ernest; somehow he was responsible for this kid who started tossing off words like *abhor* before he was reliably potty-trained.

"Where'd you hear that one, Howie? 'Abhor'?"

"The Reverend," Howie says. "It means hate."

"I know what it means, son," Ernest said, his amusement immediately dampened. He knew he should be grateful that his parents had come in from Kentucky to help with Howie while he and Lila gave their attention to the new arrival. But dear God, he hoped his father wasn't planting any overly religious (or overtly racist) ideas into Howie's head.

"Do you abhor naps, Daddy?"

"No, I *adore* them."

"Ha. That's funny. Adore and abhor are rhyming opposites."

"That's right."

"I might adore and abhor having a baby brother."

A tired smile tugged at Ernest's lips. "Probably, yeah."

"Is Baby Nathan napping?"

"Well. Sort of. Baby Nathan is sleeping, and also getting medical treatment."

Ernest thought again of how lucky they were to be living in this time and place. The first full-scale neonatal intensive care unit was established just two years earlier, in 1960, in New Haven, Connecticut. Other university hospitals took quick cues from their friends over at Yale, University of Michigan chief among them. Living in Ann Arbor, with access to the university hospital where the doctors had learned from their colleagues in Connecticut and upgraded their care of premature infants, was a blessing, and not one Ernest took for granted.

If Lila had gone into labor five weeks early a generation ago—or even more recently, but somewhere remote, like the rural bluegrass farmlands where Ernest grew up—he might have lost both her and their baby. Instead, when Lila announced in a panic that her water had broken, Ernest was able to get her to the hospital within minutes. Five days later, Lila was recovering well, and their new son Nathan was warming in his incubator. Cared for by the best of modern medical technology, he was given a fighting chance. A chance to grow up big and strong, and brilliant, like his big brother Howie.

"Neat-o," Howie said when Ernest finished explaining to him about the difference between an incubator and an intubator. "Hey! Does Mommy abhor naps? Or adore them?"

"Adores them," Ernest assured him. "All grown-ups do."

"All grown-ups do what?"

Ernest's mother, Millie, shuffled into the kitchen. Millie was a classically constructed old Kentucky woman, wide-hipped, solid-shouldered, and serious-eyed. She used to be roughly attractive, but that was a long time ago.

Other than her helmet of hair, nothing about her was well maintained. Her daily garb consisted of battered pink slippers and an ankle-length flowered housecoat. Ernest was not sure exactly when his mother had decided that getting dressed for the day was overrated.

"All grown-ups love naps," Ernest said.

"*Adore* them," added Howie.

"Nothing wrong with naps," Millie agreed. "How's Lila?"

"Doing well. Doctors say she can come home, but she wants to stay until the baby can come home, too."

"And how's the baby?"

"Better."

"Five pounds yet?" Millie asked.

Millie had no medical training and very little formal education, but plenty of self-declared areas of expertise. She proclaimed earlier in the week that once the baby weighed five pounds, that would mean the Lord had seen fit to let him live. Five, for reasons unknown, was the magic number, ordained by God according to the Gospel of Millie. Five pounds meant life.

"Not yet. But he'll get there," Ernest said firmly. "Where's the Reverend?"

"Your father went out for a walk. Should be back soon."

"All right. Come on, buddy," Ernest lifted Howie from his lap, then set him down on the floor. Ernest rose unsteadily on his spidery-long legs, leaning against the countertop to balance himself. He stretched and yawned wide enough to split his face. "You want to come nap with Daddy?"

"No, thank you," Howie said politely.

"Right. Because you abhor naps. Guess you're not a grown-up just yet, Howie-boy."

"Soon enough," Millie sniffed.

"You got him if I grab some quick shut-eye?" Ernest asked.

"Sure. What we're here for," Millie nodded.

"Thanks, Ma," Ernest said, kissing her cheek. She *aw-shucksed* him away, but seemed girlishly pleased at the gesture. She picked Howie up, grunting at his weight. The boy was growing, while at the other end of the spectrum, Millie had begun her slow but steady shrink.

"You want Grandma to make you some cookies?"

"Cookies!" Howie clapped his hands.

With a grateful look to his mother, the yawning Ernest headed for the bedroom at the back of the one-story ranch home. He hadn't slept in close to thirty-six hours, and remaining awake was a losing battle. He was ready to surrender. Pulling open the door, he fell face-first onto his bed and was instantly asleep.

A knock at the door. Groaning, unsure how long he'd slumbered and aching for more rest, Ernest got up and opened the door. His father stood framed there, unlit pipe clenched between his teeth, steel-gray eyes fixed sternly on Ernest.

"'Bout time you got up, isn't it?" The Reverend asked.

The Reverend Richard Fell was known to everyone, including his own children—as the Reverend. A God-fearing man who feared little else, the Reverend was not a man to suffer fools. He was also not a man to change his mind, advocate for anything that altered the status quo, or trust anyone not found in a church pew come Sunday morning. He slept the sleep of the supremely self-righteous, and looked down on anyone whose beliefs did not align with his own.

All of which meant he and his son Ernest didn't see eye to eye on much.

"I just lay down," Ernest protested.

"You been down three hours," the Reverend corrected.

"Sonofa—"

"Don't finish that sentence, boy."

Ernest bit his tongue, reminding himself he didn't have the energy to fight with his father. The bouts were never brief. The long list of things for which the Reverend would never forgive his son—for going to college instead of seminary or the military, for marrying a Jewish war orphan, for woeful church attendance—rendered combat futile, anyway. Battle became meaningless when the larger war was already so long lost.

"Where's Howie?" Ernest rubbed his eyes, patted his pockets to make sure his wallet was there, started going through the mental checklist of what to grab before heading back to the hospital. He had only meant to nap for one hour, not three. Lila was expecting him—

"Howie's in the living room. Your mother's reading him Bible stories."

"I'm going to take him with me. To the hospital."

"You think that's a good idea, taking Howie to the hospital?"

The Reverend's tone clearly indicated it was not a good idea to take Howie to the hospital.

"Yes. He hasn't seen his mother in five days. And we can at least let him look at Baby Nathan through the glass. He wants to see his baby brother."

The Reverend clamped down harder on his pipe. Ernest walked past him, stopping briefly in the bathroom to splash his face with cold water before heading into the living room. Grabbing his keys off a bookshelf, he rattled them at his two-year-old.

Howie's head snapped up from the *Bible Stories for Young Readers* volume he was reading with his grandmother. His serious little face was even more innocent than the pale baby-faced prophets wearing striped robes and petting lambs on the cover of the bible book. Ernest made a mental note to hide that tiny tome before his hormonal wife came home from the hospital.

"I can come with you, Daddy?"

"If you're ready, buddy."

"Ready ready ready!" Howie crowed.

"Kiss your grandma," Ernest instructed.

Howie obediently kissed Millie, then without being told to do so, ran over to the Reverend. He wrapped his little arms around the Reverend's leg. The Reverend did not react.

For the entire seven-minute drive to the hospital, Howie peppered his father with questions. Questions about his mother, his baby brother, the doctors and nurses, what other patients were in the hospital for, how long people stayed in hospitals, would he ever need to stay in a hospital, had Mommy ever stayed in a hospital before. It was truly remarkable, how much conversational ground a talkative toddler could cover in a short amount of time.

Reaching the hospital, Ernest parked the old Chevy, then looked at his expectant boy.

"All right, Howie. Are you ready to meet Baby Nathan?"

Howie clapped his hands.

"Ready ready ready!"

CHAPTER 2: HOWARD

BIG.

That would be one word to describe the hospital. It was big on the outside, big on the inside, bigger than any other place Howie had seen. But "big" was an easy word. A baby word. He needed something better.

Enormous was better.

Howie silently ran through the list of all the alternative words he knew for "big." *Huge, enormous, gigantic, massive.* Those were all good words to describe the place. *Scary* was another good word, with all the strangers and people in masks. But he wasn't *too* scared, since Daddy would protect him. That made it less scary (*creepy, frightening, terrifying*).

Smelly, that was another accurate word for this place. Howie tried to think of another word for smelly. He'd heard a fancy one the other day. *Putrescent.* Yes. The big, scary hospital was putrescent.

"Was I born here, too, Daddy?" Howie asked his father as they walked down a long hallway.

"Sure were, buddy," his dad confirmed.

"Was the hospital putrescent back then, too?" Howie asked innocently.

His father stared at him, then said slowly: "Yes. Yes, it was."

They arrived at the room where Howie's mother was recovering. Howie was so glad and excited (*exuberant*) to know that she would be coming home soon. He was thrilled for his own sake but also for hers—who would want to be stuck here?

His father pushed open the door, and Howie ran in.

"Mommy!"

"Howie!"

His mother smiled at him and he beamed back at her. She was so beautiful. (*Gorgeous.*) He held up his arms for her to lift him, like she always did.

"Easy there, buddy," his father said, scooping him up from behind, momentarily startling Howie. "Mommy can't pick you up just yet, big boy. But I got ya. Here, I'll even bring ya in close for a kiss."

Daddy held Howie close to his mother, within inches of her face. Howie grabbed her face in his hands and gave her a kiss, a big loud smackeroo. She kissed him back, nuzzling his neck. She smelled familiar, warm and good and Mommy-like. Howie beamed.

"You don't smell putrescent, Mommy."

"Putrescent," she laughed. "Biggest word yet, Howie. Where'd you pick that one up?"

"I don't remember..."

"Think hard, Howie. You can always remember if you think really hard."

Howie scrunched up his little face, thinking hard. "It was when we went out to dinner. The lady at the next table said her toilet got all clogged and overflowed and her whooooooooole house was 'absolutely putrescent'!"

He imitated the old lady's quavering voice, which earned him another tinkling, incredulous laugh from his mother. His father chuckled, too, before kissing Mommy.

"We make smart babies, my love."

"We do," she agreed. "Should we all go visit the new one?"

"Yeah!" Howie yelled, earning a *shush* from his parents, who reminded him there were sick people in the hospital, and he had to use his indoor voice. He nodded, putting a finger to his lips and mouthing *sorry*.

His father put him down, and helped his mother ease herself out of the hospital bed. His mother gripped his father's arm, and he led her out into the hallway. Howie walked right next to them, careful not to trip them and careful to only use his indoor voice.

"Where do they keep the babies?" Howie stage-whispered.

"Well, some of the babies are just in a regular nursery unit," his mother explained, walking carefully and talking slowly. "But the really little babies who came early and need extra-special care, like our baby Nathan, are in something called the neonatal intensive care unit."

Howie worked through which words he knew and which he didn't. *Intensive* meant serious. So *intensive care* must mean really serious medicine. But he didn't know the other ones.

"What's neonatal?"

"*Neo* means *new*," his father answered.

"*Natal* means *baby*," his mother added.

"So it's for new babies who need serious medicine?"

His parents nodded, proud and pained.

When they reached the neonatal intensive care unit, the nurse on duty greeted them with a smile. She donned a pristine white uniform, and her hair was neatly flipped out at her shoulders.

"Hello, Mrs. Fell," she greeted them. "Mr. Fell. And you must be Howard."

"Howie," said Howie.

"Howie, of course," said the nurse. She had a nice face, wide and friendly. "I'm Nurse Nancy. Your parents talk about you all the time. They tell me you're a very good boy. Is that true?"

"Absolutely," Howie confirmed.

"'Absolutely!' What a big word for a little boy!"

His parents smiled politely, exchanging a subtle glance; *you have no idea.*

"Which one is my baby?" Howie asked Nurse Nancy. He liked how her name had two Ns. Nurse Nancy. Three Ns: *Nice* Nurse Nancy. Howie adored alliteration.

"I can show you. We'll all go look—" Nurse Nancy began, but then a doctor entered the observation area, clipboard in hand.

"Mr. and Mrs. Fell? If you have a minute, I'd like to speak with you."

"Of course, doctor," Howie's mother replied, looking worried.

"I want to see my baby," Howie insisted, looking nervously at his parents, afraid that they'd all have to follow the doctor into another room and he wouldn't get to meet Baby Nathan.

"I can take him to see, if you like?" Nurse Nancy smiled, and looked to Howie's parents for permission. They nodded, and she picked him up. "We'll be right over here when you're done talking with the doctor."

"Thanks," said Howie's father. "Be right back, buddy. Tell your brother hello for us."

His parents followed the doctor back toward the hallway. Howie didn't watch them go; he was too eager to see his baby. Nurse Nancy carried him to the observation window.

Howie's eyes widened. There were lots of babies on the other side of the glass. He counted quickly, *one, two, three... nine, ten... seventeen, eighteen*. Eighteen babies, each one in their own little environment, some of them with tubes, some with wires, all tiny.

Nurse Nancy pointed to the center of the room. Howie followed her finger, all the way to the very smallest baby.

To Howie's surprise, he almost looked purple. His eyes were closed, there was a tube in his mouth, and all sorts of equipment, wires, and labels all around him. He was encased in a box, surrounded by plastic and metal. Caged.

"Is that Baby Nathan?" Howie whispered, suddenly scared.

"Sure is," Nurse Nancy confirmed.

Howie's eyes filled with tears. "I don't like him being in there."

"Oh, now," the nice nurse said, gently. "He's safe here. The doctors and machines and medicines are all helping him get bigger and stronger."

"I want him to come home. I don't like him here." Howie shook his head, huffing and crying quietly, not throwing a fit but obviously upset. He kept his voice low, because it was a hospital and he had to use his indoor voice and didn't want to upset the neonatals. But his request was dead serious: "Take him out."

"We can't do that, honey," Nurse Nancy said.

Howie realized his mistake; he didn't say the magic word. Gulping for air between sobs, he said desperately: "Take him out, *please*."

"We can't do that."

"PLEASE!" Howie bellowed, unable to keep his voice down any longer. "PLEASE!"

Alarmed, Nurse Nancy turned to look for assistance, and was relieved to see the Fells hurrying toward her.

"Is everything all right?" Ernest asked, taking his sobbing son from the nurse's arms.

"I think seeing the baby in the incubator upset him," Nurse Nancy said apologetically. She conveyed concern, but also seemed a little bit irritated.

Not-so-nice Nurse Nancy.

Howie nodded, then buried his face in his father's chest. He wanted to forget seeing Baby Nathan like that, tiny and purple and in that incubator-thing. He wanted him to just be a baby. Just a regular, normal, healthy *baby.* His brother shouldn't be kept in a box like that. It was wrong. *(Incorrect, unnatural.)*

It scared Howie in a way he had no words to describe. He didn't like that feeling at all.

CHAPTER 3: LILA

L ILA GOLDEN FELL WASN'T THE KIND of woman who was good at making cakes. Nor was she good at baking, generally. Or crafting. Or décor. Homemaking: not her area of expertise.

This domestic deficiency made it difficult to socialize with the other women in the neighborhood. Like most young Ann Arbor wives, Lila was married to a professor. But her husband taught at the community college, not the university, which was one strike against her. Being a former career woman herself was another.

Lila used to be a reporter. When she found out she was pregnant with Howie, she stopped working. Four years later and now with two children, she began to fear she was not "taking a break," as she kept telling everyone. She was afraid she might have gotten stuck on the Mommy track. Lila loved Howie, and Nathan, too.

But damn, she missed deadlines, cranking out stories and pinning down sources. She missed the cigarettes, the cranky editors, the clacking typewriters and ink-stained fingertips. She was good at writing articles and punching up headlines.

She was *not* good at writing out flowery words on the pale buttercream landscape of a box-made vanilla cake. The violently blue icing looked jarring, jagged; the sugary letters were barely legible in their weak declaration—"*Happy 1ˢᵗ Birthday, Baby Nathan!*"

"Mama," Howie said, tugging on her apron strings. "Daddy isn't awake yet."

"It's early," Lila said, wiping a strand of hair from her forehead. The gesture left a bright blue streak of frosting she would not notice for another hour, at which point she would not care.

"Baby Nathan is sleeping, too."

"Yes, well, that's good. That's why Mommy is able to make this cake for his party later."

"Can I see?"

"Give me a minute, sweetheart."

"I'll be patient."

"Good." Lila gave her son a wobbly smile, embarrassed at the idea of him seeing her cruddy handwriting. Maybe she could fix it, adjust the "B," make that "y" a little loopier...

"Will there be a lot of people at the party?" Howie was a constant conversationalist. He was always talking, to anyone and everyone—his parents, neighbors, strangers, sometimes rocks or sticks if no one else was nearby. "Will it be a real soiree, like Grandma says?"

"Well, a pseudo-soiree, anyway," Lila says.

"What's 'pseudo'?"

"Your word of the day, Howie." Lila never believed in baby talk, despite her neighbors assuring her it was better to talk to babies at a level they understood. Technically, Lila *did* talk to her baby at a level he could understand; it was just a much higher level than most other babies.

She never used made-up words, or even searched for simpler words. She enjoyed finding clear definitions for words when she explained them to her son. It was like introducing him to a new friend. "Pseudo means… something artificial. A sham. An… imitation, trying to pass as the real thing. Usually a poor imitation, or something mimicked."

"Sue-dough," Howie said, sampling the word. "Pseudo. Good one. I like it. *Pseudo.* Why will it only be a pseudo-soiree?"

"Oh, ah, I was only kidding," Lila assured him, looking at the cake and realizing that repeated touch-ups of the letters had only rendered them more illegible. "It won't be a pseudo-soiree, it will be a real party. The Millers are coming, and the Helmanns, and the D'onofrios. And your dad's parents should be getting in town in time for the party, too."

"But your parents won't be here, because they're dead."

"Right. They won't be there because they're dead. If they showed up, it'd be creepy."

Lila was always cavalier about referencing her long-dead parents. She should have mourned them more; and she did, occasionally, fantasize about how wonderful they must have been. But she never knew them. They had the foresight to hand her off to some cousins who were fleeing Lithuania to start a new life in America; they put their baby daughter in the hands of those cousins, promising to come for her as soon as they could afford fare to the new world. Then they died in concentration camps before they could make good on that promise.

The cousins who brought Lila to America with them, David and Sarah Golden, were perfectly nice. But they hadn't really planned on the life sentence of a child. They provided her with what she needed, but not with much else. Maybe that's why Lila never did well with the other mothers in her neighborhood; she never had a relationship with her own.

"Are you done now? Can I see the cake?"

"Sure," Lila said, putting on a cheerful voice, lifting Howie to see her handiwork.

"That's a sad cake," Howard said.

"No, it's happy. It says 'Happy first birthday, Baby Nathan.'"

"I can read the words," her toddler reminded her. "I mean, mostly. That 'y' is basically just a blob, and that 'H' looks like a guillotine. It's a sad cake."

"Yeah, you're not wrong," she sighed. "Tell you what. Instead of sad, let's call it pseudo-happy. Now. I'm going to start setting the chairs up in the backyard. Why don't you read until your Daddy and brother wake up? If Baby Nathan is up first and starts crying, just come get me."

"Okay," Howie said agreeably, and trotted off to find his book.

Lila didn't want to know what book he was reading. The last one he finished was *The Adventures of Huckleberry Finn*. A toddler choosing Mark Twain over Dick and Jane was disconcerting, especially since he was raising some pretty astute questions about slavery. She was in trouble, having a kid that smart. One more thing she couldn't talk about with the other mothers.

Not that their children were unintelligent; Anita D'onofrio was a piano prodigy, and Jack Miller was "a math whiz" (according to Howie). But brainy babies didn't seem to be the other mothers' goal. For them, as long as their children were clean and well-dressed, quiet at all times, and said please-and-thank-you-ma'am, that meant they had Good Kids.

That was the goal: not creative kids, not brilliant kids, not thoughtful kids. Good Kids.

Rubbing her eyes, obliviously furthering the blue frosting smear all the way into her hairline, Lila took off her apron and walked out into the backyard. Earlier that week, in an uncharacteristically adept hostess move, she had remembered to pick up folding chairs from the Methodist church. They weren't members; Lila was Jewish and Ernest was faith-neutral (to the biblical-level fury of his father). But the pastor there was quite friendly and always offered the extra folding chairs for any neighbor's birthday, anniversary, or cookout.

The pastor offered the chairs without her even asking. It was when Lila was buying the boxed cake mix at the A & P, staring at the rows of brightly colored boxes, wondering if Betty Crocker and just adding water really could save the day, that the clergyman appeared.

"Someone's birthday?"

Out of context, it took her a minute to place him. A nondescript blond, somewhat short, athletic build. Easy enough to glance at and assume *high school teacher* or *someone else's husband*. But when he smiled, she recognized him: the pastor at St. Luke's.

"Yes, actually. How are you, pastor… reverend… father…?"

"James," he said easily. "Just James is fine, Mrs. Fell."

"Lila."

"Lila. Is there something confusing about the cake batter selection?"

"Everything about it," laughed Lila. "I'm not much of a baker."

"But for one of your boys, you'll make a cake."

"That's about it, yep."

"How old?"

"It's my younger one's birthday. Nathan. Turning one."

"Nathan. From the Hebrew, 'gift.' Great name," the minister said. His dark blue eyes were warm, framed in crinkles ushered in early by frequent laughter. With a practiced hand, he slid a box from the shelf and handed it to Lila. "Here. Basic yellow cake. Sure bet."

"Thanks," Lila said, just grateful to have the box in hand and the decision done.

"Say, if you need folding chairs, we have plenty going spare in our fellowship room," James said. "Loan 'em out for all sorts of neighborhood gatherings. You're welcome to them."

Lila took him up on the offer, stopping by the church the next day. With the minister's help, she crammed more than a dozen white-painted wooden folding chairs into the trunk of her rattling old Chevrolet. She invited him to join for the party, but he declined. Just as well. The fewer witnesses to her ugly cake, the better.

"Mommy?" Howie said, sounding plaintive.

"What are you doing out here, little man?"

"I'm hungry."

"Why didn't you ask Daddy to fix you some cereal?"

"He's still sleeping. He must be exhausted."

"Must be," Lila said, trying to hide her irritation. *That man better get his ass out of bed.* "I'll get you cereal, then we'll wake up your sleepy Daddy. Baby Nathan hasn't woken up yet, either? You haven't heard him crying?"

"He made one cry, then went back to sleep."

"Looks like our household is suffering from Rip van Winkle syndrome this morning."

"Not us!"

"Right. Not us. Come on, let's get you some cereal."

"Yeah!"

They went inside, and Lila poured Howie a bowl of Cheerios. Thankfully, this simple dish was Howie's favorite breakfast—and also his favorite lunch, and dinner. As he munched happily on the meal she didn't have to cook, Lila kissed the top of his sandy head.

"I'm going to go wake up your daddy."

But when she reached their bedroom, Ernest wasn't there.

Odd.

"Honey?"

She tried the bathroom next, knocking on the door, then pushing it open. Empty. Had he slipped outside, somehow? Gone to get the paper, run into a neighbor?

Deciding to check on the baby before expanding the search for her husband, Lila headed to the boys' room. Baby Nathan's crib had only recently been moved from Ernest and Lila's room into Howie's room, now known as "the boys' room." She twisted the dulled brass knob, pushed the door—and it stopped short, hitting something. She pushed harder, gaining some inches though still meeting resistance. Her stomach in knots, a sudden cold tingle running the length of her spine, neck to back and up again, she slipped through the door.

It took a moment to register what she was seeing, a long beat before she started screaming. Sprawled on the floor was her husband, pale, not breathing. Baby Nathan was still in his pajamas, sitting quietly in his crib, staring silent and dry-eyed at his fallen father.

CHAPTER 4: HOWARD

A FTER HIS FATHER DIED, Howie had a lot of questions. But on the morning of the funeral, the normally talkative three-and-a-half-year-old was silent. He didn't want to talk, he wanted to listen. To pay attention. To remember. He wanted to know the word, *funeral*. What it really meant.

His grandmother Millie and his grandfather the Reverend were awake and drinking coffee in the kitchen when Howie woke up. When Millie asked him if he wanted her to make him eggs or bacon or pancakes, Howie shook his head and pointed at the pantry where the cereal was kept. He wasn't talking. He decided that as soon as he woke up. He would be quiet (*hushed, inaudible*).

When his grandmother fixed him a bowl of Cheerios, he avoided crunching them. He took them out one by one, letting the o's dissolve in his mouth silently.

"Good boy, Howie," his grandmother said every few minutes, absently. Like she was reminding one or both of them that they were still there. The Reverend said nothing throughout breakfast; his gaze was locked on his coffee, his jaw just plain locked.

The Reverend remained silent as he drove them to the funeral home; over the course of the short drive, Howie's grandmother told him seven more times that he was a good boy. It was around the third time she murmured *such a good boy* that Howie wondered where his baby brother was. He knew his mother was at the funeral home already. Someone else must have Baby Nathan. But who?

As his grandparents ushered him to the front pew of the Bowen Family Funeral Home, Howie looked around to see where his mother was—if the funeral was starting, she should be there, next to him. She promised. Was she checking on Nathan? Howie's brother probably shouldn't be there for the funeral. He was usually quiet, but when upset, he'd let out an ear-piercing shriek that made everyone jump. Then Mommy would coo to the baby *everything's fine, everything's fine.*

But that was a lie, Howard suddenly realized. Everything was not fine. His father had died, and his mother had just let it happen. Just like that.

Why didn't Mommy keep Daddy safe?

Howie used to think his parents were invincible. Maybe even magical. But his father was not invincible, and his mother was obviously not magical. Those were stupid baby thoughts. Howie grew angry at himself.

"Howie," his grandmother said, patting his head too roughly, taking him by the shoulders and smashing his face into her soft stomach. "It's going to be okay. You're going to be okay."

Smothered in the black polyester fabric of his grandmother's dress, Howie hated hearing those words again: *You're okay, it's okay.* Those were lies. (*Fibs. Falsehoods.*)

"Quiet, Millie," snapped the Reverend. "It's about to start."

Howie frantically pulled away from his grandmother, swiveling his head to find his mother. He wanted to ask his grandparents where she might be, but he also didn't want to break his vow of silence for the day.

There she is.

Dressed all in black, face pale as the marble floors in the funeral home lobby, Howie's mother made her way up the aisle. She looked thinner, older, not like herself. Howie almost burst into tears at the sight of her. It looked like all the joyful parts of her got left behind, and only the sad, tired parts of her showed up for the funeral. Like she was impersonating herself and failing.

She looks like a pseudo-Mommy.

She caught his eye. Desperate to do something, *anything*, to make her feel better, Howie blew her a kiss. It was something he'd seen his father do to cheer her up before. She stared at him, and tears began pouring down her cheeks. But then she reached up to catch the kiss, and held it to her wet cheek. Then someone walked up to her, blocking her from Howie's view.

Howie started to panic, but then there she was, even sadder, paler, and thinner up close. Howie was relieved that at least his mother still smelled like herself. A little saltier; all those tears. It was Howie's dad who taught him that tears have salt in them, telling Howie to lick his own tears after an uncharacteristic tantrum. That fascinating bit of information had ceased the tears immediately, and as Howie licked the briny sadness from his fingers, he filed away forever that tears were salty. It was one of the last things his father taught him, though not the very last.

"Howie," his mother whispered. "You're the only person I want to see today."

The room was packed with people. And all of them seemed to want to talk to his mother. So he knew she'd have to see more than just him, but he decided against telling her that. It might just make her sadder. And anyway, he'd taken a vow of silence for the day. So he just moved a little closer to her, nodding. She put an arm around him, straightened her back and stared blankly at the front of the room, where a rickety old preacher-man was taking his position at the lectern.

"Friends and family of Ernest Fell," said the preacher, looking out at the assembled. "We are united in mourning this sudden, tragic loss. Today we will remember the life of Ernest Fell. Ernest was a God-fearing man, who loved the Lord above all else. He carried Jesus in his heart."

Howie was confused. He was pretty sure that his father loved him, and his baby brother, and his mother, above all else. His Daddy may have loved the Lord—he taught them the *now I lay me down to sleep, pray the Lord my soul to keep* before bedtime, and all. But he had never mentioned Jesus. Not to Howie. The little boy began to worry that there may have been some sort of mix-up, and that this preacher was accidentally sharing the details of someone else's life.

Howie glanced nervously at the Reverend, who was staring forward, eyes locked on the preacher. Every few minutes, he sort of nodded. Howie then looked at his mother, her eyes damp with unshed tears. Howie was pretty sure she was not hearing a word the preacher-man said. She was too far away to listen. Her body was next to Howie, but her mind was somewhere else.

With Daddy, thought Howie. *Wherever he really is, that's where Mommy wants to be, too.*

Not with me. With him.

"...and now, let us pray together for our Brother in Christ."

The preacher gestured, and everyone rose. Squeaking pews and rustling shoes echoed dully in the funeral home's bland sanctuary.

Then the preacher did some sort of call-and-response prayer. Half of the assembled muttered along (the Reverend and Millie among the mutterers; Howie and his mother among the silent).

"We may be seated," the preacher finally said, and everyone sat heavily. "Now. I'd like to take a few minutes to reflect more deeply on the life of our friend Ernest."

Whose friend? Howie thought. *Your friend? You never even met him. My father was not your friend. You're a liar.*

Howie decided, right then and there, that he abhorred funerals. He would live as long as possible, and die when he was an old man. But he would never want to have a funeral. He wouldn't want anyone to talk about him when he was dead.

Because they'd probably get it all wrong anyway.

DALLAS 1963

CHAPTER 5: FOUR

EDWARD ADAMS KENSINGTON IV tugged at his signature ten-gallon cowboy hat, pulling it a little lower over his eyes. It was drizzling all morning, and although the sun was teasing, seductively suggesting that she just might step out and show a little leg, she hadn't delivered on the promise yet.

The man in the cowboy hat was best known simply as "Four." By the time he was born, the fourth of his name, his family had already run through every iteration of Edward—his great-granddaddy was Edward, his grand-daddy was Eddie, his father was Ed. Rather than go with a pansy derivative name like Ted, Edward Adams Kensington IV went by Four.

Most of his family still lived back out East, but he and his brother Bradley moved out West to oversee the family's oil interests in the great state of Texas. His Connecticut relatives saw the West as a no man's land, a place wild and uncultured, the rough-and-tumbleweed antithesis of their high-society lives. Four was just fine with them keeping their high-and-mighty distance.

He immersed himself upon arrival, wearing the hat and the boots, adding a drawl, cultivating a moneyed-cowboy image. Had they deigned to set foot in the Lone Star State, his East Coast family would have damaged his credibility in his adopted home state. He and Brad were built for Texas. They'd been somewhat out of place in Connecticut, but they were "Texas naturals," as Four would tell anyone who asked (and anyone who didn't).

"American by birth, Texan by the grace of God," Four cracked as often as he could.

Four knew he'd never move back East. And if he wanted to be a long-term player in Texas, he needed to keep a high profile. Be seen where he needed to be seen. That's why he was getting his good hat damp in the stubborn half-assed rain. The president would be coming through Dallas today, and the whole damn town was showing up just to wave at the guy. Well, the guy and his wife. Jackie Kennedy was at least as popular as the man she'd married, and most of the folks lining the streets were probably there to catch a glimpse of her.

Four wasn't a fan of Jackie; he was a Marilyn man. He also wasn't a big fan of Kennedy. The guy was too warm with those Civil Rights nut jobs, letting the country sink into the hands of inferiors. Not tough enough, abroad or at home, if you asked Four. But Four respected the office. Moreover, he believed in playing the game. If he sat in his office while every other mover and shaker was rubbing elbows, staring at JFK and Jackie, he might miss out on important conversations.

Brad appeared at Four's elbow, adjusting his own hat, which was elaborately decorated with a wide bright band inlaid with turquoise, matching his similarly-patterned belt. Bit feminine for Four's taste, but he didn't comment on his brother's attire.

"Rain looks like it's lettin' up."

"It better," Four said. "I'm not gonna stand in the damn drizzle all day just to wave at those godawful Kennedys."

"Sure you will, 'cause everyone else sure as hell is," Brad grinned. "Think we'll get a good view of Jackie?"

Four shrugged. He didn't understand his brother's fascination with the first lady—or why the whole stupid country found her so intriguing. Jackie looked like every woman back up in Connecticut. Manicured, petite, demure, jacketed and hatted and boring as hell. Marilyn, now, she was a show-stopper. That woman was the one thing he and the president agreed on.

Brad nudged Four. "Look, see. Rain stopped."

So it had; the flirty sun was beaming down, the temperature was rising. Forecast had said it'd get near on up to seventy today, a warm day for November, even in Dallas. The weather itself seemed intent on impressing JFK and Jackie, proving to the East Coast-born first couple that the Southwest had its charms.

"Yep," Four drawled. "Shapin' up to be a nice day after all."

"Speakin' of shapin' up," Brad said, his voice falsely casual. "Things are shapin' up pretty well with Sue Ellen Matterhorn. Her father's eatin' outta my hand, and so's she. Think I'm gonna go ahead and let her pick out a ring."

"Really?"

Four doubted his brother was actually interested in the reedy, androgynous Matterhorn girl, but her family was powerful in Dallas. Big landowners, lots of oil connections, and a solid old Texas name to boot. Brad marrying her would be a strategic boon. And it wasn't as if he would ever be truly interested in any other woman, either, so might as well marry up.

"Can't get a better name than Matterhorn."

Four nodded, slowly. "All right. If you're sure."

"Pressure's on you now, boy-o," Brad winked. "Any prospects yet?"

"I'll find someone."

"Don't look for a Marilyn. Look for a Jackie."

"I'm lookin' for both, rolled into one," Four said.

"Good luck," Brad chuckled. Squinting, he raised a hand in reply to someone who spotted him across the way. "That's Joe Fordham, over there. Said he had something he wanted to talk with me about. Find you later?"

"Sure," Four said, and watched his brother lope off to talk business. Maybe business and pleasure, given the lingering handshake Brad exchanged with the small, trim Joe Fordham.

And somehow he's getting married before I do.

Four had to find his mythical Jackie-Marilyn match sometime soon. The Lone Star State did not value the single. If Four didn't settle down, he'd become the brother people whispered about instead of Brad.

"Hey there, Four."

At the sound of the molasses-thick drawl, Four turned to see Frederick Andrews. Andrews was old Dallas money; he called himself a cowboy, but he didn't herd cattle, he owned them. A hell of a lot of them. And a hell of a lot of land. Rumor was, he also had a blindingly beautiful set of daughters.

Frederick Andrews turned on the thick Texas shtick even more than Four himself, which Four found irritating (regardless of the fact that unlike Four, Andrews was actually a born and raised Texan). He clapped his hamlike hand onto Four's shoulder. Three of his fingers boasted large gold rings. The weight of the meaty embrace might have thrown some people off balance, but Four held his own.

"Mr. Andrews," Four smiled, managing a shrug that slipped the other man's big hand off Four's shoulder and into his hand for a brusque, hard-gripped shake. "Good seein' you out here. Figured you'd be up in a buildin' somewhere, not slummin' it with us down here by the street."

"Well, like 'em or not, I want to be as close to Jack and Jackie as I can be. You can smell the power from here, tell you what! Who knows, get close enough—maybe some of their luck'll rub off on me."

"Don't think you need any more luck than you got already goin' for you, Mr. Andrews."

"Don't know 'bout that," Andrews scoffed. "Everyone can use a little more luck."

"You a Kennedy man?" Four asked, already knowing the answer.

"Nah," said Andrews. "No real man is. But no harm in smilin' at the White House."

"S'pose not," Four agreed, and they shared a knowing half-smile.

"Tell you what, parade's still a good ways off," Andrews said. "If you'll give up your spot here, I'll take you over to my piece of real estate. Right by the route. Gloria wanted to be sure we'd be right up there by Jackie. Just loves the woman. Speaking of women, I think it's high time I introduced you to my daughter Annabelle."

This piqued Four's interest. The alluring beauty of the Andrews girls was almost as legendary as their father's fierce protection of them. An introduction to meet Annabelle was likely an introduction to court her, which was not an opportunity to be overlooked.

"Be my pleasure," Four said quickly, in what was undoubtedly the sincerest statement he'd ever made to Frederick Andrews. Andrews winked and gave a *follow-me* jerk of his head. He strode confidently through the crowd, lesser mortals making way and giving the powerful man a wide berth.

Andrews wasn't kidding about the "real estate" his wife had secured for them being prime: Dealey Plaza was crowded as could be, but the Andrews family was right up on Elm Street near the intersection at Houston, as close as the Secret Service had let anyone get to the route. Four was about to compliment the spot, but then he saw her: Annabelle Andrews.

The world stopped moving. The swelling crowd went silent. She was everything.

Head to toe, Annabelle was stunning. Shining blond hair, blue eyes, fair skin just peachy enough to banish any possibility of pale blandness. Slim but buxom. It was as if someone had custom-built her to meet the exact design specifications Four would've laid out in his blueprints for a bride.

"Annabelle, baby girl," Andrews said. As she drew near, Four noted that she was at least a foot shorter than him, which added to her appeal. This woman was something to be pulled in beside him, tucked under him, protected.

"Papa," she said, kissing Andrews' cheek.

"This here is Four—er, Edward Kensington. The fourth. Goes by Four."

"I like a good nickname," Annabelle purred, flirtatious but demure, head down, eyes up.

"Pleasure to meet you, Miss Andrews," Four said, tipping his hat, wondering if he should remove it. He knew the rules for indoors, but an outdoor introduction to a lady like this presented a new circumstance for the man who only recently adopted the cowboy hat.

"Annabelle," she said. "Please just call me Annabelle."

Anything you want, you say 'please' like that, you're damn well gonna get it.

Frederick Andrews burst out laughing, a big, hearty, showy laugh. Annabelle giggled. That's when Four realized that his last thought, which he'd intended to keep internal, had in fact been said aloud.

"I'm sorry," Four said, reddening and hating the feel of that flush. "I didn't mean to—"

"Hoo, no, boy! Ha!" Andrews chortled, downright delighted. "You got that right, I tell you what! This one's had me wrapped round her pretty little finger since day one, and that's just the way it's gotta be for Annabelle!"

Four allowed himself a sheepish smile, which Annabelle returned. He wondered how many other men her father had introduced her to like this, and how they might compare to him. He was glad for his height, his good teeth, his enviably strong jaw. He knew he was a good-looking man, successful, savvy—but Annabelle's standards might well be as high as his own.

"She's too young for you, right now," Andrews warned Four, right in front of the girl. As if she were one of his prize breeding stock, paraded out before a potential buyer. "You're gonna have to give it a good few years, you take a shining to this one."

"Yessir," Four said, wondering just how young she was (seventeen, sixteen? Surely not fifteen?) and how long he'd have to wait. Whatever the answer might be, one year or some sort of biblical seven-year sentence, he'd wait.

"Good man. C'mon, then, son, and I'll introduce you to Gloria and the rest of my girls. Just wanted to get this introduction underway first. Never was much one for poker. I like cards out on the table at the very start of the game."

For the next hour, Four socialized with all of the Andrews clan. He knew these first impressions mattered most; that these people might well be his future in-laws. He respectfully acknowledged Mrs. Gloria Andrews, and each of the beautiful daughters (of which there were five), but always locked eyes with Annabelle between introductions.

He learned that Annabelle was, in fact, only fifteen years old. *Damn!*

Four was only a few years north of twenty, himself, but that still put a decade between them. And meant he'd be closing in on thirty before he'd be allowed to marry the girl. But if that was the case, so be it. Four always did set his sights on the long game. Just as he acquired business interests and put long-term prospects over short-term profits, he'd acquire this girl.

"Oh, look!" Gloria Andrews chirped. "Here, they're coming!"

They all pressed closer toward the street, straining to see the first couple. Four made sure to secure a spot beside Annabelle, their hips almost touching, everything in his body pulling him like a magnet toward hers.

"You a Jackie fan?" he whispered to her.

"Mrs. Kennedy is incredible," Annabelle said, then dropped her voice lower and added, just for him: "But every girl needs a little streak of Marilyn in her, don't you think?"

And so Four was staring at the beautiful creature, and not at the convertible, when the entire world changed with the crack of a gun and the screams of the crowd at Dealey Plaza under a bright and obliviously shining sun.

ANN ARBOR 1964–1968

CHAPTER 6: NATHAN

"**P**OOR THING, DO YOU MISS YOUR DADDY?"

The woman asking Nathan the question had a stupid face, saggy, with lipstick drawn way past the real line of her lips, and pathetically sympathetic eyes. She was standing in line behind them at the post office making small talk with Nathan's mother, who had accidentally let slip she was a widow. This cued the dumb woman to speak to Nathan.

"No," Nathan said, realizing it was true, though he'd never really thought about it before.

He looked at his mother, but she wasn't listening to him or to the stupid stranger. One of the two blue-shirted postal clerks had motioned her up to the counter, and she was asking for stamps, handing over a crumpled bill and some pre-addressed envelopes.

"Oh," the moron woman said, not knowing how to respond to the tiny child's confession that he did not miss his dead father. Then the other postal worker motioned for her to come up to the counter, and she looked relieved to scurry away from the disconcerting toddler.

Nathan unsettled people even when he wasn't giving the wrong answer to obvious questions. He was small for his age, and quiet. One might mistake his demeanor for good manners, since he truly embodied old idioms like *children should be seen and not heard* and *do not speak unless spoken to*—but really, he just found most people beneath his attention.

Nathan rarely spoke. But he was constantly assessing, observing, and thinking. From early on he was building schemas far beyond *red ball* and *the stove burns*. His mind whirled constantly, in stark contrast to his physicality. He moved slowly, deliberately, like he was carrying something hot. Perhaps his body feared spilling the crammed contents of his mind.

I don't miss my father.

He knew he should miss his father, although he wasn't certain why that was an expectation. Still, knowing that his answer was met with disapproval, he considered the implication. He wasn't sure if the problem was that he didn't miss his father, or that he *admitted* to not missing his father. Nothing to be done about the former, but he could mitigate the latter.

Nathan did not attend his father's funeral, but that wasn't his choice. He was barely a year old. An infant. While his mind was already firing away, his legs were not, and his presence or absence anywhere was entirely dependent upon others. If someone had carried him to the funeral, he would have attended, like it or no. Instead, he was left with a sitter. Either way, he could not be blamed for not attending the funeral.

But he was to blame for his father's death.

No one knew he was his father's murderer, but that didn't matter. Intention had little to do with outcome. Nathan's actions—whatever his intent—led to his father's demise.

That morning, one year ago, Nathan had awoken hungry. Ravenously hungry. And he hated screaming. It hurt his throat, purpled his face, sometimes made him accidentally fill his diaper, adding insult to injury. When he needed something, he did not throw the typical infant temper tantrum. He made one loud sound, almost a bark, and someone always responded. So that morning, he barked.

His father answered the call, clodding awkwardly down the hallway on his too-long legs. But then the footsteps stopped, just short of Nathan's room. At the bathroom just next door. Through the thin wall separating the rooms, Nathan heard the distinct sound of a gush of urine hitting toilet water. This irked Nathan.

His father, stopping to pee on the way to Nathan's bedroom. Giving preference to his own needs before making sure that Nathan's needs were met. That was not the arrangement. Parents cared for children. Children's needs came first. *That* was the deal.

Nathan considered letting out a second sharp bark, but decided against that course of action. Instead, he gripped the bars of his crib, hauling himself up on his fat weak baby legs. The crib was old; it had been his brother's, and his father's before that. It was made with thick, heavy wood, with wide bars—twice as wide as the gaps between each bar, making it an effective prison for the thick-bodied infant.

His unreliable balance tilted Nathan back and forth. The slight rocking caused his fingers to slip from the thick bars. He fell back onto this mattress, and hated the squelching sound his wet diaper made. He was so angry, sitting in the wet cloth while his father peed a few feet away.

Not. Fair.

In his crib, Nathan had several toys. Silly baby things, none of which interested him. A teddy bear, some wooden alphabet-letter blocks, and a bright red fire truck. No one knew yet that you weren't supposed to put babies to bed with toys; that it was a hazard to do so. Nathan never hurt himself sleeping with the toys. He shoved them into a corner and avoided them. But he did know that stepping on them hurt; he'd seen his mother and father step on them and let loose a series of whispered words he knew he shouldn't have heard.

He wanted to make his father say those words.

He wanted to hurt him.

To punish him.

Nathan grabbed the blocks, wrapping his chubby fingers around them. He tried to hold two in one hand, and use his other sausage of an arm to pull himself up on the rail of the crib. It didn't work. Down the hall, he heard the toilet flush.

Faster.

Nathan released his grip on the blocks and went instead for the fire truck. It was heavier, but easier to maneuver. He shoved it against the bars of his crib, positioning himself under it, so it balanced on his head and shoulders. Then he carefully gripped the bars, slowly stood up, then let go of the bars and before falling back down, shoved upwards with his hands, pushing the raised fire truck just enough to send it toppling over the edge of his crib.

It landed a mere two feet away.

Nathan almost wailed. It was too close to the crib. His father would easily avoid it. A wasted effort—but then his father stumbled in, rubbing his eyes and not looking at his feet. He made his way to the baby's crib and stepped square on the truck.

"Shit!" Ernest Fell swore, the muted syllable barely escaping from his lips before he stumbled, pitched forward, and smacked his head hard on the wide edge of the heavy wooden crib. Without making another cry, he thudded dully to the floor.

Nathan didn't mean for his father to die. He wanted him to hurt his foot, not smash his head. His goal was a fall, not a fatality. It was Nathan's first lesson in accidental outcomes; in the collateral damage that can come when trying something new.

It was also a lesson in how quickly things can change. When Ernest Fell walked into Nathan's room, he was one thing: a person. When he hit his head and stopped breathing, stopped moving, stopped being, he was no longer a someone, but a something: a body, empty and vacant.

That was what they buried. Just an empty body.

Why would he miss that?

Everyone assumed Ernest Fell died of a heart attack. There was no reason to suspect foul play, and autopsies weren't really done in situations like that. Not back then. So Nathan's crime went entirely undetected. Even he didn't think about it much. Only at moments like this one, when an entirely unsuspecting party asked him about his father's death.

"Okay, Nathan, let's go home," his mother said, shifting him from her left hip to her right hip. Her eyes were far away. He could tell she was already planning her next nap. "Your brother will be home from the neighbor's soon. I'll make us all TV dinners and maybe we'll watch a show tonight. There's a show I think you and Howie will like. It's called 'I've Got a Secret.'"

The title of the show intrigued two-year-old Nathan. After all, young as he was, the little boy already had a massive secret he'd never share with anyone.

CHAPTER 7: LILA

O N THE SECOND ANNIVERSARY of her husband's death, Lila Golden Fell went to his grave. Going to the cemetery was what she was supposed to do; everyone said so. But no one told her what to do once she got there. So Lila just stood and stared at the stone monument, flanked by both of her small sons. Nathan was silent. Howie was unabashedly sobbing.

I should comfort him, she thought dully. But she didn't know how.

She was thirty and a widow. The very word seemed to age her. *Widow.* It hung on her like a thick-linked chain, weighing her down, limiting her ability to move. She stood there reading and re-reading the name of the man she married, carved letter by letter into unforgiving granite. Staring at the grave of the man who promised to grow old with her, she felt her own aging process lurch forward; felt her skin wrinkle, her heart harden, each strand of dark hair inch its way toward dull gray resignation.

"I miss Daddy," wailed Howie. Five years old, having lived fully half his life without his father, he still asked about Ernest daily. *What would he be doing if he was here right now? What new word would he teach me today? What would he have bought you for your birthday this year?* Those questions from Howie used to cause Lila physical pain, but eventually she numbed to them. But his keening that morning was harder to ignore. He raised the volume: "I.... missssss Dadddyyyyyyy!"

"Howie! Hush your mouth. You're yelling loud enough to wake the dead!"

"Dangerous place to do that. All these folks wake up, place might get a little crowded."

Lila jumped, startled by the voice behind her. Turning around, her alarm quickly dissipated. She hadn't seen those blue eyes since they were looking down from the lectern at her husband's funeral, but they remained unmistakable.

"Reverend James?"

"I'm sorry. That was a terrible joke, inappropriate—"

"It's fine," Lila said. "No need to apologize. You remember my boys, Howie, Nathan—"

Nathan kicked at the dirt and did not acknowledge the preacher. Howie looked up at him, still huffing with grief. Reverend James handed Howie a handkerchief, which Howie quickly smeared with tears and boogers. When Howie politely tried to return it, the man of the cloth gestured for Howie to keep the filthy rag.

"Two years today?"

"Yes, Reverend."

"James, please," the minister urged.

"James," Lila repeated. "Are you here for a funeral, or...?"

"Not today," he said. "I'm just—visiting. At least once a week I come to the cemetery and pick a row, and visit that whole row, grave by grave. Offer prayers. Reflect on the next stage of our journey. Death is a master teacher. We're all scared of the final exam, of course, but I find that—as with all subjects—studying can help take away some of the fear."

This sentimental confession seemed odd to Lila. She assumed all Christian clergymen were like her father-in-law: men of scripture who worshipped the letter of the law and enforced God's will with rigid, unforgiving rigor. She didn't expect gentler philosophy, let alone humor. She looked a little more closely at James, his thin buttery hair, his warm blue eyes. He looked more interesting than she remembered. Not more handsome, but more—yes, *interesting*.

"Well," she said. "I guess when it comes to death, I'm like most students. I put off studying. Figure I'll just cram, right at the end. Of course, our family got an unexpected pop quiz…"

"Some teachers aren't fair," the minister nodded. *Ah yes, Death really was quite the cantankerous old so-and-so.* Or maybe he meant God, not Death, was the unjust instructor.

"I'm hungry," Nathan said out of nowhere, loud and demanding.

"Right, okay, we can go," Lila said. Then, impulsively, she said to the reverend: "Would you like to join us for dinner?"

"I'd love to," he said, triggering an instant panic in Lila.

The house is a shambles. All I have in the kitchen is peanut butter and Wonder Bread. Nathan will say something cruel. Howie will wail the whole time. I'll come apart at the seams. This is the worst idea I have ever had.

Lila realized she was staring at the reverend, as if he had just invited himself. She knew all too well that she had one of those faces that required careful monitoring; her default expression was dour, particularly in widowhood.

"We'll have to stop at the grocery on the way home," Lila said quickly, forcing a smile to sweeten any sour look she accidentally gave the poor man. "And you'll have to forgive the house. It looks like sh—sure is messy, is what I mean, but if that doesn't bother you, well, then…"

"Fortunately, I'm in the forgiveness business," smiled the minister.

He walked with Lila and her sons to the A&P. They picked up some vegetables, a chicken, and cereal for Nathan (who would currently eat nothing else). Then they went home. Nathan went to his room to do whatever it was he did, alone in there. Howie hunkered down with a handful of Cheerios and the book he was reading (Felix Salten's *Bambi: A Life in the Woods*).

James unloaded the groceries, then asked for a paring knife. Lila had no idea what a paring knife was, so she just slid open the cutlery drawer and gestured for the preacher to take what he needed. He did, and then expertly sliced the vegetables; cleaned, patted dry, and seasoned the chicken; turned on the oven. He kept a running chatter the whole time, as he rattled pots and pans, sprinkled salt, and generally gave the appearance of knowing what he was doing in the kitchen.

Lila simply watched and listened for the first five minutes, be-fore excusing herself to set the table. Before setting it, she had to clear it of the debris of their past week—pieces of cereal, aban-doned crayon drawings, unopened mail. She then hastily tidied the dining and living areas and even shoved some laundry into the hallway hamper. When she returned to the kitchen, the chicken was roasting alongside the vegetables and her home miraculously smelled like a meal.

"Where did you learn to cook?"

James shrugged. "I wanted to be a chef, before I decided to go to seminary."

"Maybe you should've stuck with the chef plan. Surely God wants His people well-fed."

"Well," James smiled. "There's always time for a second chance, isn't there?"

"I'm hungry," said a small, crisp voice, startling them both.

Nathan was standing in the doorframe, toeing the line between the dining room and the kitchen, scrawny arms folded against his chest. Howie was standing behind him, waiting to see what his little brother's demand might yield.

"I think it's a few more minutes until dinner'll be ready—" Lila started, and then her young son cut her off, aiming his next statement at the interloper in their home.

"Tell me what you made."

A command, not an inquiry.

James was unfazed. "Wasn't sure what you'd like. So I made roasted chicken and seasoned vegetables, and also some batter for pancakes, which you can have tonight or save 'til tomorrow or—"

"Cereal," Nathan interrupted, defiant and definitive.

Lila felt trapped by her petulant child, as always. She knew he needed discipline, but he'd had such a hard life. Born sick. Father died. He was so easily upset, and who could blame him? So she said nothing when he spoke rudely to their guest; she just guiltily watched James' face fall. To his credit, the clergyman quickly recovered.

"Sure, Nathan. Cereal, coming right up. Howie, how about you? What do you want for dinner?"

Lila felt Howie pressing into the back of her legs, peeking around her to look up at James and the various pots and pans deployed for the first time in months. Lila knew Howie was torn. His loyalty would make him want to take his brother's side. But he also loved chicken.

"I'll have some chicken," Howie whispered at last. And then, louder: "And some cereal."

James' resigned smile became a genuine one, and he winked at Lila.

"Chicken and cereal," he said. "Sounds great to me."

"Thank you," mouthed Lila.

The evening's feast of chicken and cereal, with vegetables en-joyed by the adults (their praises loudly sung by Lila, in a fruitless attempt to coax her children into taking a bite), became the first of a series of dinners.

The next week, James called Lila before coming by; week after that, he simply arrived with a bag of groceries—featuring a prom-inent box of Cheerios poking from the top of the grocery sack. Proving that "tradition" could be defined as "doing the same thing more than three times," the fourth Sunday evening when James arrived Lila had already set the table.

At some point, a few months in to the arrangement, Lila start-ed calling James each Saturday to ask if there was anything he wanted her to pick up at the grocery. But he insisted on bring-ing his own ingredients. Howie and Nathan grudgingly accepted the weekly dinner. Nathan hated James on principle, from day one, and never relented—despite the fact that Reverend James brought a weekly offering of Nathan's prized cereal. Nathan ate the cereal. He just didn't award the preacher any brownie points.

Howie, on the other hand, liked James. He began looking for-ward to the Sunday dinners. Although he did feel the need to pe-riodically remind his mother that the reverend was not as good or smart or interesting as his father had been.

"He doesn't want to replace your dad," Lila assured her son, wondering if he did.

She couldn't tell if James was interested in that scenario—in being the boys' father; in being her husband, or lover, or anything beyond friend. He was so respectful, so unassuming. He just showed up and cooked. Not just that, though; he showed up and talked. Listened. Made her feel, for the first time in two years, both interesting and interested. She was relieved to have some-one who saw her as more than That Poor Widow. It was a balm, soothing her crone-fears, smoothing some of the imagined wrin-kles from her skin.

"You were a reporter?" James asked, over a dinner of grilled salmon and asparagus.

The first course had been cereal for the boys, and one glass of good red wine for each of the grown-ups. Then both boys turned up their noses at the fish and went off to read and play. Alone, with real food and real conversation and a second glass of wine in-hand, Lila felt dangerously close to being on a date.

A pseudo-date, at least.

"Yes," Lila said. "Until we had Howie. I worked right up until the day I had him, in fact. He was just about born in the newsroom."

"Really?"

"I was on a deadline."

"Overlapping deadlines, huh?"

"Met 'em both," she said, proud.

He smiled, warmly. "What got you into it?"

"Oh," Lila said, enjoying the memory as she unpacked it, carefully, gently. "Our local newspaper had a competition when I was in the seventh grade. An essay contest, 'Why Newspapers Matter.' I wrote the essay that would win, got a youth-voice column in the paper, and from there—"

"You said 'you wrote the essay that would win,'" James interrupted. "Don't you mean you wrote the essay that won?"

"Well, it won," Lila admitted. "But it won because I wrote the essay that *would* win. It was strategic. I wrote what the judges would want to read. I didn't write what I believed, I wrote what they wanted to read."

"Clever little girl."

"Clever enough."

"And it worked."

"It worked," Lila agreed. "I got my fifty-dollar savings bond. I got my column. Kept it up until I graduated from high school. Parlayed that into a spot on the editorial team for my college newspaper. Majored in journalism. Applied for any newspaper job I could find. Wound up at the *Ann Arbor Gazette*."

She'd been Lila Golden then, and seeing her name—LILA GOLDEN—credited with a byline was thrilling. Her first assignments were basic and dues-paying, but not altogether boring. She enjoyed researching and writing obituaries, though they were often uncredited. She enjoyed attending city meetings, interviewing politicians, elbowing her way around the old boys' clubs at the papers, staking out her own spot in the ground upon which to press her ear.

"So I guess you liked it."

"I loved it," she said, the clacking of a typewriter singing in her ears, her nose recalling the smell of ink. She knew she was romanticizing her newspaper days, overplaying the good moments and downplaying the stress, the misogyny, the pressure to perform. Despite her love for the work, she was an unreliable witness when it came to the details of its downsides.

"Do you miss it?"

She knew she should have *said no, not really, being a mother is so fulfilling, I've never really looked back.* That's what the other mothers of Ann Arbor would expect her to say, and certainly what their husbands would assume. It's what everyone wanted to believe, to validate their own choices and pay homage to the world as they understand it. But losing her husband also helped Lila lose any ambition she had of fitting in with the successful wives, the ones who decorated cakes and kept their children in matching socks and had husbands who were still breathing. And anyway, James wasn't like them. So she told him the truth, unfiltered.

"I miss it more than anything."

As soon as the words escaped her mouth, as soon as she heard herself say them, she dropped her fork and let out a small, strangled cry. Because, of course, there was something she should—and did—fundamentally miss even more.

Ernest, Ernest, my God, I'm so sorry—

How could she have said that? She was glad the boys weren't in the room to hear her say that. She couldn't imagine what James must think of her for saying something like that. Even a man as understanding as he couldn't possibly—

"It's okay," James said, and his hand was on hers. That was all he said, and he said it again: "It's okay."

His blue gaze held hers, without judgment or expectation, just simple acceptance. He was in the forgiveness business. She knew she could trust him. She knew despite her baggage, their religious differences, despite everything, he was interested in her, the entire her. Although it had only been two years since her husband's death, she knew she could be interested in him.

She knew it all in that moment, and only for that moment.

Because as soon as she relaxed her hand under the reverend's gentle fingers, Nathan walked into the room. He saw the man's hand on Lila's, and his eyes went wide.

"NEVER DO THAT," he screamed. "DON'T TOUCH HER! I'LL KILL YOU!"

James' hand sprang from Lila's, leaping away like an independent entity, landing hard back in his own lap. Lila sprinted toward her son, but Nathan turned and ran, still shrieking his disapproval. She chased him down the hall, but he slammed his bedroom door behind him and wouldn't let her in. She sat in front of the door, pleading, but he just kept screaming.

When James came to check on her, Lila waved him away, eyes desperate. He left, quietly. She sat outside Nathan's door all night, until he finally stopped screaming. Then she opened the door, which her son had passed out against. Careful not to hurt or wake him, she pushed the door open enough to step through it, picked him up, and whispered apologies into his hair as she put him in his crib. Howie watched the whole thing from the hallway. He had to wait on the fit to end, too; the boys still shared a room.

James did not come for dinner the following Sunday.

Or any Sunday thereafter.

CHAPTER 8: HOWARD

NATHAN WAS WAY, WAY TOO BIG for his crib. He was six years old - a kindergartener! - and for some reason refused to transition from his baby crib to an actual big kid bed. Howie was getting incredibly irritated about the whole thing.

For a smart, allegedly "advanced" kid, Nathan sure was stunted on this front.

Howie shared his thoughts on the bed issue, over and over: *You're too big for a crib. It's weird that you still sleep in one.* As with most things that Howie said, Nathan ignored him. But this particular morning, Howie pinpointed exactly why it bothered him so much: It reminded Howie of when Baby Nathan was in the incubator, at the hospital.

The very first time Howie ever saw his brother, he'd been disturbed to view him trapped in a box and hooked up to machines. It was just wrong.

"You're too big for a crib," Howie tried again over breakfast, as both boys shoveled cereal into their mouths. "It's a baby crib. You're in kindergarten."

"I like my crib."

"It's for babies."

"It's not for babies. Other cribs are for babies, but mine isn't. It's for *me*. It's *mine*."

"Why do you like that stupid crib so much?"

Nathan took another bite of cereal, chewed slowly, swallowed, then looked at his big brother. He spoke deliberately, as if reading from a memorized text.

"My crib is secure. It's where I can do my best thinking."

"You'd think just as well in a big-kid bed. Maybe even better. You need a new bed."

"No, I don't."

With that, Nathan pushed his chair back, and slid out of it, leaving Howard alone at the table. Their mother entered the room as Nathan exited; she stepped around him, letting him continue on his path uninterrupted. Nathan preferred not to be touched, and his mother and brother were conditioned to automatically honor this preference. Lila absently dragged her hand through Howie's hair, tousling it on her way to the coffee maker.

"Mom," Howie said, trying to keep the whine out of his voice. He wanted to sound reasonable. Adult. At nearly nine, he figured this should be doable. "Why is Nathan still allowed to sleep in his stupid baby crib?"

(He realized too late that saying *stupid baby crib* diminished the chance of him sounding like a reasonable adult.)

"He likes the crib," his mother shrugged, having clearly already conceded this battle. "He says he wants to keep sleeping in the crib as long as he can fit in it. If it makes him happy, nu... it makes him happy."

"But doesn't it bother you?"

"No, baby," Lila said. Usually Howie didn't mind her calling him that, but when he was trying to underline the fact that his brother was, in fact, the infantile one, it stung.

"It doesn't bother you, at all?"

"Howie," Lila said, a bit bemused. "Why does it bother *you* so much?"

"It's just... *stupid*," Howie said unconvincingly.

"Ah," said his mother, before turning her full attention to the coffee maker.

Later that morning, as the boys walked to school together, Howie was still irritated.

"Hey, Howie!" Phil D'onofrio called out from behind them. "Wait up!"

Phil D'onofrio was their next door neighbor, seven and a half years old, right between their ages. Howie thought Phil was nice, but he knew Nathan thought Phil was an idiot.

"Can I walk with you guys?"

"Sure," Howie said.

"Thanks! Hey, Nate."

"NATHAN," Nathan snapped. "Not Nate. NATHAN."

"I have a cousin named Nathan, but everyone calls him Nate," Phil said blithely. "Whaddaya got against 'Nate'?"

"I'm not your cousin," Nathan said, without looking at Phil. He began purposefully dawdling, putting a half block between himself and Howie and Phil, unsubtly exiting the conversation.

"Sheesh," Phil said to Howie, rolling his eyes, *can you believe that guy?* "Hey, you wanna play after school today?"

"Sure," Howie said, grinning.

The best thing about playing with Phil was that Phil had a dog, a big yellow Labrador named Mack. Going out for hikes with Mack, tossing a tennis ball for him to chase, rolling around; there was something easy and joyful about romping around with the dog. Nathan, of course, thought dogs were dumb. (Mack's frequent butthole-licking made Nathan's case a strong one. As did the dog's tendency to run smack into walls when he got excited.)

"Great," Phil beamed. "You can bring your little brother, if you wanna. I know he doesn't always like coming over, but if you want to bring him, you can. I'll call him Nathan, not Nate. And we can put the dog up so Nathan won't scream."

"He might want to come, but probably not," Howie shrugged. Nathan found both Phil and butthole-loving Mack banal, but he also hated being left out or excluded by the older boys. He still wanted them to see him as a big kid.

This gave Howie an idea.

"Say, Phil. Did you sleep in a crib when you were a baby?" Howie asked loudly, making sure Nathan could overhear this conversation.

"Yeah?" Phil said, blinking, confused.

"How old were you when you got a big-boy bed?"

"I dunno," Phil shrugged. "Two? I don't remember. I was really little."

"Interesting," Howie said. "You were really little. Because cribs are for babies, right?"

"Uh, yeah," Phil said, having no idea what Howie was driving at with this exchange.

"Stop right now," Nathan warned. "Don't say anything else, Howard."

"Whatsa matter, Nathan?" Howie smirked, looking over his shoulder. "You don't want me to tell Phil here that you still sleep in a baby crib?"

"What?!" Phil burst out laughing. "No way! Nate, you don't really still sleep in a baby crib, do you?"

A muscle in Nathan's tiny jaw twitched. They had reached the school, and he steamed past them, saying nothing.

But the exchange wasn't over.

At recess, Phil pointed at Nathan, whispering something to some of the other first graders. Word spread, and soon what felt like the entire schoolyard began haranguing Nathan.

Weirdo sleeps in a baby crib.

Hey, baby crib. Do you also suck your thumb?

Do you wet your bed? Ooooh, sorry, I mean do you wet your crib?

Or does it stay dry because of your diapers?

Baby. Baby. Baby!

Nathan didn't respond as a normal six-year-old might have. He didn't cry. Didn't hit. Didn't go looking for a teacher. Instead, he got on a swing, and pumped his little legs as fierce and hard and fast as he could. He put himself above the fray, swinging higher, and higher, above the other children, above their barbs.

From the other corner of the playground, Howie watched as Nathan swung back and forth, frantic, too high—and then, as if in slow motion, Howie watched Nathan slide forward off the seat of the swing, let go of the chains, and plummet from the highest arc of his swing toward the crowd of swarming children and the hard-packed dirt below.

"NO!" Howie yelled, racing toward his brother.

Too slow. Too late. No way to reach him in time.

The children parted like the Red Sea, only a few caught by the small boy's flailing limbs as he dropped like a cannonball toward them. Nathan landed with a hard thud and a loud crack. He screamed, once, and then went silent.

The scattered children stared for a moment, and then gasps and cries and nervous laughter and hiccuping sobs of terror rose up in popping bursts of sound. Several of them took off running to find a teacher. Others just stared. Howie shoved the staring bystanders aside, making his way to his baby brother's side.

"Nathan," Howie panted. "Nathan, are you okay?"

"No. I'm not."

"What's wrong? Tell me where it hurts. They're getting a teacher—"

"Shut up," Nathan said.

"Nathan—"

"Shut. Up." Nathan repeated. "You betrayed me."

"I was just trying to get you to understand—"

"I know what you were trying to do."

Mrs. Matthews came running outside, her oversized round Coke-bottle glasses emphasizing the wide-eyed look of shocked concern on her face.

"Oh, my goodness! Nathan Fell, you stay right there and just stay still. The vice-principal is getting the school nurse, and we'll see if you need to go to the hospital or maybe just come in and see the nurse for a Band-Aid, or—"

Then she let out a shrill little shriek. Howie followed her gaze, and blanched at the unnatural angle of the pale, grisly bone protruding from Nathan's small leg.

"You're going to need to go to the hospital, Nathan," managed Mrs. Matthews, whose face was suddenly as pale as the exposed bone staring up at her. "You're going to need to go to the hospital."

"I'm sorry, Nathan," whispered Howie desperately. "I'm sorry."

Nathan turned his head, looking away from his brother. His voice was soft but clear, and laced with anger: "I'll have to get a real bed now. I won't be able to get into my crib. I can't scrunch up my knees. You won, Howard."

"Nathan…"

Nathan ignored Howie, gritting his teeth against the pain but reciting lines as if from a script: "I also guess I won't be able to go to school, so we won't walk together anymore."

Tears welled in Howie's eyes and spilled hotly down his cheek. He hadn't meant for it to escalate like this; hadn't meant to hurt his brother so badly, emotionally and physically. He felt terrible. He hated himself; *abhorred* himself.

"Nathan, I'm sorry. Please, look at me. I'm sorry, all right? I'm really, really sorry."

Nathan turned his steely eyes toward Howie. Though his face was red from the pain, his eyes were dry and cold. He did not smile, nor did he glare. He simply looked at Howie levelly, as if confirming that this moment was something he would never be able to forget, and would never attempt to forgive.

WALTHAM 1979

RS. AGRAWAL?" The doctor asked, eyes on his clip-board.

"Doctor."

"Yes?"

"No, not you," Nirupa said, testy. "Me. It's *Doctor* Agrawal, not Mrs."

"Oh," said the doctor. He was in his fifties, maybe sixty, a for-gettable white man, hairline retreating, eyes bored behind frame-less glasses. Nirupa noted his mild surprise at her interjection, at the assertion of her nomenclature. "Oh. Well. What are you a doctor of, then, Dr. Agrawal?"

"Anthropology," Nirupa said. "And—"

"Oh, a Ph.D.," the doctor said, returning to both his clipboard and his judgment.

"Yes," Nirupa said icily. "I found medical school dull."

That was true. Throughout undergrad, Nirupa planned on being a physician. She took and aced the courses everyone else hated—biology, physical chemistry, organic chemistry. Pre-med was a breeze and medical school, a foregone conclusion. But after the first two years of medical school, Nirupa realized she was not built for the medical life. The knowledge part was fine. But being in hospitals, dealing with insurance paperwork, talking slowly and patiently and kindly to people in pain and/or simply incapable of comprehending what she was telling them—everything she saw the doctors around her doing, she knew she could not do. She also found her fellow students mostly blandly competitive, without the savvy to back it up.

So she shifted gears, and decided to study people rather than try to fix them. A much better fit.

"Well," said the doctor, nonplussed. "You're pregnant."

The words slammed into her like a semi-truck. Dazed, she twitched her head, shaking off the news. Somehow, it was a total shock—despite her swollen breasts, despite her morning sickness, despite the "sign" that when she called around for an appointment near campus this morning, the only available doctor was an obstetrician. Of course, Nirupa didn't believe in signs. She believed in science. And science should mean she wasn't pregnant.

"But I'm on the pill."

"Even when properly taken, the pill is not one hundred percent effective," he said, giving her a look that clearly indicated *maybe you should have stayed in medical school longer, Miss Fancy Pants Ph.D.*

"Right," Nirupa said tartly, knowing this but somehow apparently believing that it would always work for her. It always had before, after all. "I know that."

"Do you have any other questions?"

"Can you tell how far along I am?"

"We can run some tests. We've got one of those ultrasound machines, big damn thing. Admin figured we'd need one, might as well be the first around here to get it. When was your last menstrual cycle?"

"I don't know."

"Uh-huh," he said, less and less impressed with her. "Well. Best guess, if you want to skip the machine, you're first trimester. But could be six weeks along, could be ten."

Still time enough to take care of it.

"Do you want to schedule the ultrasound?" The doctor asked.

"No," Nirupa said, decision made. "I'll—call my own doctor."

"Your own doctor." His words were doubtful, but his look only mildly probing. He had other patients to see and had run out of patience for this one. He might have guessed her plans, was likely judging them, but did not care enough to comment on them if so.

"That's right," Nirupa said, dismissing him.

"All right, 'Dr.' Agrawal," said the doctor, and left.

Nirupa sat for a moment on the stiff plastic exam table, gathering her ricocheting thoughts. She considered calling Michael. But what would the point be? Telling Michael wouldn't change a damn thing. Michael was facing his first major publish-or-perish deadline. He was busy. He wouldn't want to hear this news.

Though Michael and Nirupa had discussed marriage, and would make their relationship legally official down the road, neither academic had any interest in children. They had their research, their ambitions, their goals; things they discussed as passionately as other people discussed more emotional things, late at night, in bed, legs tangled. They talked nakedly about the legacies they wanted. Legacies of the mind, not of the flesh. They could enjoy each other's bodies, but they would not add to the world's overall body count. No children. Not for them, not now, not ever.

So she knew what she had to do.

She picked up her carpet bag of a purse and walked confidently out of the examination room. She stopped briefly at the billing desk, confirming her insurance information, declining again the offer of scheduling a follow-up appointment. She walked through the waiting room, where women in various stages of pregnancy or anticipation were sitting in uncomfortable chairs, awaiting their own appointments.

Nirupa had almost reached her clean yellow Volkswagen when she was halted by a familiar, cutting voice.

"What'll it be, then, Nirupa?"

She turned to see Catherine O'Brien Hess. Michael's mother. The stout, short Irish woman was planted firmly on the concrete, standing in the parking lot with arms crossed, looking unwaveringly at Nirupa.

"Catherine. What are you doing here?"

"Easy question, easy answer," Catherine said, her lilting Irish brogue taking a decidedly less musical tone. "I'm here to see you. So now you answer my question, that's the more important one: what'll it be?"

"What are you talking—"

"Are you gonna tell my son you're carryin' his child, or will it be me that's tellin' him?"

"Did you follow me here?"

"I did."

Nirupa glared at Catherine. This woman was as good a reason as any to never marry Michael. A pushy, Irish-born, Boston-hardened, old-school- Catholic mother-in-law was the stuff of nightmares.

"You shouldn't have done that. This is none of your business."

"Isn't it? My own grandchild?"

"There is no child," Nirupa said firmly.

"I'll help you with him."

"There is no child."

Catherine's eyes widened, and her fingers reflexively flew to her neck, stroking the small gold cross permanently nestled above her collarbone.

"You best not be sayin' what it sounds like you're sayin.'"

"Go home, Catherine," Nirupa said, opening the door to her Volkswagen.

But Catherine did not move.

"You tell Michael, or I'll be tellin' him."

CHAPTER 10: CATHERINE

I F LOOKS COULD KILL, the expression on Nirupa's face would've dropped Catherine O'Brien Hess straight to the ground. But Catherine's life was not the one at stake here, and she answered the younger woman's expression with just as deadly a look.

"Don't you dare say a word to Michael."

"I will. You know I will," Catherine said, swallowing the sharp profanity she wanted to insert between the words *I* and *will*. She was working on cursing less. Now that she was about to be a grandmother, she'd be watching her mouth even more. And she *would* be a grandmother. She would not let this cold, rude woman end the life of that baby.

"Fine," Nirupa spat. "I'll talk to Michael. But it won't change anything."

"Sure about that, are ye?"

Nirupa did not reply further to Catherine. She got into her odd little bug-car, slammed the door, and peeled out of the lot, leaving Catherine standing on the pavement.

Catherine swelled with righteous pride. She'd made it in time, stood up for what was right in the eyes of God. Staved off the relentless flames of hell for at least a few minutes. Long enough to make a difference.

Catherine knew her son would make that woman see reason. See mercy. He was rebellious, sure, but his soul was pure. He had morals. He was raised in the church. He would propose to that woman, they'd have a quick and quiet little shotgun wedding, and when Catherine held her grandchild, all would be right in the world.

Catherine didn't believe in prophecy or visions in modern times. Old Testament seers were long extinct. (Not that Catherine O'Brien Hess believed in *extinction*, strictly speaking.) America in the nineteen-seventies was no place for visions and prophecy, unless you were a drug user.

But she believed unwaveringly in the will of God. And she had a sense about this situation. She'd noticed it when Michael brought Nirupa over for Sunday lunch last week; the woman was green beneath her smooth brown skin. She excused herself to use the restroom more often than usual.

Catherine had been given some clues, certainly. But still, that couldn't quite explain why she had sat bolt upright at six this morning. Why she slipped the car keys from the bowl in her hallway, drove her old Chrysler to Michael and Nirupa's apartment

(Lord Jesus, the way those two lived in sin). Why she parked a half-block away, between two larger sedans, so that her car would not be spotted. Why she felt compelled to wait for Nirupa to come down the stairs, witnessed her vomit into the bushes and wipe her mouth before driving off in that stubby little Volkswagen.

Catherine knew it in her heart and soul and gut: her grandchild was inside that woman, and her job was to see that the baby was carried to term, christened, and raised right. Raised *by her*, if necessary. Catherine O'Brien Hess had very little family left. She'd fight to the death to protect and preserve what little she had.

She offered a quick prayer of thanks to Jesus, for allowing her to reach Nirupa in time. She prayed that God would guide her son, that he'd convince Nirupa to marry him, to make their child legitimate, to be a real family.

The world needed this baby.

She just knew it.

CHAPTER 11: NIRUPA

B Y THE TIME NIRUPA REACHED MICHAEL'S campus, she was seething.

The nerve of that woman.

She almost changed her mind, almost left without seeing her boyfriend. Despite what that old Irish bag thought, Michael was unlikely to be moved by the news of his potential fatherhood. Nirupa knew Michael better than his mother did. Catherine only knew the man she wanted him to be; Nirupa knew the man he actually was.

It would be a kindness to just keep him in the dark. He didn't want a baby, but the idea of terminating the pregnancy might make him feel guilty. He was of Jewish and Irish-Catholic descent. Guilt was in his blood.

So why not spare him the useless guilt?
Why should I have to say a damn thing to Michael?
Because she will if I won't.

Nirupa knew better than to test Catherine O'Brien Hess. She'd tell Michael everything she knew, everything she suspected, and her unfiltered opinion on it all. And if Michael heard the news from anyone other than Nirupa, even if it changed nothing, even though he wouldn't have wanted to know, it would trigger his temper. He'd be livid, ashamed and angry to be handed this intimate information by the mother he always tried to keep at arm's length.

It would end Nirupa and Michael's relationship, without question. It might even end Michael and Catherine's relationship. Nirupa didn't want either of those responsibilities on her shoulders. She might not want to be a mother, but she wasn't a monster. She loved Michael, and knew he loved her and his mother, even if he was begrudging with affection. She despised Catherine for putting her in this position.

Manipulative old bitch.

Nirupa pulled into a parking spot, the yellow lines so faded they practically disappeared into the pebbled old gray asphalt. She threw the parking brake on violently, then put her forehead on the steering wheel. Maybe she should just bail. That way Michael would only lose her, not her and his mother. Cleaner that way.

But she entertained this notion only briefly. Leaving Michael would make her miserable. And she had nowhere to go; even if she were willing to return to India, her parents would not take her in. Above all, her professional connections were in Boston. Nirupa was trapped in a self-selected prison of ambition.

She got out of the car and walked to Michael's laboratory, trying to staunch the new wave of nausea roiling in her belly.

Michael was a medical doctor, whose undergraduate degree was in mechanical engineering; he was also all-but-dissertation on a Ph.D. in chemistry. He would not allow anyone to surpass his credentials. He was the consummate workaholic, grading student work while checking on his chemical intervention experiments, taking notes on his next big idea, constantly in motion and just as constantly aggravated by his inability to do even more at once. As usual, his stress level was palpable when Nirupa entered the room.

"Michael."

He looked up, his face patchily bearded with several days' worth of unshaven growth. His bloodshot eyes were recessed above deep purple bags. He was so disheveled, so distracted, it took him a moment to place his own live-in girlfriend.

"Nirupa? What're you doing here?"

"What are you working on?" She asked, sidestepping.

Michael rubbed his red eyes. "Friggin' Carl's going to get that journal spot. I'm trying to beat him to the punch. Backstabbing little prick is piggybacking off of my work. That's why he has the time to write—doesn't spend a damn second in the labs anymore. Just looks over my shoulder and takes notes. Leech."

"What are you working on?"

"Oh. It's pretty high-level—"

"And I'm not?"

"Fair point," he said, and gave her a weak-jawed smile. "We're researching the impact of synthetic compound chemicals on brain function. May someday point us in the direction of re-generation, keeping our minds more limber—we don't know all the implications yet, but it could be exciting."

"Exciting enough that Carl wants to ride your coattails."

"Carl would grab anyone's coattails if it meant credit without work. He's just lucky that I happen to be brilliant."

"You know the old joke? 'Why is there so much backstabbing in academia?'"

"'Because the stakes are so low?'"

"Yeah."

"I never thought that joke was funny."

"Me, neither," Nirupa said. And then: "So. Speaking of funny."

"Uh-oh. What." Michael's question was as flat as his expression. "Funny news" might be an obstacle between him and productivity. Nirupa decided to rip the Band-Aid off quickly.

"I'm pregnant."

Michael said nothing.

"It's yours, obviously," she added unnecessarily.

He nodded; no dispute there. They both stood silently, the information sucking the air from the room, suffocating them. The silence lasted several moments; one small lifetime.

"Right, well," Michael said, finally. "You've requested some time off already?"

"Time off?"

"I hear the recovery can be a little bit rough," he yawned, his eyes already sneaking back toward the paper on the table in front of him. "I assume you'll need at least a day or two to put your feet up, take it easy."

Nirupa stared at him. Though his conclusion was the same as hers, she'd expected something more. A conversation. An emotional reaction beyond boredom and an immediate return to the more important tasks at hand.

"What if I'd decided to keep it?"

Michael laughed, a barking sound. "Yeah, right."

"Don't say that. Don't *laugh*."

He yawned again, shrugging an apology at the same time. As angry as Nirupa had been at Catherine in the parking lot, she was ten times angrier now at Michael's complete apathy. Maybe it was the hormones surging through her; she tried to calm herself, but her fury crackled.

"Nirupa," Michael said, as if talking to a failing student who came to see him during office hours to ask whether or not she should drop the class. "You don't want a kid. I don't want a kid. We've talked about this."

"We talked about it, hypothetically. This isn't a hypothetical. This is an actual outcome. You. Got. Me. Pregnant."

"Do you need money?"

Nirupa's left eyeball twitched.

"No," she said. And in the space of that single syllable, informed not by reason or intellect but emotion and indignation, Nirupa changed her mind.

She was going to have the damn baby.

More than that: she was going to marry Michael. She was going to continue on her career path and even outpace him. She was going to take back her power.

She was fine with the other option when it was her choice, but when it felt like Michael's decree, it was unacceptable. She was not one to follow orders. Like it or not, in order to preserve her fundamental sense of self, Nirupa had to subvert her earlier vision of herself. She was going to become a mother.

She just wished it wasn't going to make Catherine so damn pleased.

ANN ARBOR 1980

CHAPTER 12: NATHAN

AT EIGHTEEN, Nathan Fell still walked with a pronounced limp.

He was irritated by it with every lurching step he took. He didn't intend to give himself a lifelong limp when he launched himself off a swing at the age of six. He didn't do it to punish himself, he did it to punish his brother—even back then, he knew the best way to hurt tenderhearted Howie was to do damage to someone Howie loved. That would wreck Howie, *especially* if Howie thought it was his fault.

It had worked, but the younger Nathan's calculations were off when it came to the fall itself. He was aiming for a sprained ankle,

not a snapped fibula. A temporary inconvenience, not a permanent impediment. But at least the experience had taught him a
valuable lesson: *We can't always control the outcomes; that's the real
risk of anything worth trying.*

Nathan finished high school at sixteen, having convinced his
mother it would be best for everyone if he went to college at the
same time as Howie. He wished they'd gone even earlier, maybe at
fifteen and seventeen, but for some reason, Howie was unhurried.
He took all four years at high school, and all four years to get his
undergraduate degree. Of course, in high school, while Nathan
broke academic records and avoided all social interaction, Howie
broke hearts and won homecoming king. He *enjoyed* himself.

Nathan was mildly jealous of Howie's social aptitude, but
he was less interested in humans than he was in their building
blocks. Unraveling humans' genetic codes, exploring the potential
for merging man and machine—that was infinitely more interesting than voting on "Paris in the Spring" vs. "Caribbean Beach
Party" for prom theme.

Both Fell boys transitioned easily from high school to college.
By sophomore year, they were titans on campus at the Massachusetts Institute of Technology. Howie maintained his high school
reputation as a smart, good-looking flirt who always stayed friends
with girls after breaking their hearts. Nathan, meanwhile, was famous for his shocking youth and brilliance. He was slight of build
and steely-eyed, but alluring in his own way—a lone wolf who
limped around campus dreaming up new ways to change the very
landscape of science. He was a man of mystery, attracting the attention of many a girl and even a few sharp-eyed intellectual boys,
who wrongly thought they had guessed his closeted little secret.

Thanksgiving, sophomore year: Howie and Nathan drove
from Cambridge back to Ann Arbor, barely speaking as they sojourned from one college town to another. They rarely interacted
on campus, and had little to discuss. They would have to put on

a show and chat with each other when their mother was there to observe them—better not to waste the small talk on the way there.

Lila Golden Fell still lived in the house where the boys grew up, which was too big for her. She claimed she couldn't sell it because she'd never get what it was worth, and she liked her neighbors, and it would take so much work to get it cleaned up enough to go on the market. Her sons knew it was because their father lived there and died there, and so would their mother.

Lila never remarried. If Nathan were the sort of person to feel remorse, he would feel guilty about his mother's solitude. After all, he accidentally killed her first husband and then ran off the only man she ever came close to dating after becoming a widow. That pasty preacher. But Nathan feeling guilty would do nothing to better his mother's situation, so why bother?

Nathan was a calculator, an assessor; not malevolent, nor spiteful, but absolutely against prioritizing emotion over evaluation. This had come up recently, when he caved to pressure and went out on a date with a classmate named Linda.

Nathan and Linda went to a Thai restaurant just off campus. Nathan ordered a simple curry dish. Linda ordered an appetizer, a bowl of soup, and Pad Thai. When the bill came, Nathan took nine dollars out of his wallet—the cost of his curry, plus tax and tip—and handed it to Linda.

"What's this?" Linda asked, baffled.

"My share of the bill," Nathan said, wondering if Linda was an idiot.

"I sort of figured…" She hesitated, like she was going to say one thing, and then said instead: "…we'd just split it. Like down the middle. Dutch treat."

Nathan blinked. "Your total is twice as much as mine. I'm not covering that."

She gaped. "Do you have, like, Asperger's?"

"I don't know," he said, setting his nine dollars on the table and leaving.

The exchange sent Nathan down a research rabbit hole, and in the end he decided that he probably did, in fact, have Asperger's. He felt no need to have it confirmed by anyone beyond himself; he was certain he was correct, and appreciated the insights and strategies his diagnosis yielded him. Nathan liked being able to appropriately categorize things, himself included.

The Fell boys arrived at their mother's house on Thanksgiving Day, late-morning, having driven overnight. Lila gave Howie a hug, and nodded her hello to Nathan, before helping them unload all the laundry they'd crammed into the back of Howie's rusty old Toyota Tercel.

"Millie and the Reverend should be here in a few hours," Lila told her sons after the first overflowing load of laundry was thumping around the old washer in the basement. "I told them Thanksgiving dinner will be at three this year."

"Mind if I pop by the D'onofrios to catch some of the Lions game?" Howie asked.

"Sure, sure," Lila said. "Just be back in time to help me set the table. Nathan, you going to go watch the game, too?"

Nathan did not look up from his book. "No."

Lila chuckled. "That was a joke, kid. Howie, hop in the shower before you go to the D'onofrios. I love you, but you stink. Nathan, come read in the kitchen, keep me company while I chop onions. You know it's gonna make me cry and I'll need you to hand me a napkin."

Howie obediently hit the shower, then bounded over to the neighbors to watch terrible football players play their stupid game. Nathan hauled himself and his book into the kitchen. For the next few hours, there was peace in the Fell home.

And then the Reverend and Millie arrived.

They arrived an hour earlier than they had estimated, which was exactly when Lila and her boys had expected them to arrive. They were *always* an hour earlier than their estimates. ("That's how you know your father's family isn't Jewish," Lila had said once. "Always early to dinner, never hungry.") The household was ready for their early arrival. Howie made it back just before they knocked on the door, in time to hold it open for them with his big grin.

"Happy Thanksgiving!" Howie crowed, echoed softly by Lila.

"Happy Thanksgiving!" Millie chirped back.

Nathan and the Reverend just nodded their acknowledgment of the occasion.

Nathan generally appreciated his grandparents. The Reverend was stern, serious, and seldom spoke; all qualities Nathan admired. Millie never shut up, but she slipped him a lot of cookies back when he was small and valued such currency. She thereby cemented herself into his goodwill long ago.

"Did you watch the Lions game?" Millie asked Howie, knowing he had. He always watched the game. She always asked about it. Their holidays were less about meaningful tradition than rote repetition. Patterns, repeated annually.

"Man, yeah," Howie said, shaking his head, as if somehow the team's loss came as a surprise. "Lions were up 10-3 at the half, but then the Bears really kicked into high gear. I mean, coming out of nowhere! That quarterback, though—Evans? He's going places. Bears pulled it out with a 23-17 win. Poor old Lions."

"Lions and Bears," Millie cued.

"And how 'bout them Tigers," Howie continued the setup.

"Oh my!" Millie brought it home with the punchline.

Then the Reverend and Millie headed to the guest room to freshen up. Lila went to check on the turkey, instructing the boys to bring the good china up from downstairs and get to work setting the holiday table. And for a few minutes, it was just the Fell boys.

"So why're you reading that book?" Howie asked, gesturing to the tome on genetic disorders as he began un-boxing a set of holiday plates.

"For fun," Nathan said. The book was recreational reading for him, not assigned. He rarely felt a need to read the texts for his classes. They were rudimentary. He needed more depth.

"Ha," Howie rolled his eyes.

He's smart, Nathan reminded himself, before deciding at last to give a more candid reply.

"The subject—the book—it's related to a new theory I'm developing," Nathan said. "To be fair, I'm not the only one working with this particular theory—but I'm sort of, you know, adding my own twist."

"What's the theory?"

"That ultimately, the best way to eradicate genetic disorders—from Tay-Sachs and spina bifida to dementia—is to augment human material with better-engineered material."

Howie stopped unpacking plates. "Better-engineered material? The hell does that mean?"

"Mechanics," Nathan said. "Bioengineering. Not just 'better living through science'—better *life* through science. Better bodies, better minds. The things we're starting to be able to do with computers is also—"

"You're talking about... what, robot-people? Cyborgs? Man-meets-machine? Like on *The Six Million Dollar Man*? 'We have the technology'—"

"Not like that dumbass TV show," Nathan snapped, already regretting confiding in his brother. "I'm talking about real science. A real opportunity to improve mankind. Not something inefficient like throwing a bunch of resources into rebuilding one stupid guy. An upgrade for the entire species. Designing people better. There's so much potential for us to—"

"Nathan," Howie said, shaking his head. "Come on, man. That's messed up."

"Stop interrupting me," Nathan said quietly.

"Jesus," Howie went on. "An 'upgrade' to the 'species'? Look, I'm all for medical science, but you can't 'design' people. That's just wrong. You do *get* that, right?"

"No."

"Be reasonable, Nathan. You can't really think—"

"You're the one who's not thinking," Nathan said, hating the rising pitch in his voice. "I am the one demonstrating all the reason in this conversation. You're demonstrating emotion. Emotion is not reasonable! I want to move the world forward, you want to let it stagnate. We're killing the planet, overusing resources, refusing to evolve. That's not how it has to be."

Nathan limped angrily to the other side of the table, shoving Howie out of the way and reaching into a cardboard box for the gleaming good china, grabbing a plate roughly.

"Hey, careful," Howie said, but Nathan slammed the plate onto the table, shattering it.

Their mother entered the room, carrying a golden-roasted turkey on a giant platter. Her apron was tied loosely around her slim waist; her hair was streaked with gray and powdered white with flour, making her appear suddenly much older. She looked from Nathan, to Howie, to the shattered plate, and finally back to Howie. Her expression was tortured.

"You can't even be civil on Thanksgiving? We haven't even sat down, and I hoped—"

But Nathan limped from the room, dousing her hope with his scowl, furious at himself for opening up to his brother about ideas far too big for his small thinking.

CHAPTER 13: MILLIE

NO ONE EXPECTED MILLIE and the Reverend to die romantically. No one except for Millie.

The Reverend and Millie met on Christmas Eve. It was love at first sight. For one of them, anyway.

Millie had traveled with her family down to Kentucky from Ohio. They were visiting Millie's mother's relatives, a collection of bad Baptists, middling Methodists, and secret atheists. The entire clan had gone together to the Baptist church in the small town's center, because the bad Baptists were still the family majority back in the 1920s.

Millie had not wanted to go to the service. She was an indifferent Christian, glad to be saved but uninterested in discussing the matter. She didn't care for church much. She felt little motivation to get dressed up or make a big old show of herself like those other girls in the pews. It took too much energy. Besides, she wasn't interested in *being* the talk of the town; she just enjoyed talking about everyone else. If she had any true religion, it was gossip.

The little Kentucky church was a warm wooden building, radiating an almost otherworldly light on that cold, dark December night. Millie had to admit, as they approached the building, that it was charming; but once inside, it was like all other churches. Boring. Not bothering to stifle her first yawn of the evening, Millie was preparing to practice the handy skill of sleeping with her eyes open when instead something caught them. Some*one*: the Reverend Richard Fell.

He was young, new to the ministry and new to town. He was solid of voice and square of jaw, preaching about a tiny precious baby in a manger, and how that one child would save their sinful world. His focus shifted swiftly from the infant savior to the otherwise irredeemable world. Full of temptation, fallen souls, wicked men and women, a sinful, sinful, sinful world. He kept repeating that word, rhythmically, almost sensually: *Sinful, sinful, sinful.*

Millie felt delightfully sinful herself, sitting in that hard wooden pew. She was immediately and irreverently attracted to the young reverend. Less-than-pure thoughts danced through her mind as she hung onto every righteous and beautifully damning word offered by the serious young clergyman.

At Millie's home congregation in Piqua, Ohio (a quaint Methodist church with a stone foundation and a leaky, badly patched roof), the minister was so old, he'd had one foot in the grave when he baptized Millie, and was somehow still dangling his other foot over the abyss eighteen years later. Because of this, Millie thought of all men of the cloth as Methuselah-types, hopelessly old, tired, creaky.

She suddenly realized she could be a preacher's wife.

This had never occurred to her as a possible life choice, but now that she thought about it, it was an absolutely perfect fit.

Preacher's wife. She had heard that preachers referred to their vocation as a calling, well; preacher's-wifery was *her* calling. She could know everything about everyone. She could be an insider, without having to venture out much. She could keep home and hearth for that man at the lectern. She knew this was exactly what she was meant to do, the way she sometimes just knew things, patiently and certainly.

After the service and Millie's private revelation, the world seemed different. Expectant. Exiting the sanctuary, Millie wondered if her family could tell that she had been changed that Christmas Eve. It seemed they did not; her parents were talking about the menu for tomorrow, her sister and brothers taking guesses at what their small gifts might be. All seemed oblivious to Millie's newfound knowledge of her very own destiny.

The preacher stood waiting at the door of the church, thanking everyone for coming, giving out sturdy handshakes and solemn wishes for a meaningful holiday. As he acknowledged each of Millie's many family members in turn, shaking hands with the boys, giving a ministerial nod to each of the girls, Millie went suddenly shy. She kept her eyes on his slender hands as he passed them from person to person, verifying an important detail: no ring.

Millie's father was sharing his children's names with the preacher, nodding to indicate Jonathan, Martha, Samuel, Mildred.

Mildred. Jesus. He couldn't have said Millie?

Millie knew her full name added a good seventy-three years to her age.

"A blessed Christmas to you, Mildred," the reverend said, nodding at Millie.

"Millie," she corrected.

"Millie," he said, with a tight smile. (She would later learn that this was as wide a smile as the man was capable of allowing.) "I'll keep that in mind."

The next morning, Millie's parents were surprised when she requested that they return to church. But they went. And the family's shock gradually diminished when she kept referring to the reverend. The Reverend this, the Reverend that. Her family teased her. "The Reverend" became the sole and only name by which Reverend Richard Fell would be known.

Throughout their holiday stay in Kentucky, Millie attempted to impress the Reverend in every conceivable way. She borrowed a flattering dress from her cousin Abigail, and had her sister Martha fix her hair. She baked a casserole and took it to the parsonage— only to find that the Reverend was not there. He was at the hospital, bringing the good word to invalids who could no longer make it to church but still needed to know that the flames of hell would roast their wilted limbs and blaze right through their crutches if they didn't turn daily to Jesus before drawing their last breath.

He was a man on a mission, always. That's how Millie realized what it would take to land this man: she had to fit in with his mission. To *further* his mission. Millie would become the most biblical of women, a woman of valor, prized above rubies.

She showed up for Bible study. She sat in the front pew for Sunday services right after Christmas. She made three massive casseroles and brought them to the hospital while the Reverend was making his rounds there, delivering them to patients instead of to him, and loudly leading grace before letting anyone take one damn bite of the food she had prepared for them.

In an act of direct divine intervention, God sent a blizzard that extended Millie's family's stay. She trudged through the snow back to the church for yet another Bible study, and it finally happened. She caught the eye of the Reverend.

The class was reading an Old Testament story—the trial of Abraham, commanded to sacrifice his only son, Isaac, whom he loved, to his demanding new God. The Reverend did most of the talking. For the Reverend, nothing in the Bible was up for debate.

He was teaching his students something as straightforward as basic math, and far more vital to their mortal souls. This was not philosophy; this was law.

"God sent an Angel of the Lord to stop Abraham," the preacher intoned, as much a divine messenger as any angel. "But he sent the angel at the very last moment, only after Abraham had demonstrated his faith, his willingness to sacrifice everything—*everything*—for his Lord God."

"What about Sarah?"

The Reverend was surprised by the voice, took a moment to place it. His eyes landed on Millie, who demurely ducked her head before tilting it up again, just slightly, to meet his gaze.

"Miss Millie?"

Millie nodded. "Sarah. Isaac's mother. Did she know what Abraham was going to do?"

"This was not her story."

"But Isaac was her son."

"And Abraham was her husband. The head of her home."

For a moment, Millie considered making the case for Sarah. Sarah, the matriarch, who had her own conversations with God and interactions with angels; who must have been suspicious when her husband left so early, so solemnly, with her only son. It was her story, too.

Why shouldn't Sarah's perspective count? And Millie's, for that matter? Millie was living in a thoroughly modern era. She knew women who went to college (well, she didn't know any personally, but she knew *of* them). Then again, those women fought uphill battles—as Sarah would have, if she had ever questioned her husband. Maybe if she hadn't acquiesced to all the concubines and travel and the near-murder of her son, she would have been abandoned in the desert. Sarah didn't go against her husband, and in the end, she was still being mentioned, by name, two thousand years after her death. *That* was gossip with some real staying power.

So instead of saying what she thought, Millie said: "You're right; it isn't her story. This was her husband's test of faith. If anything, she demonstrated her faith by being quiet. She trusted her husband in all things, as the Lord says we women should. Sarah... waited."

The preacher nodded, eyeing her with more interest now. "That's right, Miss Millie."

By the next Christmas, she was a preacher's wife. She jumped in whole hog. She jubilantly abandoned Ohio, abandoned her boring old childhood, abandoned risky, pesky questions and troublesome matriarchal viewpoints.

She loved living in Kentucky and welcoming the extended family there, no longer a visitor but a local. The Christmas after their wedding, her daughter Christina was in her arms when she welcomed the Ohio family to the Bluegrass State. Two Christmases later, it was her son, Ernest, she was showing off beneath the tree.

Over the years, the preacher and his wife played their parts quite consistently. Since Millie's husband railed against vanity, Millie gave up her efforts to appear appealing. Shedding the trappings of beauty came easily to Millie, who never cared for the exertion style demanded. She was never unkempt, but "letting herself go" was practically a goal. As she'd hoped, she was also gossip central for the church community, while righteously pretending gossip was beneath her. She knew everything about everyone, and all without having to extend much of an effort. People showed up at her doorstep, she poured tea, they poured out their hearts. Easy as anything.

She was content, but did have one latent prayer, unspoken, powerful: She wanted one moment—just one—of true romance. Millie could bide her time. Patience was a virtue she and the Reverend both valued. She kept this prayer private, and her piety public. Like Sarah, she would wait.

If nothing else, Millie knew that people didn't remember what they saw, or even what they experienced. In the end, what people remember is whatever other people can't stop talking about. Millie had long known the power of good gossip, and she was going to make it work for her in the end.

The days often dragged, but the years flew by. Quietly, steadily, Millie and the Reverend ate and slept and prayed beside one another for decades. He preached, judged, went after sinful souls; she listened, waited, birthed two children, lost two others, and made plenty of small talk but always avoided discussing loss or regret.

Life tossed trials their way. Their only son, sweet Ernest, died young, leaving a grieving young widow and two little half-orphaned boys. Their quiet, skeptical daughter, Christina, moved to Maine and lived with another spinster. (Millie had plenty of questions about that situation, but knew better than to raise them.) Time aged Millie and her pious husband.

Millie knew she wouldn't have to wait much longer.

Christmas Eve, 1980: Millie and the Reverend were home alone. They'd visited their dead son's wife and the grandchildren for Thanksgiving and had planned to return to them again for Christmas. But between the snowy roads and their own cold old bones, they changed their minds. Millie, maker of the phone calls for the entirety of their marriage (or at least ever since the Reverend had acquiesced to getting a phone, back in 1950, several stubborn decades after most other folks installed telephones), called her son's widow, Lila.

"Hello, hon. Yes, yes, we're fine, but with the weather, I don't think we'll be making it up to Michigan. You know the Reverend would be mad at me for saying so, but his eyes aren't so good lately, and I haven't driven in years…"

Lila reacted appropriately, disappointed but understanding, murmuring regrets wrapped around repeated expressions like "safety first" and the obligatory "we'll miss you, but we understand." She promised to kiss the boys for Millie.

Millie liked her daughter-in-law; always had, despite the fact that the Reverend couldn't stand her. She was a reckless choice, the Reverend warned; too independent, too irreligious. Her parents were dead Jews, which didn't help, either. Lila was a foreign heathen without kin, who asked too many questions and dangerously encouraged others to do the same.

"A 'reporter,'" the Reverend snarled when he first learned that she had her own career. "What kind of woman does that? Ernest says she couldn't come to church because she was 'on a deadline.' Putting a deadline before the Lord? That's Satan at work."

Millie was careful not to defend Lila too much, but also tried to ease her husband's concerns. She told him it was a new world, the sixties, plenty of women working, and plenty of couples skipping church. The Reverend had not appreciated either of these points. But Millie was proven right overall. Lila was good to Ernest, good *for* him, right on up until the day he died and well beyond that. She did right by him, raising those two boys, and all on her own.

Those boys.

Living in the shadow of her eighth decade, Millie did not feel wise, only old. But she was observant enough to pick up some things here and there. She noticed patterns, over the course of her life. She saw lives begin, play out, inevitably conclude. She never believed as strongly as her husband did about anything, especially not when he embraced Calvinism quite passionately later in his ministry—the idea that everyone's born saved or screwed. But she believed in patterns.

Lives wove together in different ways, Millie saw that time and time again. Some patterns repeated consistently, others alternated, like in a piecemeal-but-orderly quilt—every third square being red, say. Sometimes it was hard to see close-up, because some of the strands skipped generations and bobbed back in later, but when you pulled back and looked at the whole thing, the design all made sense. The big story was just a patchwork of smaller stories, stitched together by a mighty Hand. That was her sense of faith, anyway.

Her grandsons were what solidified her belief in repeating and alternating patterns. In Howie, she saw her own son Ernest so vividly it was almost painful. The brains, the charm, the eagerness to love and be loved: Howie was a little Ernest-clone, had been since day one. Nathan was the skipped-square in the quilt. He was the Reverend. Serious. Focused. Not one to be distracted by the details of this life, because his unshakable focus was somewhere much farther away, on whatever he believed was bigger and more important than the things normal people saw.

If Millie had taken a more active role in her own life, she would have been more involved in her grandsons' lives. But she was a gossip, not a meddler. And so she prayed for those boys, and reminded them when she saw them that they had a responsibility to better their own little bit of the world, and confided in her friends about them, but otherwise, she didn't get involved. Wasn't her place.

Millie did not want drama, or heartache, or excitement in her own life. Not until the very end, anyway. That seemed like the right time to shake things up—when you wouldn't be around for the fallout. She would leave something the neighbors would talk about, when she was gone. A good ending. Good gossip. Sweet, envious, *I-want-something-like-that-for-my-story* gossip. And so she began to make plans for her storybook conclusion.

She knew it was time to implement the plan. The Reverend had cancer. Just *cancer*, nothing more specific than that—that was all he told her, and he made her swear not to tell anyone even that much. His breathing beside her at night was more and more labored; it was in his lungs, she suspected.

She also knew that things were getting tougher for Lila and the boys. The boys were in college, too smart for their own good, likely to make some sort of mistakes. One of them might get a girl knocked up or wind up in jail. Millie was not interested in either sort of bailout.

Besides, it was December. After the holidays, she would have to endure the bleak stretches of January, February, and miserable winter-clinging March. Who wanted to deal with all that snow, all that cold? After a lifetime of Midwestern winters, Millie was done with them.

And so that Christmas Eve, as snowflakes swirled through the air and piled into drifts, blanketing the yard and creating a snow-globe worthy scene, Millie knew the time was right. Her story-book ending, the one moment of romance that would leave them all talking, was at hand.

She prepared a casserole, just like the ones she'd fixed when she was trying to catch her husband's eye decades earlier. But this time, she stirred in a few extra ingredients. Not enough to over-power the seasoning, but enough to carry out their duty. Just a few shakes, a few stirs.

They got into bed, the Reverend stretching out uncomfort-ably on his side of the mattress Millie tucking herself into hers. They lay, as always, back to back, sharing the bed but not their bodies. She waited until his uneven breathing became slightly more regular. Then she rolled over, nudging herself closer to him. She pressed herself into her husband's back, wrapping her arms around him, her cheek at his shoulder.

Not quite good enough.

She shifted, tugged at her husband, rolled him over so he faced her. He was lighter than she remembered, gaunt and bony and barely there. He did not resist her movement of him, perhaps be-cause he had eaten more of the casserole than she had, and was already somewhere very far away. Face-to-face, his eyes closed and breath catching, she picked up her husband's arm and placed it around her, holding him and helping him to hold her in return. An oddly godly peace settled over her as her heart began to beat off-kilter. Her romantic ending was coming.

They died peacefully in each other's arms. Amen and amen.

She had prayed about this moment. But she also knew that God helped those who help themselves.

I am a daughter of Sarah, she thought.

"I love you, Richard," she whispered, perhaps to herself, perhaps aloud.

And as the wind blew the snow against the outside of their house, everything inside the house stilled.

Quieted.

Stopped.

The next morning when the Fells were not at church, two parishioners came around to check on them. Edna and Bob, a kindly middle-aged couple, found the door unlocked, just as Millie had left it the night before. Letting themselves in, they called out for a few moments, then began searching. With a muffled cry of shock from Edna and a *well-damn!* from Bob, they bore witness to the fate of the Fells—right there where they lay, dead in their shared bed.

Millie and the Reverend held one another tenderly, and their expressions were so peaceful. It was obvious to anyone who saw the scene or heard the story that the reverent old couple had died at the same moment, gathered back up to God together on a Christmas morning. It was a miracle.

The whole town talked about it for years.

CAPE COD 1985

CHAPTER 14: HOWARD

HOWIE ADJUSTED THE BIZARRE BOW tie around his neck. It was pink, matching not only his cummerbund but also apparently the dresses that the bridesmaids would be wearing and the bouquet his bride would be carrying. It was choking him.

"Hey, can you give me a hand with this?" He said to his best man.

Nathan turned and lifted an eyebrow. "What do you need help with?"

"This bow tie. It's askew."

"It's fine. It's empirically fine. You're just nervous. Take a deep breath and stop looking in the mirror. You're never going to think it looks right, but it has nothing to do with the suit or the tie. It's just your own stupid face."

Stunned, Howie gave a bark of laughter; for once, his little brother said the right thing.

"Do you have my—"

"Vows?" Nathan asked, reaching into his right breast pocket and pulling out the top edge of a gilded index-size card. Then he patted his left pants pocket. "Or rings?"

"You know," Howie said, bemused. "You're actually pretty good at this best man thing."

Nathan shrugged. "The expectations are pretty clear. I only plan to do it once, though, so this marriage of yours better work out."

"It will," Howie said confidently.

He was anxious about the wedding, but not the marriage itself. Sophie Eisen was his perfect match—patient, kind, wise, generous to a fault. She got along with everyone. She even liked Nathan, which was more than Howie would ever have expected or required in a spouse.

Between sweet Sophie's adoring fans and Howie's legion of friends, the wedding guest list swelled quickly. Her parents had little means, but were paying far more than they should have to finance the dress, the caterer, the small live band that would play music as their two hundred guests dined and danced in the backyard of this beautiful Cape Cod home.

One reason they could afford the wedding was that the venue was free; Sophie's wealthy great-aunt owned this charming, rambling old mansion and offered its use before anyone even had to ask her. Sophie had summered here as a child and just loved the place; she had brought Howie here for the past three summers and he, too, had come to adore the Cape Cod home. It was where he proposed to her, last summer; it was the perfect choice for where they would wed.

There was a knock at the door, and Maxwell poked his head in. "Am I interrupting?"

"C'mon in, Max," Howie said, grinning.

Max was Sophie's oldest and dearest friend, a college buddy who got her into and out of plenty of trouble. Howie was pretty certain Max knew things about Sophie that no one else would ever know, which was both charming and somewhat unsettling.

In a non-traditional move that Howie found delightful, Sophie had asked Max to be her Man of Honor. She had five girlfriends as bridesmaids, plus Max. Howie had five groomsmen, plus Nathan; the other groomsmen were already outside, doubling as ushers, handing out programs, greeting guests and offering their arms to help seat them, charming everyone and laughing at silly quips.

Nathan wouldn't have done well as an usher.

"How're things in here, Fell boys?" Maxwell asked.

"Good, good. How's my bride-to-be holding up?"

Max smiled. "Oh, she's fine. She wanted me to find out how you were doing."

"I'm… you know. Sweating buckets."

Maxwell chuckled, then looked at Nathan. "You taking good care of him, Nathan?"

"I am," Nathan said without looking at Maxwell. "You can go back to the women."

Howie winced, wishing for the thousandth time he could apologize for Nathan. He wanted, at the very least, to assure Maxwell that Nathan's dismissal of him had nothing to do with Max being gay and everything to do with Nathan being a socially graceless jackass.

Max just rolled his eyes and then winked at Howie, like he was in on this whole thing. Sophie must have told Maxwell about her future husband's weirdo brother. Howie wondered briefly what other intimate details Sophie has shared with Maxwell over the years, then pushed the thoughts from his mind. He was already nervous enough.

"See you for the big walk, man," Maxwell said, and left.

"Hey, I've got something to take your mind off your nerves," Nathan said.

"What?" Howie replied, caught off-guard.

Nathan pulled his suitcase up onto the bed, then pulled something from it. It was dark plastic, brick-like, with buttons. Some sort of giant calculator, maybe?

"What is it?" Howie asked.

"Guess," Nathan said, uncharacteristically gleeful.

"Uh..." Howie shrugged helplessly.

Nathan pulled something from the top—an antenna. "That help?"

"It's... a phone?" Howie ventured.

"Yes—a mobile phone! So you can make phone calls anywhere."

Howie burst out laughing. Nathan's glee was replaced by an irritated frown. Even at twenty-three, being laughed at by his big brother sent him into pouty childlike indignation.

"What the hell's so funny?"

"Sorry, bro," Howie said. "But what do you need a mobile phone for? You don't even like talking to people!"

"That's not the point."

"Talking to other people isn't the point of a telephone?"

"Not at all. The implications of this technology—sending the information wirelessly, transmitting from one unit to another without requiring—"

"One *person* to another, not one *unit*—"

"No, no, I'm not talking about people, I'm talking about the phone itself—"

"The phone itself isn't going to call someone without a person placing the call," Howie, the philosopher, reminded his brother. "Without the human interaction, it has no purpose."

"Well...I don't entirely disagree with you," Nathan said, tucking the phone away.

"Whoa! It really must be a special day."

Nathan regarded his brother. "Are you excited to... do this? Get married?"

"To get married, eh," Howie said honestly. "But to *be* married, yes. Absolutely."

"Sophie is... a good match for you. I doubt I'll ever find someone right for me."

At Nathan's admission, Howie's mind raced. It was rare for his brother to say anything so personal, so candid. Howie wanted to handle this moment correctly, even in the midst of his own big day. Nathan's walls were usually impenetrable. Any opening must be approached cautiously.

"Why do you say that?"

"I'm picky, for one," Nathan said, clearly having given this some thought. "I'm not very good with people. And I'm not certain I see the point of having children—other than improving the average intelligence of the next generation."

"Ha," Howie said, acknowledging his brother's attempt at a joke, then wondering if maybe it wasn't intended as a joke. "Well... you never know. And you're young. Plenty of time."

"I'm only two years younger than you. You met Sophie years ago."

"Yeah, well. We're too young to be getting married, anyway. Ask anyone. Ask Mom."

"Ha," Nathan said, acknowledging Howie's humor. "You're twenty-five. Not so young."

"Not so old, either."

Maxwell popped his head in again. "Guys. You ready to start the lineup?"

"Yes," Nathan said, looking at his watch to confirm the schedule before shoving Howie out the door. And just like that, the moment of brotherly bonding was over.

They lined up on one side of the yard, while the bridal party lined up on another. Howie took another deep breath, hoping the deafening clatter of his heart jumping around his chest was audible only to him. He looked around, at this beautiful day on Cape Cod, only one hour's drive and yet worlds away from Boston, Cambridge, and the real world.

But everything most real about his world was here. There was his mother, seated in the front row of the white folding chairs, wearing a soft lavender dress and looking relieved. She had expressed concern about Sophie and Howie's young engagement, what it would do to each of their careers; but she loved Sophie and was glad Howie had someone to love.

And there were his groomsmen, college buddies, plus his good old childhood friend Phil D'onofrio, grinning and making everyone feel welcome.

And there was Sophie.

Beautiful, smiling Sophie, probably cracking jokes with Max and the girls to ease everyone's nerves before that long walk down the aisle.

Casting his eyes about one final time, taking in the bigger picture, he spotted something else in the distance—two people, a small boy and an older woman, holding hands, walking toward the beach. They looked like a Norman Rockwell scene. Perfect. They made Howie suddenly, strangely excited to start a family of his own.

"What are you looking at?" Nathan asked.

"Oh, nothing," Howie said. But his eyes were still on the old woman and the young child, who were now looking right at him. Howie suddenly realized the iconic role he was in: a perfectly costumed groom. The people he had observed as picturesque were, in turn, watching the scene in which he was starring. The wedding scene.

Nathan followed Howie's gaze, spotting the boy and the woman. He raised his hand, which struck Howie as odd; the old woman and young boy waved back at them.

"All right, we waved at a kid," Nathan said. "Now he'll go away. Focus. Are you ready?"

"Sure am," Howie confirmed. And he was.

CAMBRIDGE & ELSEWHERE 1998–2000

S IX KIDS IS A LOT OF KIDS.

By the time they had been married for thirteen years, Howard and Sophie had six children. Three girls, three boys. Good kids, smart kids, but *a lot* of kids.

Dinah, Micah, Ellie, Tamar, Isaac, and Moe.

Six. Kids.

In addition to parenting a half-dozen offspring and volunteering as soccer coaches and room parents and Hebrew school teachers, Howard and Sophie both worked. Howard taught philosophy at two universities. Despite all his students adoring him, he was adjunct at both schools, still unable to secure a full-time position, let alone a tenure-track one. Sophie's career as a pharmaceutical rep paid the bills while affording her just enough flexibility to keep her career going despite all the maternity leave.

She liked her job, enjoyed meeting the doctors and nurses, popping from place to place rather than being tied down in an office. But she couldn't remember the last time she didn't feel exhausted.

They managed to make a lot of things work, Sophie and Howard and the kids. Eight lives under one roof. Hyper-organized Sophie kept the whole enterprise going. She was a builder of budgets. A creator of calendars. She ensured their lives were color-coded and clearly charted. Howard was a good partner, completing his to-do list assignments, keeping a good attitude, grabbing kids by their ankles and dangling them upside down until they screamed with delight.

Everything was great. Except for one small thing. While Sophie could handle having six kids, she could not handle seven. And the seventh child in the equation of their lives, the additional variable she had not counted on, was her brother-in-law Nathan.

Nathan was a tenured professor, something he blithely rubbed in his big brother's face. He was a well-funded researcher. He owned his own brownstone in nearby Brighton. He dressed well. Went to the right events. Donated money to the right causes. He was, by all measures, an adult. But when it came to emotions and basic social functioning, he was barely an adolescent.

Sophie knew early about Howie's strange, sad little family. His widowed mother, dead father, anti-social brother; even his grandparents sounded bizarre: small-town conservative zealots who made the local news for dying in each other's arms. She struggled not to see the small Fell tribe as creepy.

The trouble with Nathan was twofold. First, he disrupted their life constantly. He did things like tell the children they should think hard about the inevitability of death. Or he'd give them weird, inappropriate gifts (a mime he brought as a surprise for Dinah's third birthday, which made her cry; a dissection kit, complete with blanched fetal pig in formaldehyde, for Micah's seventh, which made him vomit).

Second, there was the effect he had on Howie. The dynamic between the brothers was something Sophie never understood. She knew the loss of their father at such a young age must have bonded them deeply, even if they didn't get along; she knew they were both protective of their mother, Lila, with her faraway eyes and absent smile. They were insanely competitive, and constantly debating—sometimes at top volume. And when Nathan inevitably got upset and stormed out, Howie always followed.

Howie felt responsible for Nathan in a way that Sophie found irrational. Nathan was more financially secure, more professionally established, had fewer responsibilities of his own—yet Howard constantly checked in on him, apologized for him, tried to help him out.

This occasionally led to arguments between Howie and Sophie about *appropriate boundaries* and *letting full-grown people sink or swim on their own*.

"Nathan needs me, Sophie," Howie pled, never raising his voice, making her feel bad for yelling at him. "He needs a compass. He's a brilliant guy, and he's doing some revolutionary work, but if he's just out there on his own—"

"He's not on his own! He works with a whole team of people!"

"People who see him as a leader, the visionary—"

"So let him be a visionary!"

"I'm not sure he's the sort of person whose... vision should prevail," Howie said heavily, shoulders stooping with the weight of this knowledge. "He's so smart, Sophie—so, so smart. And he's doing some amazing things. But *being able* to do something is one thing; whether or not he should actually be doing it—doing what he's doing, planning what he's planning... that's an entirely different matter. No one else will raise the ethical concerns with him."

"Sweetheart, you know I love your moral compass," Sophie said, placing a hand on her husband's arm, drawing him toward her. "But you're not the ethics police. I know you're worried about whatever Nathan's working on. But he can't do anything without approval from the, what do you call them, the—the Institutional Review Board, or whatever? The university has plenty of ethical measures in place—"

"He's at M.I.T. less and less, sweetheart," Howie said. "He keeps talking about starting an independent institution. Something that will be funded by big donors, won't have the same reporting and oversight he has to deal with at a university—"

"It's not your problem, Howard."

"Sophie, please..." Howie searched for the right words. "He needs a compass."

"Well, I wish he'd find another one," she snapped. "You're supposed to be *my* compass."

She hated how she sounded, harsh and uncaring. It went against her very essence; Sophie fundamentally wanted to help people, strived to extend olive branches, believed in second chances. But she was done with Nathan.

She tried to tell herself that maybe someday things would change. Maybe Nathan would meet someone. Get married. Go *away*. She wondered if she should set him up on a date. She brought this idea up with Maxwell as they watched their children sprint across the soccer field.

Micah was on the same team as Maxwell and Henry's daughter, Penelope. Game days and practices were the only times Max and Sophie could get in some catch-up time these days, clutching coffees while they watched a bunch of eight-year-olds chase after a ball.

"Nathan needs someone," Sophie said, after giving Maxwell the blow-by-blow on her latest fight with Howie. "Someone other than his brother. But he's just never gonna meet anyone. I just have this feeling. He's always going to be this albatross, sucking Howie away from me and the kids, making life more complicated. He's never brought a girlfriend over, not once—"

"You don't think he's gay," Maxwell said mildly, clearly not believing this was the case.

"Nah," Sophie said. "Gay, I could handle. Gay would be great."

"Obviously. I'd even help you set him up, if I knew a guy super into brilliant weirdos."

"God. He is a weirdo."

"Do you think he's dangerous?"

"You mean, other than to my marriage?"

"Yeah."

"No. I don't know. I think he's just... off."

"Maybe he will meet someone, then," Maxwell said. He looked at the field, raised his coffee cup. "Yes! Penny! Good hustle, baby girl!" Then, back to Sophie: "Give it time. I mean, the guy is good looking. Educated. Well-off."

"So are a lot of serial killers," countered Sophie.

"You just said you don't think he's dangerous. You changing your mind now?"

"I don't know. No." Sophie sighed. "I mean, I hope not. You know how much I love Howie, but lately, I just... I don't know. Sometimes, Howie seems more concerned about being his brother's 'compass' than he is about being my husband. Or the kids' dad. I get the feeling there's something he's not telling me. But... God. I just don't know."

Max squeezed her hand. "You and Howie'll figure it out."

"I hope so."

"You will. He's a good one."

It would be easy for a best friend to turn on a significant other, to demonize them, to want to win their friend's attention back. But by then, Maxwell loved Howie almost as much as he loved Sophie. While the worst part of Sophie felt a twinge of regret at

Max not spearheading a Howie-trashing session, the bigger and better part of her is glad he didn't. Howie was a keeper, after all.

But something was going to have to give with Nathan.

And as if in answer to her prayers, that night when Howie got home, he shared some very surprising news.

Howie arrived as Sophie was preparing the last of the lunches for the next morning's hasty exit to school. He looked dazed.

"Long day?" Sophie asked, zipping shut the final plastic baggie. "I was getting worried."

"Nathan came by my office."

"Everything okay?"

"Yeah," Howie said, disbelieving his own statement, three miraculous words that sent Sophie's heart soaring: "He met someone."

CHAPTER 16: SARAH

SARAH FELT OUT OF PLACE IN Cambridge. It was too cold, for one thing. Why the hell would anyone elect to live somewhere that regularly dropped below freezing for half the damn year? Sarah saw no charm in snow. Freezing, dangerous, bad for traffic. Nothing romantic about any of that. And the snow wasn't the only thing that was way too white about Massachusetts.

Before moving there, she was assured that Boston was supposed to be diverse. And it was, to an extent, depending on the neighborhood—but she still felt conspicuous here. This Chestnut Hill coffee shop was a particularly pale little yuppie haven. Everyone here was white. Including the man she was meeting.

Not *"the man,"* she reminded herself. *My fiancé.*

She had met the odd, limping genius at a brain research conference, inexplicably held in Choctaw, Mississippi, at one of the casino conference centers there. When she got her registration and planning packet for the conference, announcing its new venue, she had huffed aloud in surprise.

Guess they ran out of funding for the Vegas location.

Sarah wasn't a neuroscientist, researcher, or pill-pusher. She was an event planner, and her firm was taking over this conference next year. Her supervisor, Bonnie, had selected Sarah as the representative to observe this year's conference, to "get a feel for it." At first, Sarah was excited at the assignment, thinking maybe it meant she'd get to head up the event next year. But when she got the brochure, she frowned, fearing she had actually been selected because this conference was held on a reservation, and Sarah was the firm's only native employee.

She almost asked Bonnie if that was the rationale. Did Bonnie think Sarah would befriend a tribesperson, smoke a peace pipe, and get some sort of deal? Broker a special native rate? Sarah doubted that the bored Choctaw woman who handled events on the casino's end of things could give two shits that Sarah was half Hopi.

Instead, Sarah agreed to the assignment, deciding she would simply sue if she didn't get the coordination gig after scouting it. Venue aside, everything about this event was appealing. Brain surgeons were likely to be big spenders and mostly men. Rich guys were conference-goers who wouldn't balk at premium rates and wouldn't complain about insufficient carb-free dining options.

Sarah had briefly worked as a wedding planner, which probably forever ruined her for working with women. She realized it was an unfair bias, and increasingly politically-incorrect opinion to hold. So she kept her mouth shut about it, but was always relieved when her clients were men.

She knew she also shouldn't assume that a group of brain docs would be mostly men—but the gender disparity was confirmed as soon as she arrived at the Bright Sun Casino.

A sea of men, only a small handful of women. Good.

Although technically just there to observe, Sarah had been volunteered by Bonnie to help this year's coordinators with the registration table. So she was checking in conference registrants with last names A-G when the limping man approached. He had a thick head of hair, steel-gray eyes, and a serious expression.

"Name?"

"Dr. Nathan Fell," he said.

"First time in Mississippi?" Sarah asked, not really interested, but trained to make conversation. Better for business, even if it went against her generally aloof personality. She got into event planning for the logistics, not the schmoozing. Almost too late, she remembered to slap a smile on her face after asking the question.

"First and last, hopefully," said Dr. Nathan Fell.

Sarah raised an eyebrow. "That's… direct."

He shrugged, took his packet from her, and left.

She watched the stormy-eyed man limp off, still thinking about him as she checked in the next few registrants.

"Excuse me," said another registrant, young and eager. "Hi. About three people ahead of me, was that—was that Dr. Nathan Fell?"

"Oh, um, yeah," Sarah said. When she confirmed the identity of the limping man, the kid looked as if Sarah had just confirmed an Elvis sighting. His eyes bugged out from his head, making him look like a sallow caterpillar about to explode.

"It's really him," breathed the lithe young man.

"Um, are you a conference participant?" Sarah asked, eying the irritated line of registrants behind the big-eyed dude. "This line is for last names A through H—"

"Yeah, yes, yes," he said, still looking over to where Fell had headed. "Last name is Hess. Felix Hess."

"Ah, okay. Got your packet here. And here's your student badge—"

The kid grabbed his materials from her and took off like a shot. As she checked in the next participant, Sarah was bewildered. Should she have heard of that guy, Dr. Nathan Fell? The more she thought about it, the name did ring some sort of a bell. But why did she know it?

Turning to the woman registering people beside her—Carol, maybe? She didn't care—Sarah mumbled something about needing to wrap up her duties here so she could observe more of the event. As she walked away from the registration table, she flipped through the conference program, and there it was—a stern headshot of the man she had just met. Dr. Nathan Fell was the keynote speaker at this year's conference. The title and description of his session was over Sarah's head:

THE INEVITABILITY OF CYBORGANICS
The Coming Age of The Singularity and Beyond

Dr. Nathan Fell, Hodge Endowed Chair of Cyborganics at Massachusetts Institute of Technology will explain the basics of cyborganics and transhumanism, from brain mapping for initial augmentation to moving conversations about the Singularity from theoretical to practical as the inevitable merger of mankind and machinery approaches.

Sarah thought she was going to be running a brain conference. This sounded more like ComiCon shit. She was intrigued, though. So she decided to attend his lecture. She made sure to stop at the bar first, assuring the bartender that since she was staff, it was all right to pour her a glass before the official happy hour.

Flirted with him just enough to get a glass of the good stuff, please and thank you.

Clutching her plastic cup of gin and tonic, Sarah snuck into the back of the packed lecture hall. *Jesus, this has to be against fire code.* There were people everywhere: Every seat was filled, every aisle way and back row full of standing room attendees. The presentation wasn't even supposed to start for another ten minutes. She caught the eye of a gap-toothed man standing to her left, then nodded toward the podium, where Fell would soon be standing.

"You ever heard this guy speak before?"

"Fell?" The man shook his head, face shining. It was hot in the room, too many people crammed together. Sweat dripped down the guy's face. "Man, I wish. He's a legend, but also a total recluse. He was still teaching at M.I.T. when I was there, but getting into his class was impossible. And now he almost never lectures outside of this new institute he's heading up."

"Oh," Sarah said. She sipped her gin, hoping the pour was generous enough to see her through awkward small talk with this nerdy fanboy *and* a potentially boring lecture.

"They call him the Cyborganics Cowboy. No one's doing the shit he's doing."

"Huh."

Then, the man beside Sarah shut up and began smacking his hands together. Because there he was, the Cyborganics Cowboy himself, at the front of the room, limping up to take his place at the podium. Dr. Nathan Fell. The entire crowd began applauding before Fell even said a damn thing, and he raised a hand to halt their appreciation. He then gave a curt nod to the A/V booth. The main lights in the room cut out immediately, and a large, high-definition presentation illuminated instantaneously on the massive drop screen hanging behind Fell's podium.

A word filled the screen, accompanied by its definition:

Cyborganics: The science of life or living matter blended with technology; augmenting organic material with supplemental technology designed to improve and enhance existing function and potential.

"A very simple concept," Fell began. The crowd hung on his every word. "And yet this field of science has generated no small amount of criticism and ridicule. So let me make the case. The Greek word 'techne' means art, skill, craft; what we see and define now as hard science is also something beautiful. We are not mere interpreters of technology, we are its designers. Its artists. We are not separate from technology. More and more, it informs our daily experience. Yet when we say 'technology' we mean the tools of the trade, and not the craftsman. We distance ourselves in that way, and impoverish our ability to truly elevate technology. The best artists, after all, put themselves into their art."

Sarah had been an art major. She pictured van Gogh as she sipped her cocktail, intrigued.

Fell continued: "In the field of cyborganics, we offer an idea that should not be seen as radical: technology is about people. People shape technology, technology shapes people, we are already interdependent and this trend not only will continue... but must be moved forward, by those of us with the vision to be true artists. True scientists. And to prove my first point—that we are already interdependent with technology—I will use a very personal example."

On the screen behind him, the words disappeared, replaced by a vintage photograph. The image was of a tiny, yellowish baby laying in an incubator, surrounded by tubes, wires, and all manner of now-dated machinery.

"That," Nathan Fell said flatly, "is me."

The crowd buzzed. Sarah gazed at the photograph, rapt, wondering if his limp might be due to him being a preemie or a crack baby or something.

"I was born too early," continued the man at the podium. "And also at just the right time. Because I was born in an era when premature birth was not an automatic death sentence. My life was saved by machines. To those who say that the merger of man and machine is unnatural, I say: Would you be willing to cast aside the life of every child who had to be connected to a machine before he could breathe on his own? Would you pull the plug on every person in a hospital, right now, kept alive by their literal connection to technology?"

As soon as the presentation was over, the entire audience was on their feet, applauding and screaming out questions and throwing their hands in the air. It was less like a post-lecture talkback and more like a rock concert. But there was no encore. As the screen behind him went dark and his fans screamed, Fell limped offstage without taking a single inquiry.

Sarah's mind was racing with a thousand new thoughts. When was the last time she had been challenged to think like this? It was exhilarating. She wanted to talk with Fell. To ask him questions. But more than that, she wanted to rip every shred of clothing from his body and have her way with him.

She didn't know why. He was attractive, but not incredibly so. Sarah wasn't drunk, she hadn't just been dumped—none of the reasons that usually drove her to pursue a lover were at play. But there was something electric about him. About knowing how everyone else wanted a piece of him, and he had denied them all. She had access that no one else did, and for the first time in her lackluster career, she was going to exploit that access.

She slipped out of the room, chugged the last of her gin for courage, tossed the cup into a trash can, and hurried to the locked room where the company computers were being stored between sessions. Knowing she could get fired for what she was doing, Sarah logged into the server and looked up Fell's room. Penthouse suite. Figured—a nice perk for the main presenter.

Head down, Sarah hurried to the nearest elevator. She pressed the PH button, hoping her room key allowed access to that level; it did. She dug through her purse frantically as the elevator rose smoothly upwards; finding her Tic Tacs and lip gloss, she crunched hard on the mints and swiped the gloss across her lips, stepping out of the elevator as soon as the door slid open. She walked to the penthouse suite, and knocked confidently.

Fell opened the door, mildly surprised. His tie was loosened around his neck. He had deep circles under his eyes, indicating a lack of sleep she had not noticed earlier. But he looked hotter, casual and disheveled like this. And those eyes—so gray, mysterious, penetrating…

"You're the woman who checked me in," he said mildly.

She was thrilled that the conference celebrity recognized her.

God, this really is like being a groupie at a rock show.

"Yes. I am. I'm Sarah. Sarah… Proudtree."

She hated how she always hesitated before saying her last name. She wasn't born Proudtree. She was born Loloma. But she had a contentious relationship with her father, a man as moody and damaged as she was. So at eighteen she legally changed her name. At the time, Proudtree signified everything her adolescent self valued—independence, nature, artistry; she wanted a poetic new name that distanced her from her father while still staking a claim in her native heritage. As the years passed, her self-selected name started to feel clunky. She wished she had gone with something simpler. But the paperwork was a pain in the ass the first time, and she never got around to changing her name again.

"Miss Proudtree," Fell nodded. Somehow, when he said her name, it didn't sound awkward at all. "Is everything all right?"

"Yes," she said. "I was just hoping to…"

And then, because she had come up with nothing further to say, she kissed him.

An hour later, after the kissing and everything that followed had reached its conclusion, they lay in bed together, arms and legs entangled. Nathan was looking at her intently; curiously.

"Why did you come up to my room?" he asked.

"I'm—impulsive. But not usually this impulsive."

"You were at my presentation."

"Yes. I guess I found it… stimulating."

He smiled. At the time, she didn't know how rare a reward that was. "Ah."

"Especially what you said, towards the end—about implications for mental illness."

"Are you mentally ill?" He asked the question without judgment, as if he were asking her if she lived in the area, or if she preferred regular or decaf.

"Yes," Sarah said, in her second most impulsive move of the evening; disclosing this fact was far more intimate than removing her clothing. "I'm manic-depressive. Or bipolar, or whatever we're supposed to call it now."

"Are you on medication?"

"Yeah. But I hate it. What you were talking about sounded… I don't know. You were talking about things that would obviously be more invasive, but also more…"

"Integrated."

"Yes. So it's just… part of you?"

"Cyborganic tech is wholly part of you. Not like rudimentary supplemental medications that regulate and restrict you. You're grateful for your medications, but also resent them?"

She nodded so hard her jaw hurt. "Yes."

"How old are you?"

She considered lying, but once again, didn't: "Thirty-nine."

"I'm thirty-seven," he offered.

"Guess you have a thing for older women," she cracked, surprised and a little embarrassed to learn she was older than the world-famous brain researcher.

"Not really, no," he said, apparently missing her joke. He rolled on to his side, propping himself up on an elbow, looking at her intently. For all his sharp edges, his leanness, there was a softness to his belly, to his arms. Skinny-fat, her friend Jae would call it. She doubted this brainiac had ever seen the inside of a gym. "Where do you live?"

"Arizona."

"Do you like Arizona?"

She shrugged, her shoulders shifting beneath her curtain of smooth, dark hair. "It's fine, for a desert. I grew up there. I have a job that doesn't totally suck, so that's something. Some old friends. Some plants. It's a commitment, raising plants in the desert."

"Arizona is far from here. Why are you staffing this conference?"

"The company I work with—we're going to run this conference, next year."

"This conference used to be in Vegas." He chewed his lip. "If it were in Vegas, we could go get married right now."

She burst out laughing at this. "Yeah, right. Talk about impulsive."

"Have you ever been to Cambridge? Massachusetts?"

"I've been to Boston."

"Come to Cambridge," Dr. Nathan Fell said, sitting up and sliding his white button-down shirt over his arms, fastening it swiftly. "At the end of this semester. Come to Cambridge, and we'll get married then. It will be less impulsive. We can get to know each other a bit between now and then. I'll give you my card."

It was the most surreal moment of the most surreal day of her life. This stranger, this brilliant and sought-after scientist she'd just slept with, telling her they should get married in a few months. Casually suggesting it, like a restaurant recommendation—*here, take my card, drop me an email, I'll send you the name of that Thai place, oh, and you can take my last name.*

But she took the card when he handed it to her.

And the next day, she emailed him.

For a week, she heard nothing. It was long enough for her to decide that he was a sadist, a man who had taken most men's stereotypical "I'll call you" line and raised it all the way up to "I'll marry you," evidently just to be cruel.

She hated him. *Hated* him.

But when he wrote her back, seven days after her email, his reply was apologetic. He confessed that he had re-written it time after time, wanting to get it right. Explaining that he was not very good with people in general, and women specifically. His experience was limited. He spent his life in classrooms and laboratories. She had shaken his focus, which he endearingly described as "a welcome revelation." He hoped she would forgive his tardiness and tell him more about her. He had been serious about the marriage proposal, he added.

He wasn't kidding. Three weeks after the conference, and after only a half-dozen e-mails, he mailed her an engagement ring. A massive, gleaming stone, nestled in a tasteful white gold band. Sarah knew it must have cost two years' worth of her salary.

A week after he sent it, she decided to put it on, which meant answering more than a few questions.

Dear old Bonnie very nearly dropped dead of apoplexy twice—when she saw the ring, and when she heard the (edited version of the) story behind it. The version Sarah told people, Bonnie included, was that she met Dr. Fell at the conference, it was love at first sight, they had started a long-distance relationship, and now they were engaged. Which was sort of true, possibly minus the love part.

"Twenty-five years in event planning, and I never..." Bonnie gaped.

December 2000 came quickly. By the time the plane ticket arrived, Sarah had already decided that she would use it. The ticket arrived at her apartment just as the engagement ring had, expensively overnighted and requiring a signature on delivery.

It was accompanied by a simple note, written on a post-it in Nathan's scrawling hand:

> End of the semester is the 18th. Plane lands at 2:30. Car will be waiting. Will meet you at The Daily Grind coffee shop, 4 PM. –Nathan

And there she was, sitting at The Daily Grind in Chestnut Hill, waiting to see the man she might inexplicably be marrying. Her luggage was jammed uncomfortably under the table, her feet scrunched up against the roller bag's wheels.

She glanced at her watch. 3:59. She wondered again if this was all one big prank, the joke of a sociopath. She had nothing worth taking, but money clearly wasn't a problem for this guy. If he was gaming her, it was a sicker game. A brilliant man with deep pockets and limited social skills. Maybe he was planning to lobotomize her.

With each sip of her coffee, each yoga-mat carrying white girl walking in and ordering a skinny latte, Sarah's anxiety grew. She was torn between wanting him to show up, and becoming convinced that if he did, it might well be only so he could cut her into little bits later.

At four o'clock on the dot, Dr. Nathan Fell limped in to The Daily Grind, and smiled.

L ILA GOLDEN FELL HUNG UP THE PHONE, shaking with small earthquakes of gratitude.

At last, her Nathan had found someone.

Howie had been secure with Sophie for years. He was fine, well-loved—and now, Nathan, her baby who arrived too early and never seemed to settle into this life, had finally found someone. Lila feared it would never happen, that she and Howie would forever be the only ones who attempted to connect with her brilliant but volatile boy. But this phone call—this unexpected, glorious phone call from Nathan, informing her that he was marrying a woman named Sarah—it was a gift. It was everything Lila had been hoping for, for so many years.

It's all right, Ernest. They're all right. My work here is done.

LOS ANGELES 1995

CHAPTER 18: CLAUDIA

"CHAUFFEUR.   C—H—A—U—F—F—E—U—R. Chauffeur."

"Correct."

Claudia Lee slumped lower in her seat and sucked loudly from her grape juice box. This earned her quick, sharp glares from the riveted audience members all around her before their idiot heads swiveled forward again.

For some reason, everyone in this stupid school thought that things like spelling bees were important. That they actually *mattered*. This was dumb for many reasons, primarily because being able to spell flawlessly from one's own recall was a totally useless, outdated skill. Every word processing program out there could already correct common spelling errors. Those corrective systems had their flaws, which tended to play out on the easy stuff—not catching when a *they're* should be a *their* or a *there*. It could reliably tell you how to spell a distinct word like *chauffeur*.

Claudia was, as it happened, an excellent speller. But she felt no need to flout that skill, because it was such a superfluous one. She had refused to even participate in the first round of this year's spelling bee, claiming her science classes and extracurricular projects were too time-consuming to allow her adequate time to study for the bee.

Study for the bee. What a joke.

"Contestant Eleven, your word is 'excruciating,'" called one of the three intensely focused English teachers seated behind the rickety card table. It was Mrs. Owens, the one with the round eyeglasses and bad bowl cut, who looked more than a little owlish. She was Claudia's favorite teacher, because she allowed her students to read whatever they wanted for extra credit. Her wide eyes always went wider at Claudia's selection of complex computer science and robotics texts, or, most recently, *Zen and the Art of the Internet.*

"Can you use the word in a sentence?" Contestant Eleven, squeaked. Contestant Eleven, AKA Miles Majors, was a big hulking kid who could barely keep from crying when put on the spot like this.

The moment we're all currently trapped in is excruciating, Claudia thought unhelpfully, slurping the last of her grape juice box and counting the minutes until she could be done with all this provincial crap and on to bigger and better things.

THE EAST COAST 2000-2010

CHAPTER 19: HOWARD

"**S**TILL WORKING?" Sophie asked, nuzzling her husband's neck. "It's July, by the way. You do know that, right, babe? Summer break, and all?"

Howie took a step back from his standing desk, leaning into the softness of his wife, her comforting scent. He removed his glasses and rubbed at the growth on his face. He hadn't shaved in weeks. It was the one visible sign that he was, in fact, on vacation.

"I really want to finish this before the semester starts up," Howie sighed. "When the students are back, their papers are the ones that matter, and then this never gets written…"

"This is still the pendulum swing thing?"

"Yeah."

Howie had been picking at an article for some time now, about what he was calling the generational-spiritual pendulum. Two generations ago, religious affiliation and identification was high; his grandparents were all people of faith, of varying origin but all religiously observant to some degree. His parents' generation, if not irreligious, was statistically less religiously inclined than the generation above them. The pendulum typically swung back in the third generation.

But his own generation appeared to be an anomaly. Rather than completing the traditional pendulum swing, they looked more like a wagging finger, back and forth back and forth, across the board. Some were spiritually starved and perpetually seeking, like Howie; others, spiritually dismissive to the point of aggression, like his brother. He had already interviewed several sociologists and religious scholars for the piece, and conducted several surveys over the past few years. He was wondering if he should interview his brother, get his perspective.

He should call Nathan, even if not to interview him for the paper. They hadn't really talked since Nathan's wedding, eight months ago. Howie knew it was a huge relief to his own wife that since committing himself to Sarah, Nathan had virtually vanished from their lives. But the lack of communication was odd for Howie. Though the brothers were contentious as sparring lawyers their whole lives, their debates had never ceased before. The silence was deafening.

And while Sarah seemed pleasant enough—not warm, but socially adept—Howie had no idea what sort of support system she provided Nathan. Was she a sounding board, a mediator, an enabler? Would she raise questions of ethics and implications when Nathan discussed his work with her? *Did* Nathan discuss his work with her?

Nathan needed a compass. He always had, he always would. Howie was not sure if Sarah could provide him with that sort of guidance, and that uncertainty unsettled Howie.

"Where'd you go, baby?" Sophie asked softly, already knowing.

"Sorry," Howie said. "Just—drifting. Where are the kids?"

"They're all out back, asking to fill up the kiddie pool for a splash party. You in?"

"Yeah, sounds fun," Howie said, hitting save and turning around to smile up at Sophie. "I'll just go shave, then meet you out back."

"You know what?" Sophie asked, combing his beard with her fingers, then kissing him, long and hard. "Don't shave it. That beard's kind of hot."

CHAPTER 20: FELIX

F ELIX HESS HAD NEVER BEEN MORE NERVOUS for an interview in his life. He spent the past semester in the only course offered by Dr. Nathan Fell. He worked his ass off. Just getting into the class had taken plenty of finagling. There were only eleven students in the classroom, and each of them was as accomplished as Felix.

It was unsettling. Claudia Lee had been his one and only worthy academic adversary, back at Stanford. But here, half the students were already post-docs, so eager to learn from Dr. Nathan Fell that they took the class for no credit and worked three times harder than the average graduate student. So Hess doubled down and worked four times as hard, studying until he could no longer keep his eyes open, reading ahead in the impossibly dense textbooks and then re-reading them to hammer in the knowledge.

He shouldn't be so nervous. He had earned this, and he was owed this: his program guaranteed him a faculty mentor in his second year. There was no guarantee of who his mentor would be. But it had to be Nathan Fell. It *had* to be. This man, this great mind, this Synthetic Moses was the entire reason Felix had chosen this program. This school. This path.

Felix Hess would do whatever it took to get this mentorship.

The office door opened and a female student stumbled out, looking dazed and slightly sick. Felix recognized her, one of only two girls in Fell's class. Amy. Felix wondered if she'd gone in asking about a mentorship, or requesting a final rewrite on her term paper. Either way, it did not appear that her supplication went well.

Nathan Fell stepped into the doorway. He clutched a fat file folder. He didn't look at Amy as she shuffled down the hall. He barely looked at Felix as he called his name.

"Felix Hess?"

Felix rocketed out of his seat. He followed his awkwardly gaited idol into the man's small, neat, uncluttered office. The professor gestured toward the chair across from his desk, and Felix forced himself to sit, though his nerves would rather he stood. Nathan Fell dropped heavily into his own desk chair. He set the thick folder gingerly on the desktop, eyeing Felix appraisingly. Waiting.

"Professor Fell," Hess began. "It's imperative that I—"

"You want me to be your faculty mentor."

"Yes," Hess said, brought up short. He was unaccustomed to being cut off. "And I believe you'll find that—"

"All right."

"What?"

"All right, Felix Hess," said Nathan Fell. "You've proven yourself this year, in my class. I'm not going to be teaching after this term, but I'll be your faculty advisor. And depending on how things go, I may be in need of some ongoing assistance with a long-term project. Would that be of interest?"

"...yes," Hess barely managed to squeak.

"You're very lucky, Mr. Hess," said Fell. "I'm in a good mood. Got married recently. I'd told the dean I wasn't taking on any new mentees here this year. But your resume is impressive. Your work in my class has not gone unnoticed. And as I said, I'm in a good mood."

"Th-thank you."

"You can go."

Hess rose, his knees clacking together. After all the anticipation, all the preparation, all the anxiety—it had gone well, but he was almost shaken by how quickly it had gone. He felt he should say something else, but instinctively knew that once dismissed, he was expected to leave.

"One more question, Hess," the professor said. He looked up from the papers in front of him. His expression had shifted, an almost-smile playing at his lips. "Do you have a girlfriend?"

"Oh, uh, sort of," said the young Felix Hess, almost apologetically. "This girl Marilyn, we just started seeing each other, and—"

"Lock it down," Nathan advised. "Marry her. Just get it over with, so dating or love won't distract you from what really matters. Take it off the to-do list. Focus on the work. Got it?"

"Got it," Felix said. It wasn't advice he was expecting.

But whatever this man told him to do, he'd do.

CHAPTER 21: PASSENGERS

AMERICAN AIRLINES FLIGHT 11 was scheduled to depart from Boston's Logan Airport at 7:45 that Tuesday morning. The passengers had to rise early; five in the morning, maybe earlier.

They arrived at their gate with coffees in hand, bleary-eyed, some showered and dressed, others in sweatpants still smelling of last night's sleep. Some barely made it on time, snapping at their spouses as they fretted about missing the plane and needing to re-book a later flight. They were mothers and fathers, brothers and sisters, sons and daughters. They were mostly good people, perhaps an affair here and there, petty crimes, flaws, but so many gifts and talents and goals. Some had songs stuck in their heads. Others were halfway through a good book. They kissed their loved ones goodbye, cursed themselves for forgetting toothbrushes, went to the bathroom one last time before boarding.

A jumpy passenger who hated flying glanced at her boarding pass and thought, *Flight 11 on the 11ᵗʰ, sounds lucky*, and felt a little calmer.

There were eighty-seven passengers who boarded American Airlines Flight 11, intending to travel from Boston to Los Angeles.

There were five more men who boarded the plane with other plans.

The plane did not make it to Los Angeles. It went instead to New York, taking all those people with them.

The eighty-seven passengers aboard American Flight 11 shared a fate that day with nearly three thousand other people— people on other flights, people in each of the Twin Towers in New York, people in the Pentagon, people who brought their own hijackers down in a fiery crash in a field in Somerset County, Pennsylvania.

But for the passengers on American Flight 11, the people whose lives and deaths were most entwined were those working in the North Tower of the World Trade Center. Professionals at their desks, in meetings, wishing their elevators would go a little faster, enjoying a donut, jotting down a note to call their mother for their birthday.

Travelers. Workers. Humans expecting a day like any other.

At 8:46 that fateful morning, their lives came together and ended all at once, blue skies suddenly seared by smoke and fire and screams.

They might have gone on to be anything. Everything. Because one person can make the world an entirely different place, and these souls, all taken in one day, could have changed the world in so many ways. The five hijackers on American Flight 11, and their compatriots, proved this beautiful truth in the ugliest and most violent of ways.

Just a few people can do so much.

Just a few people can take so much.

The nineteen hijackers who carried out the evil deed, stealing so much potential when they stole the planes and aimed them toward death.

The eighty-seven on the first plane.

The two-hundred-sixty-five on all three planes.

The sixteen hundred in the first tower.

The three thousand, in total, who would die that day.

The thousands who would die in years to come, in retaliations and conflicts related to or forcefully associated with that day. They could have done anything, amongst them all. They could have changed the world, all of them or any one of them. Any or all of them might have been the key figure in a revolution, or a revelation.

But that morning, surprised and sorrowing souls went up; the twin towers went down. And while some things seemed to go back to normal, nothing was ever really the same.

CHAPTER 22: SARAH

S ARAH HELD ONE DAUGHTER in each arm, still uncertain how she had gotten into this situation. How *this* was her life now; how she arrived at this moment in time, where she was a mother to not one but two girls.

Ruth and Rachel were born just minutes apart: Ruth first, screaming and wailing and sucking all the air from the room as soon as she arrived; Rachel came second, clinging weakly to Ruth's ankle, and attacked by her own amniotic fluid, which was clogging her nasal passages. The smaller girl required assistance before she could breathe on her own. She barely made it.

They were beautiful, angel-faced babies, each unique, far from identical.

Fraternal twins.

Shouldn't that mean they belong to their father?

They are not me.

They are not mine.

Sarah tried to shake these thoughts from her head, but they clung like static, crackling and relentless. They were not just his, she reminded herself. They were his-and-hers, equally, albeit they favored their parents in unequal measure. Even physically, each child seemed sprung from one parent more than the other. Ruth resembled Sarah; Rachel favored Nathan.

Four months old now, no longer wrinkled and interchangeable with any other baby in the world, Sarah's daughters were also sharpening their personalities. Ruth was the bigger, stronger twin, with a thick thatch of dark hair, ruby lips, a stubborn curiosity. She did not like being held by strangers. She was not fussy, but she was particular. Discerning.

Rachel was smaller, softer, with patchy light-brown hair and a sweet, wide-eyed look of perpetual amazement on her little face. Like she was surprised and grateful just to be there. Rachel could be passed from person to person without complaint.

They were both lovely girls. Healthy. Endearing. Any mother would be proud of them. Sarah was proud of them. But she knew they would be better off without her. They would be *safer* without her.

She followed a story in the news, not long ago, about a mother who drowned all of her children. Sarah stared at the woman's round glasses and pale face, the face of a woman people reviled but also pitied and even considered forgiving.

They wouldn't forgive me as quickly as they'll forgive a white woman. And their hearts won't break for my children the way they broke for hers.

The thoughts swirling like angry leaves through Sarah's autumnal mind terrified her. She shivered as she crunched through them. The crunching carried whispers, whispers from other mothers, dangerous whispers, whispers about putting babies to sleep, forever.

No. No. I won't.

I won't.

Back when Sarah first learned she was pregnant, her first call was not to her husband, but to her psychiatrist.

"I'm pregnant," she told Dr. Karen Adelson. Sarah liked Dr. Adelson because she pulled no punches and offered no apologies. "If I want a healthy baby, should I go off my meds?"

"Probably," Dr. Adelson replied, her voice tight but certain, informed by the best studies available at that time. "But let's get you in here to talk it through, see what all the options are."

"Do you think I can handle it? Nine months, no meds?"

"What do you think, Sarah?"

"I think it's risky."

"Let's talk through the options. Wednesday good for you? I can try—"

"I don't have my calendar in front of me just now," Sarah said quickly. "I'll call back later today, to schedule an appointment."

She didn't.

Sarah also did not bother to discuss her medical quandary with Nathan. He was spending more time in New York these days than in Cambridge; his institute was moving there, but the transition was gradual. Nathan and his staff all still lived in Cambridge, finishing up research projects and staving off the inevitable cost of living increase that would come with the move to Manhattan.

When he returned home the weekend after Sarah learned she was with child, Sarah cooked a big meal. Nathan's favorite comfort foods—spaghetti and meatballs, Caesar salad, sweet wheat rolls. Sarah rarely cooked, and could tell Nathan was pleased when he came home to find her in the kitchen, spaghetti sauce simmering on the stove, rolls warming in the oven.

"What's all this?" He asked.

"Spaghetti night," she said. "Welcome home."

"Smells great," he said. "Should I open a bottle of red?"

"Only if you feel like drinking alone."

"Not drinking tonight?"

"Not drinking for the next eight months."

Quick as Nathan was with most calculations, this one took him a minute. His brows went from knit to split as he realized:

"Holy shit."

"Yes."

"You're pregnant."

"It happens sometimes, when people have sex."

He stared at her. And then he just kept staring. The timer dinged; the rolls were ready. She turned her back on him, pulling open the oven door, clenching her jaw, forcing back the tears that threatened. She had already gone off her medication, without seeing her doctor. She already felt altered. It had only been a few days, though, so maybe it was just a sort of placebo effect. Maybe. When she turned back around, tray of rolls in hand, her husband was still just staring at her.

"So, are you still hungry, or did I kill your appetite?"

"I'm still hungry," he said, and followed her into the dining room. He sat, rubbed his eyes, tried to find his balance in a world suddenly tilted. "I—you know I'm going to have to keep up this schedule. Projects here, overseeing things in New York. I'm not going to be able to be around more just because you'll be pregnant."

Just because you'll be pregnant.

Like it was something small, insignificant.

Just because.

Just.

"Yeah, I figured," Sarah said, hoping she sounded breezy. Unaffected. Conversations with her husband always went better when she could match him logic for logic, calm for calm. "I wouldn't have told you at all, but the next time you came back, you might wonder why I was fat. And when there was a little mini-you running around, you might wonder—"

"I don't appreciate sarcasm."

"Well. We're at a standstill, then."

Sarah's responses that evening were her own, and not her own. Normally, when her medications were helping modulate her moods, she could bite her tongue and keep the upper hand. She was not the brilliant mind her husband was, but she wasn't a dumbass. And she was better at reading emotions. She knew sarcasm pissed him off, and reason calmed him.

But the new version of Sarah—the pregnant, hormonal, off-her-medications version of Sarah—found remaining calm and reasonable a painfully difficult assignment.

"What do you want to do?" Nathan asked, his expression neutral.

"What do I want to do?" Sarah whispered, her soft words running like hot lava from her mouth, the entire volcano within her seething, ready to explode.

"If we have a child, it'll be your responsibility. You know I don't have the bandwidth—"

"Shut up," Sarah whispered, fearing she might explode. And then instead of exploding, she ran to the car, peeling out of the driveway so fast that if any unfortunate jogger or dog-walker had been strolling down the sidewalk at that moment, they would have been flattened. She pointed the car west, and started driving. She stopped when she got to Marlborough, Massachusetts. Far enough away that she wouldn't run in to anyone she knew. It was night, and Sarah didn't like driving in the dark.

Easing her car off the highway, she followed signs to a nearby set of hotels and motels. She picked the one that seemed most middle-of-the-road, not the cheapest, not the nicest. A motel almost nice enough to be a hotel. She knew the distinction between a hotel and a motel was that a hotel had a main entrance you had to go in before accessing the rooms, while motels had individual room entry. Someone told her once that the real difference was that a motel was for cheap sex and a hotel was for expensive sex.

Which one is for holing up in and bemoaning the consequences of sex?

She paid for a room, just one night, in cash. This made the attendant raise her eyebrows, but she said nothing. Single woman, no luggage—Sarah knew what she looked like: a refugee of a domestic violence situation. How could she explain that she was escaping domestic apathy?

Before even going to see the room she had secured, she drove to a gas station, went straight to the counter and bought a pack of cigarettes. Marlboros.

Smoking a Marlboro in Marlborough.

I wonder how many stupid teenagers do this and think it's funny.

She didn't find it funny. She walked back to her car, opened the pack, and put a cigarette between her lips. Then she realized she didn't have a lighter. She hadn't smoked regularly in a decade and no longer carried a little fire-starter in her purse. She didn't find that funny, either.

Hot tears pricked at the back of her eyes as she realized that even if she had a lighter, she wouldn't light this cigarette. If she was keeping the baby, she was going to do it right. Go off her meds, and not replace them with cigarettes, even though the appeal of those little cancer sticks would go through the roof when she wasn't regulated. No cigarettes. No meds. After all, as her jackass of a husband had pointed out—this was going to be her responsibility.

As if her idle thought a moment earlier had conjured them, a stray pack of teenagers wandered into the gas station parking lot.

They strolled in from nowhere, going nowhere, aimless as feral dogs who once had nice homes. Three boys, two girls, with hair unwashed and shoes scuffed. Sarah, the unlit cigarette dangling from her lips, called out to them.

"Hey, you want some cigarettes?"

Five heads snapped toward her, mildly suspicious. One of the boys, lanky and good looking in a dirty delinquent sort of way, slowly smiled at her, revealing surprisingly white teeth. He gave an easy shrug of the shoulders, nodded.

"If you're offering, lady."

She tossed him the entire pack; he fumbled, caught it, pulled out a cigarette and stuck it somewhat awkwardly in his mouth, then offered the rest to his friends, distributing a cigarette to three of them (one of the girls turned him down, making a face). Then he turned to give the remainder back to their benefactor. Sarah shook her head.

"Those things will kill you," she said, and got into the car.

Sarah turned off her cell phone when she returned to the hotel. This was unnecessary, as Nathan would not call her. He had a firm policy of not dealing with anyone he deemed unreasonable. Sarah was unquestionably being unreasonable in this situation, running away from the conversation, leaving dinner uneaten, taking the car and disappearing. Sarah knew all this as she lay in bed, hand over her stomach, feeling her blood circulate, playing out in her own mind how the next chapter of her life would go. Weighing her options. Making her own decision.

She fell asleep fully dressed, atop the covers, clutching her lifeless cell phone. She dreamed of her ancestors, strong Hopi women, surviving pregnancies and births and life without medication. Setting their jaws and getting it done. Not relying on moody men, or chemicals, or therapy. Ancestors who turned their dark eyes on her, in quiet judgment, then morphed into wolves and ran into the woods, disappearing when Sarah gave chase, the woods twisting and shape-shifting, trees wrapping themselves into roads and becoming old tires and car corpses. Sarah found herself standing in front of the small trailer she grew up in. She opened the door, expecting to smell alcohol and hear ridicule, but the trailer was empty except for a small black and white television, turned on. Onscreen was a nature show, something about wolves and grandmothers.

The next morning, Sarah woke up to the sound of a garbage truck slamming a dumpster back onto the pavement of the motel parking lot. It beeped as it backed up, out of the parking lot, heading toward the next load of garbage.

She sat up, rolling her fuzzy tongue around her stale mouth. A wave of nausea crashed over her, and she lurched to her feet. She made it to the bathroom just in time, and spent several long minutes expelling the limited contents of her stomach. After vomiting, she sat on the bathroom floor, noticing the shitty cleaning job, dirt lining every edge of the floor, walls, ceiling; shoved aside rather than removed. She sat there, waiting to see if her stomach would rebel again. It would be morning soon, and Nathan would not be home. He was due in New York, and would not delay his flight for her. Wasn't his style.

As soon as she felt well enough to drive herself, she decided she should go home. She would still have privacy, and the bathroom was cleaner. *The better for puking in, my dear.*

Sarah listened to classical music as she drove home. It was something someone had told her once—classical music was good for fetuses. Improved brain development. Maybe it made them dance or helped them get in touch with their ancestors or prevented bipolar disorder. She doubted that last one. But the music soothed her own nerves a little, so she kept it on.

When Sarah let herself into her home, her husband was standing in the hallway.

"Sarah," Nathan said, his voice flat but not insincere. "I was worried."

"You were—what?" She said, still shocked that her husband was standing there, in their hallway, and not on a plane to New York.

"I was worried." He said, again.

"You were?"

"You seemed upset. You left, never came home, your phone went straight to voicemail. I know I may have come off as brusque last night, and I—I'm sorry."

In a half-dozen years of marriage, it was the only time Sarah's husband had ever apologized to her.

"You're supposed to be in New York," she whispered.

"Yes," Nathan said. "I moved my flight to tomorrow. And if you hadn't come home today, I would have moved it back and back until I had found you."

Giving a small cry, Sarah collapsed into her husband's arms. He almost didn't catch her, so surprising was this intimate move; but he did catch her. It was all she had wanted from him, to be held and affirmed, and against all odds, her detached and dismissive husband embraced her.

He stayed home all that day, and they didn't talk about apologies or babies or where Sarah had been, but they were simply together. Occupying the same space, and demonstrating their commitment to that simple thing. Before bed that night, Nathan asked Sarah if it would be all right with her if he did go ahead and take the plane to New York the next morning. She said yes. And that night, he held her again. She slept dreamlessly, and awoke to less nausea, kissing her husband before the taxi carried him off to the airport.

He was gone for a week. While he was away, she saw her doctor, had a blood test, confirmed what she knew. She scheduled her first ultrasound, selecting a day that Nathan would be in town to accompany her. When he returned, their life resumed fairly normally, and for several weeks, this was the case. They had Howie and Sophie and their brood over for dinner, and shared their good news, earning claps from the children, a sharp gasp from Sophie, and an uncharacteristic expletive from Howie, who immediately apologized. Howie then clapped his brother heartily on the back, and gingerly hugged his expecting sister-in-law.

For a little while, Sarah thought she had staved it off. Sheer force of will. Blessings of the ancestors. She was well, in body and mind. This would all be okay.

And then the morning of the ultrasound, Sarah awoke with a feeling of dread. She did not feel nauseous; she felt empty. She had dreamed of wolves and ghosts, an endless set of howls in duet, a wolf and a ghost-ancestor crying together.

Dead baby, she thought. *Inside me there is a dead baby.*

Nathan drove her to the doctor's office, and neither of them said anything. Sarah would not remember the time in the waiting room, the paperwork, the details that blurred into a thousand other similar moments in their lives. What she would remember is the moment in the ultrasound room, clutching the sides of the examination table since her husband's hands were jammed into his own pockets. The technician spread the cold jelly onto Sarah's flesh, then slid the transducer around Sarah's slick skin. Sarah trembled slightly against the mechanical exploration of her body.

"Open your eyes," the technician chuckled.

Sarah didn't realize she had closed them. When she opened her eyes, they went immediately to a fuzzy screen that she could not interpret—the crowded dark interior of her own womb. She looked to Nathan; he was just as mystified by the image. They both stared at the technician.

"You're a little farther along than we thought," said the technician, a petite black woman with two little teardrop pearl earrings, which seemed a bit formal for her white lab coat and scrubs. "Just about the end of your first trimester, I'd say. And that means that we can easily count the number of fetuses, the number of heartbeats… and I count two."

"Count the—what?" Sarah said, confused.

"Twins," Nathan said, catching up faster. His face was softly illuminated by the screen, where he was transfixed by the two lives that he had played a part in creating. Sarah could not swear to it, but he almost seemed happy. "Twins."

Not a dead baby inside me, Sarah realized, relief and terror flooding her at once. *Not a dead baby. Two live babies. Two things, two lives, two possibilities, two responsibilities. A wolf and a ghost. Two howling things.*

"Congratulations," said the technician. "Do twins tend to run in your family?"

"No," Sarah said, then realized she did not know if that was true of her husband's family. She looked at Nathan, and he shook his head. No. No, this was not the sort of thing that ran in either of their families.

"I'll give you two a minute," the technician said, and stepped out of the room.

"Are you happy?" Sarah asked Nathan.

"I am… fascinated," Nathan said, and for a moment Sarah's heart soared. She was not certain she had ever fascinated her husband. Then he kept talking. "Since twins don't run on either side of our family, and we certainly weren't utilizing hormones or in-vitro or anything else that often yields multiples… are you certain they're mine?"

Sarah's soaring heart slammed into the windshield of an oncoming vehicle and shattered.

"What?" She whispered, not shrieking because the technician was just outside the door, not saying more than one word because that was all her ruined heart had the strength to support.

"I've been traveling a lot these past few years. And our own first sexual encounter was—unplanned. I should have been aware that such a scenario might be possible. I would not be pleased to learn of an infidelity, but I feel I have a right to know if—"

"They're yours," Sarah snarled, feeling slapped.

The technician knocked, re-entered. She smiled lightly, adept at using machines to detect unexpected fetuses, but less adept at realizing such news might not be greeted with joy.

"Doctor should be here in a minute, and I'm sure you'll both have some questions…"

My husband already asked the most important one, thought Sarah, closing her eyes again.

For the next half-year, as Sarah grew in size, she shrank in her sense of self. She stayed off her medications, but felt as if someone were slipping her something. A medication designed not to regulate, but to sedate. A little something to make her simply the docile incubator in this process. She moved numbly through her pregnancy.

When Sarah's water broke, Nathan was in New York. Sarah sent him a text message, alerting him to the situation, then called Howie and calmly asked if he would take her to the hospital. So it was Howie who took her to the maternity ward. It was Howie who was there when the labor intensified and when two infants slipped surprisingly swiftly from Sarah. One howling, as expected; the other eerily silent.

A wolf and a ghost.

Then the silent one was smacked, and began to scream.

Two howling things.

Sarah did not hold her daughters that first day. She passed out shortly after the delivery; she was pumped full of drugs and grateful to slip into the warm nirvana of painkillers. Nathan returned from New York the next morning and came to see her before seeing the twins, who were in the nursery, where Howie stood watch over them. Howie, who always would.

By evening, the day after her daughters' birth, the hospital told Sarah she was "good to go." She was wheeled out of the hospital, a baby in each arm. Nathan was waiting outside, and there were two rear-facing car seats in the back of their sedan.

"Don't worry," Nathan said, before Sarah could ask. "Sophie installed them."

They took the babies home. Howie, Sophie, and their whole tribe brought casseroles and soup and presents. The whole herd of children *oohed* and *ahhed* over their tiny pink-faced new cousins.

"What are their names?" Micah asked.

"Oh," Sarah said dully. "They don't have names yet."

She ignored the look that she could practically feel Howie and Sophie exchanging.

"They need names," Micah said.

"Okay," Sarah said. "Thing One and Thing Two. Like in that Dr. Seuss story."

"Aunt Sarah," Micah said, reproachfully.

"They need real names," Dinah added.

"Tell you what," Nathan said, stepping in unexpectedly. "If the six of you can select two names that you agree on, and tell us the rationale for your selections, you may name your cousins."

"Seriously?" Micah asked, eyes huge. "For real?"

"Nathan, I'm not sure that's—" Howie began, but Nathan cut him off.

"Seriously," Nathan said. "For real."

And with the naming of his children thus assigned like any term paper, Nathan went to his study. Sarah sat on the couch, looking at the small humans who had escaped her body. Howie held one, Sophie held the other, while their children flocked around them and commenced naming them. Now that they were outside of Sarah, they already seemed so far away from her. They seemed fine with that. She felt fine with that.

That's when the seed that would bloom and blossom into her escape plan was planted.

One week after the girls were born, the children of Sophie and Howard Fell gathered in their aunt and uncle's living room to make a presentation of the names they had selected for their new cousins. Micah, Dinah, Ellie, Tamar, Isaac, and Moe lined up in order of their own ages. Each held a picture they had drawn or essay they had composed, depending upon their age and ability. But it was Micah, the eldest, who did most of the talking.

"Okay," he began. "I'm gonna keep this brief, but we have lots of—Dad, what did you say we should call it?"

"Supporting evidence," Howie coached, with a wink from the sidelines.

"We have lots of supporting evidence for our recommendations," Micah continued. "And research, and stuff. But basically, we decided that our cousins should have Bible names, since their parents both have Bible names. And we all have Bible names, and we thought since they're part of this family, they should also have some sorta Bible names—"

"*Biblical* names," Sophie finally interjected, unable to hear this error one more time.

"Biblical names," Micah agreed. "And then we also decided that they should have names that start with the same letter, because that's something special for twins."

"And it's super cute," Tamar added.

"It's not just for twins, sometimes whole families have same-letter names," Moe offered.

"But it is something special for twins, sometimes," Micah said, trying to steer things back on track before he lost control of this whole enterprise. "Anyway! We wanted two Bible... *biblical* names that started with the same letter. And after extensive research—"

"Research starts with the letter 'R'!" Moe crowed triumphantly.

"Moe, *shhhhh*," Ellie hushed. "Don't jump the gun."

Micah rolled his eyes. His siblings had trampled and peed all over his chances of making a credible presentation. So he hurried to the end: "We found two 'R' names for girls that are biblical and that we all liked, and we think you should name the babies Ruth and Rachel."

There was a pause, as six sets of eager eyes stared at Nathan and Sarah, waiting.

"Which one for which one?" Nathan asked.

"Ruth is the loud one," Ellie said.

"Rachel's the quiet one," Tamar whispered, for dramatic effect.

Sarah looked at the two girls, sleeping now in their bassinets, which had been dragged out to the living room for the naming ceremony. Ruth and Rachel. The wolf and the ghost was how she still thought of them, but she couldn't very well call them that. These names were as good as any, she decided.

"Sure," she said, without even checking in with Nathan. He shrugged. The half-dozen namers cheered and high-fived, thrilled that their hard work had paid off and they had successfully named their own real-life dolls.

Sarah tried to join in on their cheer, but found that she could not. She could no longer even fake it. She was back on her regular medications, bottle-feeding the girls so they would no longer rely on her body for anything. Her breasts ached for a few days, swelling with milk, but eventually acquiesced and deflated.

In the weeks following the non-traditional naming of Ruth and Rachel, Sarah too seemed to deflate. A darkness wrapped itself around her. Her dreams became more violent. The sound of her children's cries pierced her eardrums by day and tortured her by night. Nathan's travels continued uninterrupted, leaving Sarah alone with the girls every other week, for a week a time.

She watched a lot of television. She became more immune to the girl's cries—Rachel's intermittent yelps, Ruth's unrelenting scream. She did not get used to the sounds; instead, she got used to ignoring them.

And so four months in, on a bright and sunny Saturday, she drew the curtains. The time had come. Her thoughts were too dark and dangerous. The girls' cries were too desperate. She was dreaming again about the mother, the one who drowned her children in the bathtub. But in her dreams, she was not watching the other mother. She was the mother, filling the tub, hearing the screams of her daughters nearby, and further off, the howls of wolves and grandmothers.

Sarah loved her daughters. She loved them more deeply than she could ever have loved Nathan, or anyone. And she *did* love Nathan. Her strange, stoic husband loved her, too, in his own way. She saw it in the way he looked at her now and then, with the same wonder he usually reserved for new discoveries. He was not a man to whom connection came easily, but he was capable of love, and he loved her. Although she sometimes felt a chasm between them, it was not one carved out by some slow erosion of love. It was always there; they were both wrapped in gaps, always distancing themselves from everyone and everything. But they did love one another, against all odds.

She wished she could be as strong as her own mother, who could steel herself and get through anything. She wanted to find some great reservoir of strength, a path toward motherhood and mental health and marital satisfaction.

But she did not know how to find her way to these things, and she knew it was too risky to stay where she was with no salvation in sight. She had to leave before she ruined everything. Before desperation became violence. Before she began filling the bath with water.

She wasn't leaving her daughters because she didn't love them. She was leaving because it was what her love demanded that she do for their survival. And as she buckled them carefully into their car seats, there was no question in her mind about where to take them.

"Hi," Sarah said with a smile, when she showed up unannounced at Howie and Sophie's house. Her hair was clean and she was dressed well, unlike any other time her in-laws had seen her those past few months. She had already set both car seats on the front porch before ringing the bell. Rachel was asleep in her bucket; Ruth stared up from hers.

"Sarah, hi," Sophie said, surprised. She was still wearing a robe; it was nine in the morning, a lazy Saturday. "Howie, Sarah's here—"

From the seat on the porch, Ruth gurgled and reached up— not for Sarah, but for Sophie.

Good girl, thought Sarah.

Giving an apologetic little laugh, Sarah gestured to the infant: "Look, she wants you! I have some errands to run, I was hoping maybe the girls could spend the morning with you?"

Before Sophie could respond, Sarah was already turning to go. She nearly tripped over Rachel's car seat in her haste. Seeing that sleeping baby, she hesitated. Rachel was quieter. Easier. The prospect of a life with two children and Nathan and her depression was too much for Sarah. But what if she had just one perfect baby? A wild woman and her daughter, two wolves ranging out far and wide…

But just then Rachel opened her eyes, and looked around— seeking not Sarah, but Ruth. Her twin. Rachel was not a wolf; that was Ruth, the difficult one, the strong one. Rachel was the ghost. The shadow-child. She needed her sister, not her mother. Her sister would care for her. Yes, the girls would be better off, together, with Howie and Sophie. Just like Sarah planned. Just as she'd written in the letter tucked into Rachel's car seat, for Howie and Sophie to find later.

It never once occurred to Sarah to leave her children with their father.

He was never really there to begin with, and would never have known what to do with two babies and no wife. He would be relieved, Sarah assured herself. He would see the logic here, and appreciate it.

Howie was on the porch by then, looking questioningly at the women and the babies.

"Thanks for keeping them for me," Sarah said, looking straight at Howie.

Then she turned and walked back to the car.

"Sarah?" Sophie called, probably wondering when they might expect her to return. Maybe wondering if Sarah was okay. Either way, Sarah pretended not to hear her.

She got into the car and drove away, her heart and mind echoing with howls. She did not know how to stop the howls. All she knew was that they heralded danger, and misery, and everything she wanted to spare her daughters.

My wolf.

My ghost.

May your paths be easier than mine.

CHAPTER 23: HOWARD

THREE YEARS AFTER SARAH LEFT HER daughters behind, Howie was still trying to convince their father to play a role in their lives. He called his brother weekly, pleading his case, trying to make his brother do the right thing.

"They could at least stay with you on weekends," Howie seethed one Sunday night at the end of yet another weekend wherein Rachel and Ruth had not seen their father. "You're just across town, it's not as if it'd be difficult to arrange—"

"I'm in New York every other weekend."

"So on the weekends you're here, then."

"I don't... do babies."

"They're not infants, Nathan. That excuse has expired. They're three. They can use their words. They use the potty."

"'Potty.' Jesus Christ—"

"They're just kids, Nathan—very good girls, not a burden—"

"She didn't want me to have them," Nathan said bitterly.

"They're still your daughters," Howie argued, catching and releasing the heartbreak in his brusque brother's voice.

"Biologically. Sure. But you know they're better off with you. And didn't you just say they're not a burden? I'll keep sending money. Life with me would be uncomfortable. For all of us. And when I move—you really want me to take them? You'd never see them, Howard."

Howie heaved a sigh. His household would be devastated if the two little girls were gone. It would break them all. With this argument, Nathan had won.

"When exactly are you moving to New York?"

"Later this year. New year, at the latest."

"And what are you working on, these days?"

"Keeping busy," was all Nathan said.

It made Howard nervous, how tight-lipped his brother had become about his work. Nathan was never quiet about work. He was uninterested in commercial fame, but it was important to him that his achievements be noted as *his* by his peers, and ultimately by history. He wanted to be part of the collective conversation. He had taken the science community by storm for a while, talking about cyborganics and the coming synergy, but the past few years he had all but disappeared from public view. The past few months, he had faded further from his family. He never discussed work. Didn't debate ethics with Howie. Nothing.

It compounded Howie's metastasizing concern. He was certain Nathan was working on something big—all those trips to New York, this new institution building he kept talking about. What sort of building took a decade to build, in Manhattan?

Only something massive. Only something with extraordinary laboratory capabilities. Howie knew Nathan had funders who made sure he never need worry about money. They must have made him sign something, some sort of non-disclosure agreement.

Sarah was gone, and Howie doubted she had ever provided the steady compass Nathan needed. Now Nathan was pushing Howard further away. He had no relationship with his daughters. He was constantly shattering any compass Howie tried to press into his hand. Howie had hoped the girls would root Nathan, even if they did not alter his course. That was why Howie kept pushing for Nathan to spend time with them. He believed his brother would ultimately fall in love with the sweet, smart girls he helped create. If only he spent time with them.

"Children should know their parents. These girls need their father—"

"We didn't have a father," Nathan retorted. "We turned out just fine."

"Did we?" Howie asked, sharp.

Nathan hung up on him.

That phone call, almost two months ago, was the last time Howie had spoken to his brilliant, broken brother. He decided that, while it might be risky, the next time that he talked with Nathan, it should be in person. More specifically, it should be with one or both of the girls in tow. Because if Nathan saw them, it would be harder for him to deny them. Howie loved his own wife and children with such intensity, he could not fathom a complete lack of paternal connection. It was just dormant in his brother, he told himself, not entirely missing.

Howie loved his children so damn much. All of them.

All *eight* of them.

He sighed, because the seed planted two months earlier by his brother had taken root. He couldn't imagine writing off Ruth and

Rachel, handing them off to someone else—even if that person was their own disinterested father. They were Howie's children, as much as the other six, and he would do anything for the girls.

So he changed his plans. He no longer pushed for Nathan to step up to the plate when it came to fatherhood. He just wanted him to interact with the girls. Hell, back in the day, Nathan used to give Howie and Sophie's kids more time than he gave his own girls. It wasn't unrealistic to think he could show up sometimes. Send a birthday gift, even if it was poorly selected. Send something more than money.

Although, setting emotion aside, the money mattered more than Howie cared to admit. If he and Sophie kept the girls, they needed Nathan's money. Raising six children was expensive, even with both parents working. Raising eight was impossible. Howie hated cashing the check from Nathan each month, but it was necessary to their survival.

Sophie felt no such qualms.

"He should be sending us double this," she said. "He can afford it. And he's completely pawned parenthood off onto us. We deserve top alimony. Half of everything he has. Let's take him for all he's worth, and tell him in exchange he never has to see any of us again!"

She was kidding, but she also wasn't.

Howie should be grateful for Sophie's ability to joke; when Sarah had initially left Ruth and Rachel with them, Sophie was spitting fire. She unwaveringly and immediately cared for the girls like they were her own, because she was a good person; but she carried a constant rage in her pocket, snapping at Howie constantly, always on the verge of exploding. She had six kids of her own, she finally screamed at Howie one night, since she could not scream at Sarah or Nathan. Six was already insane. This was not fair. This was not *possible*.

But eventually, something clicked within Sophie. When it came to Nathan and Sarah, her fury was unabated; she never spoke to either of them again. But her daily fury abated, and she stopped snapping at Howie and moaning behind closed doors about how unfair it all was; Ruth and Rachel were hers, period. When the girls were two years old, the courts confirmed Howie and Sophie as their legal guardians in a simple process wherein Nathan eagerly waived all rights.

Sophie made sure those waived rights included visitation. Though Howie wanted him to have a relationship with the twins, Sophie was dead set against it. Nathan had given them away. He was not welcome in their home. And Sarah was just as evil, in Sophie's estimation. If either of the biological parents ever showed up out of the blue and tried to collect the girls, they would have to go through Sophie first, and Sophie would murder them. This was why it was Sophie who initiated the court proceedings to make sure the girls were legally hers and Howie's. Once she was in, there was no backing out; and once you were on the outs with her, as Nathan was, as Sarah was—there was no getting back in. Sophie was kind, and generous, and open-hearted. But in the face of heartless acts, Sophie felt no mercy.

Howie stared at the still-loading computer screen, stroking his beard as he waited for the technology to wake up and answer to him. The semester had just resumed, and he once again felt buried alive in the avalanche of his academic career. He loved teaching, loved his students. But he was on the verge of giving up his own professional dreams. His pendulum paper hadn't been written over the summer; there were too many Little League games, neighborhood barbeques, family road trips. Now that school was back in session, he was beholden to the demanding masters of teaching, grading, advising, being a father of eight, trying to maintain his relationship with Sophie, mowing the lawn before the grass grew taller than the twins…

Logically, Howie knew he was doing noble things; things that "made a difference." Being a teacher. Being a father. A partner. Those things mattered. But he envied that it was his brother contributing to history on a global stage, and not him. Howie knew he was as smart as his brother. He wanted to use his considerable intellect for the greater good. But it felt whittled down now, splintered down into something blunt, diminished by the sharp blade of his brother's relentless, cutting focus.

Was teaching the wrong path? Was fatherhood? His days were filled with dissertations and diapers, term papers and toddlers. What if he had chosen another career, or foregone family life?

Howie had, at one point, considered the clergy. But his mother was Jewish, he was raised with no formal faith, and he abhorred his grandfather, the Reverend. So he nixed that potential path. He loved the notion of being there for people at their darkest hours and in the moments of their greatest joy. It was just the organized religion part he couldn't quite abide.

No one could say Howard was a failure as a teacher. He was consistently voted favorite faculty member in the student publications, he was a sought-after advisor, he knew he was good at his chosen career. But even if he was undeniably successful in the small campus bubble, what about the world beyond? He hadn't written a textbook everyone used or shed light on anything world-changing. He'd done a thousand small things with his life, and maybe the sum of those things adds up to a meaningful enough contribution. But his large pile of small acts of goodness does not feel as meaningful as discovering the atom or writing *To Kill a Mockingbird*.

Or founding a mysterious neuroscience enterprise, like Nathan.

If nothing else, it was the fraternal competition that kept him going. Howie might have given up on doing something remarkable, if not for the fact that his well-funded baby brother was clearly out to change the world. Howie couldn't let Nathan be the sole and only Fell boy to leave his mark. That would be wrong. Possibly dangerous. And definitely irritating as shit.

That competitive drive was embedded in Howie, as intrinsic as his intelligence. It ran through his veins along with his blood. It would lay dormant, then surge, sometimes waking him in the middle of the night as a slippery thought darted around, silvery hints of genius circling the murky waters of his mind. That was what led him to sit at the still-firing-up computer, stroking his beard and trying to pin down the flitting thoughts while he waited. He tried to still his mind, like when he stood stock still in the shallows of Seven Lakes Beach as a child, watching thousands of minnows, as slippery-silvery as his thoughts, swarm his feet. If he moved, the fish dispersed; and when he tried to think too hard about articulating the ideas teasing his brain, those ideas would slip away just like those little echoes of fish, fast and fleeting, there and then gone.

The computer was finally up and running. He opened the file he'd hastily saved as "minnows.doc" the last time he was jolted awake by some sort of philosophical muse. He scrolled down to the last paragraph he'd written:

> *The way we interpret a perceived transgression is shaped by our own past guilt, past trauma, past regret. It is our perceptions—our past experiences—that magnify or minimize a new transgression, far more so than the transgression itself.*

Howard Fell stared at the words on the screen. He barely remembered writing them, but they were his; a minnow he caught when wasn't even looking. And as he held still, staring at the screen, tentatively, then quickly, the slippery, silvery thoughts began to swarm.

CHAPTER 24: NATHAN

A S THE CLASSROOM EMPTIED, Nathan felt no reaction to the official end of his teaching days. He thought he might feel relief at being done with this obligation; maybe a tinge of wistfulness at the quiet conclusion of a lifelong career. But no. He simply noted the event as another box being checked off a very long to-do list, and there were much bigger boxes a little farther down the list.

Everything he valued about this teaching position—access to hungry assistants, fiduciary sponsors for grants, credibility—would be at his disposal in his new position. The Synthetic Neuroscience Institute of Technology's state-of-the-art new building in New York was a facility ten years in the making; it would give him more resources at his disposal than any university, or in the offices here of the fledgling little think-tank, the precursor to the institute. The only thing he wondered if he should pocket before leaving this dump was his current top student—Derek Abelson. Abelson was sharp. No one since Felix Hess had shown as much promise.

He glanced idly at the stack of papers on his desk, research projects his students had slaved over, only a few of which Nathan would give more than a passing glance. Hess had done most of the grading over the weekend, and would be dropping off the last dozen graded assignments shortly. Nathan knew his assistant resented the menial task of grading; Hess would much rather spend his valuable time going over their own experiments and results. But Hess did not complain. He would not risk falling from Nathan's good graces.

Hess was conniving, Nathan knew. Given the chance, he would usurp Nathan in a heartbeat. Nathan admired that. Hess was hungry. Insatiable. He would do whatever it took. It was exactly why Nathan had selected him as his protégé, and also why he dared not trust him.

"Professor Fell?"

Speak of the devil.

"Hess."

Nathan noted the two bags Hess carried; as instructed, in addition to his briefcase he had packed an overnight bag with toiletries, a business suit, and two forms of identification. With a disdainful look, Hess added another thick stack of papers to the neat piles on Nathan's desk. Even with just a quick glance, Nathan saw the angry red everywhere, Hess' bloody judgment smeared across every earnestly submitted paper.

"Good," said Nathan.

"Well, I wouldn't say good," Hess snickers. "Half of them failed, even with the curve. These students are mentally deficient."

"Not all," said Nathan. "Derek Abelson. How was his paper?"

"Solid," Hess admitted. "He even caught the implications of the outlier we threw in there. He pays attention, I'll give him that."

"I want to read his paper. We should think about offering him an internship."

"Fine, fine," Hess rolled his sallow eyes. "Did the grant come through?"

"I wanted to mention, Hess," Nathan said, pretending not to have heard Hess' question about the grant. "I liked your suggestion for the post-procedure testing. Your whole multi-pronged, cognitive, physical, emotional assessment structure—I have some revisions we'll work in, but it's the right base, I think."

"Professor!" Hess said, almost whining now. "The grant! Did we get it, or didn't we?"

"No. We didn't."

"Government assholes! Small-minded, partisan *pariahs!*" Hess was beside himself. "What are we going to do? Dammit. I mean—*shit hell dammit.* We were counting on that. We'll stall out. We needed that funding!"

"We did," Nathan said. "But now we don't."

Hess' expression changed, from devastated to expectant; he could see now that Nathan had been holding something back. Toying with him. He waited. There it was: the hunger.

"Our funders increased the ceiling on our budget," Nathan said, sharing the news that had allowed him to quit teaching. "The new facility is ready for us. What I'm saying is screw the grant. I know you worked hard on it, but trust me, this is better. We already know our funders. They already know us. And now we won't owe anyone quarterly reports. We're good to go."

"YES!"

"We'll need to find more funders," Nathan said, almost enjoying Hess' enthusiasm. "But for now we have enough to get started with—"

"Nathan. Yo, Nathan."

Nathan and Hess turned to see Howie standing there. Howard was a real bohemian mess these days. The bushy beard, the plaid button-down shirts, the widening gut. It was disgusting.

Howie was also holding a young girl in his arms, her gangly legs dangling halfway down Howie's body. No longer a baby—a child. A girl.

Seeing the two of them, Nathan was instantly exhausted. He didn't have time for this.

"Daddy!" The little girl cried, scrambling down from Howard Fell's arms and running toward Nathan. She ran behind his desk, tried to crawl up into his lap, but Nathan instinctively stood, thwarting her attempted embrace.

"Not now, Ruth," he said sternly. Why did she even still think of him as her father? He had tried to minimize contact, tried to keep expectations clear. Her lip trembled.

"But Daddy, I made you a picture…"

For a split second, Nathan glanced at the artwork she waved in the air. A few scrawled lines, boxes and triangles. Houses? They were in no way accurate depictions. Hard, dry little macaroni glued haphazardly here and there, representing—what? Rain? Small turds?

Who could say. The kid was no van Gogh.

"We need to meet with the funders immediately," Nathan said to Hess, returning his attention to his assistant. "That's why I asked you to have an overnight bag—there's a car picking us up right after class, and straight from here we're heading to the airport. We need to scout a few more of the options in Manhattan—"

"Hey, whoa," Howard said, stepping forward. "Nathan—you're moving to New York?"

"Yes. This shouldn't be a surprise, Howard. That was the plan."

"The plan before you had kids," Howie said hotly. "When things change, plans change."

"My plans don't change."

"Maybe they should."

"Maybe they shouldn't," Nathan snapped, feeling a familiar frustration with his self-righteous big brother. "Maybe if you were a little less willing to make compromises, you would have more of a career. But we each made our own choices."

Howie was clearly pissed, but stepped forward, lowering his voice, not wanting the little girl to hear their exchange: "You know we love having Ruthie and Rachel with us, but are you sure you can't take some time out for your own daughters, at least before you move—"

"It will be easier when I move now; it would be harder on them if we were attached."

"Do you really think this is what Sarah wanted?"

"Sarah?" Nathan spat. Hearing her name still made him seethe, made his skin itch. "She wanted you to have them. Period."

"Her mistake doesn't have to be yours," Howard said softly.

"Don't talk to me about mistakes," Nathan sneered. "Everything I do is to correct mistakes. Humanity's mistakes. Like overpopulation, which I regret having contributed to."

"Nathan!" Howie gasped. "Having children is not a mistake—"

"Says the man with six children. Maybe if people could live long enough to create true legacies, we wouldn't feel the need to preserve ourselves by having children—"

"You think people only have children to ensure a legacy?"

"You make a good case for that theory," snapped Nathan. "You squandered your potential, did nothing meaningful or valuable, but there's your consolation prize. A half-dozen little clones. Why not make it eight? That's your legacy, Howard. Not mine. Now. Get her out of here—I have work to do."

Howard's wounded look was so sincere that Nathan regretted his outburst. He was not as heartless as his cutting words made him out to be. He was logical, yes; distant, sure. But Nathan didn't think of himself as cruel. Howard's expression argued otherwise, and that bothered him.

For an instant, Nathan considered telling his big brother everything. Getting his advice, perhaps even his approval. After all, Howie was bright. As bright as Abelson, as Hess, maybe even as bright as Nathan himself—he'd always just been too social to tap into his true potential. Nathan could hire him as an ethics consultant, something stupid like that.

In that same moment, Nathan wondered what it would be like if he allowed his daughter onto his lap. Or if he went to visit his other daughter, Rachel, who no longer called him Daddy. He considered attempting to dismantle the wall constructed around his heart, brick by brick by brick.

Then Hess cleared his throat. Reminding Nathan there were bigger things at stake. It's what Hess was truly good for: unwavering commitment to the cause.

The instant was over as quickly as it began. All of that sentimental stuff would take too long. Yield undesirable outcomes. And an ethics consultant was just a flat-out process killer. If he did things like what he considered in that instant, he wouldn't be Nathan. He would be, well—Howard. So Nathan said nothing.

And Howie opened his mouth as if he might say something else, but he too seemed to decide that there were no more words the brothers needed to exchange. He picked up the little girl, held her tight, and left with his Ruth.

CHAPTER 25: RUTH

ET HER OUT OF HERE—I HAVE WORK TO DO. Ruthie would always remember those words. She would carry them with her, stones in her pocket, always weighing her down. The ten little words would be drummed out over and over again by her small fingers on every available flat surface, tapping out her sad rhythm. They would haunt her, urge her on, torture her by reminding her that both of her parents ultimately chose to abandon her and her twin sister.

Though neither of them knew it that day, those ten words were the last ten words she would ever hear him speak. Her father, dismissing her as easily as a horse flicking away a fly with its tail. Just as thoughtlessly. He didn't even really say the words *to* her. He said them to Uncle Howie. Ruthie wasn't worth apologizing to or even directly addressing. She was just an object in her father's way. An object he needed to have removed, so his focus could remain on the objective.

Get her out of here—I have work to do.

NEW YORK 2012

CHAPTER 26: DEREK

D EREK ABELSON WAS NOT A RISK-TAKER. That's what differentiated him from his mentor, Nathan Fell, and the professor's assistant, Felix Hess. Professor Fell took risks; each was meticulously calculated for months or years before it was taken, but they were still risks.

Hess, too, took risks. He didn't give a damn about what anyone else thought. He was driven by an insatiable desire for advancement. But where Nathan always took decisive action, Hess hesitated. His pauses were never due to doubt; they were always a matter of calculation. Hess waited and watched before making a move. Even when it came to the big game Hess had studied and stalked and aimed at for years, he was wary about loosing his bullet too soon. He waited for Fell to fire the first shot. But at the end of the day, Hess had what it took. He'd cock the hammer and pull the trigger once he was certain of the target.

While the others took risks, Derek took notes. Although trained as a scientist, Derek was more of a documentarian. He wanted to be in the room where it happened—where the world-changing work was done—but he didn't want to design or implement the changes. He just wanted to witness them.

It wasn't a question of capability. Derek was smart. He just didn't want anything quite enough to "do what it really took," as Fell might say. He could go toe-to-toe with his colleagues intellectually. But he lacked Fell's vision; did not share Hess' hunger.

He sure enjoyed watching them work, though.

Interning for Fell was a trip. When Fell and Hess got all stressed out about something, Derek would just slip out of the room, head back to his cheap apartment, smoke a joint and order a pizza. By the next day, back in the lab, Hess and Fell had usually made some headway and had a new assignment for Derek to follow up on. Derek would do whatever number-crunching or results analysis they needed, and everyone was content.

Derek had initially considered declining his first internship with Fell. He knew it would mean doing actual work, which was something he usually managed to avoid. Of course, Derek had actually worked pretty hard as a student in Fell's classes. He'd taken two lecture courses and one lab section with the legendary teacher, despite all the rumors about how impossible his classes were to pass. Derek purchased and read the books ahead of time, comprehended most of the theories at first go, and decided he could handle it.

He figured having coursework with the legendary Nathan Fell on his resume was the cherry on top of an already sweet C.V.—the final garish garnish that would assure him a solid, well-paying research gig. Something that would always keep his liquor and gaming cabinets well-stocked, and wouldn't be too taxing. His post-doctoral goals were pretty modest: earn big money, expend minimal effort, keep his nights and weekends free.

Derek had seriously considered, more than once, the likely possibility that he was the world's smartest stoner.

He wondered if there was any way to test or prove that theory,. Then he chuckled and decided just as quickly that he didn't really give a shit.

It's not a competition, man.

"My institute is moving to New York," Fell said at the end of Derek's last semester of classes. "We'll be doing some really groundbreaking work, and I'd like you on my team. You'd be well-paid, and your living expenses will be covered—the new Manhattan building has an apartment within the complex. You'll have spacious accommodations, right on-site."

Derek knew that working for Fell full-time, not as a student intern but as a salaried employee, would mean working much harder than he had in-class or as an intern. There would be no phoning it in, no skating by on being the smartest guy in the room. He'd have to be more like Felix Hess—working every waking hour, uninterested in having a life.

"I still have a year of doctoral work," Derek hemmed.

A year that could be stretched into a fully funded two or three more years, if he played it right, with only one easy-breezy dissertation due at the end of that time...

"You have enough credits to graduate," Hess chimed in from behind Fell. "You're ABD."

Nosy little bastard.

"All but dissertation," Professor Fell agreed, giving Derek a knowing nod. "And the university will certainly let me oversee your dissertation research. Your work with me will likely double-count, anyhow. Won't even have to write a separate dissertation, you can just submit some of the papers I'll have you do, and voila."

Those had been the magic words: *double count.*

Derek might have to work hard, for once in his life, but the work would pay off on two fronts—a salaried internship with benefits, and the completion of his doctoral work. All in one Fell swoop, he thought, knowing he was neither the first nor the last to make this stupid joke.

He took the gig.

A few months later, he was living at the newly up-and-running Synthetic Neuroscience Institute of Technology. It was positioned in the heart of Manhattan, within steps of every kind of culture, cuisine, and curiosity. There were parades, readily available weed sold on the same corner as dollar slices of New York thin crust, there were two baseball teams and discount tickets to Broadway shows and a whole world of possibilities.

None of which mattered, because Derek had not set foot outdoors in more than a week.

This was not an exaggeration. The whole staff lived at the Synt (Derek and a few others had started calling the place that, mostly because it bugged Hess so much). The facility included a state-of-the-art cafeteria. The chef was pretty decent, but it was all weird healthy quinoa-and-oat sort of stuff. Here he was, living in New York City, and Derek had yet to get pizza, a bagel, or gelato. Which was bogus.

Derek was eating and sleeping and living and breathing his work, without interruption. The algorithms and logic models he was tasked with designing and discerning swam before his eyes at all times. The intensity of their work was ever-increasing all that week. Derek knew they must be on the cusp of something. But despite being in the mouth of the wolf, Derek still had no idea exactly what prey they were hunting.

Obviously it was something in the cyborganics field. Fell was the Cyborganics Cowboy, after all. But when he was asked to do data analysis, Derek was rarely presented with more than one slim piece of the puzzle, not enough to piece together what they were aiming at with all the recent tests.

Then one drab Tuesday morning, Derek was handed a report. Atop the report was a bright yellow note, which read in Hess' scrawling hand:

Read this. Then meet us in the central lab.

The report itself was brief, outlining a few key findings from some of the experiments to which Derek had not been privy. Experiments with monkeys, apparently.

This dismayed Derek, on multiple levels. First, he had mixed feelings about using apes in experiments. Second, he always wanted a pet monkey and would much rather have spent the last few months working with monkeys in the sub-basement of the Synt than holed up staring at computer screens all the time. The more he thought about it, the more he wished he'd been assigned to work with monkeys, assuming nothing bad befell them during the experiments. In this pleasant monkeys-at-the-office scenario, Derek imagined he would have fed them bananas between tests and give them names like Business, Suit, and Wrench.

He might have been a little high.

But as he kept reading, about the monkeys being connected to machines, his buzzy glow subsided and his rosy monkey playtime picture quickly wilted. He read about the brain stem augmentations and the synthetic genetic material introduced to make the organic and augmented elements communicate. Derek recognized a few of his own theoretical models embedded in some of the techniques—well, models he worked on, even if he didn't develop them. He read quickly, familiar with the language and processes, riveted by the realization that this report was not theoretical, but actual.

The final case study summarized the results of a monkey called Coal 42, who was "successfully synched and fully functional." Seeing those words, something knotted and flipped in Derek's stomach.

He hurried to the central lab, clutching the report. It was only upon arrival that he remembered he didn't have adequate security clearance for the central lab; his badge wouldn't get him into this room. He swiped it once, just in case—and the laboratory door slid open.

Guess I've leveled up.

When Derek entered the laboratory, it was silent. No one in the room but Fell and Hess, and both were staring at a screen. On the large wall-mounted flat screen, a live feed showed footage of the monkey designated Coal 42. Coal 42 was leaning back toward an electrical socket. This momentarily alarmed Derek—was the monkey about to be shocked? Why? But as soon as the monkey's neck was level with the outlet, there was a soft click, like a magnet connecting. The monkey's eyelids slowly closed, and he sat comfortably, chest rising and falling—asleep.

"It's working," Fell breathed.

Hess glanced at his boss, then returned his gaze to the sleeping monkey. "You're sure?"

"Absolutely," said Nathan. "Don't you agree, Derek?"

Both men turned to look at Derek, who startled. He had assumed they were unaware of his presence; he felt like a ghost in the room, observing, haunting, not intending to be noticed. He stared stupidly at his supervisors.

"Don't play dumb, Abelson," snapped Felix Hess. "It doesn't look good on you."

Derek tried to recall the last reports he'd reviewed, data comparing electricity levels against a new data transfer/recharging system. Something similar to cell phones or electric cars, from what he'd gathered—a system where the plug-in vehicle (or smartphone; or... monkey?) could be charged while it was also checked or updated, and would then be able to run on the electric power stored from the charge until the battery depleted, then switch over to the primary system. He thought he was looking at numbers about how much electricity was safe to surge through an electronic system, not an organic one. But as he recalled the other studies he had been spot-checking—impacts of electricity on tissues; feasibility of data-sharing across platforms; tiny interlocking chips that could collectively contain a universe of data all while easily fitting within a cell—they began connecting in his mind all at once. Pieces flying into place, constructing a puzzle he would have finished months ago had he just given it a little more thought.

Shit, Derek, you lazy pothead. You know this is cyborganics. How did you not realize you were helping develop some sort of plug-in system for mammals with mechanical components?

"He's charging?" Derek asked, eyes on the monkey. Coal 42.

"And uploading his memories from today," Fell said.

"And downloading new information we've shared with him," Hess added eagerly.

"We're ready for the next phase," Fell said.

At this, even Hess looked surprised. A cold ball of panic formed in Derek's stomach. He was done being two steps behind. The next phase meant a human subject.

God. What's one step up from a monkey?

A goddamn assistant, that's what.

"Who's the one?" Hess asked. Unlike Derek, his excitement was mingled not with fear, but with an uncanny hope.

Professor Nathan Fell's eyes remained on screen. And then he smiled, lips slowly curving up, which did nothing to melt the icy ball of fear bouncing around Derek's stomach.

CHAPTER 27: NATHAN

DESPITE HOW LONG NATHAN FELL had been preparing for this day—two decades, in one sense; his entire life, in another—it still felt sudden. And, to be fair, the long-awaited day was arriving ahead of schedule.

According to the strategic plan, this milestone was due in 2020, not 2012. And those timelines were very carefully constructed. Truth be told, the plan was still accurate; 2020 was a more realistic goal, allowing for additional testing, course-correction, preparation. But as Fell's assistant, Hess, was fond of reminding him, the pace was continuing to accelerate. There were rumors that China was developing similar technology, and that

Russia was hacking both American and Chinese tech to try to steal the intelligence and win the cyborganics race.

If they didn't pull the trigger now, someone else was going to take the shot first.

And things had gone well with the latest monkey, better than expected. The creature was given a series of injections, organic and synthetic material to build up immunities and prepare his system to accept the merger. The port installation had gone well. The docking system worked. The monkey appeared to be thriving.

Coal 42 was a healthy, spry simian, an ideal specimen. All monkeys used in Fell's tests were named Coal, a nod to the canary in the coal mine. The first few Coals sacrificed to the cause made the staff—even Fell, to an extent—feel bad. But the disappointment was sharper for the failed science than the dead monkey. By Coal 7, the team was getting numb to the loss of life, and more determined to figure out the errors. By the time the simian cadavers numbered in the twenties, Fell felt only anger as monkey after monkey made it all the way through the preparations, everything right up until the final full synch. Once fully synched, they never lasted more than a few minutes before a brain bleed or massive heart attack flat-lined them.

Until Coal 42.

Three days post-synch, Coal 42 was still very much alive.

He was alert, interactive, his vitals were normal. Moreover, he was sleeping less than he used to, utilizing new signs when communicating with his trainer, and had already learned to plug himself into his port for his nightly recharge. He was obtaining and retaining a tremendous amount of new information daily. The only question mark on the chart was about his diet. His appetite had diminished, but not in a way that seemed to indicate illness. As Hess pointed out, the first day that Coal 42 ate less than usual, when fully charged his machinated parts were keeping his system running, so the traditional fuel of his normal food might not be quite as necessary. It was a plausible theory. They would find ways to track it in the weeks ahead.

That was the plan, according to the timeline: Find ways to track and monitor the monkey's progress in a more deliberate way. Determine which measures were most instructive, identify which variables yielded the best outcomes. Then they would move from monkeys to men—only after best practices had been established, only after important lessons had been learned, only after the monkeys had taught them a technique that would pave the way for successful human synching. But then one of the key funders sent word that the Chinese laboratories were already preparing for a human test.

And there was no way the Institute could let anyone else get there first.

Nathan was fairly certain they were ready, but under normal circumstances that would be inadequate. *Absolute* certainty was the goal. But he was out of time. He couldn't risk someone else winning the race; he had to reach the finish line first. He earned it.

"Coal 42 means we're ready," Hess assured him, even more eager than his mentor to make sure theirs was the winning team. "We are. We're ready."

Hess' words rang hollow, echoing his own ulterior motives. Though their collaboration had been extremely productive, Nathan and Hess' goals remained somewhat divergent. They sought the same end, but for different reasons. Hess worked in pursuit of power, because he believed he knew best; if he had more power, he could fix more problems, his way.

For Nathan, it was simply about knowledge. Knowledge broader and wider than human issues; knowledge that would unlock new doors, new possibilities. He didn't want to fix something broken. He wanted to build something better. He wanted to align the stars, illuminate the world anew, bring minds together in an entirely different way. He wanted to delete past errors and usher in a calm tranquility unimaginable in the haphazard world as-is.

He couldn't blame Hess for thinking small, for focusing only on the known world and not beyond it. Not all minds were capable of projecting past their own experience. Hess might eventually get there. He had the intellectual potential. He was simply too insecure, too vainly competitive, too young and egotistical and hungry for accolades. Which was fine, because Nathan didn't want Hess to share his precise motivations and intentions. If Hess were in the same headspace as Nathan, he would be vying to be the first synch.

And that right was reserved for Nathan himself.

Nathan Fell had to be the first human to experience and control this brand new sort of intelligence. And the only way to do that would be the first one to successfully evolve.

"It will be me," Nathan Fell had calmly announced yesterday to his assistants.

Both of them responded with widened eyes and shocked expressions—Hess showing surprise tinged with jealousy, Derek surprise tinged with relief.

"You?" Hess sputtered, then recovered. "That's—unexpected, but if you're sure—"

"Whoa, hold up," Derek interjected. "We've had one successful monkey, that's it. Shouldn't we try for a few more? Or if we really are ready for human subjects, shouldn't we stick with the plan—volunteers and shit? I mean, come on. I can't be the only one who thinks this is nuts, allowing the pioneer of this technology to be the first to test it—"

"'Allowing'?" Nathan said, almost amused. As if Derek could grant or withhold permission. As if anyone could.

"I just mean, it's a ludicrous—an *unmitigated* risk. If something goes wrong—where the hell would that leave us?"

"We'd still have me," Hess quipped.

Or maybe he was being serious. Always hard to tell with him.

"I appreciate your concerns, Derek," Nathan said, acknowledging the protégé who actually cared about whether he lived or died. "But it's the only way. We're only moving the timeline because of external pressures—similar studies closing in on us. We haven't recruited any subjects yet; even if we began that process now, it would be months before we would be ready for the first human trials. Participants would need to sign confidentiality waivers, be screened, begin the series of cocktail injections required to prepare for the procedures…"

"…and you've already started the cocktail series," Hess said slowly, as realization dawned. He looked at Nathan with something akin to awe, likely wondering why the hell he hadn't thought of this first.

Hess. When will you get it through your thick skull that I'll always be a few steps ahead?

Everything moved quickly after that. The circle of power was small. All they told the funders was that they would proceed with the first subject; they didn't reveal the identity of said subject and implied such knowledge at this stage might open the funders up to dangerous vulnerability. Better to have plausible deniability. The funders didn't argue. So there was no one else to bring into the loop, no procedural processes or red tape to slow them down. There was only a doctor to put on call, an already-prepped test subject, and a machine re-calibration to adjust the subject size from monkey to man.

The augmentation machine was sleek, cylindrical, made of steel. The top of the tube slid open to reveal a padded bed, lined at the base, on the sides, and even along the top of the tube; the monkeys had taught them that thrashing during the procedure was common. For that same reason, there were restraints for the ankles, wrists, torso, and head. For anyone with even a touch of claustrophobia, heavy sedation would be required, because once closed the subject would be belted firmly into what essentially appeared to be a high-tech coffin.

The base of the machine was lined with a neat little network of wires, connecting it to the monitors to evaluate the subject's vitals and brain function throughout the procedure. There were speakers and recording devices throughout the machine, for documentation and two-way communication. Once the subject was secured within, he would be visible only via images illuminating the large, flat monitors that will be watched intensely by the scientists. The video monitors, the heart monitors, the brain scan monitors—a series of screens would keep the scientists' eyes flitting back and forth to read each new development in the story of their subject.

The procedure would go like this: The subject would be secured, strapped in, the tube would slide shut. Just above the wrist restraints, a series of needles waited expectantly in a sliding panel. As the procedure began, the panel would slide open for the needles' delivery of a series of swift injections: sedative, final dose of synthetic-organic cocktail, microchip insertion, heavy painkiller in case the initial sedative wasn't enough. Flush with the base of the subject's neck was the port installer, which would begin its work as soon as the needles finished theirs.

A small laser then sterilized and completely shaved the back of the neck, leaving not one stray hair; then a small piece of metal, flat with two prongs bookending a circular opening, would surge upward. The two prongs pierced the subject's neck, securing the flat metal base to the neck and leaving a small stretch of skin exposed in the circular opening. The placement of the metal base was crucial, aligning the implant with the brain stem. Then the port, the critical piece of hardware synched with the embedded microchip and the larger computer program, would twist upward, burrowing through the skin and muscle and bone of the neck, securing itself forever to the brain stem like an insatiable tick. The exposed end of the port would connect to the augmentation machine, wired and wireless technology linking the subject to the computer.

This was not the end of the full process; installing the port and synching the central nervous system to the technology was only the beginning. Once the tech was installed, there would be a twenty-four-hour monitoring period; as the merged organic-synthetic brain tech took hold, it would—theoretically—begin to "teach" the organic body to accept the components. Upgrades would be a routine part of life—a life that will now have the potential to be extended, perhaps indefinitely; acceptance and incorporation of the tech was critical.

Nathan watched the procedure over and over on monkeys, which provided cold comfort, since until Coal 42 the monkeys died of gruesome neurological catastrophes within minutes of the procedure. That's not how Nathan wanted to go, brain-first and trapped in a tube. He'd seen it too many times to imagine it as anything other than what it had been for the unfortunate simians: several moments of pain and fear, followed by a merciless death.

Not for Coal 42, though.

And hopefully not for Nathan.

There were more than a few fail-safes in place. The augmentation machine was built to inhibit movement and keep installation precise; the cocktail delivered by needles should minimize pain and maximize the body's acceptance of the process. Hess and Derek were both trained EMTs with extensive medical knowledge and Dr. Kansal would also be on hand. The young prodigal neurologist would not be allowed in the room, but would be no more than one minute away in case of emergency. (The good doctor, who came on recommendation from Hess, was provided no information on the intricacies of the procedure, merely paid an exorbitant sum by the funders as a retainer to be "on call in case of a neurological crisis," for the day of the procedure and indefinitely, post-op. The requirements of the retainer are simple: If summoned, appear. If another patient was on the operating table, they would be abandoned. Period.)

"You're ready, Professor?"

Hess was eerily calm, but his passivity was offset by Derek, who was on the verge of melting within his own skin. The younger man crowded in at Nathan's elbow, sweating through his lab coat, the dampness evident beneath his arms, down his chest, across his brow. He looked so nervous, one might assume *he* was the one about to be thrown into the box.

"No," Nathan said honestly, and watched Derek's knees buckle.

It was his call, but for the first time in a long time he didn't know if it was the right one. There was no one here to truly question him, to challenge him (Derek had tried, but Derek was weak). He felt an odd pang in his chest, and stupidly wished that Howard were there.

"But professor..." Hess swallowed, more nervous about the idea of delaying the procedure than rushing it, "The pace continues to accelerate—"

"Enough," snapped Nathan Fell. *If that little prick says 'the pace continues to accelerate' one more time, I'll murder him.* "No one is ever truly ready for change when it comes. That doesn't mean we back down."

He walked toward the center of the lab, deliberately tortoiseing his way to the machine. He felt the anticipation crackling in the air. Limping heavily, his bones vibrated with a humming certainty that this was the moment everything would change.

Waving away a muted offer of help from Derek, Nathan eased himself into the machine. He lay flat on the narrow metal slab, unflinching as the restraints automatically snapped around his wrists, ankles, forehead. This rapid metallic embrace had sent each monkey into a panic, but Nathan knew what to expect. The large top panel above him slid shut, walling him in. The small panels above his arm restraints hissed open. He braced himself for the punctures; he never liked needles. But after the thin pinch of the first slim steel point sliding into his flesh, he felt nothing. No pain at all after the initial prick. Not as bad as he thought it would be.

He began to feel almost calm. Probably just the sedative kicking in. He neither felt nor saw the laser, but a faint sizzling sound and whiff of burning hair told him his neck was shaved and ready.

For an instant, Nathan felt placid. Ready. Almost pleasantly expectant.

Then the sudden upward surge of the metal base slamming into his spinal cord jolted him into a new universe of pain.

Nathan Fell stifled a scream. The prongs forcing their way through his flesh and bone seared through his very being, seemed to peel his flesh and blood and bone and mind away from one another. He had no time to absorb this pain before he heard the whirring of the port itself, spiraling its way up, then twisting its way through his neck and into his spinal cord. The brain stem. His synapses were firing haphazardly, connecting to all of the computers and—

No. This is wrong.

It was another miscalculation, like leaping off the swing in his youth, jumping at the wrong time, landing too hard. Shattering his leg instead of merely breaking his ankle. Permanently damaging himself, causing that cursed limp. The impact had been too much. He could see it now! He knew they needed to adjust the calibration to account for this error—

He tried to say these words, to instruct his assistants in the necessary course-correction, but he could not move his mouth. He tried to signal to Hess, to get his attention so at least they would be alerted to something being wrong. But the steel cylinder kept him hidden, and moreover Nathan realized with a cold, icily-spreading dread that he could not move his hands, his fingers, his feet, his toes. Not his head. Not even his eyes.

Nathan Fell was completely paralyzed.

And for an instant that seemed to last an eternity, he was terrified. It was every nightmare brought to life; trapped in a coffin, unable to move, unable to scream. His adrenaline surged through his useless body, his mind raced, his heart thudded. But then he began working through the problem, running new calculations, guiding his thousand-mile-an-hour-mind toward things that mattered. His breathing normalized. His panic ebbed.

Tucked into this box, connected to this machinery, everything around him slowed and slowed and slowed. There was something familiar and comforting about the box; a small space that would allow him to grow. He felt secure, unhurried, unburdened by all of the world's frenetic movement, pressure from funders, pressure from the media, pressure from other scientists, pressure to rush and finish. For the first time in decades, everything stilled.

For the first time in decades, it was quiet enough for Nathan Fell to think.

CAMBRIDGE 2012

CHAPTER 28: HOWARD

WHEN HOWIE GOT THE CALL, he was in the midst of preparing dinner. It was spaghetti night; he was stirring the sauce, little red bubbles rupturing on the surface of the simmering marinara.

Tiny, stubbornly helpful Rachel had declared that she would set the table, *by herself,* and was lugging ten heavy ceramic plates toward the dining room. Howie was listening for her inevitable crash when instead he heard the jangling of the phone.

"Hello?"

"Is this Howard Fell?"

"Yes?"

"This is Felix Hess," said the unfamiliar voice on the other end of the line. "I work with your brother. He has you listed as his next of kin."

Howard's breath caught.

"What happened?"

"There's been an—accident. I'm sorry, but he's… brain-dead."

Silence.

A buzzing silence that numbed Howie and paused the entire universe.

Then a small red bubble popped from the pot, splattering onto the stovetop. In the dining room, Rachel dropped the ceramic plates, shattering two of them, bursting into startled tears.

NEW YORK 2014 – 2016

CHAPTER 29: JORGE

JORGE MARQUEZ SHOULD NEVER have been imprisoned. Yes, he was driving the car when his cousin Ricky robbed the gas station. Yes, when his cousin leaped into the car and said "Go go go," Jorge had driven him away from the scene of the crime. Yes, technically speaking, everything the prosecuting attorney had said was true.

But that was not the real story.

What really happened was Ricky called and said he needed a ride, which was something Jorge's deadbeat cousin did all the time. He asked to go to the gas station for some cigarettes. Jorge pulled into the station. Ricky went inside, and Jorge stayed in the parking lot in his crappy old Tercel. He pulled a comic book out from the backseat. He'd just picked up some trades and needed to know what Deadpool was up to. He was sitting there in the car, happily reading his comic book, snickering at Deadpool's snark, completely oblivious to his stupid-ass cousin flashing a gun to the kid inside the store.

When Ricky ricocheted into the car and said "Go go go, man!" Jorge rolled his eyes, put the comic in the backseat, started the car, and eased it out of the lot onto Front Street. Used his frigging turn signal and everything. No rush. No hurry. Because he had no idea he was driving a damned getaway car.

Unfortunately, the public defender who represented Jorge was an idiot, and couldn't make the judge see the situation for what it was: Jorge, clueless, giving his carless cousin Ricky a ride; Ricky, a piece of trash who had been getting his cousin into trouble for two decades.

The trouble was always minor before. But Ricky used the "threat of force" to get the kid at the counter to give him all of the money in the till. Apparently, that whole "threat of force" thing elevated Ricky's crime, converting it from misdemeanor to full-on felony. No slap on the wrist this time. Ricky had wielded a gun, which made his crime an armed robbery; he clutched that gun in brown hands, which meant he was truly screwed. Ricky was looking at thirty years.

And Jorge was the accomplice.

The unwitting, unwilling, but nonetheless-found-guilty accomplice. He was pretty sure Ricky'd sold him out to get a slightly more lenient sentence for his own crime. Even if they'd just offered him a damn reduction of six months, that kid would sell out his cousin Jorge.

Prick.

Jorge had hoped the jury would be sympathetic. He had a clean record, a good job at an auto repair shop, and he was a good looking young guy. His amber eyes, his well-groomed dark hair—

but he had skin the same shade as Ricky's, which was his only flaw. An incredibly punishing flaw, it turned out.

He was given the maximum sentence: three years. Three. Damn. *Years.* For doing Ricky a favor. For looking down at his comic book at the wrong time—because if he'd looked up and seen Ricky with the gun, he would have peeled out of there and called the cops himself before that jackass ever got back into Jorge's car.

Jorge's incompetent lawyer, a sad-eyed public defender with terrible breath, assured him that with good behavior, he could probably be out in only a year and a half.

"Oh, only a year and a half?" Jorge replied. "And then I'm out with a felony on my record. Who's gonna hire me? Who's gonna take care of my ma? This is a death sentence, man."

The public defender said nothing in response to this; he was already thinking about the next case he was going to lose.

So Jorge served his eighteen months, working hard to maintain that good behavior, ignoring every catcall and slur (Goldeneye, Pretty Boy, Hey Mexican; he was Puerto Rican, but he doubted that the leering supremacists were much interested in the intricacies of his background), never taking the bait, always sidestepping any situation that could get him off track. He shaved his head, in an effort to look a little tougher and a little less like a golden-eyed pretty boy. He sure as hell didn't want anyone in there to guess he was gay.

And after eighteen months, the good behavior paid off, and he was out, just as his lawyer had predicted. And just as Jorge had predicted, he was utterly unemployable. His job at Johnny's Auto Repair was gone. He couldn't make it past the online applications for any office gigs. Even the fast food joints didn't want him, not when the economy had tanked and plenty of other people were vying for the jobs. People with clean records. People who had assistant-manager uncles instead of loser cousins who ruined their life.

So Jorge was doing mostly under-the-table work. Handyman stuff, moving jobs, auto repair for friends and family, day labor crap. The sort of stuff he'd sworn to never do. It was taking a toll. He was as bitter back on the outside as he'd been behind bars, and this time there was no release date in sight.

His mother prayed and cried but was unable to do much else to help him. She had never really recovered from the stroke that left the right side of her body immobile and landed her on disability at forty-one. His four little brothers and sisters were growing like weeds, and between trying to keep the older ones out of trouble and the younger ones in shoes that fit, Jorge was on edge constantly. But especially after a year and a half of being away, he wouldn't entertain the thought of bailing on his family. If he didn't take care of them, no one would.

First Monday of the month, Jorge had to check in with his probation officer, Mario. Like the defeated public defender, or the wary corrections officers, Mario was yet another older white man theoretically entrusted with keeping Jorge in check, despite Jorge absolutely and unequivocally being the more competent and trustworthy party in the situation.

Mario was a shifty-looking guy with a broom-like mustache. Built like a garden gnome, squat and short and wide, he was always clutching a Styrofoam cup of cold coffee. He told Jorge to grab free coffee wherever you can, even if it meant crashing an AA meeting, because Starbucks was a goddamn racket. Mondays with Mario were high up on the list of things Jorge hated about his life—a list full of stiff competition.

Mario showed up at Jorge's house early. He had missed their appointment last month due to "personal reasons"; had given Jorge a quick call to say that he'd just note it was all a-okay. Mario was able to get away with missing meetups. If Jorge did, he risked jail.

"How's it goin', ah-mee-go?" Mario asked, standing in the doorway, scratching his ass.

Jorge hated it when Mario tried to act chummy, and he especially hated it when the fourth-generation Italian-American gnome deployed his Sesame-Street-level grasp of Spanish.

"It's goin', man," Jorge said, and let him in, because he was required to do so.

Mario waddled in, clutching his foam cup. He cast a disinterested glance around the front room. The kids were all at school. At least, they better be, or Jorge would be on their asses like an avenging angel. His mother was asleep in her bedroom, as she was the majority of most days.

"Looks good, looks pretty good," Mario said, without really looking at a thing. "You workin', these days?"

"Here and there."

"Goin' to the employment office?"

"Yep. If you need to verify—"

"Oh, don't you worry, om-bray, I'll verify," Mario said. He wouldn't. He'd just sign the form, dot the I's and cross the T's. Jorge was not one of his problem cases, and they both knew it. "Look, I got an opportunity for you to look into."

This was new. Mario had never brought Jorge any "opportunities." Instinctively, any offer of help from his probation officer made him wary.

"Opportunity, huh?"

"See, see," Mario said, nodding. His teeth were stained yellow, too much bad coffee and cigarettes, not enough fluoride. It took Jorge a minute to realize that he was saying *si*.

"What kind of opportunity?"

"Opportunity to make some good money. Some solid dee-nay-ro, way I hear it." Mario reached into the pocket of his weathered leather jacket and pulled out a crumpled flyer.

DO YOU WANT TO LIVE FOREVER?
HEY, WHO DOESN'T?!

WE CAN'T GUARANTEE LIFE ETERNAL JUST YET.
NOT WITHOUT YOUR HELP!
SIGN UP FOR THE VOLUNTEER SYNTHETIC TEST PROGRAM,
AND AT NO COST TO YOU, YOU CAN EXPERIENCE
THE WONDER OF CYBORGANICS.

MAKE HISTORY. BE A PART OF THE FUTURE.
COMPENSATION PROVIDED TO VOLUNTEERS AND/OR
THEIR DESIGNATED BENEFICIARIES.

*YOUNG, HEALTHY, PHYSICALLY FIT VOLUNTEERS ONLY. SAFETY NOT GUARANTEED.
SIDE EFFECTS UNKNOWN. ALL VOLUNTEERS MUST PASS
A RIGOROUS SERIES OF TESTS BEFORE BEING ACCEPTED INTO THE PROGRAM.

He read it once, then read it again. It made no sense—was it a joke? A viral marketing campaign for some weird new "theater experience" in the Village or something? Jorge stared at the paper, wondering if this was the garden gnome's idea of a hilarious prank to pull on his under-employed ex-con client.

"Is this, like… Scientology or some shit?" Jorge finally asked.

"Naw, her-man-oh," Mario grinned. "Shit's not Scientology. This is actual *science*. Whole lab-type deal—cutting edge stuff. It's at a real reputable place, what I understand. And the money's good. Real good."

"How good is real good?"

Mario shrugged, chewed his lip, and then—out of nowhere— the wide lips beneath his stiff broom of a mustache split into a cavernous opening. He giggled, trilling and high-pitched, an un-expected sound from the squat man. It made Jorge flinched.

"Ten grand." Mario giggled again. "For every week you manage to stay in the program."

It took Jorge a minute to process that information.

"Shut up. Sorry, I didn't mean to say—no disrespect, I just— did you say *ten thousand dollars a week?*"

"For every week you manage to stay in the program."

"What does that mean? What does it take, to stay in the pro- gram?"

"Dunno," Mario shook his head, still grinning a stupid grin. "But I sure as shit know I'm applying. And there's a referral bo- nus, so hey, more the merrier, right? A rep from this place, the— synthetic-science something—came and talked to me. Said they'd take ex-con apps, long as they were healthy and not violent, and at least consider 'em. Wanted me to spread the word to 'my guys.' You're the first one I'm coming to with this, ah-mee-go. See what I do for you?"

Jorge shook his head, looking at the flyer. "You sure we're not about to get pranked on some reality show?"

"Nah. Rep seemed pretty serious. I think it's for curing diseas- es and whatnot. End cancer and whatever. Noble as shit, right?"

"So it could be some pretty invasive stuff."

"Guessing it is, for ten grand a week."

"A *week*," Jorge repeated, incredulous.

"Yup. Make it a full month, that's forty-kay, compren-day?"

"And you're gonna try to get in too, huh?"

Mario sipped the last of his cold coffee from the sad Styro- foam, squeezing the cup slightly, eliciting a raw squeak that made Jorge squirm. "Gonna try, yeah. How much you think probation officers make, Jorge? Shit. I could use the dee-nay-ro, too."

Jorge rarely set foot in Manhattan. He was a Bronx guy. The moneyed island full of tourists always felt like another planet to him—a paranoid planet that saw him as the alien. He resented the way too many of the tourists and pearl-clutching Upper East Siders looked at him, like he might pounce. He hated even more that at this point in his life, everyone giving him the once-over could be vindicated by his paper trail. He'd done time. He had a record. Somehow he had become the stereotype he never, ever wanted to be.

Ten grand a week, he reminded himself, and walked unhalt-ingly toward the Synthetic Neuroscience Institute of Technology.

The building was massive, and still under construction. It took up an entire city block already, and seemed poised to consume the neighborhood. Above the first dozen completed floors, wide beams rose upward like new metal bone, skeletal steel awaiting its flesh.

It took Jorge a moment to locate the door.

The entrance was well-hidden, consisting of tinted glass windows an entire story tall—one of which happened to have a subtly-embedded door, also dark glass, cut into one the panes and rendered flush with the windows. On the door was a small silver keypad; when Jorge had called to make his appointment, they had given him a code to enter: 48103.

Jorge keyed in the numbers, and nearly stumbled backward when a sharp beep was followed by a soft hiss, and the glass door swung open before him. He stepped through it, and it shut just as quickly. Soft classical music surrounded him, disorienting as he took in the slick surroundings. The ceilings were so high, the corridor so wide, it felt like being in a hangar. Or the Batcave.

In the middle of the wide hallway, several yards in front of Jorge, was a massive desk, black and sleek and unadorned. Behind the desk sat a woman. She had waxy skin, and wore lipstick so pale it gave her face a monochromatic look. Her slicked-back platinum hair only added to the effect. She looked very much like a mannequin. And also very much like the sort of woman who would grip her purse a little tighter at the sight of Jorge.

Jorge had an appointment. He was supposed to be there at nine sharp, and it was nearly nine now. He reached for the crumpled flyer in his pocket, ready to explain that he was there for the volunteer program, he wasn't trespassing. But before he could identify himself, she did.

"Jorge Marquez?"

"Yes?" Jorge said, startled.

"Right on time. That's good. Do you have a cell?"

"A what?"

"A. Cell. Phone." She spoke each word deliberately, as if addressing an idiot child.

"Ah, no." He didn't. He recently gave his to his fifteen-year-old sister Mariposa, who had wailed that she *needed* a smart-phone, that *everyone else* had a phone, that she was *the last person on the planet without a smart-phone*. Jorge had given her his, so now *he* was the last person on the planet without a smart-phone.

"No?" The receptionist repeated dubiously, proving Mariposa's point.

"Nope."

"All right. Down the hall to my left, third door on your right."

"Thanks."

Jorge took a step to the left, and the woman clucked her tongue, once, halting him.

"*My* left."

"Oh. Sorry."

Feeling like a complete and total moron, Jorge hoped that his evaluation was not already underway. Trusting nothing and expecting cameras everywhere, he hurried down the hallway, away from the flat white receptionist and toward whatever awaited him. Reaching the third door on the right, he almost second-guessed himself (*my right or her right?*), then slowly opened it.

The room was a movie-set version of a doctor's office waiting area, down to the cracked leather seats and end tables littered with magazines. Two dozen people sat in the waiting room, men and women, all ethnicities, all ages, all nervous. No one was touching the magazines, or talking to one another.

Jorge began to take a seat when a woman in a lab coat opened a door on the other side of the room, glanced at the clipboard in her hands, and looked straight at him.

"Jorge Marquez?"

His butt didn't have time to hit the seat before he was scrambling to his feet.

"Come with me, please."

He felt everyone's eyes on him as he approached the woman in the lab coat. He wondered the same thing they must all be thinking—he was the guy who just walked in. Why was he getting called back, and they were all just left to continue waiting?

The woman with the clipboard gave him a tight smile, and gestured for him to walk past her, through the door and into the hallway. She pulled the door shut tight behind them, and turned a lock with a definitive click. She was attractive, with tilted cat-eye glasses and honey-colored hair twisted up into a bun. Her lab coat was unbuttoned, revealing a silken blouse and a surprising amount of cleavage. She looked almost like she was dressed up to play the part of a sexy lab tech at a Halloween party or something.

"You a, uh, scientist?" Jorge asked.

She shook her head. "I'm just here to get you started on your paperwork. Right this way."

She led Jorge down the hallway, then turned left down another hallway, then right—a third hallway. Jorge was completely disoriented by this point. The hallways were all windowless, interchangeable. He felt like a rat in a maze.

A lab rat.

Shit. I am a lab rat.

What am I doing here?

Finally, the sexy not-scientist woman in the lab coat stopped in front of a door with a keypad, swiftly entered a code, then opened the door and nodded at Jorge to walk into the room. She herself stayed in the hallway; Jorge looked at her, questioning.

"Your paperwork is on the table, in the folder," she said encouragingly, nodding toward a table in the middle of the small room. "Someone will be back to get you in a bit. You'll want to get started on the paperwork—it's a good bit to wade through. It'll take you a while."

"You're not staying—?"

She shook her head, giving him a pouty little smile and a final glimpse of the cleavage likely meant to distract him, and then pulled the door shut behind her, locking him in. His chest tightened; being locked in a small space was still a fresh wound in his memory.

Turning to look at the table, he saw the brown folder the woman had pointed out. Across the filing tab at the top, a neatly printed label read MARQUEZ, JORGE. There were two plain folding chairs on either side of the table. Jorge took a seat and flipped open the folder.

Shit, Clipboard Girl wasn't kidding.

The folder contained a thick stack of paper, an intimidating collection of forms for him to fill out. Each sheet included a long dash at the bottom for Jorge's signature, and a shorter dash at the top right for his initials. Every single page—and Jorge groaned aloud when he picked up the first page, flipped it over and realized the whole damn thing was double-sided.

His mother always told him not to sign anything without reading it, but there was no way he could read all this. He made a good faith effort, wading his way through the legal jargon and overly-wordy descriptions.

He delayed signing, tied to understand it all—passages like "[Subject] shall hold harmless [Synthetic Neuroscience Institute of Technology, henceforth 'The Institute'] in the event of death, dismemberment, damage to organs, tissues, bone, or any resulting paralysis, decreased mental acuity, visual acuity, auditory acuity... neither [Subject] nor any proxy thereof will receive compensation or damages following the volunteering program...this non-disclosure agreement shall in perpetuity render [Subject] unable to discuss in full or in part any of the information, processes, or any other insights into [The Institute] and its research on this or any other project..."

The small black print swam before his eyes. He rubbed his face, trying to think.

In high school, before he got honest with himself about his identity and who he might actually want to date, he had a girlfriend. Because all of his boys had girlfriends, and he needed one too. His was named Tanya. Jorge was never in love with Tanya, but he liked her. She was interesting and offbeat. He introduced her to comics and she introduced him to horror films. She always teased him about being too serious, too much of a perfectionist.

"You gotta chill, Jorge," she'd tell him, tracing his jawline with her hot-pink fingernails, then drawing circles around his chest. "You don't gotta make everything so hard."

"You make *me* hard," he'd lie, and they'd make out for awhile. She tasted like mint and apples, which made it more difficult for him to pretend that she was her hot brother, Tony. More difficult, but not impossible. They lasted about three months. Until Jorge couldn't live with the lie anymore, and decided he would rather fly solo than fake a relationship. It was the first time he really listened to his gut. Too often, he still ignored his instincts, which were going haywire right about now.

Then he came across a clause that made his heart skip a beat: "For participation in the Volunteer Synthetic Testing program, for every week's survival, [Subject] shall be compensated at the rate of ten thousand dollars."

Ten thousand dollars is what Jorge noticed first, pulse pounding at the confirmation of the rumored compensation.

Survival is what he noticed next, upon a second reading of this almighty sentence. Surely, this meant survival in a hyperbolic sense, and not a literal risk of dying in whatever—

"Mr. Marquez?"

Jorge's head snapped up. A guy in his forties was standing in the doorway. His skin was dark, but drawn and somehow sallow; he had a tight salt-and-pepper goatee and serious eyes, no glasses even though he looked like the type to wear glasses. He was waiting for Jorge to respond.

"Oh. Yeah?"

The man stepped into the room and let the door click shut behind him. He walked to the table and sat in the second chair. Introducing himself, he did not offer Jorge his hand.

"Dr. Felix Hess. I'm the director of the Synthetic Neuroscience Institute of Technology."

"Oh. Nice to meet you, man. Sir," Jorge quickly corrected himself.

The man was not holding a clipboard, or anything else. The intensity of his stare made Jorge uncomfortable, as did the prolonged silence following the brief introductions.

"We still have a few more tests to run," Hess said abruptly, as if continuing a conversation that Jorge somehow had not heard. "But your pre-screening moved you to the top of our list. You are very fortunate, Mr. Marquez. Only one percent of the people who will apply for this program will be accepted. You will be a part of history."

Jorge couldn't have heard him right.

"Wait, so I'm—I'm in?"

"As I said, a few more tests to run, but I'm confident you'll pass with flying colors, assuming you have not contracted any terminal or chronic diseases since your last medical examination."

"No, but I…" Jorge faltered, unsure what to say. Surely they knew of his criminal record. How could he be in this top-one-percent? Something wasn't right. He wished he had more time to figure out just what. Wished he didn't need the money so badly. But he did. His family did.

"You…?" Hess asked, testing.

"Nothing," Jorge said, knowing he had the right answer. "Me… nothing."

Hess nodded. Correct. Then he launched right into instructions: "Everything is strictly confidential. All phones, cameras, and recording devices are confiscated. You will also be bound by our non-disclosure agreement. This is revolutionary, proprietary science and confidentiality is of the utmost importance. Your treatment begins with a series of injections, and a healthy diet and daily exercise. Then you will receive a… transplant, of sorts. Of a new technology. And then… well, the next step is contingent on how well your body accepts the 'transplant.' But before you ask anything, let me add: Yes, the money is real. This project is very well-funded. Just for showing up on time today and completing your paperwork, the first ten thousand dollars has been wired to your mother's bank account."

"What?"

"You can walk out right now—you already signed the nondisclosure—keep your mouth shut and keep that ten thousand dollars. Or you can stay here, begin your injections, and ten thousand dollars will be transferred into your mother's bank account… on a weekly basis."

I can walk out right now and we'll have ten grand. That's enough to cover Mariposa's phone bill, pay off Javi's dental work, close out the car payment, this month's rent, maybe even get us started chipping away at the credit card bills. But there's still Mama's doctor bills, and tuition soon for the older kids, and car repairs, and the loan debt, and next month's rent…

Jorge swallowed. "You said—begin my injections. Now?"

"Yes. If you begin the process, you stay here. In the building. No leaving the premises."

"If I participate, I can't leave, starting now?"

"Yes."

"But I didn't bring—"

"We will provide clothing, meals, lodging, everything you need. Since you are not on any prior prescription medications, and you are allowed no contact with the outside world during this testing project, it appears that you have everything you need—"

"But my family. I didn't even tell them—"

"Don't interrupt me," Hess commanded. "A courier will deliver a message to them, informing them in the broadest terms of your selection for an extremely confidential scientific study. It will explain the money. It will say that the study is long-term, but you will be in touch as soon as you are able. The courier will tell your family to think of it as military service. And that's really what it is, isn't it, Mr. Marquez? You are on the frontlines of science. And you are here as a soldier. To protect your family. Isn't that right?"

"Yes," Jorge said, mind racing, jaw clenched. He had only come to wade into the waters of this opportunity; he wasn't prepared for this deep dive. What had Mario gotten him into?

Mario.

How could he miss probation check-ins? As soon as he opened his mouth to ask, Hess smiled.

"And don't worry," Hess said blandly, looking perhaps proud of himself. "Your record has been cleared. No more probation. You're not a felon here. And your room here has been well supplied with the comic books you enjoy."

This small detail chilled Jorge's blood.

How the hell would this guy know…?

Hess nodded, frowning slightly, as if this whole part of the process was distasteful in its foregone nature. They both knew that Jorge needed this opportunity far more than the program could possibly need him.

"Finish your paperwork and a technician will be down to take you for your injections. I assume you'll prefer if I send Eric to escort you, rather than the pretty female option." Hess' grin was more unsettling than his frown. "Welcome to VOST."

CHAPTER 30: ANGELA

*S*HE BETTER NOT CRY. *I am not in the mood for that woman's tears.*

Angela Childress eyed Marilyn Hess, her longtime friend who had started to feel more like some sort of punishment from God. They were sitting at Marilyn's dining room table; as usual, Marilyn had prepared an unnecessarily elaborate set of snacks to accompany their weekly coffee date. Angela was neither surprised nor impressed by the spread of cheeses, crackers, fruit, and teacakes. Marilyn's overboard approach to hosting was just as predictable as her bursting into tears within minutes of the women taking their seats.

"It's Felix," Marilyn sobbed, clutching at a pink cocktail napkin, crumpling it in her fingers, though making sure to never fully hide her absurdly large and sparkling diamond ring. Not that any paltry little paper napkin could hide a rock like that.

"Oh?" Angela said, feigning interest. Marilyn had been doing these monologues so long, Angela could practically mouth the words along with her.

"This work he's doing, I mean, it's completely taken over his life. Ever and I haven't seen him in weeks, and he won't take my calls, and I just don't know how much more I can take…"

Angela said nothing. She didn't have to; she determined years ago that her job was not to counsel, or contradict, or offer any instructive insights. Her job was to show up, sip coffee, and give the occasional sympathetic murmur or head shake punctuated by a sigh. That was the gig.

"…and that's why I want you to come with us, Angela," Marilyn said.

It took Angela a moment to register Marilyn's words, and their need for a response.

"Sorry, that's why—what?"

"I want you to come with us," Marilyn said, watery blue eyes aimed at Angela. "To New York. To—whatever's next."

"Oh, come on, now," Angela chuckled, taking another sip of coffee. "Be serious."

"I am being serious. Dead serious." Marilyn said.

Angela stared at the complicated, difficult woman. Marilyn Kensington Hess, the privileged Texas white girl, who had never worked a day in her life; soft-handed Marilyn who had always been cared for (or at least provided-for), first by an oil baron father and then a science-prodigy husband. Marilyn was not a bad person, but she was an infuriatingly oblivious one. Self-centered and ridiculously unaware of how she came across, demanding and needy and attention-starved.

But she had her share of hardships, too. Mother who died giving birth to her, estranged father, distant possibly-sociopathic husband. Angela didn't envy the woman, despite all her privilege. Marilyn was also genuinely kind to Angela. If ever Angela needed help, be it financial or emotional, Marilyn would be good for it. She'd show up. But Angela had never made that call, and meanwhile Marilyn never took her finger off the speed dial.

"Come to New York with me," Marilyn said again.

"My life's here, Marilyn," Angela sighed, patience thinning.

"It hasn't always been," Marilyn pointed out.

She had Angela there. Even after nearly two decades in Boston, it still didn't quite feel like home. Angela was born and raised in Jackson, Mississippi. Being born black in Mississippi in the seventies wasn't exactly a cakewalk. She was raised by parents still vibrating with the energy of the movement, still yearning to breathe free, seeing the ugly underbelly of the smiling south, smelling the stench of rotting magnolias.

Haunted as her hometown was, eager as she was to leave it behind, she missed it every day. She missed the comforting sensation of humidity seeping into her skin, the syrupy smell of sweet tea boiling on stoves, the soft cracking creaks of rocking chairs on porches. She knew all too well that she romanticized the South more than was reasonable. But that was how every toxic relationship functioned—all the good parts asserting themselves, trying to crowd out the abuses and manipulations, all the fading memories of bruises.

She should know better. Mississippi was what it was, and it was dangerous to sugarcoat past sins. But it was just as dangerous to demonize one place, one state, one era, when the evil embodied there was a sickness infecting so many others. The same shit her parents protested in the sixties, her son was protesting now, decades later.

Angela's son, Leroy, was just shy of twenty-one. He was marching that very morning in Chicago, while Angela sat there pretending to care about Marilyn's manufactured problems. Angela worried about Leroy constantly. Not due to anything he might do, but simply because of who he was and how he looked. There was nothing safe about being a black man in America. Angela was equal parts proud and terrified of her son's commitment to be on the frontlines of social change. A junior at Northwestern, the boy was swiftly becoming an activist living up to the legend of his grandparents.

Leroy never met his grandparents. Although they were politically liberal, they were also deeply and devoutly Christian. They believed in equal rights for people of color, but they had little tolerance for other deviations from social norms. They were straighter-laced than most of their other friends in the movement. Church came first, everything else, distant second. Angela was not allowed to date, let alone do the sorts of things that might get her into "real trouble."

When Angela discovered she was pregnant, her senior year of high school, she kept quiet about it. She said a quick prayer of thanks that it was already well and deep on into March, and she'd be able to hide it until she graduated. She had walked across that stage, waving her diploma and pointing at her parents, hoping her ear-to-ear grin didn't look too forced. That very same night, she got on a northbound Greyhound and left Jackson forever. Before her rounding belly could shame her parents, or tie her down to the idiot football player who'd knocked her up. Johnny wasn't a bad guy. But he wasn't anyone Angela planned to stay in touch with, either.

She had an aunt in Boston, so that's where she headed. The aunt was her father's sister, but she was a lesbian and he was a full-throttle Missionary Baptist, so they were not in touch. Aunt Sharon-Lee opened her home and her heart to her frightened young niece, taking her in without a word of judgment and only one rule: If she was going to stay, she had to make something of herself. She had to go to college, community or otherwise, and then get a job and make sure she was setting herself up to provide for that baby.

Angela promised she would, and she did, going to community college while pregnant and then while nursing. When her baby boy was a thunder-thighed toddler, she transferred to Boston University and got an accounting degree. She did Aunt Sharon-Lee proud.

Unbeknownst to Angela, stubborn Sharon-Lee sent Angela's parents periodic postcards with updates on Angela. She never mentioned their grandchild, figuring that was Angela's own business to tell them. But as a sister, she felt an obligation to let her brother know his child was alive. He might have been a self-righteous lunatic, but he was still her brother. Thus Angela's parents went to their graves thinking their daughter was probably a lesbian who sought refuge with That Lesbian Sharon-Lee, praying for her daily, but not trying to track her down.

Angela eventually left her aunt's place in Boston, moving out to Cambridge, where she had a good job as the accountant at a small law firm. Her son, named Leroy Shane in honor of his great-aunt Sharon-Lee, went to good schools and got a scholarship to Northwestern. When he left for Chicago, Angela moved from a two-bedroom to a one-bedroom apartment, telling him he was always welcome to the couch but that she fully expected Leroy to be taking care of her, not moving home for her to keep taking care of him.

He'd rolled his eyes, but grinned. He was a good kid.

So Angela's life was in Boston, as much as it was anywhere. It wasn't home, but it was close enough. She would never go back to Mississippi, because the guilt she still carried about her parents weighed too heavily in her heart. What was funny was that most of her friends in Massachusetts—her white friends—assumed she wouldn't go back down there due to racism.

It almost amused Angela, how convinced Northern whites were that racism somehow dissipated on the upper side of the Mason-Dixon. Even now. Even while the prisons were packed with black and brown bodies. Yes, it was better up North, in some ways. But not in most ways. And at least down South, racism was acknowledged—a ghost still howling and heard.

Maybe that's why Angela and Marilyn managed to remain friends: though they come from different strains of Southern soil, they were both transplants to the North. Marilyn, a native Texan, naively told Angela when they met that they were destined to be friends, since they were both Southern girls who somehow wound up living in Yankee land. It genuinely did not seem to occur to Marilyn that a rich Texas white girl and a poor Mississippi black girl who found their way up north by way of two very different trains were not likely to share much in common with one another.

But it was oddly charming, how she proclaimed so guilelessly that they were "destined to be friends." Marilyn's sugary Southern hospitality and Angela's embedded Southern politeness meant that Marilyn was bound to extend an invitation to come over, and Angela would be compelled to accept. One coffee led to another, and over the years, they became close. Which was destiny, according to Marilyn, and completely bizarre, as Angela saw it.

"Come with us," Marilyn said, voice cracking, swinging toward desperation. "Please. It would mean the world to me. And to Ever! God, she'd be thrilled."

Ever.

Angela did have a soft spot for Marilyn's daughter. Poor Ever had drawn the short straw early. Marilyn *chose* Felix. She could thereby also choose to leave him ("*I would never!*" Marilyn would always retort, shocked and thrilled by Angela's brass). Ever had not chosen her parents. Like any baby born into this world, she got what she got. And what Ever had wound up with was an absent father and a neurotic, narcissistic mother.

Ever was always fed and clothed and well cared for, and no one ever laid a hand on her or said nasty things to her. But her parents rarely said anything to her, one way or another. The kid spent all her time at the next door neighbors' house, which is where she was now. Probably. Hopefully.

"You told Ever about the move?"

Marilyn shook her head. "She'll just pitch a fit."

"She's a smart kid. Won't go well if you just keep leaving her in the dark."

"Well, if Felix were ever here, we could both tell her," Marilyn snapped, irritable. "But he isn't. It's all on me, always. When I married him, I had no idea he would leave the whole parenting thing to me. It's terrible."

"Terrible," Angela muttered. Incredible how Marilyn could misappropriate yet another helping of pity, feeling bad for herself instead of her daughter.

"The last time Felix and I talked—God, like a week ago—I mentioned you might come with us. And you know what? He liked the idea."

Hearing this, Angela suddenly felt like the television a toddler gets plunked in front of, a distraction that freed up the grown-ups to get things done. She'd interacted with Felix little over the years, but when they crossed paths, she always feels vaguely unsettled. Like he was looking down at her—not because she was a woman, or black, or not as prestigious as he; no, she was pretty sure he disdained Angela because she was dumb enough to befriend Marilyn.

"He says he could get you a job at the Synt, even. They need people who are good with numbers, Angie. It would pay well— they're a bottomless money pit."

"Bottomless money pit, huh?"

This whole thing already sounded six shades of crazy. As a certified public accountant, Angela knew that words like *bottomless money pit* constituted a wildly waving red flag.

"Yes," Marilyn nodded. Sentence by sentence, she kept building her case: "And Felix says with the big stuff coming in, there'll be even more money. There's gonna be a whole lot of demand for what they're doing over there."

"Which is?" Angela pressed, a little curious on that front, at least.

Marilyn looked around, which was bizarre. Did the woman think there were spies tucked behind her expensive pillow cushions? She leaned in, dropping her voice conspiratorially.

"When I met Felix, he was studying this new field of science—cyborganics. Bringing man and machine together, like—you know. Some embedded chips or whatever. Improving our life and health and minds through the 'augmented' parts, he said."

"Yeah, I've read some articles on that," Angela said. She had; she'd subsequently written it off as bonkers. "I didn't think that was anything, you know, for real."

"It's real. It's the whole focus of Felix's group. And I think it's about to really blow up."

"You mean blowing up in a good way, or a bad way?" Angela asked.

"I meant it in a good way," Marilyn said, blinking her wide mascara-clad eyes. "How could it blow up in a bad way?"

Famous last words.

"Well, thank you for the invite, Marilyn," Angela said, finishing the last of her coffee and eager to get back to her desk and the sane, not-robot-building people at her office. "And you know I'll miss you and Ev when y'all move. But me coming along, it's just not in the cards."

The tears that had been brimming and swimming in Marilyn's eyes for the past hour spilled over the edges of her lids now, running down her pretty face, tracking delicate black mascara lines along her cheeks.

You'd think she'd've invested in waterproof by now. Bless her heart.

Angela pushed back from the table, resenting herself a little as she wrapped Marilyn in a comforting hug. Marilyn, still seated, burrowed her streaked face into Angela's bosom, clutching her arm and wailing like an infant. Angela gave her a good squeeze, then firmly extracted herself. Maintaining boundaries was something her therapist Gracie was coaching her to do. *Don't get guilted into what you don't want to do; don't stay longer than you want to stay.*

"I can't do this without you," Marilyn blubbered.

"You can, honey," Angela said. "And I gotta go pick up my dry cleaning and get back to work. I'll see you soon."

Angela walked from Marilyn's oversized home to the dry cleaners, just a few blocks south. She could have driven, but Angela usually preferred taking the train the short ride from her office in Kenmore Square to Marilyn's home near Harvard's campus. It was chilly that day, though, and Angela squeezed her quilted-coat arms tight against the brisk early-winter wind.

She replayed her conversation with Marilyn, wondering what Leroy would say when she told him about it later. She could already hear his heavy sigh, could clock the rolling of his eyes. Leroy loved Marilyn, but he sure didn't like her much.

"Marilyn's a lunatic," he'd told her on more than one occasion.

"She's my friend," Angela would say, countering him without quite disagreeing.

"Well, you got yourself one crazy-ass friend."

"Watch your mouth," Angela told him, trying not to laugh.

As she walked into the dry cleaners, her phone rang. She glanced down at the screen; it was her boss, Ed. Odd; Ed never called her. And she'd been gone less than an hour, no reason for him to be checking in on her. Their firm had been acquired by a corporate conglomerate awhile back, and lenient hour-and-a-half lunches were now frowned on, but Angela had kept a strict eye on the clock. She wasn't violating any rules.

"Hello?"

"Angela? Hi. Jesus. I don't know how to tell you this."

Her stomach dropped. "Tell me what?"

"Especially so soon to Christmas... Dammit. Look, don't come back after lunch. You can come back Monday, to get your stuff, but—I just got a call. From those new bastards, corporate—we're done. We're out. All of us."

"What?"

"I'm sorry, Angela. I am really, truly sorry. They're shutting us down. Our whole office is just... erased. We're all unemployed. Happy friggin' New Year."

CHAPTER 31: FELIX

F ELIX HESS LIED TO HOWARD FELL when he
told him about Nathan. "Brain-dead," that's what he told
Nathan's brother. "He's brain-dead. He's gone." He knew
for Howard, that would truly mean the end of Nathan; without
his mind, he was nothing. But when it came to Nathan's actual
fate, "brain-dead" could not be further from the truth.

After the lights stopped flickering in the lab, while Derek was
on the phone calling Dr. Kansal, Felix Hess had re-booted the
monitors. He started with the ones tracking Nathan Fell's brain
activity, and what Felix glimpsed on the monitors did not reflect
brain death—instead, the lights and intersecting lines reflected
more brain activity than Felix had ever seen. Synapses were firing

at lightning speed through an unbelievably illuminated mind, mapping new information, working overtime, running calculation after calculation, making discovery after discovery, connection after connection.

But the mind was no longer interested in operating the body that housed it; it was focusing on something else. It certainly wasn't dead. It was on fire. Despite Nathan's paralysis, his vacant eyes and unresponsive outward appearance, that luminous mind of his was working harder than it had ever worked before.

Dr. Kansal had arrived on the scene within minutes, shoving Derek out of the way and rushing toward Hess, who quickly snapped off the monitor and pointed instead to the augmentation machine.

"Open it up!" The small woman bellowed, sliding her stethoscope out of her pocket.

Hess had pressed a button, and the top panel slid back from the machine, revealing Nathan Fell and his staring, lifeless eyes. Dr. Kansal leaped into action, listening for a heartbeat, checking Fell's breath, his pulse.

"He's alive, but barely," the doctor barked, like a commanding officer to a sluggish army. "Hopefully he's stable, for now, but he's unresponsive and his pulse is quite weak. We need to get him to a hospital!" She tried rolling him over, and saw the port in his neck, connecting and binding him to the larger machine. "What on earth—?!"

"Dr. Kansal," Hess said, calm. "Thank you, but your services are no longer needed."

"What are you talking about? If we do not get Dr. Fell to a hospital—"

"We have a hospital on-site," Hess said, lying only a little. "He will be well cared-for. We only retained your services as a neurologist. Since his medical needs are more basic—"

"But we have no way of knowing—"

"Thank you, doctor," Hess said firmly. "It's all under control."

"Felix—" Derek began, and Hess glared daggers, cowing him. The younger researcher, pants still damp from wetting himself, said nothing further.

A few hours later, after ensuring Fell was indeed stable, and then securing a death certificate from a clerical paper-pusher only too happy to accept a ridiculously exorbitant bribe, Hess called Howard Fell, told him Nathan was brain-dead, and that his wish was to donate his body to science. Which was also technically true.

Yes, he told Howard, *we're pulling the plug now; no, there was no time for a visit; yes, it was just terrible.*

Hess' next call was to the funders. What he told them was closer to the truth—Nathan had survived the procedure but was currently unresponsive. Hess was optimistic about the ultimate outcome. But it was imperative that the work go on, and that the leadership torch be passed to the only other man on earth who knew the ins and outs of their cyborganics work.

And thus Felix became the new director of the Synthetic Neuroscience Institute of Technology. Effective immediately.

After all, there were no other promising candidates. No competition in the field, anywhere—unless the funders wanted to try to go poach a few Israelis, Russians, or Chinese. Hess had made sure of that. Hess knew he could control Derek, keep him from deviating from their story, and get him to continue working to advance their agenda. Hess also knew that they potentially had an extremely powerful new tool in their fingertips.

Things moved quickly when Hess' appointment was announced. The media descended on his family in Cambridge, forcing him to bring Marilyn and Ever to New York earlier than he would have liked. There was a slew of paperwork and hysterical hubbub around the death of the Cyborganics Cowboy; some intrepid reporters theorized he wasn't really dead. Hess worked hard to discredit the "Elvis lives" contingent. By the end of 2012, almost all of Nathan's earthly affairs were attended to; his memorial was well-attended, his debts were paid, his significant personal funds disbursed, a department at MIT named in his honor. His laughable parental rights were posthumously relinquished (apparently his sister-in-law Sophie had started a court process to adopt Nathan's children years ago). The inquiries about Fell from outsiders finally slowed, freeing Hess to focus on the internal inquiries about Nathan Fell that were far, far more interesting.

He had monitors tracking Nathan Fell's brain activity, and the results continued to be amazing. Unbelievable. A galaxy of cerebral constellations, comets sailing, stars being born, all within the mind of a man staring blankly from the reinforced-glass window of the tight tube in which he was contained.

Hess had swiftly realized the potential of this unintended outcome. Nathan Fell without a functioning body, without a voice, unable to call the shots, but with his beautiful brain churning away at maximum capacity. Hess had no way of knowing exactly what was going on within that mind, but the sheer energy it was generating was incredibly powerful. It had taken Hess a few weeks to catch on to it, but he eventually determined that the relationship between Nathan and the machine to which he was connected had shifted.

The machine was not powering Nathan's body, keeping it alive—no; Nathan's mind was powering the machine. When Hess cut out all power sources, the machine kept churning, the electricity of Nathan's brain continuing to surge through the system. It was incredible. So Hess began building the machine around Nathan. He brought in specialists, who had to sign confidentiality agreements and join the permanent staff of the Synt (he didn't need more loose cannons out there—Dr. Kansal was enough, though she surely believed the public reports of Nathan Fell's death). He expanded Nathan's augmentation machine to be a life support system, complete with catheters and feeding tubes, everything necessary to keep Nathan's body alive, simply to serve as a vessel for the mind. Hess built several new augmentation machines, in preparation for the next round of testing—and all of the shiny new machines for synching connected back to the original machine, which now housed its own original creator.

Nathan Fell was where he always wanted to be, Hess rationalized. He was at the literal center of the technology. He was the heart of this new collective consciousness.

No! He was not the heart. Nor would he have wanted to be. He was *the mind*.

Hess was relentless, working round the clock and forcing Derek and their team of underlings to work at maximum capacity as well, designing and building upon this mighty machine and the cloud system to which it connected, storing information. Hess decided they needed a name for this central machine. Since it was Nathan Fell's final resting place, he considered *The Tomb* or *The Mausoleum*, but that seemed too grim. Hess wanted something savvier. More savage. He appreciated some sardonic humor here and there. Then, the perfect name came to him.

The center of the new world, created by intelligent design, surrounded and protected by cloud technology, would be called Heaven.

Hess initially saw the sacrilegious name as hilarious. Later, he would pat himself on the back for it also being somewhat prophetic.

The funders knew that Hess wanted to keep the work going, but put their foot down when it came to next steps. They could not skip a full-fledged testing phase. No more brilliant minds were to be sacrificed.

Find expendables, they told him.

It made Hess recall Derek's half-joking suggestion of experimenting on prisoners. But of course, they couldn't really do that. So they did the next best thing: they developed the Volunteer

Synthetic Test program, which Derek dubbed VOST (Hess could never understand the obsession with acronyms and nicknames). The VOST premise was simple. It was time to move beyond monkeys, without risking the lives of those pushing the program forward. So they had to recruit young, healthy volunteers willing to participate in experimental trials to test each element of the augmentation process. People who would trade their autonomy and health for enough compensation. So—not prisoners, but the poor. The desperate.

Hess waved around money, subtly enough and through the right channels. Probation officers, he decided. Folks out on parole, that would a good base. Hard for them to get good jobs. Many had families to support—and Hess knew how the system worked well enough to know that not all ex-cons were bad guys.

They got more than enough volunteers. They grabbed those with the fewest social connections, and got to work.

Unfortunate incidents peppered the first round of VOST testing. Unfortunate, but instructive; Hess and his team learned a lot. But the first group of volunteers did not fare well. Blindness. Brain bleeds, debilitating migraines, aneurysms; none of them survived. Hess was quietly grateful that the "lowlife" perception of those first volunteers meant almost no one noticed when they disappeared from society. No one who *mattered* noticed, anyway.

In the second round, things were a bit rosier. There were still incidents. Paralysis on the left side of the body for some. Seizures for others. But there were more successes. Only a handful of the second generation volunteers were terminated, unlike the entire population of those unfortunate first few volunteers.

As the technology improved, Hess felt the need to drill down on quality control of the volunteers. After all, now that the technology was starting to work, Hess didn't want a bunch of augmented psychopaths running around. The first few recruits were not ideal. But they taught Hess something, not only in terms of the technology but also in terms of the test subject themselves. They had to be a certain caliber. They had to fit a certain profile.

Ideal candidates would not be missed much in their community; had already done time or served in the army or skipped town here and there. But they would not be violent. Most of all, they would be hungry for money—and ideally, not for themselves, but for someone else. Someone they loved more than themselves. A spouse; children.

Hess' team would call in hundreds of people each day, dividing them into smaller rooms so no one there ever saw more than a few dozen other potential participants at a time. Of the hundreds called in each day, ninety percent were for show. They were there to be seen by other participants, to give credibility to the general, vague testing program in case too many rumors started floating around. But the pre-screening, of which all participants were unaware, was so thorough that it knocked almost everyone out of the program before they even walked through the door.

To get in to the small pre-selected subset, you had to be smart. Fit. Ethical, but willing to compromise and sacrifice for what you loved. You had to be in a tough spot, willing to leave everything behind, despite how much you loved those you would be forced to abandon.

In short, you had to be Jorge Marquez.

Hess was glad that Jorge had been brought in at this later stage, the third round of the VOST program. The third generation was near-perfect, technologically speaking. In Hess' estimation, they could have gone ahead with full-on, pay-to-play synchs for selected citizens—but the funders had been insistent, saying a ninety percent success rate with volunteer subjects was mandatory before the program could move from pilot into full launch, made available to the public.

This third generation was the ninety-percent success Hess has been awaiting. And just as predicted, Jorge Marquez was the most successful synch yet. A full year post-synch, Jorge was just as fit, just as healthy, just as bright. No side effects, physical or neurological.

But Jorge wanted out. Wanted to see his family. Wanted to quit.

Jorge knew too much and had done too well for Hess to release him. Conveying this information firmly would not go well, but Hess took precautions to ensure that he would keep the upper hand. He never played cards any other way.

"Jorge," Hess said when the Vost entered his office. "How are you today?"

"Fine," Jorge said. "As soon as I see my family."

"Sit," Hess said, gesturing to the low chair in front of his desk. "Let's talk about—"

The electronic beep of Hess' phone intercom cut him off. A secretary's voice comes timidly through the speaker.

"Sorry to interrupt, Dr. Hess, but it's your wife. Says it's about Ever—"

"Tell her I'll call her back," Hess snapped, pushing a button to sever the connection.

"You're married?" Jorge's eyes shot to Hess' left hand, which bore no telltale ring.

"Yes," Hess said. His irritation at the intercom's violation of his privacy sent his mind spinning in new directions. *I need to find a way to upgrade this place to some sort of silent messaging system—no, not the place; the people. Heaven could connect us all and we could message directly, mind to mind...*

"I've never seen your wife."

"What? Oh," Hess said, almost snapping at Jorge for interrupting him before realizing he had not been speaking aloud. "Yes, well. Our daughter keeps her busy."

"You have a daughter?"

"Yes," Hess said through gritted teeth, kicking himself for all the accidental oversharing.

"You miss her?"

As a matter of fact, no.

But Hess did not say that aloud. He knew it would make him more distant and dislikable. An unfair penalty for telling the truth. And as it happened, Hess did not *dislike* his daughter. He just had no daily need to monitor her.

"Jorge, I have something important to tell you. I am telling you this in the strictest confidence." He cleared his throat, drawing out the moment. "We think that the program is ready to move from pilot to practice. Several of us—some of the funders, some of the researchers—will be undergoing the process in the coming weeks. I will supervise the first few, then undergo my own augmentation. This has been in the works for quite some time."

"And you're telling me because...?"

"Because assuming this is all successful, we're going to change the world," Hess said, eager. "We are about to change the world. Everyone is going to want what we have. All eyes will be on us, and our work will intensify. And there may even be some... initial resistance, let's say. Protests. It could be dangerous out there for anyone affiliated with the program. You could be seen as... unnatural."

"So what does that mean?" Jorge asked, hand moving to the back of his neck, stroking the hard metal of his port.

"We're not sure yet. And until we know, we can't risk your safety."

The flash in Jorge's eyes reflected a thousand emotions at once. His voice was tight, controlled. "How long."

Hess shrugged.

"No, man," Jorge said, shaking his head. "Look, I'm sorry, but no. Only reason I did this was for my family, and now I haven't seen them in a year. I appreciate your concern, but I'll take the risks. I gotta get out of here."

"I'm afraid that's not possible, Jorge."

Jorge's mouth twitched. "What if I just decided to walk, right now?"

"I'm afraid you wouldn't make it past the front entrance."

"What. Are. You. Talking. About."

Hess fought back a sigh, wishing everyone were as reasonable as he.

"It was in your paperwork, Jorge. All the mechanic material used to augment your body—that all belongs to us. To the Synt. And it's central to your operating system now. You can't survive without it. And, well—you know those old grocery carts that had wheels that would lock up if you took them too far from their home store? Restaurant table pagers that wouldn't work outside of their home restaurant? I'm afraid our technology—*your* technology—is like that. You walk too far from home base, and, well… same thing, really."

"This was a volunteer program—"

"You entered this building, voluntarily. Signed up, voluntarily. Allowed this technology, our property, to be embedded in you, *voluntarily*. No one put a gun to your head, Jorge."

"But you what—put a bomb in my skull?"

"You signed every page of that waiver, Mr. Marquez," Hess said coolly. "Every. Page. I would advise you to watch your tone, and choose your words carefully."

A vein bulged in Jorge's forehead, but he held his tongue. Thinking before acting. Hess admired Jorge's balance of reason and fervor. He liked that the man could intimidate people, give the impression that at any moment he might crush them. He already decided, way back when he was reviewing potential volunteers, that Jorge Marquez was someone he wanted on his team, long-term. Hess didn't have nearly enough muscle around him.

"There's gotta be an off-switch. Or an extraction procedure, or something. You can make it possible for me to leave."

"Extracting your technology is not in the institute's best interest."

"What about *my* best interest?"

"You signed the paperwork, Jorge. If you didn't read it, that's your problem. Your liability. Not mine. I am quite familiar with the content of the contract. We have held up our end of the bargain. Your family has received over a half-million dollars in compensation. They are doing well. Because of you."

Hess watched Jorge trying to control his emotions. The clash of gratitude and frustration played out as a series of small twitches at the corner of Jorge's left eye.

"Of course," Hess continued, "...the weekly allowance will be cut off now that we're easing out of pilot phase. But if you join my staff, your family will continue to be cared for, you have my word. The half million will never run out. Your mother will have five hundred thousand dollars in her bank account, anytime she checks it. Your brothers and sisters will all go to whatever college they wish. They'll never have to worry, and they'll have you to thank for it."

"But they'll never get to thank me to my face?"

Right on cue, as per Hess's request, the receptionist buzzed through again, this time not with an unwarranted interruption, but reading from her assigned script.

"Funder's here. Shall I send her to the conference room?"

"Absolutely," Hess said to the phone. "Send her there and tell her I'll be right with her."

"Yes, sir." The intercom clicked off.

Hess aimed for an apologetic smile, although he was not sorry. "Looks like I have to go."

And looks like you have to stay.

CHAPTER 32: RUTH

F OR A PRE-TEEN GIRL, Ruth wasn't much of a talker. But she was very much a thinker. And, as her Uncle Howard said, she was a world-class worrier.

She didn't stress out about tests or crushes or making the cheerleading squad; she worried about climate change and global epidemics. She worried about racism and sexism and senseless violence. Most of all, secretly, she worried that she was meaningless. A nobody, incapable of making a difference, unworthy of notice. Despite being a good student, a beloved sister, whatever else—she was afraid that someday the mask of competence she wore would fall off, and everyone would finally realize she had no face of her own beneath the heavy mask.

She wore a lot of different masks. More than masks: whole costumes. Whole personas. When Ruth was sweet to her Aunt Sophie or to her sister Rachel, she felt as if she were putting on someone else's soft cashmere sweater, stepping into the role of the good, gentle girl; the sort of girl her sister Rachel actually was, and Ruth could never be for more than an hour or two at a time. When she mouthed off to Howard or got into a fight with one of her brother-cousins (or punched a schoolmate for telling her that "brother-cousin" sounded incestuous), she felt as if she was sliding on a badass leather jacket and becoming a real rebel. But this, too, was just another costume change. She wasn't really defiant.

She wasn't really anything.

Each costume change gave her a momentary sense of self, all too fleeting. But when she lay in her own slim bed at night, listening to the heavy rhythmic breathing of her twin sister in the bed across the room, she was gripped by fear. She had no idea who she really was; why her parents left her; what she was meant to be. She was starting to believe that if she didn't figure herself out soon, it would be self-evident proof that she was nothing.

"Ruth," Rachel said from the darkness. "Stop thinking so loud."

"Sorry," Ruth told her twin. "I'll try to think quieter."

"Ha. What's on your mind?"

"Stuff."

"Oh, stuff," Rachel said, a little miffed at this lack of intimacy. And then, she offered a more generous truth than her sister had: "I've been thinking about our mother."

"You mean Aunt Sophie?" Ruth asked, knowing that wasn't who was on Rachel's mind.

"No," Rachel said.

"Why were you thinking about her?"

"Do you think, if she knew... if she knew Dad died, would she come for us?"

Ruth considered this; somehow it had never occurred to her that their mother might not know. Or that she might know. Ruth had never considered her mother at all when it came to their father's death.

It was years ago already that Uncle Howard had called them into the kitchen and told them that he had some bad news. Then, his eyes wet and bright, his voice thick, he had informed Ruth and Rachel that their father had suddenly passed away.

Rachel had cried, because Rachel always cried at news of a death, be it an innocent victim on the nightly news, or a character she didn't even like all that much on a television show, or an unfortunate rabbit squished into a furry brown street pancake.

Ruth had not cried. She had not said anything. She simply stared at the wall. Stupid as it was, Ruth had secretly believed that their father would one day come back for them. He had known them for longer than their mother had; he would realize how great they were, how wrong he'd been, and he would come for them. But now he couldn't, because he was dead.

"It was in the news," Ruth said, abruptly and more harshly than she intended. "When Dad died. The whole lab-accident thing."

She flapped her arms in a sort of there-you-have-it gesture.

"Maybe she doesn't watch the news—"

"You seriously think she doesn't watch the news or listen to the radio or use Google or, like, anything?"

"I guess you're right," Rachel said, her voice smaller.

"Hey, I'm sorry," Ruth apologized sincerely. "I didn't mean—"

"No, it's fine. You're right. It was just a stupid thought I had."

"It's not stupid."

"It is. And so is she. I guess I got the stupid from her."

"Rach, come on," Ruth said, feeling terrible. She hated upsetting her sister. Being the first twin, a little older and a whole lot bolder, made Ruth feel like the big sister. She was protective of her little sister; she wasn't supposed to be the one hurting her.

"Do you think she's a bad person? Our mom?"

Ruth hesitated. On paper, their mother was terrible. She left them when they were soft little babies, and never looked back. She sent no birthday cards or letters or presents, attempted no phone calls or emails. But Uncle Howard said she'd been trying to do the right thing, giving them to him and Aunt Sophie. She wanted good things for them, things she couldn't give them.

She was sick, Uncle Howard had told Ruth, confidentially, one night in the kitchen.

Sick like a cold? Like the flu?

No. Sick in her mind—in her heart. She was troubled, Ruthie.

Will I be... troubled?

Don't you worry about that, Ruthie. You're a strong girl.

What about Rachel?

...Rachel will be fine, her uncle had replied, just a second too slowly.

Ruth never shared this conversation with her sister. But it shaped her next reply, softening its edges: "I think... I think she was probably a confused person. She was trying to do what was right, she just didn't know what right really looked like."

"Yeah, sure," Rachel muttered, uncharacteristically bitter. "'Confused.' Confused about how to be a good person."

Maybe she thought she was nothing...

Feeling a sudden possible connection to her mother, Ruth's defenses kicked in; she suddenly didn't want Rachel to write their mother off. It might mean, in some deep and not yet knowable way, that she would someday write Ruth off, too.

"We don't know what was going on in her mind," Ruth said, trying to stay calm. "Anyway, why... why are you thinking about her now?"

Even in the dark of the room, Ruth could sense her sister's movements, could practically see her shifting, shrugging, shaking her head as she struggled to find the right words. "My teacher gave us an assignment. We have to write an essay, about what family means to us."

Ruth and Rachel had been in different classrooms since second grade. Separating twins, even non-identical ones, was something their school "strongly recommended." Otherwise they might just socialize with each other or do some other weird twinning-thing. The teachers all agreed that it was a Good Idea for the girls to have their own, separate school experiences.

Ruth and Rachel thought this was ridiculous, but they got used to it. It was harder on Uncle Howard and Aunt Sophie, who had to navigate another two nights of parent-teacher-conferences, another two sets of homework assignments and field trip duties; another two on top of the other six they already had. Now that half of their biological kids were in college, it was a little easier, schedule-wise. Finally.

"I didn't get that assignment," Ruth said.

"It's 'cause Mrs. Myers is pregnant," Rachel said, her eye-roll audible. Everything irritating about fifth grade, Rachel blamed on her teacher's pregnancy. (A trick she learned from Mrs. Myers herself, who also blamed everything on her pregnancy.) "Family on the brain."

"So write about Uncle Howie and Aunt Sophie and the whole gang of kids we grew up with. She'll love it. Big happy family."

"It's just weird to always leave out our parents. Our *real* parents."

"Well, writing about them would be a real short essay. 'My mother left us when we were four months old. My father moved away a few years later, then he died too. Luckily, I'm not too sad, because I have an incredibly beautiful twin sister. I wish we were identical, because then I too would be beautiful'—"

A pillow sailed across the room, landing just shy of Ruth's bed and plopping to the floor.

"Missed me," Ruth smirked.

"I was aiming for the floor," Rachel said sweetly. "Now you'll slip on my silky pillowcase and get a concussion in the morning."

They both giggled. Ruth loved this secret late-night version of her sister, with the wicked sense of humor. By day, Rachel was mild and a total goody-two-shoes. But she was much more fun in moments like this one.

"You're right," Rachel said, sober again. "I'll write about our real family. Not our parents. I'll write about the ones who stuck around. That's who matters."

"I'll always be here for you. You know that."

"Maybe. If you stop smoking. Otherwise you'll die of lung cancer and I'll be alone."

Ruth froze. Somehow, she had convinced herself that her dirty little secret was under the radar. That she was an eleven-year-old stealth agent, who chewed gum like a maniac and used apple-scented shampoo and made sure to never, ever smell like the cigarettes she smoked with the seventh graders under the bleachers every day after school.

"I am *not* smoking—"

"Don't lie to me, we have twin telekinesis."

"We do not. And I'm pretty sure you mean telepathy. And we still don't."

"Well, whatever. You're a terrible liar."

Ruth was very comfortable being the Bad Twin. It was at least a *partial* identity; something to define her. But she didn't want to disappoint Rachel.

"Fine. "I'll quit smoking."

"Good," Rachel said. "I'm going to pretend that you're telling the truth."

"I *am*—"

"Whatever." Rachel paused. "You really think Mom knows about Dad, and just decided not to come check on us? Because I was thinking, we could ask Uncle Howie to tell us her last name—like, her maiden name—see if we could find her, to let her know, and then—"

"Rach," Ruth said, gently but sternly. "That's a bad idea."

"Why? Why is it such a bad idea?"

"Well, maybe we wouldn't like her. I don't think Aunt Sophie liked her."

"Why do you say that?"

"It would… it would hurt Aunt Sophie's feelings."

This quieted Rachel. "I don't want to hurt Aunt Sophie's feelings. Or Uncle Howie's. I don't want them to think they… weren't enough for us, or something. They're the best."

There she is, sweet Rachel.

"Yeah. The best."

Ruth waited to see if her sister had anything else to say, but Rachel rolled back over, turning her back to her sister and burrowing into her remaining silken pillow. Ruth, too, rolled over, hugging herself around the giant question-mark shaped hole within her, hating the knowledge that her twin had an identical hole in her own gentle soul. Ruth wondered if they would ever be okay. Broken bones heal. She wasn't so sure about broken hearts.

THE SINGULARITY

CHAPTER 33: HOWARD

OWARD WAS ALONE when Felix Hess announced, via livestreaming video, that he had successfully augmented himself.

"I have successfully merged with machine," Hess boasted, moving the camera toward his neck and showing off the glinting metal embedded in his flesh. "The future is no longer something we are awaiting; it is something we are creating."

Sitting in his cramped office, the one he shared with two other adjunct faculty members, surrounded by philosophy texts and tomes on ethics and morality, Howard felt something in him crumble. Watching Felix's broadcast, he knew that he was seeing the culmination of his brother's work—and the beginning of the end of the world.

There was no going back. The stock market was going crazy; social media was immediately exploding with theories about which billionaire would be the first to buy his way into the technology. Howard knew that a powerful, wealthy subset of the population augmenting and leaving everyone else to fend for themselves was going to lead to chaos; to modern monarchy; to all-out war.

He began moving quickly, reaching out to like-minded activists and academics. He had heard the news alone. He needed allies to tackle its dire implications.

The world was already on the brink, tempers rising, rifts widening, the whole world spoiling for a fight. Religious wars, turf wars, terrorism, the poisoning of water and sky, the pillaging of the earth, deadly dichotomies of oppressors and oppressed, the continued other-ing of anyone perceived as different, disease, famine, violence, apathy. Hurricanes. Hunger. Hopelessness. Mass shootings. Despair.

For millennia people survived threat after threat, disaster after disaster, incursion after incursion. But Howard believed deeply that people survived because they were, in the end, *people*. Fundamentally one and the same. Interconnected, interdependent. Sure, they veered off track individually and collectively, but as a whole species, they had course-corrected and saved themselves. But if people were no longer all *people*—if some were more, and some were less, not in the minds of bigots but on a very measurable and scientific level—they were doomed.

So after Felix Hess' ostentatious press conference, where he preened and showed off the port at the base of his neck, Howard sent out a message. He summoned the crack team that he believed could make a difference, could band together and organize, could come up with a way to stop Hess' work. Yes, that megalomaniac had already been augmented—but he was just one man. If they could get a bill passed, cut off his funding, make his work illegal, they could still head off widespread human synching. They could still prevent the Singularity.

The first meeting was attended by about two dozen people, all crammed in to the Fell family living room. A few of Howie's colleagues from Harvard, a few from Bunker Hill; some former students; Sophie's best friend Maxwell and his husband Henry; the Garrisons from next door; and Howie's physician, Gregory Chapman, who brought a handful of other doctors from his hospital. Howard and Sophie welcomed everyone as their large collection of children (most of whom were now young adults) offered their guests coffee, tea, and light refreshments.

"I, uh, I'm not sure where to begin," Howie said, putting his hands in his pocket and shuffling his feet, the same way he often began lecturing in his classrooms. "We've all been following the news. We're aware of the implications—as aware as we can be. And this has been on our radars, mine at least, for some time. This man, Felix Hess, is continuing my... my brother's work." Howie offered this statement tightly, acknowledging the elephant in the room. "I feel a personal responsibility, for that reason... but also because I truly believe that this is a dangerous, divisive path. We can't just moan and debate around our own tables about whether or not this is right or wrong. We need to take real action on this, and we need to do it now. Get some bills passed. Organize a movement, against transhumanism, or augmentation, or synching, or whatever they're calling it. So that's why—that's why we're here."

Howie took a hand out from one of his pockets, stroked his beard, and thus ended the first of many speeches that he would give as the somewhat reluctant de facto leader of the resistance against a synthetic society.

One of Howie's Harvard colleagues, an ethics professor named Stan, cleared his throat.

"I, uh, fear we're going to meet some challenges, if we try to go the legislative route. Felix Hess—the Synt—they have a lot of funders. Funders he inherited from…"

"My brother Nathan," Howie said, granting permission.

"Right," Stan nodded. "Nathan Fell's funders. They've been backing Hess for years, ever since—well, ever since. It's all dark money, as the politicians would say—anonymous funders, encrypted transactions… off-shore banks, all sorts of protections in place. No one knows who all of the funders are. But there are rumors… rumors that it's people like…"

Stan paused, looking nervous.

"People like…?" Howie pressed.

"People in the Senate. Congress," Stan said, swallowing. "People in the White House."

The room went quiet at this direct statement of what immediately seemed obvious, as they considered the wealth and ego of the new administration. Of course rich politicians would be supporting this; they wanted it. They wanted *in*. The air chilled.

"So you're saying a bill would be an uphill battle," Howard said heavily.

"I'm saying the odds of getting anything actually passed are nil. And even if by some miracle we got it through, soon as it hits the executive desk… veto."

Sophie's brows drew together like a curtain pulled suddenly shut, blocking out the promise of any light breaking through.

"So… we shouldn't even *try* the legislative route?"

"It's a bunt, at best," Stan said.

Sophie went white. Howard looked slapped. No one knew what to say.

"Having a petition to get a bill underway or whatever is something," Maxwell finally said, giving a reassuring look to Sophie while squeezing his husband's hand. "I mean—yeah. The activist in me says it's a start. Call it a bunt, whatever, but I think if nothing else, it'll flush out some more folks who see things like we do. Get us some more allies."

"It'll also get us on our opponents' radar," added Stan, with a nervy swallow.

"Raising our voices against this shouldn't be something that puts us at risk," Sophie said.

"It shouldn't," Stan echoed, in a way that meant *but it probably will*.

"This is still America, right?" Dr. Chapman cracked, eliciting some nervous laughter.

They chatted for a few minutes more, planning next steps. An email group, list-serve or something, would be a good start. They all agreed on that. Continue the conversation there, set a next meeting, dole out tasks and get people working on action items. Bunt with the legislative stuff. Figure out what to do after that. Howard thanked everyone for coming. Sophie told them all that they should really take some cookies with them.

As the crowd began to disperse, one of Dr. Chapman's colleagues made her way to Howard. A small Indian woman with short dark hair, she was the best-dressed person by far in her expensive dove-gray blazer and sleek heels. She walked toward him with purpose, planted herself in front of him and stuck out her hand.

"Professor Fell," she said. "I'm Dr. Preeti Kansal."

He shook her hand, impressed by the strength in her grip. "Pleased to meet you."

"Yes," she said. It seemed to take some effort for her to hold his gaze. "I am pleased to meet you. I am also sorry."

"Sorry...?"

Her voice wavered: "I was... I was the on-call neurologist when your brother...I'm sorry, I can't—I signed a confidentiality agreement, so I can't say..."

"Dr. Kansal," Howard said, voice low and steely. "You signed a confidentiality agreement with—with them?"

Her eyes flashed. A tight nod.

"You were called in when my brother... when Nathan..."

And then he got it. How could he have been so stupid?

"Nathan attempted to augment himself. Before the technology was really ready."

Flash. Nod.

A low ringing began in Howard's ear, a ringing that would last for the next week, making him feel hollow and only half-real. It pulsed behind every other sound and thought he encountered, like a flat-line alert in the background as a doctor tried vainly to resuscitate a patient. Fighting against the ringing, he asked another question:

"Are you the one who declared him brain-dead?"

"No."

"No?"

She shook her head. "When I got the call, I came right away. They had transportation—I was there in minutes. He was unresponsive, weak pulse, shallow breath, but the monitors weren't working. I had no way of knowing—I told them to take him to a hospital, let me treat him there, but Hess had me escorted out of the building—"

That opportunistic prick. That monster.

The ringing in Howard Fell's ears got louder and louder, echoing throughout his entire body as blood pounded through his neck, heating his face, coloring his vision until he was seeing nothing but red. Seething.

"You're saying..." Howard said through gritted teeth, fighting for control, voice barely a whisper, "...that as far as you know... Nathan was still alive, when you were escorted out?"

"He was alive, but barely," she whispered back. "I could make no determination of the status of his brain. He was unresponsive, but that could have been shock or a stroke or a thousand other things. I do not know. But if they did not immediately get him to a hospital, I told them… well. There's a death certificate. He is officially dead."

"But is he actually dead?"

"If I had to guess. Yes. I believe it is likely that he is actually dead."

"But you were the attending physician. And you don't know."

Her eyes were downcast, a parishioner seeking absolution. "I do not know. I am sorry."

"It's not your fault," Howard said through his anger, and he meant it. Absolution came easily for Howie. He could forgive anyone but himself. Himself, and his brother—and Felix Hess. "Thank you. For telling me."

"If you don't want me to come to any more meetings—"

"Come to the meetings," he said swiftly. "For as long as you feel safe doing so. You may be our greatest asset, Dr. Kansal. You're the only one who's been in the belly of the beast."

"Hey," Dr. Chapman called from the doorway, waving at Dr. Kansal. "Bus is leaving."

She lifted a hand back in his direction, acknowledging the summons, then turned back to Howard. "I'll see you at the next meeting."

"Good," Howard replied. "And hey, your confidentiality agreement with Hess is something you should feel free to piss on. Tell me everything you know. Everything you can remember. Okay? I'm an ethics professor, so if I say it's cool, it's cool."

His weak joke earned him a tight smile as Dr. Kansal accepted her penance and left. Howard turned to find Sophie—and instead locked eyes with his niece Ruth. He didn't ask her if she overheard the whispered exchange between him and the doctor. She obviously had. He opened his mouth, not sure what to say. Ruth beat him to the punch.

"He's dead to me either way," she said.

Sophie continued doling out the leftover sweets to the handful of friends who lingered past the meeting's end, and the conversation turned from the impending global shift to the vagrant who had been poisoning neighborhood cats. Not dogs; only cats. A weird, targeted takedown of Cambridge felines. People were sick.

Preparing for sleep that night, Howie lay uneasy on his pillow, waiting for Sophie to come to bed. She was in the adjacent bathroom, taking out her contacts—a task her husband never could get used to watching. It was just weird, seeing his beloved peel off the top layer of her eyeball and then tuck it into its own little watery bed for the night.

"Sophie," he called softly.

"Yeah?"

"Do you think—do you think people are paying attention? Are we doing enough to convince them how serious this all is?"

She moved to the doorway, standing on the threshold of the bedroom, illuminated by the bathroom light behind her. She held some eye drops in hand, and leaned her head back to drop them in as she replied.

"You're doing everything you can, Howie," Sophie said diplomatically, blinking back emotionless saline tears. "You are." She paused. "Oy, babe. It's Tuesday. You forgot to take the trash out, didn't you?"

The group kept meeting. Maxwell was spearheading the legislative option. Stan and Howard recruited more intellectuals to their cause. Dr. Kansal wrote up a confidential report about her inside knowledge of the Synt, though she would not attach her name to it. Within months, their small collection of activists had grown from two dozen to five dozen; within a year, their numbers were in the hundreds. Mrs. Rainey, a librarian who was easily in her eighties, offered the library's large basement meeting rooms for their gatherings.

Maxwell and his team collected thousands of signatures online. Howard and Stan's peers on campuses in Maine, New Hampshire, Washington, and California began organizing chapters of the anti-augmentation movement. Everyone agreed they needed an actual name (preferably one that didn't sound like they were boycotting boob jobs, snickered one young volunteer), but things were moving so fast that they had not yet reached consensus on what to call themselves. Throughout 2017, there seemed to be real momentum in their movement—and very little news from Hess' institute. In fact, after the initial splash of media, the buzz around cyborganics died down quickly; *too* quickly. Almost as if a moratorium was passed on its coverage.

That made Howard nervous.

The less they heard from the Synt, the more the Synt's work was kept behind closed doors, the harder it was to combat them. No one was interested in fighting an enemy they were not being constantly reminded to fear. Especially not an enemy that has never bombed, invaded, or otherwise attacked them. Especially not when there were so many things to get mad about on Twitter, so many phones to stand in line to buy, so many shows to watch.

One weirdo who put some machine-parts into his neck? Who cares? Didja hear about the woman who had a second set of octuplets? That's crazy! She's getting her own show, it's gonna be trash but you know it'll be worth watching...

Soon, the general public had all but forgotten Felix Hess and that hot, hedonistic second where it looked like cyborg-life might someday be an option for all. It was like back when some nut jobs were reserving pieces of real estate on Mars. A joke. A blip on the radar.

Which was probably what spurred that egomaniac Felix Hess to call another press conference.

Much as his funders wanted their progress kept under wraps, Hess could not bear the thought of his work going unacknowledged. When Howard saw a press release announcing Hess' upcoming appearance, an emergency message went out over the list-serve. Dozens of folks crammed into the Fell living room once more, to see Hess' press conference play out onscreen.

"Exciting news," Hess said with an expansive sweep of his arms, standing again on the steps of the Synthetic Neuroscience Institute of Technology. The Synt appeared twice as large as it had been a few years earlier, looming mountainous behind him, its highest floors disappearing into the angry gray clouds crowding the sky. "An extremely small number of citizens will be invited to apply to become the first generation of synthetic citizens, augmented by technology that will enhance every aspect of their life. I myself am living proof of the safety and success of the synching process. And as further show of good faith, I would like to introduce you to another enhanced individual—my wife, Marilyn Kensington Hess."

There was a gasp from the reporters at the press conference, and the activists in the Fell's living room, as Marilyn stepped up beside Felix at the podium. Marilyn was from an old, iconic American family. She was a known entity, stately, attractive, relatable—and now, apparently, part-machine.

"Holy shit," Stan said. "He made his Stepford wife into a real…Stepford wife."

Marilyn raised a slender arm and waved, like the pageant queen she was born and bred to be. The crowd of reporters went wild, shouting questions, snapping pictures. Though she had seemed nervous at first, Marilyn's smile swiftly solidified. She seemed to gain confidence with each flash of the camera bulb, each screamed inquiry about how her neck felt, what it was like to be the first female to synch, and who she was wearing.

"The application is available on our website." Hess continued. "Although you can only apply if invited. If you want to request an invitation, a small number of lottery spots will be available. First-round of applications are not due until January, and none will be reviewed before then. No questions today. Thank you for your attention."

"Get on the goddamn website!" Howard yelled.

Beside him, Rachel flinched. Ruth put an arm around her.

"Going there now," said Sophie, already seated at their down-stairs desktop. And then, within seconds: "Jesus."

"What?" Howard asked.

"Site crashed," Sophie said. "I'm guessing it just got mobbed."

Requests for invitations had indeed crashed the site. Seeing not only the somewhat off-putting Hess but also the beautiful Marilyn as evidence of the procedure's outcome, hordes of people became hell-bent on securing a spot. Felix Hess had officially split the world in two.

By January 2018, when the application process closed, more than twenty million people had applied for the first-generation spots at the Synthetic Neuroscience Institute of Technology.

Hess issued another statement, warning people that the review process would be lengthy. It would be at least a year before initial selections were made and notifications were sent—probably two years before those selected could begin their treatments.

"We will do what we can to expedite the process," Hess promised, the public face of synthetic citizenry smiling coyly for the cameras. "We strive to accelerate the pace."

Howard and his small tribe tried to accelerate their own efforts. They began meeting one on one with elected officials, delivering signed petitions in person. But they didn't have a fraction as many signatures as there were applications sent to the Synt. As official after official pointed out, this seemed to be something that the vast majority of their constituents *supported*.

Howard knew they were losing ground.

Then Hess made a mistake.

Six months after the applications process closed, the Synthetic Neuroscience Institute of Technology began mailing out its first round of rejection letters. Those who requested invitations, and even some who were granted invitations but then failed some element of the screening process, learned they were being denied eternity. Hundreds of thousands of people found out that they had not been chosen. They were informed in passive, careless form letters that their petition for a better life had been summarily denied. Many rejections were issued on the basis of "financial disqualification," meaning that a review of the economic situation had shown that the applicant in question could not afford the procedure.

Being told they were too poor to qualify for a shot at something better did not sit well with people. They took to the streets.

Having been rejected from the program, many people began to resent and reject the notion of synthetic citizenry. They changed their position, realizing that if only reserved for a few, it was a dangerous, unjust privilege. There were outraged riots. Public outcry. In Times Square, an angry mob sets fire to an effigy of Felix Hess.

"They look pissed," Maxwell said, sitting in the Fell's living room, watching protestors screaming on the news. "Maybe we should see who their leaders are, if they have any, and ask them to take it down a notch?"

"No," Howard said, eyes glued to the screen. "We need to join forces. And ramp it up."

New Year's Eve, 2020. Another broadcast.

"Happy New Year!" Hess crowed from the steps of his institute. It was snowing softly in New York, fat flakes falling prettily, clinging to his black cap and the shoulders of his wool coat. Marilyn was standing beside him, a vision in politically incorrect ankle-length mink. "And it is a new year, indeed. 2020 will truly be, if you'll forgive me the wordplay—a year of clear vision. A year of change, and progress."

"He sounds like he's running for president," Rachel said, looking haunted.

"I think he's aiming even higher," growled her twin, smelling of cigarettes and gum.

"Shh," Howard said, willfully ignoring the third scent coating his adopted daughter—the whiskey Ruth had been nipping at every opportunity. Peripherally, Howard knew his niece was developing hazardous habits. But the world was a dumpster fire. He didn't have time for discipline. "Let's hear what the bastard's planning."

The cameras zoomed in on Hess, who hadn't aged a day in the better part of a decade. Howard's heart twisted when he saw Sophie's fingers move to her hairline, subconsciously stroking her gray-streaked locks. He wanted to tell her how beautiful she was, how much he loved the way the years shaped and marked her. Claimed her; claimed them both, bound them together. But rather than comfort his wife, he listened to his nemesis address the world.

"The first generation of synthetic citizens are recovering from their procedures," Hess said triumphantly. He gripped his wife's hand, a showy and loveless move. "We are no longer test cases. Anomalies. We are part of a larger whole. We are the future."

From somewhere nearby, the small assembly at the Fell home heard a scream. Then several loud *pop-pop-pops*—celebratory fireworks in a nearby wealthy neighborhood, perhaps—or gunfire a few blocks over, where incomes were lower and tonight's news would not play well.

"I'm not really one for praying," said Henry, Maxwell's husband. "But does anyone… maybe just want to hold hands and think or hope or pray or whatever?"

Maxwell nodded, clutching Henry's hand, then slipping his other hand into Sophie's. Sophie accepted Maxwell's hand and reached for Howard, who gripped Ruth, who grasped Rachel's hand for dear life, on and on until they were all connected to each other, fingers intertwined, intentions shared. The small tribe held hands, closed their eyes, and offered silent petitions in the face of the unknown.

The Singularity had arrived.

A CHANGING WORLD 2021 – 2039

CHAPTER 34: ANGELA

A FTER MARILYN'S AUGMENTATION, it was only a matter of time before she began hounding Angela to do the same. Angela called Leroy to give him the latest insane update.

"That tech is bullshit, Mom," he said immediately, and she didn't chide him for swearing. She could picture him in his little apartment in Chicago, the one he had to move into when Northwestern shuttered earlier this year, costing him his teaching assistantship and his housing. She hadn't seen his new place yet, but he'd described it: a one-room efficiency he was sharing with three other guys, ratty old posters on the wall of Martin and Malcolm, alongside the one nice framed print of Maya Angelou's words she had given him last Christmas. "Don't do it."

"I know, I won't," she assured him.

"I can't believe you're so close to the first family of all this synthetic shit," he said. "You know we're doing another protest. Next week. They're diverting resources from social services to pay for this, you know. That asshole in the White House is all about it."

Something sizzled in Angela, prickling the hairs on her neck; an instinct she could not explain. She said quickly: "Don't talk like that over the phone."

He was quiet on the other end. She could sense him nodding. "Got it, yeah. Look, Ma—I gotta go, I'm meeting—" Leroy stopped so abruptly Angela almost wondered if they'd been disconnected, then realized her clever boy had let her comment sink in, and would now assume he was being bugged "—people. I'll call you soon, okay? I love you."

"I love you, too, baby," she said.

She hung up, and looked around her own sparse new efficiency, tucked in to the Lower East Side of Manhattan. When she'd been unable to find a new job, and the whole world seemed to be falling apart, she was ultimately unable to turn down Marilyn's offer. She had moved to New York, taken the job she was offered, at a small accounting firm that she assumed was connected to one of the Synt funders. She didn't like thinking about that.

But she was a single woman of color nearing fifty, alone, with a child who kept putting himself on the frontlines. If she could at least save up a little, until she could move closer to him, figure something out—all she was trying to do was buy a little time.

Buying a little time, that's all; I'm not purchasing eternity. I'm not. I won't.

She knew Marilyn's offer was sincere; she could get Angela on the list, guarantee her the augmentation process generally

reserved only for the hyper-rich and connected. Angela doubted there were very many people of her demographic on that list.
Power was always in the pale hands of the privileged few, but it
was being seized unapologetically and in broad daylight these
days. The powerful were grasping for everything while everyone
else fought for scraps.

*It won't last. The pendulum will swing the other way; it has to.
Regular people will reclaim their power. They will.*

We. We *will,* she corrected herself swiftly, shuddering.

Two weeks later, her son showed up on her doorstep. He was
shivering against the sudden cold. One of his eyes was swollen
and purple. She gasped when she saw him, shocked, appalled, immediately ready to burn down the world and crucify whoever had
beaten her son.

He winced when she embraced him, then whispered in her
ear: "I can't stay long, but Ma—you gotta do it. You need to synch.
We need someone on the inside."

CHAPTER 35: RUTH

RUTH WOKE UP EARLY, before her sister was up, before the sun was up. She crawled out of their bedroom window, using the old fire escape Sophie had insisted Howard install years ago. She shimmied up to the roof of the house, sat down cross-legged, and lit a cigarette.

She felt a dark, punishing pleasure at the burning in her throat, the tightening of her lungs. She knew she was poisoning herself, shortening her life expectancy. But if she lived long enough to die of lung cancer, well, that would be a nice damn surprise. She was expecting an earlier and far more violent death.

If Rachel knew what I did last night...

Ruth pushed the thought away immediately, almost afraid her sleeping twin might somehow read her mind. Delicate, determined Rachel; if anyone could hone telepathy, it would be her.

And these days, Ruth couldn't afford to have her sister tiptoe around her brain.

The twins were the last children still living with Howard and Sophie. Dinah, Micah, Ellie, Tamar, Isaac, and Moe were all in college or working. But Ruth suspected she'd be seeing them soon. Universities were suspending their semesters due to rioting anti-augmentation groups, and bomb threats from synthetic sympathizers. The air smelled of fear and fatigue, frayed nerves and suspicion. It was chaos, as her uncle had predicted. And it was only the beginning.

Beneath the still-starry sky, glinting in oblivious beauty, Ruth stubbed her cigarette out on a gritty shingle. She didn't bother to brush away the ashes or discard the butt, she just ground it down and down and down and then released it.

"Ruthie."

Startled, Ruth sat up too quickly, nearly losing her footing on the shingled roof. Digging in with her heels and keeping her rear planted, she turned to see her uncle on the fire escape.

"Howard. Hey."

"You all right?"

"I'm fine, just…" Ruth's eyes went guiltily to the cigarette butt. "…thinking."

"Me, too," said her uncle.

"What's on your mind?"

"This morning? You, mostly."

"Oof. Boring."

He gave her an unconvincing smile. "Mind if I join you?"

She shook her head, and he eased himself down onto the rough rooftop, huffing a little as his butt made contact with the shingles. It occurred to Ruth that her uncle was getting older. He should be thinking about retirement, not revolution.

He eyed her decimated cigarette. "You're smoking again?"

Again. He thought she'd quit, which she never had.

"Yeah, sorry," she said, not really sorry and certainly not sorry enough to attempt a lie.

He sighed. "I should give you a hard time about that."

And that's all he said about her smoking, which made Ruth's jaw twitch. If he wasn't busting her on the cigarettes, there must be some truly serious shit going on.

"Ruth, there's... something we need to discuss," he said haltingly, his words balanced as precariously as he was, an old man sitting on a rooftop as the world around him cracked and crumbled. "You're special, you know."

"Yeah, right," she said uncomfortably. Ruth didn't do well with compliments. At best, they felt unearned. She wasn't special; she was the opposite of special. She was nothing.

"Don't talk back to your old uncle-dad. You're special. And it scares me. Because you, Ruth Fell... are a soldier. And I wish we lived in a world where I meant that as a metaphor for your moral convictions, your strength of spirit, your fortitude—but Ruthie, God, my little girl. That's not the world we're in, and you're not a metaphorical warrior. You are an actual goddamn soldier." He paused, waiting for her. Then prodded: "Aren't you?"

"I don't know what you mean," she whispered at last. Lying.

"Were you part of the bombing last night?"

Her heart stopped; her blood froze in her veins. She swallowed hard, a cold lump of dread barely making it down her throat. And then she nodded.

"Okay," he said. Calm. Not condemning. "Thank you for answering honestly. Now that we're on the same page about that, we need to get on the same page about a few other things."

Ruthie whispered, at once thrilled and terrified, exhaling an icy breath: "Okay."

The night before, when she crept through the dark to the original site of the Synthetic Neuroscience Institute of Technology, a modest brick building near the MIT campus, Ruth knew she was taking her resistance involvement to the next level.

She'd overheard some of the younger movement members, talking in a small cluster on her family's porch after the larger meeting had ended. They were smoking and whispering about something they were working on; something "explosive." At some point she realized they were talking about an actual bomb.

"I want to help," she said.

They looked at her dismissively. She was a teenager, growing out some bad bangs which hung heavy and awkward across her left eye. They were college dropouts who saw themselves as legitimate resistance fighters. But they'd only been to a few of the meetings her uncle spearheaded. She'd been there since the beginning.

"You?"

"Me."

"You're too young," said one of the long-limbed boys, maybe five years older than Ruth.

"Really?" She glared, hands curling and uncurling into fists, thighs stiffening as she dug in and held her ground. "That's too bad. I guess I'll have to go ask my uncle Howard what the age limit is for this assignment…"

Their expressions went from bemusement to narrow-eyed irritation. Ruth hated using that tattletale tactic, but she knew they wouldn't take her seriously otherwise. She was only sixteen, and a girl to boot—which shouldn't matter, but did. And she didn't really know any of these guys. They had just shown up this week, after their campus shut down. They didn't know her, either; not enough to gamble on whether or not she really would rat them out.

"Fine," said the lean boy tightly. "You can come. Just stay the hell out of the way."

"Does anyone still work there?"

"What?" The lean guy snapped.

"The old Synt building. That's where you're attacking, right? Anyone work there?"

"You shouldn't be asking questions," said a dirty blonde kid with severe acne.

"Seems like an important one," Ruth pressed.

"There's no one there," chimed in a third boy, a little older than the others, with a respectable Afro and an unlit cigarette dangling from his lips. "We did check. No one lives nearby, either. This ain't about bloodshed. Just making a statement. You still in?"

"I'm in."

"Then shut up and come on. We got this."

So she shut up and they started walking. When they reached the long, low brick structure, it was full dark. But even in the moonlight, Ruth recognized the place and immediately felt uneasy. She didn't think it would seem so familiar, but it did. Sensory memories came rushing back, flooding through her. She remembered coming here with Howard. To visit Nathan Fell.

Her father.

This was his old office building; where he worked, where he spent all his time. This was the place that he had loved more than he loved her and Rachel. She did not tell any of this to the young men she was with; she didn't even know their names, she certainly wasn't going to lay bare her past scars. She didn't say a word about her connection to the building.

But she did volunteer to be the one to plant the explosive.

The boys turned her down at first, but Ruth was insistent. Her smaller size meant she could slip through the chain link fence, which they probably couldn't. She was fast, too; she ran track, she told them. (A lie. Thanks to the cigarettes, she wheezed at a slow jog.) It just made sense, she insisted. Reluctantly, but also with some relief, the boys relented.

Thanks to being built by a crack team of recent college dropouts, one of whom had been studying engineering (the boy with the Afro), one of whom had watched far too many episodes of *Mythbusters* (the lean one), and one of whom was a budding sociopath (the one with the acne), their bomb was rigged with a remote detonator. All Ruth had to do was get it far enough into the building to center the blast, then get out, and they could trigger it from afar. The plan was to plant it, then sprint to the wooded clearing up a hill a little way from the building—close enough for the remote to work, far enough for shrapnel to miss them.

Hopefully.

Ruth was handed the device. It didn't look like she thought a bomb would look. Not that she really knew what a bomb should look like. She had only seen explosives in movies and cartoons, red sticks of dynamite with a fiery fuse or little boxes with LED countdowns taped under the seat of a bus. This thing was awkward, boxy and patched together, wrapped in some wires. It was small but heavy.

"You sure this'll work?"

"Positive," said Afro.

"It better," said Lean.

"It'll make a good mess, at least," Zits grinned in the dark.

She shivered, then forced herself to still. "After we do this one—if it works—"

"It'll work," Afro said.

"—will you teach me how to make the next one?"

There was a pause. The boys stared. Zit picked at his chin.

"Sure," said Lean, finally. "You don't screw this up, sure."

Ruth nodded, started to walk away, then stopped, needing to confirm once more: "You're sure there's no one in there?"

They were sure.

The boys ran up the hill, to the meeting point under the tree. Ruth strode carefully towards the building, holding the bomb gingerly in front of her. The boys had assured her that she wouldn't accidentally set it off, unless maybe she fell and landed on it, but she didn't trust them and she wasn't taking any chances. When she reached the chain link fence, she paused. She had used her size to make the case that she could slip in most easily, but she wasn't seeing any breaks in the fence. Scaling the chain link might be an option if she were empty-handed, but she couldn't climb it with bomb in hand, nor could she toss it over and follow it in.

As she looked back and forth, the device still held out and away from her chest, she suddenly realized the gravity of the moment. What she was holding. What she was doing.

The world intensified around her and within her. She could feel the weight of it all; the weight of the actual explosive clutched in her hands, the weight of its implications. Her senses all heightened, she smelled the damp woodsy scent mingling with the musty dust odor of the old brick building ahead. She heard the soft crunch of the boys' footsteps, growing fainter behind her. Her eyes widened, adjusting further, like a cat, taking in all available light and letting her pupils expand to better see—*yes. There.*

A gap.

The chain link fence was relatively new, installed only after this building had been shuttered. To keep out curious trespassers. Or young women with bombs.

New meant *no holes*, but in this case it also meant quick installation with no supervision by fussy tenants. This was a slapped-together, hasty bit of work by laborers who knew they were just putting up a deterrent around an empty building no one cared about.

Bathed in moonlight, as if someone above was helping shine the way for her, Ruth could clearly see a gap between the east-west side of the fence and the side running north-south. It was the corner nearest her, and it was several inches wide.

With a little grunt of thanks, running as quickly as she dared while carrying a bomb, Ruth bolted for the corner. It was going to be tight, but she was pretty sure she could make it. She decided she'd get her body in first, pull the bomb through last. If she could hold the bomb in one hand, she could go in flat as possible—right arm, then right leg, then her torso sideways, then her left leg, and then, *slowly slowly slowly*, she would pull in her left arm, hand clutching the device.

Reaching the gap, Ruth didn't hesitate. She wrapped her left arm around the bomb, trembling a little as she pulled it close to her. It was hard against her soft chest, but at least it felt stable, for now. She quickly slid her right arm through the gap; that was easy. Then her right leg, a little tighter, but not a problem. Pressing her back against the tall metal pole, she began navigating her torso through the small space. She stopped; stuck. Her head was wedged in the gap between the poles. Fearing her cranium might crack, convinced her nose was breaking, she forced her head through. Her heart pounded. She sucked in her breath, further flattening her smooth stomach, lifting her ribs. Cursing her bones, those pesky hips, her whole stupid too-wide skeleton, she exhaled and painfully squeezed herself through the gap. As her body slipped through, she nearly dropped the package, but managed to press it with her hand against the fence, wrap her fingers around it, *steady steady steady*.

Now she was in, all but her left arm clutching the explosive. All she had left to do was get the bomb in. Her left fingers were gripping the device so tightly they were beginning to lose sensation. She pulled her left arm through the gap; up to her elbow, up to her wrist and now she could reach back through with her right hand, too. Gripping the device with both hands, she slowly began drawing it through the gap.

It won't make it.

It was too wide, any way she turned it. She didn't want to try to force it through, get it stuck; a bomb caught on the periphery of the property was useless. She needed to get it in. She tried sliding it down, wondering if maybe she could dig a hole in the ground, widen the gap there. *No... dammit...* For some reason the gap seemed to narrow, the closer she got to the ground. She looked up. *Yes.* The pole was crooked, leaning. It got wider toward the top. Ruth's arms flew upward, clutching the bomb, lifting her arms as high as she could, praying that now the explosive device would make it through. *No, no no no*—it was wider, but not wide enough. Not with what she could reach with her arms fully extended. She wished she were taller. She wished—no. No need for wishing. She could be taller.

Tightening her stomach, focusing on balance, aiming for balance chanting it like a mantra over and over, *balance balance balance*. She looped her left foot through the chain link fence, then her right. The chain link pressed into her flesh as she leaned into it, *balance balance balance*, and stepped higher up onto another link. Exhaling, she lifted her arms.

The device slipped easily through the gap.

The unexpected ease of its passage through the high portion of the fence surprised Ruth; the weight of it held by fingertips above her head when she was balancing on chain link tipped her backward.

Ruth fell straight back, landing hard on the ground, her stomach providing a cushion for the bomb still clutched in her hands. For a moment, she was still, ears ringing, head pounding, eyes closed. She lay for one long second in the dark, wondering if the bomb had gone off; wondering if this unnatural stillness was death.

Then one of the boys from the hill whistled, checking on her, catching her attention. She opened her eyes. She was there, alive, through the fence, bomb intact. She slowly rose, pressing the bomb to her chest with one arm, no longer afraid of it going off, no longer afraid of anything at all. She raised her other arm to the boys, signaling she was all right.

Then she headed for the building.

The boys had said that putting it on the front step would be enough. No need to infiltrate the building, the front entrance placement would mean plenty of damage. But that wasn't good enough for Ruth. She walked up to the front door, already intent on finding a way in. The small pile of spare bricks stacked near the entrance felt like divine intervention. Carefully setting down the explosive, she picked up a brick, and smashed the glass of the entryway. Reaching through the jagged glass, she unlocked the handle without so much as scratching herself. She opened the door, picked up the bomb, and walked inside, wishing she could see the boys' faces.

Once inside, her vague memories swirled into something more solid. She walked with purpose through the reception area, past the central lab, to the large office in the middle of the building. Her father's name was still displayed on a name placard by the door.

DR. NATHAN FELL

Carefully, she set the bomb outside his office door, below the placard bearing his name. Like a package delivery. Like a present, just for him.

Surprise, Daddy. Look what I made you.

Then she turned and ran, down the hallway, out the door, shoving herself roughly through the gap in the fence, banging her knee, wincing, limping up the hill to the boys. She was panting by the time she reached them, sweat pouring down her back, wild-eyed.

"Now," she said. "*Now.*"

Afro pushed a button. There was the briefest of silences.

Then a deafening boom.

They watched the night alight for only a moment, transfixed. Then, a scream in the distance shattered their reverie. The young rebels scattered, running different paths back to their different homes and outposts, fleeing the scene. Ruth ran faster than any of them, ears ringing, heart singing, knee throbbing.

She made it home. She was safe.

Whatever that meant.

"Ruth," Howard said. "I'm proud of you."

"You're…?"

"What you did took a lot of courage. I think you did it for the right reasons. But there are a few things you need to know. There was no one in the building—"

"I know," Ruth said quickly. "I asked—made sure—we wouldn't have done it if—"

"There was no one in the building," Howard continued, talking over her, no longer gentle. "But after you left the scene, someone else came. They had bodies with them. Cadavers, hopefully from the morgue but maybe—I don't know. They put the bodies in the building."

"I don't understand," Ruth said, gripped with a fear she could not comprehend.

"It's a setup, Ruthie. They want to discredit the movement. Make us look violent, irrational. Like we're savages. Like we're the bad guys. When the news breaks, everyone will believe that... that we killed three people."

"But we didn't—"

"We didn't. That's right. You didn't kill anyone. Okay? I know that. You know that. No matter what the news reports or Felix Hess or anyone else says. The bodies are plants. We know the truth."

"But how could they know—"

"Maybe one of those boys had other motives. Maybe we've been bugged."

A sob caught in Ruth's throat as the reality of her situation closed in on her, suffocating her, cutting off her air. Even though her uncle had said that the bodies thrown into the building were already dead, the image of bodies smoldering in the inferno, an inferno she had caused, made her feel sick.

"You didn't kill anyone, sweet girl," Howard said, hugging her tight. His voice was like the sound of a heart breaking. "But... there were security cameras on the property. None of the boys were seen. But you were."

She pulled back from the embrace, shaking. "How can you know all this already?"

"Well, I'm afraid we might have a rat in our midst—but our enemies definitely do, too. I trust this information. You being on camera, well, that'll mean a few things. First of all, we're going to have to lay pretty low. You're a minor, but this is going to be a helluva charge. And we can't trust the system. I'm not letting anyone take you in—we're going underground."

"You mean… leaving this house?"

Ruthie had lived in the Fell family home since she was a little girl. It was the house Sophie and Howard had dreamed of, two rambling stories in the center of Cambridge, white with green shutters, sprawling porch, shoddy old asphalt-shingled roof. So familiar. And it had been home not only to her family, but to so many others. Students, activists, wandering artists who needed a hot meal. The Fell family home was practically an institution itself.

"Yes. We're leaving."

"Where will we go?"

"For now, one of my friends has a house up just outside Kennebunkport, in his mother's name, pretty far off the grid. So we'll go to Maine. Regroup and plan from there."

"Uncle Howard, I'm sorry—"

"A soldier doesn't apologize for doing the right thing. You hear me, Ruthie?"

Ruth was drowning, but in the midst of the whirlpool threatening to pull her under, she grasped the life preserver tossed her way, which buoyed and ultimately anchored her.

A soldier.

An acknowledgment; better, an assignment. She finally knew who she was, what she was meant to be. This was not another costume change, a role to play in lieu of discovering the real Ruth. A resistance fighter, a protector, a mission-driven mercenary.

A soldier.

Finding herself at last, Ruth Fell would live and die by this identity.

*T*HAT LITTLE BITCH.

Reviewing the footage from the bombing of the old Synt building, Felix was stunned to recognize the skinny teen girl squeezing through the shoddy chain link fence. She looked unmistakably like her father, even from a distance. Lean, unhesitating, fierce; when she limped up the hill as she fled from the crime scene, she was practically his ghost.

Nathan Fell had rarely discussed his family with Hess, but Howard was constantly popping by the lab with Nathan's spawn. Twin daughters Nathan had dumped on his more paternally-inclined brother.

Hess had written Howard off back then—another boring bleeding heart liberal with a crazy mountain man beard. Someone to be ignored and forgotten. But now Hess was getting reports that the old kook had formed an actual movement. And if he was positioning his niece, the daughter of the Cyborganics Cowboy himself, to become the face of the resistance, that was going to be a problem.

If the public discovered that Ruth Fell was against synching— if she were seen as a darling, an orphan girl pushing back against this scientific progress for whatever righteous reason—that might generate more of a following. The fringe movement might actually gain some real traction.

But on the other hand, if she were presented as petulant teen-ager lashing out, a terrorist who had always hated her brilliant father—*that* was an image that Hess could work with.

A knock interrupted his thoughts.

"Come in."

Jorge entered. "You needed something?"

"A meeting with the media team, in an hour. And call my wife. Tell her I won't be home tonight."

"It's not even nine in the morning—"

"It's going to be a long day."

"Yes, sir," Jorge said, his tone a fine line between polite and trite. "Also, your nine o'clock appointment just phoned. He's going to be late."

"My nine o'clock appointment?"

"The interview. For an assistant," Jorge reminded him, almost hopefully.

"For a second assistant," Hess snapped, reminding Jorge that his own position was not up for grabs. Hess knew he ultimately needed a second assistant, but was uninterested in onboarding someone new now. He needed someone who already knew the program, knew the procedures, knew Hess. He needed Jorge, in other words, which is why that man would never be replaced.

But one of Hess' funders had been insistent about hiring more help, pushing a nephew Hess' way. A nephew that Hess had agreed, under duress, to meet with that morning. A nephew who was now running late, which was a bad sign—but he still had to interview the kid, because Hess was still beholden to the ones with money, which he resented to no end. His wife had piles of money, but he still needed to access other piles. And the funders all thought they deserved favors, or worse, input. Just because they happened to have amassed wealth, mostly through questionable means.

Another knock at the door startled Hess.

"Who the hell is that?" He snapped, making a note to fire the current receptionist and hire someone who would be a better barrier between him and the rest of the whining world.

A thin-faced, nervous slip of a man stuck his face into the room.

"Um, hi, hello, sorry, I thought I was running late but turns out parking wasn't as much of a pain as I was anticipating and anyway, I'm right on time now so figured I should just come in?" The man spoke all those words without a single breath, then gulped and added almost apologetically: "I'm Kennedy."

CHAPTER 37: EVER

E VER'S LIMBS FELT LIKE DEAD WEIGHT. Her mouth tasted dry and coppery, unnatural. She tried to sit up, and found she could not. Trying to stave off panic, she attempted to wiggle her fingers. When one of her fingertips made contact with a hard bedframe, it landed with a heavy metallic thud.

No. It can't be.

She'd told her parents, in no uncertain terms, she did not want to augment. Especially not now, at age seventeen, when all she wanted to do was grow up and get the hell away from them. She didn't want their world, their Heaven, their technology. She just wanted to be herself, whatever that might someday mean.

But now she lay supine in an unfamiliar room, with an unfamiliar finger. Tuning in to her body more, she knew it wasn't just her finger. Her mind felt different, churning, aching as it learned to incorporate its new system. Its synthetic system. She was a Syn.

297

God. No.

Her father walked in, wearing a lab coat, dressed for work. Because, Ever half-consciously realized, he was at work. She was one his projects now—one of his *products* now.

He was looking at her not as a father looks at a daughter, but as a doctor looks at a patient. No; worse. He was looking at her the way an artist studies his canvas, trying to decide if he had effectively rendered what he was attempting to create.

"Good, you're awake," said her father, as if congratulating himself. "Don't be alarmed by temporary paralysis. Common side effect."

He moved to the side of her bed, took her hand in his. To an outsider, the gesture might look tenderly paternal, until he held her hand up, twisting her wrist and rotating it back and forth to admire it from all angles, appreciating his own handiwork, tapping on the metal port embedded in her finger like a mechanic might kick well-installed tires.

"Third generation tech," he said proudly, eyes not on his daughter but on her metal fingertip. "Only a handful of people will get the finger-port instead of the neck port. A handful! Ha!"

She tried to speak, and could not; tears welled in her eyes, and she wondered if she would rust like the Tin Man from the *Wizard of Oz*. A soundless sob caught in throat.

"Clever Ever," said her father, still not really looking at her. *Clever Ever.*

A nickname she had loved when she was a baby. Something her father had not called her in years, and her mother had always resented. Why was he being nostalgic now? Was he about to gather her in his arms, apologize, tell her he loved her? She ached, wondering.

"And now you're the smartest Syn of all. Smartest designed, anyway. Clever Ever." He chuckled softly. "No need to worry about aging, ruin, or being left behind."

I wasn't worried about any of those things, she thought but could not say.

"The funders are pushing for a new regulation," he continued, reaching out and touching her face, another act of almost-tenderness, but he was probably just checking her temperature or something. "No synchs for anyone under eighteen—which was always the recommendation, but it will now be the rule. And meanwhile we're hitting capacity soon, so you're in under the wire in more ways than one."

And then with no kiss, apology, or further explanation, her father left her alone in the recovery room.

She didn't know how long she lay there, alone and silent. She had not yet incorporated the internal clock, a program that constantly calculated time and sent alerts at the merest subconscious thought about time. She just remained still, trapped in the newly-remodeled version of her own body, unable to move or scream. Finally, there was a soft tap at the door. As it slowly creaked open, an irrational remnant of hope within Ever thought it might be her mother.

A female figure stepped through the door, but it was not her mother. It was Angela.

"Baby girl," Angela said, putting her hand to her heart. "I didn't know. I'm so sorry."

She practically lunged forward, erasing the distance between them. Leaning against the bed, Angela put her arms around Ever. Angela sobbed then, sobbed for both of them. As Ever regained a little more mobility in her arm, she wrapped it heavily around Angela's neck.

When she tapped her new finger-port against the port resting at the base of Angela's skull, the clinking sound of metal on metal echoed deep within Ever, reverberating throughout her body, slicing through her, forever scarring her.

CHAPTER 38: RACHEL

AS TWINS, Rachel and Ruth had once shared a snug, small universe. Their lives were interconnected, intertwined, crammed against one another. Yet somehow in the years that intervened between birth and adulthood, the two wound up worlds apart.

At eighteen, Ruth was a full-fledged warrior. She was a woman of few words and nonstop action, always out on missions Rachel wasn't allowed to ask her about. And at the exact same age, give or take a handful of minutes, Rachel, quiet but certain, staged her own small rebellion by announcing that she intended to take a different path.

"I'm going to college."

"Honey," Aunt Sophie said, squeezing her knee. "I know you want to go to college, but it's just not possible. Schools are shutting down, your name means that you could be a target—"

"I'll use another name," Rachel said firmly. "But I'm going."

Despite her generally diminutive demeanor, Rachel was not backing down. And so as her family fled to Maine and went into hiding, Rachel enrolled at New England College, a small liberal arts enclave that had decided to keep offering classes for as long as faculty and staff felt safe attending. She registered with forged papers identifying her as Elle Golden.

Her freshman year looked nothing like the college experience she'd imagined before the Singularity. The security measures on campus were intense. There were coded identification tags, checkpoints, metal detectors, armed guards, keypads to get into each building and each classroom. Rachel was terrified that her falsified paperwork would be discovered. But her uncle had a lot of connections, and she did her part to keep a low profile.

The courses offered were limited. Everyone was simply a Liberal Arts major. The student body numbered only around a thousand, and almost everyone shared at least one class per semester. A sense of community was quickly formed. Everyone looked out for one another. Some kept a closer watch than others. Rachel was pretty sure that fellow freshman Gregory Harper was watching her quite closely, and she hoped she was right.

Gregory Harper, with his magnetic smile and thick dark hair. He was a big guy. Coach after coach had tried to convince him to try football, but he hated football. What he loved was running. He went jogging on campus every morning, and Rachel swiftly took up the habit of walking with her morning coffee the same route Gregory ran. He would lap her two or three times during her leisurely walk, grinning and shaking his head each time he passed.

One Thursday morning, after lapping her twice, the third time he ran by her, he did not slow or turn his head to smile at her. She was momentarily disappointed—but then he whirled around and began jogging backward, comically high-stepping with his knees. He slowed, then jogged in place, stopping right alongside her. He kept his expression flat and grave while his legs flailed like a puppet beneath him. She burst out laughing.

"You stalking me?" he asked her.

"Yeah," she said, holding up her coffee. "World's slowest stalker."

"Well, ya caught me," he grinned. "Slow and steady wins the race. You're Elle, right?"

"Rachel," she said, and then clapped her hand over her mouth. She hadn't done that before, not in all her weeks on campus; she flushed red, cursing her mistake. "I mean—Elle. Just call me Elle. I didn't mean to—I shouldn't have—"

"It's all right," Gregory said, and his eyes were gentle. Safe. "Whatever it is, it's cool. I'll call you Elle in front of other people. But when it's just us... Rachel?"

Rachel's cheeks flamed. "When it's just us."

He looked around, making a big show of swiveling his head this way, then that way. "Looks like no one else is around... Rachel. So here we are."

"Here we are," she smiled back.

There they were, and there they stayed, side by side. They took classes together, went through security together, stayed up late talking together. Elle and Gregory became campus darlings, adored by students and faculty alike. Everyone was hungry for anything that tasted like hope, and the sweet young couple provided that nourishment.

They were both serious students, racing against the clock to earn degrees before the campus shuttered. After two and a half years, they had amassed enough credits to graduate. There was no commencement parade, no pomp and circumstance, but they were college graduates. And twenty years old. And in love. So it seemed as good a time as any to get married.

It was Rachel who proposed to Gregory.

After the makeshift graduation ceremony, they walked along the path where they first bantered. Rachel dropped suddenly to one knee. She took Gregory's hand and pressed it to her cheek. She looked up at him, eyes as full and serious as her heart.

"All of this will sound cliché, but I like clichés," she said. "I love you, Gregory Harper, and we don't know what tomorrow will bring. Whatever happens next, whatever tomorrow or the day after that sends our way, I want to face it with you. Will you marry me?"

He got down on his knee, too.

"Rachel," Greg said, shaking his head and momentarily panicking her. "Damn. I had a whole thing planned. But slow and steady wins the race, right, baby?" Then he drew her face up to his and kissed her, three times, affirming with each kiss: "Yes. Yes. Yes."

They called his family that night. Gregory had brought Rachel home for Christmas the year before—introducing her as Elle. By that time, Gregory was intimately familiar with the details of her life; who her father was, who her outlaw twin sister was, who her uncle was. Gregory kept this information from his parents. Better to take things one step at a time. Let them first get over the fact that she was a white girl. Well, a white girl with Native American and Jewish ancestry. Once they waded through all that, he'd throw in the whole Fell-family thing.

When they called to share the news, it was Mr. Harper who answered. Gregory asked for his father to get his mother and put them both on the line. That simple request tipped them off, and when Greg's mother got on the phone, she started talking before he could get a word in.

"You're too young, Gregory, and you're not considering—"

"Maybe we should talk in person," said Gregory, wrapping his fingers around Rachel's, trying to stop his mother from saying something she would later regret.

"You want us to come to campus? But you just finished—"

"Yes," Gregory said, ending the call as soon as they confirmed they'd be there in the morning.

Rachel sent word to her family through an encrypted email sent to a business account that appeared to be a rural lawn mower repair company. She, too, asked her family to come to the campus. *Tomorrow,* she said, carefully avoiding suspicious words like 'surprise' or 'event.' *Whoever can make it.*

Gregory and Rachel decided that life was short. They weren't going to debate the merits of their decision. They were uninterested in anyone's lectures about their youth, the recklessness of this move, or anything else. They weren't inviting their parents to come to campus for an engagement announcement. They were inviting them to come for an impromptu wedding.

The day of their secret nuptials dawned drearily, a soupy fog rolling in thick and gray, obscuring the campus. Rachel's stomach was in knots. She was certain of her feelings for Greg, but certainty did little to dispel fear. She wished her sister could be there. But Rachel knew Ruth couldn't come. The campus was secure, but the roads were not. And Ruth was a wanted woman, a terrorist with several outstanding warrants. She couldn't risk an appearance.

The Harpers arrived first, dressed to the nines, somehow guessing the true nature of this invitation. Gregory's mother wore a soft blue blazer and charcoal slacks; his father was striking in a three-piece suit and blue tie. When they made it through security, they embraced Gregory. Then, more gingerly, they embraced Rachel.

"We know you think we're too young—" Gregory began, and his father raised a gentle hand to silence him.

"We're here for your wedding," the older man said before flashing the charming smile that his son had inherited. "We have our reservations... but we trust you, son. And you, Elle."

"Rachel, actually," Gregory said, and his father raised an eyebrow.

"All right," nodded Mr. Harper. The knots within Rachel loosened ever so slightly.

"Let's head toward the chapel," Gregory suggested. "Rachel's family isn't coming through the main security gate."

Wordlessly, Mrs. Harper reached for her husband's hand. Rachel knew they both must be wondering: *Who, or what, is this girl's family?*

The chapel was an ecumenical sanctuary, tucked into a corner of the campus where a large, windowed building overlooked a small reflection pool. Rachel and Gregory both loved the site; it was where they agreed immediately that their vows should take place. As they approached the chapel, Rachel was confused to see a rather large assembly.

With the fog still blurring details, she couldn't tell who was standing there. She wondered if one of the weekday masses was convening, and cursed herself for not double checking the campus calendar. She hoped whatever it was wouldn't take long; visitors were not allowed to remain on campus for more than an hour.

But then, the fog lifted just enough to reveal the crowd, and Rachel gave a small cry of joy as she recognized each face, and realized she was looking at her wedding guests. Clustered that misty morning were all of their classmates, the entire faculty, and Uncle Howard and Aunt Sophie, Micah and his family... and there, her hair lopped off and her clothing oversized, unrecognizable to anyone but her own twin, was Ruth.

Rachel rushed forward, throwing her arms around her sister. They had not seen each other in more than two years. Each was sobbing, grasping, shaking, holding the other up. Having her sister miss her wedding would have forever dimmed the day for her. Now, if only for a moment, the whole world glowed.

"I know you won't think this is a good idea—" Rachel began, but her sister squeezed her tighter, suffocating her apology.

"He better be a good guy," Ruth whispered.

"The best," Rachel promised.

Howard walked up to them, putting an arm around each of his adopted daughters.

"I wish we could make this beautiful day last forever, but—"

"I know," Rachel said, wiping her eyes, her heart full of more gratitude than it could contain, joy radiating from her. She kissed her sister's cheek, hugged her uncle, and then reached for Gregory. "We're ready."

CHAPTER 39: JORGE

"**D**O YOU THINK DR. HESS LIKES ME?" Kennedy asked.

Jorge exhaled sharply. His new co-worker was a sniveling, neurotic pile of uselessness.

"No, Kennedy," he said flatly. "I don't think he likes you."

"Well, I don't think he likes you either," retorted Kennedy, wounded.

"I really don't care," Jorge replied. "Are the latest Vost test reports compiled?"

Jorge loathed this testing process. He knew the history of the Vost program all too well, including the phases that took place before he signed on. He knew about the termination of those poor early participants and the ongoing studies to monitor the success-ful Vosts, who still served as guinea pigs for new glitches, patches, and upgrades. Vosts were second class citizens, not afforded the same rights and privileges as their fully-vested Synthetic counter-parts. They were condemned to a life sentence—for a really, really long life.

Jorge's own designation as Vost was branded on the back of his left hand—5/333, the fifth person selected for third genera-tion Vost testing. A reminder of the poor decision he'd made, at-tempting to protect his family all those years ago. His punishment continued to be enduring, and cruel. As a Vost, Jorge had to par-ticipate in these degrading semi-annual studies; as Hess' assistant, he also had to supervise their implementation.

"I'm working on it," muttered Kennedy.

"Work faster," Jorge snapped. "I want to get this over with."

A Vost shouldn't speak to a Syn like that, which Kennedy would have reminded him if he wasn't such a chicken shit.

A message flashed before Jorge's eyes. Another new annoy-ance—Hess was experimenting with a direct-messaging system, utilizing their wireless connections and the synthetic components in their visual cortex, making it appear that the words were pro-jected right in front of them, visible only to the recipient. Worst of all were messages sent urgently, accompanied by what Jorge de-scribed as a "brain pinch."

This message, thankfully, was not marked as urgent:

COME TO MY OFFICE WHEN YOU WRAP WITH KENNEDY.

Jorge knew Hess wanted an update on the Vost results, and also a report on Jorge's coworker. He didn't like being in the posi-tion of tattletale, despite disliking Kennedy. In some ways, Jorge did feel for the guy—Kennedy clearly didn't really want to be here, and Hess didn't want him here, either; they were bound together at the will of one of Kennedy's wealthy aunts. If Hess could fire Kennedy, he would, in a heartbeat. Everyone knows that, including Kennedy.

"Want to hear something funny?" Kennedy asked, then rushed on, knowing Jorge definitely didn't want to hear it. "I had this friend who took me to my first transhumanism meeting, because they thought trans-human meant something totally different—"

"I have to go," Jorge said. "I want this done today."

"Are you meeting with Dr. Hess? Right now? Tell him I'm doing the best I can—"

Jorge let the door slide shut behind him. Kennedy was whiny, not stupid. He had been thrown into an impossibly complex role with a demanding boss, so he was initially sinking, but with enough time he'd learn to swim. And that's what Jorge would tell Hess. Just because Jorge didn't like someone didn't mean he was going to throw them under the bus. Wasn't his style.

Jorge strode quickly to Hess' office, avoiding eye contact with the few Syns he passed in the corridor. He resented the disparaging looks he got from those who felt Vosts shouldn't be in positions as prominent as his. With the ballooning number of synthetic citizens, soon to be capped but still swelling, each day Jorge was outed anew as inferior. Looked down on. And he hated it. The more synthetic citizens there were, the lower Jorge sank on the totem pole.

The numbers couldn't keep increasing at this rate. A recent piece of transhumanist legislation limited augmentations—per year, and overall. Only a million people were approved to live as synthetic citizens. And as of the last census, they were approaching the half-million mark.

Jorge knew the rebellions outside of the Synt fortress were raging. When he connected to Heaven each night, he downloaded as much information as possible about the rebels, the protests, the acts of "terrorism" which he saw as heroism. But the news was biased and largely redacted. Hess didn't want his fresh new synthetic citizens panicking about the teeming masses pounding at their gates.

To Jorge, the rebels weren't a reason to panic. They were the only reason he had to hope. He wondered if any of his family members had joined the anti-augmentation movement. Were they rebelling? Or fleeing from a city overtaken by rioting in the streets?

The pain of missing his family was an ever-festering wound. Infected, inflamed, unable to heal because he was denied the salve of seeing them. Since being informed that his head would explode if he exited the premises without permission, Jorge had barely interacted with anyone representing any sort of intimate connection. He didn't date. He didn't have friends. And it had been years since last he laid eyes on anyone in his family.

Jorge longed for a reprieve; for years he hoped in vain that at some point Hess would relent and release him. But he had run out of any expectation that his automaton of a boss would ever reward his years of service with any meaningful recompense.

Despite not being a violent person, if Jorge had the ability to murder Hess, he would do it in a single synthetic heartbeat. But he knew there were failsafes against any assassination attempts. He had helped oversee their design.

Upon reaching Hess' office, Jorge squared his shoulders. The Synt director had requested that rather than knocking or phoning, everyone get in the habit of utilizing the messaging system, to continue testing the glorious new communication option. So Jorge projected his missive.

HERE.

Jorge was no poet.

The door slid open, and he stepped through.

Dr. Derek Abelson was seated across from Felix Hess. Jorge rarely saw the silent partner in the Syn enterprise. Though his position was second only to Hess himself, Abelson was rarely heard or seen. He was Hess' opposite in many ways. He shied away from the spotlight, avoided the media, and seemed almost embarrassed at his association with the technology. Which is why Jorge actually didn't hate him.

"How are you, man?" Abelson asked, somewhat nervously.

"Jorge," Hess acknowledged.

Jorge wondered at what point he went from being "Mr. Marquez" to simply "Jorge." There was a time when Hess used Jorge's last name. Had its erasure been due to familiarity? Or was it that he was the one and only Jorge in this rich, cold new world?

"I should be going," Abelson said, grabbing a flat tablet from Hess' desk and rising quickly, halfway out the door already. "Always good to see you, Jorge."

Jorge stood in front of Hess' desk, not sitting. Sitting implied the meeting might last longer than two minutes; Jorge preferred all meetings with this man be under two minutes. This was usually possible; Hess preferred minimizing interaction with all people at all times.

But this time, Hess said: "Sit, Jorge."

Jorge considered arguing, then sat. He wondered who he hated more—Hess, or himself.

"If this is about the Vost tests, Kennedy is still working on—"

"This isn't about that," Hess waved away Jorge's words. "You're not happy here."

Understatement of the year.

"I have always appreciated your candor. Your capability. But I cannot have you so dissatisfied. It's bad for business."

Bad for business. Of course. Hess was famously meticulous; he identified risks, course-corrected, and moved on. Jorge had watched him do it with everything from engineering issues to employees. And now the laser focus was on Jorge. Jorge kept his mouth shut, reigning in his churning reply.

Are you worried I'm a risk? Yes. I am a risk. Not just to your system, but to you personally, Felix. As soon as I can figure out how to dismantle the bomb in my head, I will leave this place and join the rebellion and do all I can to end this world. To end you.

Jorge volunteered for this program to save his family. To make amends for having been ripped away from them for a year and a half, serving time for a crime he never intended to commit. But the sentence he brought upon himself by becoming a Vost made his last incarceration feel like a joke. Hess wasn't a boss, he was a warden; Jorge's room at the Synt was just a nicely-furnished cell. Visiting hours at this prison were nonexistent, making it a thousand times more horrific than the county correctional facility where Jorge spent a measly eighteen months, a lifetime ago.

"I want to expand your duties, Jorge," Hess said. "Get you out of the building a little. Would that interest you?"

Jorge gaped. For the first time in more than a decade, tears threatened; the thought of leaving these walls, breathing outside air, and maybe even seeing his family, was more than his fractured heart could grasp.

"I was going to offer you that option. Until a few red flags came into view."

As quickly as the carrot was dangled, it was snatched away. Jorge's insides hardened, everything in him becoming steel, guarding himself against this man he knew better than to trust. He tensed, waiting to see what the red flags costing him his imagined freedom might be. He always dotted every I and crossed every T. He knew his family's continued security rested on his ability to satisfy Hess.

"You've been downloading a good bit of information about the rebels," Hess said mildly.

They track what I download?

Of course they do.

Stupid, Jorge. Stupid stupid stupid...

"I..." Jorge's mouth went dry; cornered into the truth, he said: "Yes. I have."

"Why?"

"Isn't it obvious?" Jorge stalled, searching for that allegedly obvious answer. And then he found it. "My family. I'm wondering if any of them are involved, or have been harmed in any of the incursions. I care about what's happening out there, because they are still out there. My family is out there. That world—*their* world is still my world."

"*This* is your world," Hess warned. "I understand that you're only still here because I blackmailed you into staying. But I had hoped that by now, you'd be a bit more invested in our work. You have played a large role in building our synthetic society, Jorge. In building a better world."

"I do what I have to do, sir," Jorge said, the words burning his tongue, souring his soul.

"Yes. And you'll continue doing what you have to do. We will live for many, many years, Jorge. I cannot hold your family over you forever, because your family will all die off long before you do."

A knife long lodged in Jorge's heart twisted, tearing him from within. He made no sound.

"Did you know they're calling themselves Originals? The rebels? I mean, really. 'Originals.' They say they're fighting to preserve the original way of the world. As if the world wasn't constantly evolving. As if there was ever one original way. Ludicrous."

"Ludicrous," Jorge said flatly, not agreeing, but unwilling to be baited.

"Jorge. I'll give you a promotion. You will be permitted a limited range of travel—assignments to be conducted off-site. You might even be permitted to visit your family, under the right cir-cumstances. But such favors would be quid pro quo."

Jorge had trouble hearing anything past *permitted to visit your family*. He thought this was off the table. The yo-yoing conver-sation was about to give him an aneurysm. Trembling, he asked: "I... could see my family?"

"Perhaps," Hess smiled wanly. "We can discuss that later. I didn't actually call you in to discuss any of this, it just—came up."

Jorge frowned, sensing a trap. "What did you call me in to dis-cuss, then?"

Hess coughed, and for a split second, seemed almost apolo-getic. Then he dropped the information heavily, sharply, like an executioner loosing a guillotine.

"Your mother died."

CHAPTER 40: RUTH

THE ONLY TIME RUTH was really able to breathe was when she was carrying out a mission. Danger snapped everything into focus; serving a purpose heightened her senses. Just as with her first act of anarchy, planting the bomb as a teenager, in the moment of action—readying for an ambush, preparing for sabotage—her fullest self unfurled.

Her spirit lifted so much when she was in warrior mode that Ruth would subconsciously hum to herself as she barreled toward her mission; almost always, the melody was the Song of the Original Resistance. No one knew who wrote it; some claimed it emerged from their collective sorrow and simply *was*, like love or faith or humanity itself. The song was sung at protests and campfires, lifting morale when they were together, uniting them when sung softly alone, as when Ruth hummed it:

Standing here, I almost see

The girl I was, the crone I'll be

The blessing of age, the passing of time

Teaching us all, profane and sublime

We will never relent, we will never rely

Thus we will live. And thus we will die.

But now the missions were changing, and Ruth had stopped singing.

Back when the rebels were seen as an unorganized mass of ants, the synthetic citizens had responded through law and legislation. Police in riot gear would sometimes be deployed, gassing and roughing up the rioting rebels. But the crowds were still small; the rebels still seen as fringe. Too many ordinary citizens still somehow believed that eventually augmentation would be extended to them, as well. Like lottery addicts and those who voted against their own economic interests because they believed they would someday be rich, most people gave the hyper-powerful plenty of leeway, hoping to curry transhumanism favor in the end. Which allowed the Syns to swiftly rise and seize all of the power, right out in the daylight.

Soon, the wealthiest one percent were almost all augmented. They began hoarding resources as well as technology, knowing they would need everything for decades upon decades. It was not in their interest to advocate for the Originals.

And so Original rights were stripped away. Social services were defunded. Voting rights suspended. Originals were denied medical care, representation, the basic dignities they thought they had been promised. When the Syns of North America, Russia, China, and the other world powers began unifying and promoting synthetic status as superior to the old system of sovereignties, everything swiftly metastasized.

This united the Originals, once and for all.

Only a handful of idiots still clamored to be included in the augmented world; the others finally woke up and realized that joining the Syns was not a realistic option. Overthrowing them was the only answer. The uprisings intensified because their ranks were finally significant enough to be taken seriously.

Instead of responding on an incident-by-incident basis, like a massive dog scratching at the occasional bite of a flea, the Syns saw the masses of Originals as a growing problem that needed to be dealt with once and for all. Which is when the Syns started actively attacking the Originals, and rebellion escalated to full-out war.

Active battle was harder than stealth resistance. Defensive action didn't make Ruth breathe easier, the way an offensive mission once did. It hardened her. Changed her.

She tried to hide these changes from her sweet sister Rachel. There was no streak of soldier in Rachel; she was too gentle a soul to fight, even in the face of oppression and enemies and violation after violation. Rachel spent her days as far as possible from the field of battle, venturing out only into cleared areas around whatever basecamp they called home that week. She was not oblivious to the situation. She tended to the wounded. She saw firsthand the impact of the incursions. She'd patched Ruth up on more than one occasion, binding her torso when her ribs cracked, awkwardly stitching a gash on her arm. That angry cut was beginning to scar, the haphazard sewing job rendering it far more visible than it should have been. Ruth wondered if her inner scarring might someday be as obvious as her ruined exterior.

They were not anticipating another drone attack so soon, and so early. Dawn was still an hour from breaking when the Syn drones began buzzing overhead, taking down three Originals before a warning cry went out and Ruth's people began running for cover.

The drone attacks were particularly vicious and effective. The Syns went to great lengths to avoid hand to hand combat, preferring technology to wage war on their behalf. The sleek synthetic drones, the Originals learned, were synched to the Syn operating them. Their cameras reported images as if the Syns were seeing the battlefield with their own eyes. Like a giant video game, Syns remotely took aim, set Originals in their crosshairs, and pulled the trigger from miles away. The battles that tore Originals limb from limb didn't require Syns to even show up to the battlefield.

Yesterday, watching her people scream and bleed, it was hard for Ruth to remember to breathe. Each breath felt forced, ragged; each breath threatened to be her last. But at the end of the day, she was still breathing. And so, this morning, she and the other survivors in her battalion would be coming together to punish their Syn attackers.

A scout had confirmed that a small cadre of Syns were operating the drones from well outside the protected fortress walls of the Synt, at an outpost base ten miles from their camp.

"A very doable hike," said the scout, a man called Aaron. Aaron wore his long blond hair in a thick braid; he had only recently joined their ranks. He'd been traveling with a band of rebels from Missouri, who sojourned upriver and had a nasty encounter with the Syns. Aaron had arrived alone, hungry, and disheveled, and was immediately taken in by the Fell crew. He had volunteered to serve as a scout, and over the past few weeks had proven himself nimble and astute. "I say we send a team there to take down the outpost. Boom."

Everyone agreed that the move made sense. A swift, efficient mission to potentially prevent further attacks. Attacks that were nearly impossible to fend off once underway. Howard wanted to lead the mission himself, but Ruth refused this suggestion.

"This is not a mission, Howard," she said. "This isn't a bomb in an empty building. There will be Syn operatives there. This will be another battle, which is why—"

"Which is why I should go, and not you," Howard interjected.

Prepared to fire back her disagreement, Ruth saw something in her uncle's eyes that made her stop. His look was pleading; protective. Howard was in denial about their recently reversed roles. He still saw himself as the strong one, the protector, and still saw Ruth as his vulnerable little girl.

But he was somewhere in his seventies. The lines on his face traced year after year, loss after loss. Yet somehow Howard Fell was still of the mind that he could spare his niece the worst of the war.

There was no easy way to tell him that she was already damaged beyond repair, and he was too old to fight.

"They need you, here," she told her uncle, slipping her hand into his and squeezing it with gentle strength. "Rachel, Sophie—everyone. Please. Protect them. Let me do this."

He did not want to agree. But he had little choice. So now Ruth, flanked by two dozen rebel soldiers, was trying to find her breath as she headed toward the Syn outpost.

The base was small, Aaron had assured them. Only five Syns running the drone program there. If they could destroy the building, dismantle the control room, and take the five Syns hostage, they could stave off the onslaught of drones and buy themselves some time, maybe even some leverage if the hostages were worth anything to the Syn Council.

Ruth was the commanding officer on the mission. Hector was second in command, which was problematic. Hector had been in love with Ruth ever since he joined the rebellion some six years earlier. Everyone knew it, although Ruth pretended not to know. Romance could prove a dangerous or even deadly distraction.

Hopeless as his cause might be, Hector remained smitten. But knowing Ruth valued mission-minded focus above all else, as her second in command he bent over backward to prove his swooning eyes were on the prize.

"Do you think his report is accurate?" Hector asked as they moved briskly through a thickly wooded area, the least-monitored path to the old building. "Aaron. You think he's right about the location, the details?"

Ruth shrugged, triggering a knowing smile from Hector. When in mission mode, Ruth was known to avoid conversation, only growling or guarding silence as a wolf guards its bones.

Unlike Ruth, Hector was serious only when necessary. A born goofball, he often joked that living in a dystopian hellscape was no reason to be a downer. He approached life with an enthusiasm that mystified Ruth.

"We'll make it," he'd say, over and over. "*Arból de la esperanza, mantente firme! Tree of hope, stand firm*! Frida Kahlo had it right, amigos."

Hector was the tree of hope standing firm within their small band of resistance fighters. Everyone adored him; Ruth was alone in rolling her eyes at his unrelenting optimism.

When he'd told Ruth she was fiercely beautiful, she nearly punched him in the mouth; when he presented her with a bouquet of wildflowers, she asked him what the hell she was supposed to do with a wad of weeds. He told her he was a moth, ever drawn to her flame. She asked him how to extinguish the light.

Hector finally gave up on grand gestures and pretty words, but his feelings for Ruth never changed. Ruth continued to will his affections away, knowing it would be better for both of them if Hector saw her as simply a sister-in-arms. He was too protective of her. He might put others at risk to save her, and she could not allow that.

It was late morning when Ruth, Hector, and their crew reached the small Syn base. It was exactly where Aaron had told them it would be, and appeared as reported: small, isolated, a perfect mark. There were no windows and only one door; the whole thing was not much larger than a small barn in an old farmyard.

"Ready?" Ruth whispered to Hector.

He nodded. But then, as Ruth began to move forward, Hector caught her arm, pulling her gently but firmly behind him. He gave a nod, and two of the other rebels instantly appeared, each holding her by an elbow.

"Sorry, Ruthie," Hector said, apologetic but unusually curt. "I promised your uncle I'd go through the door first."

Hot-faced, furious at the undermining, at the sexism, at the physical restraint, Ruth nearly exploded. She kept her voice a whisper only so their enemies would not hear them.

"Hector, so help me God—"

"Promise is a promise," he said. And with that, Hector loped toward the building, armed with one of the automatic weapons from their dwindling stockpile of munitions. Ruth struggled against the two men restraining her, and within seconds broke free. She took off after Hector, running as fast as she could.

She was still well behind him when he reached the perimeter, the front door flew open, and the gunfire began.

The first bullet caught Hector in the shoulder, torquing his body and twisting him toward his companions running behind him. He locked eyes with Ruth, his face a mask of shock as a dozen more bullets ripped through his spine, forever silencing his infectious laughter. Suspended for a moment like a puppet on strings, like some terrible joke, the next bullet cut the string and Hector collapsed to the earth.

Pouring out of the building, trampling over Hector's lifeless body, dozens of Syns rushed toward Ruth and the other rebels, spraying bullets as they advanced. Their aim was poor, but they had little need for accuracy. Their numbers, their artillery, every last damn thing was on their side. Ruth and her people were fish in a barrel, wide-eyed and unprepared.

We're all going to die.

Finally finding her breath, Ruth sucked in enough air for a bellowing cry, following her own command as she screamed it.

"Run!"

NEW DELHI, INDIA 2040

CHAPTER 41: PREETI

D R. PREETI KANSAL WASN'T A WARRIOR. But she was a keen strategist. For decades, she had overseen the successful underground development of an Original resistance network in New Delhi. Upon her return to India, having been part of the Fells' inaugural movement meetings, having seen the interior of the Synt in its earliest days of augmentation, she returned to her homeland with a plan in place.

We will go underground before there is a need to go underground.

The Singularity began as an American phenomenon. Naturally, billionaires in other countries, including her own, were swept up in the project. But other nations were not as fast-tracked as the United States. No one around her believed that the apocalypse was at hand, but Preeti wasn't going to wait around for the fire and brimstone. She took action early.

Dr. Kansal was fortunate to have money. Money she earned in her burgeoning medical career, and money that she had inherited from her parents. Preeti had been a prodigy, completing her high school education at a finishing school in London and graduating at sixteen; going on to study at Georgetown in America, and then at Northwestern, before landing a residency at Mass General in Boston. The brain was her specialty, from the very beginning of her studies. Even in high school, every science project, every essay, every assignment for any class—if she could make it about the brain, she would. She was focused, which served her well as a doctor and also as a conspiracy theorist.

She knew her money would eventually lose its purchasing power. So she began spending it, quietly but thoroughly, building one massive underground compound and a series of outposts. She brought in experts to install self-contained communications platforms, water purification systems, underground greenhouse facilities, and to develop areas for tremendous long-term food storage capacity. She began actively recruiting friends and family who she believed would be receptive to her warnings, and discreet in their responses.

The Singularity was a global event, but its epicenter was far from Preeti's world. By the time man melded with machine, the Indian elite eager to lap up the synthetic Kool-Aid had almost all relocated to the States. They left their poorer countrymen behind, condemning them to unkind fates and hungry deaths.

Preeti took as many as she safely could underground. And then she did her best to block out what was happening in the world above—the one just overhead, where her own people were starving and dying; and the one far away, where a privileged few were being provided with enormous power, courtesy of one Felix Hess.

Her cousin.

She remembered meeting Felix when he was a small, quiet child—her cousin Nirupa's overlooked son. She doubted that she made much of an impression on him at that time, but apparently he remembered her well enough to track her down when he was in need of a neurologist. It was Felix who introduced her to Nathan Fell all those years ago, convincing her to sign the nondisclosure agreement and be the doctor on call for that fateful procedure.

It was also Felix who ushered her from the room, not allowing Nathan Fell to be medically assisted after the terrible augmentation accident. It was Felix who had taken over the synthetic steering wheel. Felix Hess, no longer small, no longer overlooked, no longer someone Preeti recognized as family.

She knew she could not stop him from creating a race of synthetic citizens. But she also knew that all organic matter would eventually rot. The Syns were augmented, but their base component was human flesh. Even with augmentation, Hess and those like him would need continued course-correction. There would be unintended outcomes within the Syn population. The early rebellions would die down, but at some point there would be another opportunity to swing the pendulum the other way.

But only if Originals survived long enough to see that swing.

"Do you know why the Syns are winning?" Preeti asked her husband John, late one hot summer night, curled beside him on the futon in their underground home. "Why they *won*, at least for now?"

"Why?"

"Because of the apathetic middle-grounders. The ones who didn't pick a side."

John nodded. "Like the old political joke—stand in the middle of the road, get run over by both sides?"

"It's not funny," Preeti said, somber. "All of those people who decided that they would just try to avoid involvement, keep their heads down… they are why our world is in flames. The ones who kept quiet, or defended the Syns in conversation—it's not because they thought Syns will go away. It's worse. It's because they believed that eventually, the shining new technology would be within their grasp."

"You mean, they're Americans," her American husband joked.

"Yes," she said seriously. "Americans raised on this idea that anyone can achieve absolutely anything."

"You don't believe anyone can achieve absolutely anything?"

"*Anyone*, maybe," Preeti said. "But *everyone*, no."

"That's a fine distinction," John said.

"Too fine for most to grasp," Preeti agreed. "And so they act against their collective interest, thinking it is in their individual interest. 'Yes,' they said, 'yes, the elite Syns are immoral and awful and hoarding all the resources… *but when I'm a Syn…*'"

"… 'I'll be different,'" he finished for her.

She nodded and shivered despite the heat, huddling closer to the man she loved. He put an arm around her, drawing her in, holding her tight. She felt safe in his arms, but that night she could not stop thinking about this notion. How even knowing the statistical improbability of attaining a shot at synching, all too many people saw themselves as destined to number among the special few selected to become Syns.

That's why the masses saw the rebels as too radical. It wasn't just a fear of death or dismemberment; it was a fear of throwing their fate in with the wrong lot. They didn't want to be starving resistance fighters. They wanted to become fat, preening Syns.

They saw the Syn lifestyle as something more than selfish. They saw it as something *attainable*.

And so, rather than band together to democratize the process, they split and splintered. They supported the Syns by ignoring the rebellion. They swam upstream individually, convinced that one more lap, a few more strokes, just around the riverbend, they would find their reward. They did not see themselves as passive. They saw themselves as patient. Aspiring.

And soon, they will be extinct.

Two decades had passed since Preeti left the States, bringing John with her. The messages she was able to receive from the American resistance were becoming briefer, more urgent, more infrequent. She knew their access to technology was more and more limited. They had several older and less traceable cellular and satellite phones, which had served them well. But even finding consistent electricity to recharge the phones, let alone penetrable wireless services across which to send their messages, was becoming increasingly difficult.

Preeti knew that sometime soon, all communication between her hidden enclave and the active Western resistance fighters would cease. And then it would be time for a long round of the waiting game—staying quiet, staying off the radar, finding a way to secure an informant from within the Syn world, and hopefully someday connecting with any of the survivors who made it through the brutal war for the Original way in North America.

If there were any survivors.

THE INCORPORATED SECTORS
2040 - 2045

R EVIEWING THE MORNING REPORT, Hess was repulsed, not by the images of the bodies littering the ground but at the small black insects covering them. Millions of flies, jockeying for position, swarming and scrambling over corpses like commuters running late. The industrious flies were multiplying, eating the plentiful rotting organic flesh, fattening and buzzing and asserting that even in this new world, their place was secure.

Hess was sick of flies. He was sick of warring with the Originals. He was sick of their predictable deaths becoming his logistical nightmare. There was still so much building to do, so much refining, so much progress to be made. Contending with a protracted series of uprisings was getting in the way of much more important tasks. He was a *scientist*, he reminded the Council. He was spending far too much time lately deploying teams to fight Originals, and sending out Vosts to clean up the mess after the battles.

"I'm not an army-guy," Hess told the Council, swatting at a fly that had bumbled its way into the meeting room. Missing it. "We need to end this cold war. Now. Yesterday."

After a moment of muttering and blank stares, Lorraine Murray stood. As svelte and well-dressed as a mannequin, she spoke in a clear and unhalting voice.

"What if we stop fighting them—and just take other measures to ensure that they run out of soldiers in a less bloody manner? After all, time is on our side. We can play a slower, cleaner game. And they will lose."

Interest piqued, Hess asked: "What do you have in mind, Lorraine?"

"Stop them from reproducing," she said.

The mutters around the table ticked up again, more energetically this time, soft distant rumblings rolling into a thunderous, boisterous, un-moderated storm of debate within minutes.

"Enough—enough!" Hess barked, banging on the long meeting table. "One at a time. Questions, concerns, suggestions around Lorraine's proposal."

Henrik Reed, a thin-faced man with a well-maintained mustache, chuckled. "How exactly do we 'stop them from reproducing'? Ask them nicely? Tell them to 'wait'? Show them blown-up photographs of gonorrhea and syphilis? Maybe we'll screen *The Miracle of Life*! Abstinence education failed in the old world, Lorraine. I doubt it'll work better in this one."

This earned him several nods and chortles, but Lorraine was nonplussed. A fly was circling her head now, but she ignored it.

"Abstinence education provided inadequate information, and then expected compliance. We're not offering information, or seeking compliance. We're imposing a new reality."

Henrik's smirk went sour. "And what 'reality' is that?"

"I've been thinking about it for some time, actually," Lorraine purred. "And I believe the water supply will be an effective means of regulation. We simply prioritize the water in all of our expansion areas—ensure that we control all supply, adding chemical compounds at the source that will cause infertility. We'll ensure the elements are untraceable and irremovable. The very water they drink to stay alive will be the death sentence of their race."

That sounded cold, even to Hess.

Cold, and clean, and brilliant.

The Council agreed. Lorraine's ready reply and simple solution hit the nail on the head. It had all the elements of a brilliant plan—feasibility, utilizing existing infrastructure, achieving maximum goals with minimal exertion. The fly circled Lorraine a final time, then landed on the table beside her hand. Without hesitation, she lifted her water glass and crushed the bug.

"Lorraine," Hess said, admiring. "Allow me to pour you a scotch."

CHAPTER 43: MARILYN

MARILYN HESS WAS FIXING HERSELF a cup of coffee. Two creams. No sugar. Like always.

She was waiting on Angela to arrive. Angela came over every Sunday to regale Marilyn with her tales of working at the Synt. Sometimes the stories were mundane—bureaucratic politics here, frustrations with new uploads there—but occasionally there was good gossip. Co-workers still slept together in the new world. Scandals still popped up on occasion.

Marilyn believed Angela was happy, or at least satisfied. She was no longer in touch with her son Leroy, who had joined the rebels. That was sad. But otherwise she had it pretty good. Angela had been a mid-level Synt administrator for years now. With the lengthening of their lifetimes secured through synching, the Synt took a new approach to most work, encouraging personal enrichment that would be applicable in their ongoing information acquisition and dissemination. Angela had decided that *languages* would be her enrichment area. She was learning all sorts of crazy languages, and Marilyn half-listened when Angela would tell her about the interesting words she was learning in French and Spanish and whatever else.

Frankly, Marilyn was a little irritated with Angela and all of her intellectual pursuits. Marilyn had asked Angela to join them because she wanted an ally. Angela was supposed to be there for her, and instead she worked almost as much as Felix, leaving very little time for Marilyn.

This arrangement is no longer working.

Marilyn had devised a new idea. She'd ask Angela to move in with them. To quit her job at the Synt and work as Marilyn's full-time assistant. (Not that Marilyn had any tasks to complete. But "assistant" sounded less politically incorrect to her than "help.") To Marilyn's way of thinking, there were endless reasons for Angela to move in with them, even if none of them had anything specific to do with, well, a job. But just having another person in the house would be so helpful, in general. Since Ever's involuntary synch, the girl was unbearable. Sullen and churlish, constantly lashing out at Marilyn. Taking it all out on her mother, since her father was never there. It was incredibly unfair, really. Angela would be the perfect buffer.

Besides, Angela liked Ever, and Ever liked Angela. It would be nice, the three of them. A better balance than mother and daughter alone and constantly at odds, with no one to serve as referee or distraction. Maybe in the end, Marilyn would wind up with two friends. Maybe Angela could help her win Ever's affection.

Marilyn walked from the kitchen to her master bathroom, set-ting her cooling mug of coffee on the white marbled countertop and leaning forward, looking into the mirror. She dabbed a bit of concealer beneath her eyes, added a touch of lipstick, then gave her lashes one quick flick of the mascara wand. It was all she need-ed. She was preserved at a young enough age that it took minimal effort to look fresh and dewy.

As she beautified herself for this conversation with Angela, it never occurred to her that perhaps she should try to catch her husband's attention rather than her friend's. Marilyn had at last done what her husband did years ago: written off this marriage as a loss. Without ending it, they both accepted the reality of their situation. It was never going to work, Felix and Marilyn, as much affection as they had shared at the beginning of their relationship. A lifetime ago.

Even before Ever arrived, Marilyn's demand for love and at-tention always exceeded Felix's supply. At some point, Felix shut down production altogether. Marilyn would still make demands of him, now and again. But she had no remaining expectations that he would supply her with anything at all.

She looked at her pretty face in the mirror. Was the minimal mascara and lipstick enough? Come to think of it, for this weep-ing petition, a little blush might not hurt. She wanted to look good, but also sad. Borderline blotchy.

But still beautiful.

CHAPTER 44: RUTH

*T*HIS IS NOT A WORLD FOR CHILDREN.

Holding her baby nephew gingerly in her arms, Ruth was uncertain how to feel. She knew this innocent child was born into a world not worthy of his purity, his potential. Loving him seemed too great a risk; there was no way he would last long in this hellish landscape.

Three years earlier, in the massacre at the drone station, Ruth was the sole survivor. Hector and two dozen others, dead and gone in a matter of seconds. The bullets that somehow missed ending Ruth's life instead shot and shattered the last of her hopes.

Aaron, the scout with the long blonde braid, disappeared from camp during the massacre. He turned out to be a Syn sympathizer who had promised to deliver two dozen of the fiercest Original rebels in exchange for an augmentation of his own. *In a world of such betrayal, such pure evil, how can my sister still want children?*

Ever since Rachel and Gregory wed, so long ago, their goal was to become parents. They wanted a large family, like Howard and Sophie's family. At least six children, Rachel said; six *minimum!*

This irked Ruth.

Ruth, who was frequently out risking life and limb on movement missions; Ruth, who could not show her face in public for fear of being handed over to the Syn authorities. Ruth, who knew the true cruelty of this ugly world.

Rachel and Gregory tried for years to get pregnant without success. Rachel would weep, and Ruth stroked her sister's soft hair with her own roughened soldier's hand. She expressed sympathy, but was secretly relieved. It seemed a small act of divine mercy, if God still existed. Denying a child entry into this wicked world was an infinite kindness.

Ever since the massacre, and the ongoing legislative oppression, and the massive losses they suffered by drone, by poisonous gas, by targeted fires... it was all too much. This world was irredeemable, and bringing a child into it, unthinkable. Beyond selfish.

Ruth had long since stopped believing that things would get better. She no longer fought for change. She fought to punish. To destroy. She fought because it was all she knew anymore.

And then came the rumors that the Syns were poisoning the water supplies in order to render Original women barren. They were treating it with chemicals that inhibited fertility. Rachel's already-toxic, empty womb would soon be further damaged simply by sipping her morning glass of water. They would boil the water, of course. But it wouldn't be enough.

Then, against all odds, Rachel got pregnant.

When she shared the joyful news with her twin, Ruth spewed rage at her sister.

"Why, Rachel? Why are you doing this? How can you plan to bring a child into this world? A world where they'll have no rights, no opportunities, know nothing but hunger and battle and a life of endless, nomadic wandering? Why?"

In a rare show of temper, fueled by hormones and mother-bear rage, Rachel snapped back: "If you really believe that, what are you fighting for, Ruth? What the hell is the point? If there's no one to inherit the world you're trying to protect, why protect it at all?"

Ruth hung her head, too tired to confess that she was only fighting out of habit.

Her anger remained, but she resisted the urge to lash out at her sister and remind her that even if this tainted, water-poisoned pregnancy resulted in a live birth—the water Rachel was drinking may well have damaged the fetus. It would be born misshapen, or brain damaged. If it was born at all. Rachel and Ruth were nearing forty. Even in a world where they had adequate medical care, in a world where they were not weary and poisoned and under-nourished, her pregnancy would be high-risk. That's what frightened Ruth most of all.

The risk is not just to the baby. You could die, my sister...

But throughout pregnancy, Rachel swelled and blossomed. Despite a diet consisting mostly of canned foods and root vegetables, for the first time in her life, she gained weight and became larger than Ruth. Rachel's cheeks rounded and filled, and her belly grew and grew and grew. A terrible new thought occurred to Ruth.

My God, what if she has twins? We're twins. What if there are two damaged twins, two little lives that we will have to fight to nourish and protect in this cruel environment?

Rachel did not give birth to twins. She gave birth to one massive boy. Helena Garrison, who attended the birth, held him and crowed that he weighed eleven pounds if he weighed an ounce. He had all his limbs, all his digits. He wailed with powerful lungs and nursed hungrily. No one was more shocked than Ruth.

"Takes after his dad," Rachel said joyfully, beaming first at her husband (*I love you*) and then at her sister (*I told you so*).

Calvin James Harper was named for two of Gregory's cousins who had died in the earliest days of the resistance. They called him Cal.

Gregory doted on his son whenever he was around and able to do so. Like Ruth, Gregory was a warrior. They were rarely deployed together, since each represented the best of the resistance. Rachel had long hated that each of her dearest loves was almost always fighting on one front or another. She hoped that the birth of their son would re-focus Gregory. Make him stop fighting, stay around base more often.

It did not.

When Cal was still an infant in arms, Gregory was part of the battalion implementing a surprise attack on the Synt outpost in Burlington, Vermont. He kissed his wife and son the night before, knowing he would be gone before dawn. When they woke, his sleeping-space beside Rachel was already cold.

As the day wore on, an autumn chill further cooled the world around them. As the temperature dropped, an ominous feeling grew in the pit of Ruth's stomach. Somehow, she knew something had gone wrong with this mission. She knew it, and she hated herself for not going in Gregory's place.

It was almost two full days before the news reached the tribe: For the first time in three years, it had been another absolute massacre. Not bullets, this time; but chemical warfare.

Gregory had been on the front line, tall and wide and bold, bellowing and encouraging everyone forward. So he was one of the first to inhale the toxic chemicals that were released when they burst through the doors of the outpost building. The mighty man had been brought to his knees, collapsing before he could turn

and give warning to the loyal dozens following him into the building—a building which had been cleared of all Syn staff, and now
served as crypt for Gregory and all of the other Original soldiers
who perished within.

Ruth was with Howard, planning their next mission, when
the scout arrived. His words stooped Howard's already-sunken
shoulders, and turned Ruth's entire being to lead. The memories
of her own experience of ambush and massacre stabbed through
her, Hector's face appearing and twisting and screaming, then
Gregory's, and all of the others. This news might break them all.
Gregory was not only Rachel's husband, but also a community
favorite. Still and always the big man on campus, even when the
campus in question was a rebel base nestled into an abandoned
canning factory in rural New Hampshire.

The scout lowered her head, and scurried away.

"I'll tell Ra…" Ruth began, trying to offer that she would be the
one to tell her sister, and finding that her words abandoned her.

"No, Ruthie," Howard said, using the old nickname she hadn't
heard in years. "I'll tell her. I'll do it. But Ruth—this is where it
ends. This will be the last of the uprisings. To lose so many this
morning, and Gregory… we cannot continue. This cannot go on."

"If this is the last of the uprisings," Ruth choked, "I swear we
will give them a last fight to remember. They will pay for this.
They will pay for Gregory. They will be punished."

"Is there news?" Asked a small voice from behind them.

Howard and Ruth locked eyes, panicked. It was Rachel. She
stood with her large sleeping son balanced on her slim hip, whispering so as not to wake him. Howard walked away from Ruth,
taking Rachel by the elbow and guiding her away for a private
moment between them, with only a sleeping babe to bear witness.

Ruth wanted to run, to hide, to protect herself from seeing her
sister's pain. But she found she was rooted to the spot, staring at
the small figures in the near distance, watching with horrified eyes.

She did not have to watch for long. As soon as Howard delivered the news, Rachel turned wordlessly from him, walked to Ruth, and shoved her child into her sister's arms. All color gone from her, already a ghost, she walked into the woods. Ruth watched her sister silently striding until eventually she fell straight down and a keening wail of mourning broke free of her, a spectral sound splintering the sky and the morning and the hearts of all who heard her.

Ruth held her nephew as her sister's ghostly cry pierced her soul. Though she had not intended to, she loved this child as ferociously as she had ever loved anyone or anything. This child, who had already lost one parent, and would know loss after loss throughout his life. This child, who would probably be best spared of this existence. Who could still be spared, if Ruth just slipped her hand over his mouth…

I could. I should. It would be mercy.

She placed her hand over the boy's mouth, over his nose. He shifted beneath her, scrunching his nose, sleepily trying to open his eyes. He began to squirm and resist. She pressed her hand tighter across his little face, wanting to save him from all the agony ahead—

No.

Her hand flew from the front of his face to the back of his head, holding him close to her, soothing him back into a deep and safe sleep. She couldn't do it. She couldn't save him without destroying her sister, and herself. Instead she whispered tightly into his ear: "Things are bad, and they may not get better. But I will do whatever I can to keep you safe. I will be your protector. I swear it, Cal. *I swear it.*"

DEREK ABELSON HAD BEEN STRUGGLING with the ramifications of his work for some time now. Back when he worked for Nathan Fell, he had at least been somewhat inspired. Professor Fell was a true visionary—a difficult person, yes, but one that Derek could respect. He wasn't warm, but he was reliable. He kept his focus on the big picture. He believed that the work they were doing was intrinsically good. More than good, it was *necessary*, to address things like climate change and depleting resources. Maybe he didn't always calculate the human costs correctly. Maybe his idealism blinded him to some of the consequences of his actions. But he wasn't driven by ego. He was driven by a hunger to do something meaningful.

With the shift of leadership from Nathan Fell to Felix Hess, there had also been a shift in philosophy. Their work stopped feeling noble, and started feeling... Derek didn't even know. Competitive. More than that—*showy*.

It had been important to Nathan Fell to *be* the smartest person in the room. Over the years, Derek realized that one subtle but intrinsic difference was that for Felix Hess, it was important to be *known as* the smartest person in the room.

Which was why it mystified Derek that even after all this time, Hess still kept his greatest scientific achievement a secret. Other than Derek and Hess, no one knew that the core of Heaven was powered by the still-churning brain of Nathan Fell.

When Hess was figuring out the mechanics of connecting Fell to the core, he needed help. It was a promising but complicated proposition; even Hess had to admit that more brainpower was needed in order to figure out this... well, this new kind of brainpower.

So he assembled a small and spectacularly brilliant group. He told them they were there to unlock the secret of fusing a massively powerful brain to the cloud system and base computer, in order to create a connected system for all of Syn society. But no one on the team knew to whom the brain belonged. The donor in question was referred to simply as Patient X. Hess did not reveal that the donor was Fell. Or that no consent for said donation had ever been attained. Derek was the only one in on the secret. Only he and Hess knew that Patient X was Nathan Fell. Which is probably why Hess preferred to keep him close. To make sure his mouth stayed shut.

Derek and Hess were never close. They respected each other's intellect, but resented each other on all other fronts. The only thing cementing their bond was that each held the key to the closet where the other's skeleton was kept: Derek knew Hess was keeping the shell of Nathan Fell alive to power the Syn world.

And Hess knew that Derek was terrified of being publicly outed as one of the architects of that very same world.

Derek and Hess established a functional working relationship. They met weekly to review the latest reports—Vost testing, patch development, strategy around the rebellions, long-term sustainability planning, all of the various spinning plates. They had such a large team working beneath them that Derek had to do very little beyond read the reports (or at least skim them) and meet for one hour with Hess, once every seven days. The rest of the time, Derek was free to sleep in, and paint, and take attractive Syn women on elaborate Synt-funded dates, and generally be the glorified frat boy that he had always wanted to be. Being one of the only remaining people in the world with dirt on Felix Hess was not without its perks.

But what Felix didn't know was that Derek's glamorous bachelor life was a bit of a front.

Yes, he slept in most mornings, and went on dates periodically to keep up appearances. He maintained his rouge-ish good looks, sandy brown hair falling into his eyes, charming smile. But Derek wasn't as shallow as he pretended to be. Sure, he enjoyed his downtime. But Synthetic life gave him plenty of that. So he filled his hours building apps, running internal programs—and about a year ago he began working on a book. A book that required extensive research. He had the title selected before he even began the first chapter.

Cyborganics Cowboy: The Story of Nathan Fell,
American Legend

He wondered if he should leave out "American legend." It made the title just that little-bit-too-long. Clunky, like a middle school textbook. And Nathan was not particularly patriotic, so "American Legend" felt a bit off-brand. Derek decided to strike that final descriptor.

\

Cyborganics Cowboy: The Story of Nathan Fell

Yes. Better.

Derek saw this project as a tribute to his teacher. A chance to remind the world that Hess was not the father of the Singularity; he was its evil stepfather, at best. Nathan Fell deserved credit for all he had wrought.

Credit, or blame?

Derek pushed the thought from his mind. He couldn't go there. He thought instead about the book, how it would play out like an epic story. Almost like a Greek myth. One of the aspects of the story that Derek found most fascinating was Nathan's large, haphazard family. His brother, Howard, the good-natured soft sciences professor turned rebel leader. Their parents, a father who died when Nathan was an infant, and a single mother who raised them alone. But most fascinating of all was Nathan's marriage and fatherhood.

It took Derek some time to track down the information on Nathan's wedding; older marriage certificates had not yet all been scanned and entered into the Heaven system. He had to go through the older internet for those records, and even then had to search in the appropriate state records archives, and that took some doing. He found it at last—Nathan Fell, groom; Sarah Proudtree, bride. And the birth records for the children, girls that Derek just barely remembered meeting. Ruth and Rachel. They were five or six when Derek had last seen them, when he was maybe twenty-three. It was a long ago—before his own synch, before the Singularity—and he was fairly certain that the last time he saw either of the girls may well have been the last time their father saw them, as well. Sarah had left Nathan, abandoned their daughters when they were still infants in arms.

The girls were raised by the brother, professor-turned-vigilante Howard. Which is how Ruth also wound up a rebel terrorist. Rachel seemed to disappear from the records; maybe she'd died? He had to find out.

The Fells were so much more interesting than Derek's own family. The Abelsons were like the world's drabbest Arthur Miller play: an older brother who enlisted in the army but then died in a motorcycle accident the day before he was supposed to ship out to Afghanistan, show-boating with his buddies and dying like an idiot instead of a hero. A mother who worked as a minimum-security prison corrections officer and never talked about her feelings. A father who worked as a mailman and never got over the death of his favorite son, who spent the last three decades of his sad life reeking of alcohol and regret.

By contrast, the Fells were smart, sexy, tragic, and fascinating. Writing the no-holds-barred biography of his fallen mentor had become Derek's true passion. But he lived in constant fear of Hess discovering the project and shutting it down. Derek was all too aware of how much information was uploaded each time he connected to Heaven. Just as with an old world computer backing up to a cloud, everyone's augmented mind had a two-way link to Heaven: downloading what they needed, uploading what they had to offer. Everyone had at least some understanding of this extremely basic fact of synthetic life, but they did not think about it much. They didn't fear the violation of privacy.

Thanks to the recently-passed Limited Autonomy Act, Derek was taking full advantage of private mode. This was a simple shift in one's internal settings that allowed an individual to use the bathroom, or make love to their spouse, or experience any other intimate moment without also recording it into their day's memory log, which might later be searchable. These memories were stored only in the organic corners of their brain, and could also be copied to private files, accessible only to the creator of the internal file. This setting was one Hess had disdained, but Derek had pushed for; he developed the technology, and utilized it more than any other citizen. Whenever he was working on his Nathan Fell biography, he made sure he was in private mode.

Hess had become suspicious recently. When he asked about his inordinate amount of time spent in private mode, Derek had his answer prepared. He shrugged and said: "Yeah, truth is—I masturbate. A lot. I think it might actually be more than what you'd call normal. Maybe it's a glitch? But yeah. Jerking off. Several times a day."

Hess looked sickened, and never asked him about it again.

Still, Derek decided he should develop a new program for himself—something to mask how long he spent in private mode. Copy footage from earlier memories and string them together into some sort of false real-time log, like rigging an old security camera in a James Bond movie. Derek invented new programs and applications constantly, and kept the vast majority of them to himself. He felt no need to hand them over to that capitalist bastard Hess.

While everyone still acted as if the Synt was some paragon of academia, Derek saw it for the cold corporation it was, designing products and controlling markets and keeping investors happy. Even if money was no longer the only currency, the game was the same. So when Derek invented something new, he tailored it to his own needs, and hoarded it. A small act of defying the man.

COME TO MY OFFICE. NOW.
EXCITING NEWS!

Did that dude seriously just use an exclamation point?
Derek blinked and re-read the uncharacteristically jubilant missive from Hess. Everything about this cryptic message was odd. *Exciting* was not a word that Hess just tossed around, with or without enthusiastic punctuation. So Derek dragged himself

out of bed to go see what the fuss was about. He was still more ir-ritated than intrigued by this late-night summons, and had almost made up his mind to just turn around and go back to his room and pretend he'd been asleep when the message came through—when he suddenly heard a tremendous BANG.

Derek hit the floor, heart pounding. Threats from the rebels about attacks on the Synt slammed through his mind, as loud as the actual bang. The threats weren't as frequent as they were a few years ago, and the security here was unparalleled. But still. Panting, he crawled army-style the last few feet to Hess's door. He hesitated at the doorway, looking around—there was no one in the hallway, no bullet holes in the wall. Slowly, he rose, and entered the guest keypad to open Hess' door—a code that would only work when Hess was accepting visitors. The door slid open. The scene within made Derek's jaw drop.

Hess was standing in the middle of the room, grinning, a fresh-ly popped bottle of champagne in hand. Fizzing, bubbly froth ran down the side of the bottle, dripping onto the floor.

"Derek!" Hess cried jovially, as if they were friends. As if he was the sort of person who had friends. "Just in time! We're about to toast."

"What are we toasting?" Derek asked, finding his voice.

He looked around, recognizing the other people in the room as the funders who had enabled their work over the years. What could possibly have them all grinning like idiots? The Singularity itself hadn't yielded such a reaction.

"The President—excuse me, *former* President of the United States, has just tendered his resignation," Hess said, the grin on his face nearly splitting it in two. "He'll be undergoing his aug-mentation procedure soon, and will serve as an advisor to the new governing body."

"The new... what?"

Hess beamed. "The Syn Council is the new governing entity

of the Incorporated Sectors, formerly known as the United States of America and her territories. We may expand at some point, of course—all of North America, at the very least. But this is still worth celebrating!"

The council members all laughed, buzzing as Hess poured champagne into their flutes. Derek wondered if he was hallucinating, as the laughter of the world's richest and most powerful people bounced off the walls around him. Was he understanding this correctly? Had Hess just said what he said? The dissolution of the government? America going from a democracy to an oligarchy overnight?

Not overnight. This was in the works for years. The uprisings, the rebels… they saw this coming. Hess, getting the leaders of the free world to turn over the keys. Letting these people, who have secretly been calling the shots for years, finally step out of the shadows and call the shots right out there in the sunshine. Now Hess won't even have to strong-arm legislators into passing his bills. He will be the law. He'll be the most powerful man on the planet.

"There will be a formal announcement tomorrow of our nation's new structure," Hess said. "Probably followed by a bunch of riots. Ha!"

"Ha!" The Council members all responded, practically in stereo.

"There might be some bumps, but this will usher in a much smoother system, swiftly implemented," Hess intoned, a practiced pitch, and everyone nodded. "We'll still have our work cut out for us, but we'll get everything done right. We're moving on up. Oh, and Derek, that reminds me—more exciting news! You're moving."

"What?"

"Yes, all the residences in the Synt are going to be converted into offices for our expanded departments—health and synthetic citizen services, military council, cultural affairs. We'll need a lot of office space, moving the entire government into the building!

Ha! So all residents will need to move outside the building. We'll only keep a skeleton resident staff on hand. My residence. Maybe my assistants. But you, my friend, will be free to have your pick of places on this beautiful island of Manhattan—if we decide to keep calling it that. Ha!"

"Ha!" crowed the Council members.

"Come on, let's toast and I'll introduce you to Pamela here. She's in real estate, and has a number of properties protected from the rioters and with beautiful views—"

Derek shook his head. "This is—a lot to process right now. Maybe tomorrow. For now, I really just want to go—"

"Sure, sure, you can talk to Pam tomorrow. But for now, let's toast!"

Hess sloppily poured a glass for Derek. Everyone else raised their champagne.

"To... living in Syn!" Hess winked, swigging straight from the champagne bottle. Everyone laughed and applauded and drank.

Derek quickly downed his champagne, made his excuses and fled. He got in the elevator, feeling more panicked than when he had thrown himself to the floor, mistaking the champagne cork for a bullet.

It hadn't been a bullet.

It had been a bomb.

CHAPTER 46: ANGELA

THIS IS PROBABLY THE STUPIDEST THING I'LL EVER DO.

Angela hadn't said yes, not yet. When Marilyn had launched into the over-the-top bit of performance art, begging Angela to quit her job and become her "assistant," Angela had simply watched the production without comment. Everything in her revolted at this request, at what it represented; Marilyn, imposing on Angela again. Marilyn, thinking she was the one who had the hard life. Marilyn, still unsatisfied by everything Angela had already done at her behest—befriending her, moving from Boston to New York, becoming a goddamn Syn...

358 BORN IN SYN

But I didn't really augment for Angela. I did it for Leroy. For the movement.

So when Marilyn was taking her final bows, mascara streaming down her cheeks, asking Angela to just please, please, think about moving in with her, Angela said: "I'll think about it."

And then she went to her apartment, to do just that.

Angela still had trouble thinking of her apartment as "home." It was a sleekly renovated Manhattan loft, with high ceilings and vaulted windows, park views, a stainless steel kitchen, and of course, embedded tech in every appliance and Heaven docking stations conveniently located in each room.

It was the sort of place she could never have afforded in her previous life. But with the incorporation of Manhattan as the first entirely synthetic city, all Original inhabitants had been evacuated, and the Synt staff displaced from their Synt residences were each matched with an apartment, brownstone, or freestanding home determined to be the most appropriate to their profession, family structure, and so on. Hess had his team put together a program that ran the variables and generated the housing matches. It was entirely systematic. Angela's loft was, according to the algorithm, perfect for her needs. But like everything else in the synthetic world, even if it met her needs, the gorgeous apartment fell far short of addressing her wants.

Letting herself in, Angela walked straight to the far end of her clean-lined living room. She sat cross-legged on the floor, her back to the wall, positioning herself beside one of the many connection outlets. But she didn't connect her port. She just sat there and closed her eyes. If anyone were watching her, it might look like she was immersed in some sort of zen yoga practice.

But she was practicing something else entirely.

Angela had been tuning in to the fact that she could perceive things that others couldn't. It had taken her some time to know this for sure; soon after her synch, when she heard a constant crackling, like a radio station drifting in and out, she assumed that was a common side effect of augmentation. She thought about mentioning it when she went in for an examination and recalibration, but instinct—the crackling, itself?—told her not to mention it. She did some research instead, and found no evidence of anyone else reporting a similar side effect.

So she started fiddling with the dial. Closing her eyes, focusing her intention, and trying to tune in to the station. It seemed impossible, at first; like anything worth mastering. But gradually, she began cultivating her ability to interpret the ever-present waves of information, washing over everyone and everything but perceptible to Angela in a way that no one else could even imagine.

Her latest trick was sitting beside Heaven docking stations, and rather than plugging in to the outlets, tuning in to everything buzzing below their surface. She could extract information from Heaven, and even from other unplugged but relatively-proximate Syns, without connecting directly to the system. She didn't know why she was given this ability, and whether it was a blessing or a curse, but as soon as she was certain she could control this function and use it under the radar, she'd find a way to weaponize herself on behalf of her son and his movement.

Angela still wasn't entirely certain that she was clandestine enough, but she knew the time had come to make contact—especially if she was about to move in with the Hess family; sending missives from the mouth of the wolf would be even riskier. So she closed her eyes, took a deep breath, and aimed a message toward the encrypted device designated for emergency use. Within an instant, a rudimentary text swam along her closed eyelids.

Meet me at the border.

After exiting her loft, taking a light rail to the western edge of the island, and then recording a few images of herself sitting at a café, reading, Angela shifted into private mode and began walking hurriedly toward the border.

She kept her head down as she walked, not wanting her face spotted by security cameras, and uninterested in the city views. She had spent a decent amount of time in New York City prior to the Big Apple becoming the Big Genetically Modified Apple. It was a very different piece of fruit these days.

The old New York was a place teeming with people, full of life, illuminated by the lights of skyscrapers and flashing billboards and braking cabs. That was before the Original expulsion. Millions of people, forced from their homes by court order. It ripped the city apart. The rioting was so bad, no Synt employees were allowed to leave the premises. The Synthetic Neuroscience Institute of Technology was a fortress in the center of the city, a skyscraper with a base widened by cement walls serving as a barricade, rising several stories high and ending in a tilted row of electrified spikes.

Fort Synt, the employees living within it had jokingly dubbed their building.

Hess assured everyone the cement border wall was temporary. Just a matter of keeping the rabble out, until they were permanently rid of rabble. After a month, the riots had died when after nearly all the Originals were forced out, in part by an army still populated with Original soldiers, following orders. Though given curfews, Synt staffers were allowed to leave the building, go through the courtyard and through the monitored gate of the massive barricade. A year after the expulsion was announced, the newly-renamed Central City was declared a safe, fully incorporated sector.

But the cement walls stayed up in front of the Synt. They would stay up for several more years. Just for safety. Just until the Originals were nearly all extinct.

Though Hess characterized Central City as "the bustling epicenter of the synthetic world," it was barren compared to its past life. In 2014, a few short years before the Singularity, there were eight and a half million people living in New York City. More than a million and a half in Manhattan alone. Forty years later, the same area was populated with six hundred thousand synthetic citizens.

Despite the shiny veneers the synthetic leadership quickly slapped into place, the city felt flat and gaunt. It was not the living, breathing work of art that once it was, although echoes of its former self were everywhere. It had become its own monument, a memorial to itself—although even that effect was ruined by the bright Synt-sponsored signs that sprang up in front of rebel-wrought rubble, jovially proclaiming areas *Under Construction!* and masking the unsightly piles of old Manhattan's collapsed buildings.

The surrounding boroughs were largely empty; they were still transitional sectors, eventually destined for energy or agricultural use, since there was still plenty of room left in Manhattan for residential life. Most transit only ran throughout Manhattan, ending at the various boroughs' borders. Which was fine for Angela's purposes that morning; walking was a less traceable way to travel, anyway.

When she reached the Queensboro Bridge, remarkably intact after all the uprisings, she pulled an olive-colored scarf from her bag. She wrapped it around her neck, high enough to obscure her face. This strategic bit of fashion would, she hoped, protect her twice—masking her identity if anyone happened to be monitoring the Syn bridge and hiding her neck port so any unfriendly Originals on the other side of the bridge would not see her augmented status and take her hostage, which might be time-consuming.

It was a brisk morning, bright and crisp and colder than usual. A strong wind sweeping over the bridge forced Angela to hunch and bring her shoulders up against the gale. She made it across, and then faced her final hurdle: getting through the Syn checkpoint at the edge of the bridge, designed to keep the rebels at bay.

The checkpoint was unmanned on Sundays, a particular convenience of this timing. But unmanned did not mean unmonitored.

To exit the bridge, she would need to get through the automated system. That meant entering a passcode, at the very least. And upon arrival at the edge of the Queensboro, she still had no idea what the code might be.

Reaching the checkpoint, Angela kept her shoulders lifted, head bowed, scarf secured. She was careful to touch nothing, and resisted the urge to look and around and try to determine exactly where the security cameras were. Instead, she stood as close as she could to the shining metallic keypad, as close as she could get without touching, and then she waited. Listened.

For a long, long moment, she was getting nothing. There was a deadly silence at the end of the bridge, on the border of the new world and the old. She told herself to be patient. The information would come. It always started like a humming. But maybe the wind was getting in the way, interrupting the waves, obscuring the channel—

There it is.

Her sharp relief exhaled itself, releasing the breath she did not realize she had been holding. The hum took shape, morphing from a dull hum to a melody before winding itself into lyrics. Words. Numbers. From within the wireless chatter of Heaven, a voice distinguished itself and sang for her. Sang her the letters and numbers that comprised this particular passcode. The code for staff with all-borough access, no red flags.

Angela brought her leather-gloved fingers to the keypad, and entered in a long series of digits, letters, and symbols. The solid steel gate, tall and deep as an old semi-truck, groaned and yawned and separated into two sections, pushing back, and allowing Angela to get off the bridge and in to the unincorporated sector.

Once off the bridge, she hurried to the meeting point—an abandoned gas station just blocks away. The trip had taken exactly as long as anticipated, and unless he had encountered more trouble on his side of things, she knew her arrival should be timed to coincide with his.

*Let him be there, please, God. If you ever did or do or will exist,
let him be there.*

Angela reached the gas station, its pumps and fuel lines ripped
out for use in battles, the skeleton of its convenience store still
standing. The door was shattered, shelves ransacked, but the tinted windows made it a mostly-safe meeting point. Once inside,
away from the shattered door, inhabitants were invisible. He had
assured her that this station was cleared out by the rebels, that it
was a safe meeting place. No cameras. No synthetic technology.
Stepping through the broken doorway, Angela prepared herself
for the worst—but there he was, standing behind the counter.
Like he might ask her if she needed to fill up, or wanted a pack of
cigarettes.

"Ma," Leroy said, his voice breaking, and she ran to him.

For a moment, they simply held each other. All communication since she had joined the Syn world was limited; when it was
possible at all, it was encoded, remote, stilted and cold. She had
not laid eyes on her boy in years. Part of the plan they devised
all those years ago was the importance of convincing the Hesses
she had cut all ties with him, especially as his involvement in the
movement made him a target. As she wrapped her arms around
him, saw him up close, she could see that her boy was a man. A
middle-aged man, gray streaks in his hair. Almost as old now as
she had been when she left him behind, and joined the ranks of
the synthetic citizens.

"Leroy," she whispered, ashamed to find herself so taken aback
by his signs of aging. "You look wonderful."

Leroy chuckled, subconsciously dragging his knuckles across
his chin—where, Angela suddenly noticed, there was a long, jagged scar. "Not as good as you, Ma."

Her shame increased, choking her, as she realized she looked
exactly the damn same as the last time he saw her, more than a
decade ago. She tightened her scarf around her neck like a noose.

"I'm sorry—"

"No," Leroy said, shaking his head. "Don't be sorry. You're right where you need to be. There's a lot of good you can do. For the movement. For all of us."

"Anything," she swore. "Anything."

She meant it, and she was beginning to feel that maybe she really could do anything. After all, she'd managed to convince those around her that the person who mattered most to her meant nothing to her. She'd managed to specialize in languages as her Synt enrichment area because if the rumors of Original resistance bands in other nations proved true, knowing a dozen or more languages might be useful. It also helped her hone the chatter constantly surrounding her. She would do anything and everything for her son, and in her case, "anything and everything" might mean a whole hell of a lot.

"Thanks," Leroy said, and she could still see his little-boy eyes set in his tired, aging face. It melted her heart. "Now, listen. We— Originals, I mean—we're losing this thing. We're about to have to go from being soldiers to just being survivors. Staying out of the way. Staying alive long enough to regroup and… I don't know how much I should be telling you."

"You can trust me," Angela said.

"Can I?" He looked dubious, guilty for doubting her but protective of his people, his loyalties divided. "I know you wouldn't intentionally share anything, but with the—the way you're all connected—"

"I have some control," Angela assured him. "It's a protected right. 'Limited autonomy.'"

"Yeah, sounds great," Leroy said. "Limited autonomy. God bless the synthetic states of America. Or what are you calling it? The Incorporated Sectors?"

"*They* are calling it that, Leroy," Angela said. "*They*. I'm not one of them."

She looked at her son, and thought of him how he was, before. Before the move, the synch, the Singularity. When he was a political science student at Northwestern, marching in rallies to protest the early cyborganics initiatives. He had still been so young, so idealistic. The man who stood before her was strong, hardened, exhausted. As muscular as he was, he was also thin. An ancient maternal admonition, *you're not eating enough*, played over and over again in her mind, but she did not speak the words aloud.

"So tell me how we're going to do this," her son said.

"I have... ways of getting around the interconnected system," Angela said carefully, not sure she could provide a better explanation. "I think I can figure out a way to get messages your way. We'll come up with extra layers of security, encryption, code words—"

"Some of that, we already have," Leroy confirmed.

"And whenever there is information—about other rebel movements, or glitches in the Syn systems, chinks in their armor, new chemicals in the water—"

"The chemicals in the water," Leroy said bitterly. "Sterilizing us, like we're animals..."

"Leroy," Angela said quickly, knowing their time was limited. "You're right. It's bad and getting worse. But look—I have a unique opportunity. It's why we needed to meet now, today. I've been working for years at the Synt, and my position there is secure. I get alerts before the general public, certainly before you would get wind of anything. But I was made an offer yesterday. I can leave my job at the Synt ... and work in the Hess home."

"Felix Hess?"

"Yes."

"You can work in their home. Have direct access to the leader of the Syn world."

"Yes."

"How soon could an assassination be planned?"

Angela stared at her son. Was this the baby she had nursed, the little boy she had raised? A weary soldier, staring at her and asking her how quickly she thought she might be able to murder her friend's husband?

"I wasn't.... I wasn't thinking about an assassination. I was thinking about access. Living in the home of the most powerful man in the universe, being able to access the network but also have insight beyond the office and laboratory walls... I think that could prove useful."

"More useful than killing him?"

"Potentially. Yes."

Leroy looked unconvinced. "How so?"

"He's the leader, but it's not as if—look, even with old-world terrorist organizations, when we took out one leader, another stepped up. They're like the Hydra, right? Cut off one head, two grow back. Hess is at the top, and there's only a few right up in there with him, the funders who greased the wheels for all of this, lower-profile senior staff like Derek Abelson—"

"Derek Abelson," Leroy repeated, memorizing the name.

"The point is, just killing Hess wouldn't end anything."

"I don't think we should *just* kill Hess. We have to take down the whole system."

"See, son, *there*." Angela said approvingly but sternly, donning the mother-hat she had so missed wearing. "*There* is where your head needs to be. Taking down the system. Long-term. And I think you should let me see what I can learn, share, provide you with so that you and yours are armed with information and insights that will go a lot farther than taking down one man."

"Hess is more than just one man."

"No," Angela said firmly. "He really isn't."

"Take the job in the Hess house," Leroy said, relenting. "Let's set up a check-in system. I don't want to be your only point person. You'll need multiple contacts within my network—"

"Agreed," Angela said. "But they can't know who I am. And I shouldn't know their real names, either. Double blind. Set up code names, and don't give me anything that could be easily unraveled about your whereabouts or plans."

"Code names, huh?" He chuckled, which made her ache. She was glad to see her boy had the sort of humor that even the end of the world couldn't kill. "Like James Bond shit?"

"More like *Mission Impossible*," she corrected, and he smiled. She wondered if he, too, was remembering their life together in that little two-bedroom apartment in Cambridge. When he was a teenager and she was his mother; when she was running numbers and he was running track, and the world was simpler and smaller.

"So we're doing this?"

"We're doing this," she said. "I'll move in with the monster. I'll find out what I can find out. I'll be in touch." She heaved a huge breath, looking at him, not wanting him out of her sight, now or ever again, then forced herself to say: "I should go."

"I know," he said, hugging her. "Be safe, Ma."

"You be safe. I love you, baby."

"I love you, too."

As soon as they separated, Angela felt colder, her metallic components freezing her down to her very soul. She barely remembered her journey back to her apartment, crossing the bridge, riding the train, walking the under-populated streets. The next night, she invited Marilyn over.

Marilyn arrived wearing a soft pink cashmere sweater and an excessive amount of pink blush. She looked nervous, almost shy, as she handed an expensive bottle of Chablis to Angela.

"Thank you for having me over, Angela. Your new place really is lovely."

"It is," Angela agreed, gesturing for Marilyn to sit at the table set for two. "But I guess it's good that I'm not too settled in here just yet, since I'll be moving again at the end of the month."

Marilyn's face lit up. "Does that mean...?"

"Gave my two weeks' notice this morning," Angela said, a forced lightness in her voice, trying to make it seem as if she were excited to be moving in with Marilyn. Like it would be one non-stop slumber party. "You sure you're really ready to have another woman in the house?"

"Oh, Angela! That's just wonderful!" Marilyn said, hand going to her heart. "I'm almost afraid to ask, but...but... can I ask what made the decision for you?"

Angela bit her lip, a move she'd practiced in the mirror earlier, and gave the response she had readied for just this question: "You were right, Marilyn. My life is here. I'm not in touch with my son, and the only real family I have now is... you."

Angela watched the predictable tears swim in Marilyn's eyes at this; she knew her well enough to be able to tell the woman exactly what she wanted to hear.

You come first. You are the priority. You really do deserve to get your way.

"I feel the same way, Angela. Exactly the same. Oh, this is perfect. So, so wonderful. There's a little room off the back of our quarters, like a little maids—I mean like a mother-in-law suite sort of thing. Oh! I'm just so glad. You'll be around all the time, and it will just—it will just feel right, you know?"

Try and tell me it's a progressive new world when the black lady ends up in the maid's quarters again? You're real good with the bull, Marilyn, but I thought even you wouldn't be dumb enough to try to paint a pretty picture with this shit.

Recovering enough to form a safer reply, Angela aimed a smile at her new boss.

"Just think of me as your shadow."

CHAPTER 47: RUTH

R UTH DIDN'T LIKE BEING A PAWN in someone else's game, nor did she like toying with other people. The mission she was about to undertake made her feel as if she would be both played and player, which curdled her stomach.

This move should have been months in development, but instead it was pulled together in days. It was ambitious and dangerous, but that was not what bothered her. She was fine with the risk. But the risqué—*that* was the part of this particular plan that made her so uneasy.

The unorthodox plan had come together after Leroy brought back news from his informant. News about a man named Derek Abelson. Leroy had been with Ruth's tribe for several years now;

his merged with hers when both were dwindling in number. His Midwestern rebels and her East Coast refugees had quickly become family. She trusted Leroy. But she remained suspicious of Leroy's informant. Whoever the guy was, he'd certainly provided the best intelligence they'd ever had regarding the inner workings of the Syn center. But Leroy still wouldn't reveal the identity of his informant. And after being burned so many times in the past, the Drone Massacre still tormenting her nightly, Ruth didn't like being kept in the dark.

There had been a concession, recently; while at first Leroy was the only point of contact for his informant, now several people—Ruth included—were designated as points of contact. The clandestine network, Leroy called it. They all had small rigged cell phones, which could receive encrypted messages from the insider-informant. But no one knows who the informant actually was; no one but Leroy, whose lips were sealed.

The informant claimed to be able to get protected information from the Syn wireless networks, without being detected. Though Leroy assured them that everything his informant did was discreet, Ruth still didn't trust any communications utilizing synthetic technology.

"We have to go after Abelson—he's second-in-command," Leroy said, making the case for this mission. "Works directly with Hess. Tries to stay out of the spotlight, but he's been there since the beginning. He was on the first cyborganics team—your brother's people, Howard."

That triggered a memory in Howard, enabling him to verify the initial intelligence.

"Abelson, you said?"

"Yeah," Leroy confirmed. "Derek Abelson."

"I met him. Years ago. He was a doctoral student… Didn't realize he was still around."

"That's the guy," Leroy said, nodding. "Goes all the way back to the Fell days. He was in the room when Nathan attempted the augmentation. And apparently, he's obsessed with the Fells. Nathan, in particular—but he's a big ol' fanboy when it comes to all of you people. He's working on a book. And he's a little bit stuck on the chapter about you."

He was looking at Ruth when he said that.

"About me?"

"You and Rachel." Leroy nodded. "He doesn't know what happened to the Fell girls—the mysterious twin babies Nathan lost touch with—*you*. Can't finish the book. It's driving him crazy, apparently."

"So?"

"So I think we can lure him out of his safe zone, if we let some information trickle in about your whereabouts. I think he would venture out to find you, and you can take him hostage. Getting someone like that, it will send a strong message—hurt their morale, give us a real bargaining chip."

"And I have to be the one to lure him out."

"Yes. You're his holy grail, Ruth. The trick will be tipping him off to your existence, without alerting any other Syns to your whereabouts."

Ruth had managed to avoid Syn detection for years. Between the massive ransom out on her, and her lingering post-traumatic stress following the most traumatic ambushes of the uprisings, she finally stopped petitioning to be allowed to venture out on the offensive. She stayed behind to cover defense. But every time one of her people was wounded or killed while Ruth stayed behind, her guilt and trauma metastasized—so she didn't dismiss this crazy new mission out of hand. If the only one at risk was her, there was an appeal to that.

"Assuming I could... draw him out. How would I capture him?"

"I don't think you would have to capture him," Leroy said. "I think he would go willingly, wherever you asked him to go. You're... you know... the incentive."

"Incentive?" Ruth spat. "You mean bait?"

"I only mean that if he is attracted to you, that's an asset. We can't overlook any advantage we might have. It could use a, y'know, delicate touch, and maybe—"

"I throw hand grenades," Ruth growled. "I don't give hand jobs."

"I didn't mean—" Leroy said, the consequences of his implications hitting him all at once, rendering him unable to backpedal fast enough.

"What are we talking about?" Asked Howard Fell.

Everyone stopped, staring at their leader. They were all seated inside their makeshift community meeting room, a bland beige cafeteria inside a squat old office building, ripe with asbestos and shuttered long before the Singularity. Howard had risen from his battered plastic chair, unsteady on his feet.

"Uncle Howard?" Ruth asked, concern melting her anger.

"Why didn't we..." Howard said, not aiming his question at anyone. His eyes were cloudy, distant. "Why didn't I...?"

Eyes still elsewhere, fixated on something or someone unseen, the great Original leader wandered out of the room. All conversation about abduction ceased. Sophie hurried out after her husband. Everyone else gaped open-mouthed at Ruth, awaiting explanation.

"I—I've never seen him like that."

"Ruth, if you're protecting him—" Helena began, but Ruth shook her head.

"No. No. Sophie mentioned—just recently—that Uncle Howard had one incident. One. Where he seemed to just sort of—get confused about where he was. Just for a minute. Just... just like this, I suppose. But she said it wasn't any sort of regular—"

Howard and Sophie re-entered the old cafeteria, arms linked, as if nothing had happened. Howard took his place at the table again.

"Where were we?" He asked, eyes clear, voice steady.

Ruth looked at Leroy, his eyes reflecting her own thoughts. Howard's days as leader of the movement were numbered. Their resources were limited, their options few; these were the very last days of the resistance, unless something drastic happened. A miracle.

Like abducting a top Syn official.

"I'll do it," Ruth said, snapping the focus away from Howard and back to the proposed mission.

"Good," Leroy said. "Excellent. I'll let my contact know, we'll get Derek's attention—"

"How will you 'get his attention'?" Helena asked, and Ruth wondered if the old woman saw herself as Howard's successor. Helena was sharp, but only ten years younger than Howard. Not exactly fresh blood.

"A handwritten note," Leroy said. "You'll write a note, Ruth, and my contact can get it directly to Abelson. No electronic footprint."

"That will take days."

"A day or two."

"Why will he believe it's from me?" Ruth asked.

Leroy gave her a tight smile. "It'll have your fingerprints on it. Plus I bet he'll run a handwriting analysis. Everything is stored in their Heaven database. He'll compare the letter against, I don't know, whatever the last test you took in school, and everything else you ever wrote pre-Singularity, and verify it's you."

"And that won't tip anyone off, when he runs that analysis?"

"My informant says he's very careful about his book, his research into the Fells," Leroy said. "Doesn't want anyone to know about it. It's a secret. I'm sure he'd be careful, looking you up. He'd want you to be his own find—he'd want you all to himself."

"If his book is a secret, how the hell does your informant know about it?"

"My contact—has ways," Leroy said, cagey. "Trust me."

"It's not you I mistrust," Ruth said. A half-truth: she half-trusted him.

"Well," Jonah Harper said, squinting his failing eyes, scratching his beard and looking very much like his nephew Gregory, the brother-in-law Ruth missed daily. "Let's do it, then."

"All right, if we're going to do it…" Helena said, before sprinting from the cafeteria, surprisingly spry. They all heard her loudly rummaging around in one of the adjacent rooms. A moment later, she returned triumphantly with a faded yellow legal pad and a ballpoint pen.

Ruth took the legal pad and sat at the table, staring at it. She felt suddenly self-conscious, with everyone watching her. Not that this was a private note, but it felt oddly intimate to consider writing someone a handwritten message. Like passing a note to a schoolmate.

I like you. Do you like me?

Ruth has also not wielded a pen much in her adult life. She worried her penmanship was sloppy—just like in her student days, come to think of it. Maybe that'd help match it. She popped the plastic cap off the ballpoint, held the pen like a needle above the paper, then stitched together a brief and awkward missive to lure Derek Abelson to her.

> *Mr. Abelson: This letter is for your eyes alone.*
> *Most people assume I'm dead. If they figure out*
> *I'm not, well, then soon I WILL be dead. I un-*
> *derstand you have an interest in my family, and I*
> *would like to speak with you. If this is of interest*

Here she stopped, uncertain where to tell him to meet her. It would have to be outside Central City, but she was sure someone as high up as him could find a way to slip unnoticed from his heavily monitored abode. She didn't want to bring him anywhere near where her people were currently camping, in the squat old office building in rural Connecticut.

"Somewhere in between," she muttered aloud. "A day's journey for each…"

"New Rochelle," Jonah suggested. Though his untreated macular degeneration had rendered him almost completely blind by now, he had once been a trucker and knew all the routes and spaces between states better than any of them. Closing his eyes, he still saw all the creased and well-worn maps stretching out before him. "A long day's walk from here, but a day's walk. For you, anyhow, Ruth. Might take Helena better part of a week…"

He was rewarded with the grunt and shin-kick he'd been fishing for, and everyone smiled at the momentary levity.

"All right," Ruth said, bringing them back, as everyone nodded. "New Rochelle. How do I tell him exactly where, and exactly when…?"

Helena started giggling, a sound so out of place that it made everyone jump. Ruth stared at the aging woman, her former neighbor and sometimes-babysitter, a woman known for her calm and reason. She was laughing so hard that her eyes were beginning to moisten.

"New Rochelle," she gasped. "New Rochelle! That's where Norman Rockwell used to live. *Norman Rockwell!* And now it probably hasn't had a real old-fashioned human being living there in decades. I mean, come on! Our Ruthie is going to meet a founding father of the Syn world, destroyer of our once-great nation, to kick his ass right in the heart of Americana… *Norman damn Rockwell!* It's too much. Ahahahaha!"

Sophie, arm still linked through Howard's, looked stricken. Ruth reckoned her aunt was wondering if she might be the only remaining mentally-functional senior citizen in the group. Staring at the howling Helena, Ruth saw the real picture of lives spent too long in hunger and desperation; too long at war. They were

coming apart at the seams, this collection of desperate aging soldiers. They were drowning in scars unable to heal, ill-conceived
hail-Mary strategies, and unsettling peals of misplaced laughter.

Ruth returned to the letter.

> *Mr. Abelson: This letter is for your eyes alone.*
> *Most people assume I'm dead. If they figure out I'm*
> *not, well, then soon I WILL be dead. I understand*
> *you have an interest in my family, and I would like*
> *to speak with you.* ~~*If this is of interest*~~ *I will be wait-*
> *ing Saturday. Evening Post. Fresh Lady. —RF*

"Will he figure this out?" she asked dubiously after reading
it aloud. The clue about where to meet was flat out stupid. She
could come up with something cleverer, if given just a little more
time. But time was too expensive for the impoverished rebels, and
anyway, why should Ruth care if this Syn found her clever?

"He'll figure it out," Leroy said. "He's supposed to be a genius."

"I'm elected to outwit the genius," Ruth said glumly. "Pickings
must be slim."

But she folded the letter and handed it unceremoniously to
Leroy. He nodded, and carefully pocketed the note.

"Make a plan while I get this note to Abelson," Leroy said.
"You have three days before you need to be in New Rochelle."

So Leroy left. And Ruth and others began to develop a plan—
although "plan" felt like an awfully generous term for the half-assed ideas they pieced together before Ruth had to start hiking to
Rockwell's old stomping grounds.

Once home to immigrants and artists and college students,
New Rochelle was now a ghost town. Upon arrival, Ruth was un-
surprised to find that the haunted hamlet had been vandalized,
damaged and abandoned. Another casualty of augmentation.

She walked the streets alone, unsettled by the silence. She had never noticed the omnipresence of sound—traffic, buzzing street-lights, the thousand small instruments forming a symphony of daily background noise—until it was abruptly cut off.

Standing in front of a cottage that once belonged to Norman Rockwell, the entire scenario facing her felt even more surreal.

All set to kidnap someone. If he shows up to be kidnapped like a good abductee.

She'd had no update from Leroy since he left. No way of even knowing if his leg of the mission had been successful. Had the message been delivered? Had the genius been smart enough to decipher her meetup instructions—and stupid enough not to realize it was a trap?

"Ruth?"

Hand flying to the knife at her hip, Ruth looked up the street, empty moments earlier. There, offset by the purple-orange clouds crowding out the setting sun, was a man with messy hair the color of sand and wire-rimmed glasses. He stared at her with open wonder.

"Dr. Abelson," she said.

"It really is you..."

Ruth's fingers were still wrapped around the hilt of her knife. She forced a smile, as if this were some perfectly normal old-world blind date and not the prelude to an abduction. She felt ill at ease, wondered what she should do with her hands. She worried that she was walking funny as she took a few steps toward the man. She inclined her head toward the cottage behind her, remarkably intact, perhaps protected by someone with a fondness for the man who once lived there, painting pictures of a now-extinguished world.

"You got my message," Ruth said, her voice unnatural in her own ears.

"Yes. Norman Rockwell's cottage in New Rochelle. I just... wow."

"Are you in… the privacy-mode?"

"Private mode—I mean, er, yes, I am," the man said quickly, shoving his thin glasses up the bridge of his narrow nose. "Have been since I left home. And I set up a program that will run the whole time I'm gone, pulling from images of my past few days. It'll look like I'm there, if anyone checks in on me. Handy little app I came up with recently."

Almost none of that meant anything to Ruth, but she nodded. She opened the unlocked door to the cottage, and smiled again at the Syn man, hoping she looked friendly, and not like a dog baring its teeth.

"Why don't we go inside?"

CHAPTER 48: HOWARD

HOWARD FELL STROKED HIS WIFE SOPHIE'S face, no longer fresh and unlined as in their youth, but still lovely to the touch. Soft and papery thin. She was still so very beautiful. More than beautiful; precious. *Beyond rubies,* he thought, recalling an old psalm. *Beyond rubies.*

Sophie, keeper of his secrets, guardian of his heart. She was always the one to push him, challenge him, expect more of him. Start the movement, lead a rebellion—without Sophie, none of it would have been possible. He got the credit, but she got the job done.

Lately, when he slipped, she covered for him. He was self-aware enough to recognize the edge of dementia creeping in, but for the most part he was still himself. And Sophie was there to ensure that when he wandered off the path, there was always someone to pull him back on track.

Still sharp as a tack, Sophie.

He wished he could get her new glasses. In the old days, she wore contacts. He used to find it so weird when she fished around in her eyes for the invisible little slips of glass. But it had been years since she had been afforded the luxury of contact lenses. She wore glasses these days, a visible reminder for him of both his wife's vision impairment and the downfall of society. But after awhile, he got used to the glasses. (The end of civilization as he knew it, he still hadn't quite absorbed.) The specs were rusted and bent now, and the prescription barely aided her at all.

A visit to the optometrist. What an odd luxury to suddenly miss.

A nice pair of corrective, un-cracked glasses was just one of the many things Howard Fell wanted to bestow upon his loyal wife. A real bed was another. The makeshift cot on the floor of an office building, a refugee base camp shared with dozens of other nomads—this was not the retirement plan he had pictured for them, when he and the gregarious Sophie Eisen had walked down the aisle. Had he known then the weight of the vows he was asking her to take…

She probably would have married him anyway. He wouldn't have been able to talk her out of it. Like Howard, Sophie knew that life's greatest treasures and assets were often also their greatest liabilities and burdens. This was certainly true for Howard; there was almost nothing he adored without ambivalence: His brother. His children and his adopted daughters, his brother's children—all of whom he loved, and all of whose lives he had put at risk. His own mind.

He felt a familiar cloak of guilt settle around his shoulders. He should have put his mighty intellect to better use—to more proactive, combative use, earlier and more relentlessly. He should have been covert and conniving, joined his brother's research team, so that he would have been in place to dismantle the bomb Nathan developed. There was no greater guilt than the near-certain knowledge that, with just a little more effort, one could have saved the world.

Howard's mind contracted, yawning into a momentary blip of nothingness, stretching across the waiting abyss.

And then he was back, trembling, the memory of the gaping expanse of nothingness still hovering at the back of his mind. He forced himself to calm, to focus, to count the blessings still surrounding him.

My people. My children. My brave Ruth, out to save us still. My Sophie. My Sophie…

He kissed her cheek, dragging his rough snowy beard gently across her jawline. This usually woke her, causing her mouth to twitch and curve, lips moving down and then up as the bristles tickled her. Then she'd open her eyes, squinting and slow, blinking and readjusting until her gaze finally found his. That's when she'd whisper good morning, and start asking him about his dreams or nightmares. But this morning, her mouth stayed still; her eyes remained shut.

"Sophie?" Howard whispered. He propped himself up on shaking elbows, knowing something he did not want to know. He called her name again, louder, his old voice cracking like a young boy's. "Sophie!"

Sharp as a tack, but wearier than she had let on, his Sophie had somehow slipped away from him.

His reeling mind replayed a million moments—Sophie, across the room, laughing at someone else's joke; Sophie, walking toward him in that gauzy gown on their wedding day; bringing their first-born into the world; chasing after their adopted toddlers; dashing out the door to work; sobbing at the Singularity; grimly opening their home for movement meetings; leaving their home behind;

gripping his hand, always, always there. But now she had exited the world as graciously as she had moved through it, not troubling him with a long goodbye.

All breath gone, all vows kept.

CHAPTER 49: DEREK

WHEN HE FIRST SAW RUTH FELL, she seemed an apparition. When he called out her name, she held so still that she almost seemed to flicker and disappear entirely. Derek was momentarily concerned that he might be having some sort of prolonged delusion, wandering around in a fugue state.

Are fugue states something my synthetic system would override?

(He made a Mental Note to add "fugue state" to his list of phenomena to study. Mental Notes was one of his favorite new synthetic applications, a handy little program he developed earlier this year. Handy for writers, teachers, almost everyone; but as with most of his apps, he went ahead and just kept it to himself.)

He considered pinching himself, but instead just stared at her, because if he were in the midst of some hallucination, he wasn't sure he wanted to end it. Assuming that she was not a specter, but indeed a flesh and blood figure, there was no mistaking her identity.

Standing in front of Norman Rockwell's getaway cottage—
thank God he'd guessed right on that ridiculous clue—Derek
knew that ghost or no, this woman could be no one but Ruth Fell.
He had seen so many pictures of her as a child, as well as every
single one of the small handful of images of her as a young woman. She was in her thirties now—forty, on her next birthday. She
and her twin, both entering their next decade. Assuming her twin,
too, was still above ground.

I should ask her about Rachel...

(Another Mental Note.)

Yes. He should ask her about Rachel, and Howard, and all of
the other characters in the world of Nathan Fell. But this character, the strong and strange and possibly dangerous daughter Ruth,
was taking up too much of his attention for him to think about
anything else for long.

She was lithe and muscular, alert and alive. Her hair was short,
cut unevenly, probably with a knife-blade. But it was flattering,
falling haphazardly but nicely framing her face, calling attention
to her high cheekbones. When she invited him to join her inside
the cottage, he nearly tripped over himself hurrying inside. After
entering the abode, he found it difficult to collect his wits. Or say
anything even remotely clever. Or say anything at all.

"So," she said, after sweeping the room, checking for cameras
or booby traps or whatever else might threaten. "You worked with
my father."

"Yes. He was a great man," Derek blurted immediately.

Her eyes flashed at this—he was pretty sure, anyway; the
cottage was dark, save the moonlight sneaking in through wide
cracks in the shuttered windows.

"I see. And you are writing a book about him? About my family?"

How could she know that?

He had kept this hidden even from Hess, encrypting his research and writing in security so deep no Syn could unravel it, let
alone an Original. There's no way this woman could know about
his book project.

Unless she really is a ghost. Or fugue state hallucination. Corner of my own mind.

"Yes," he whispered to the possibly-imaginary Ruth. "I was stuck on… you, actually. You and your sister, but mostly you. Because you're the one who made a lot of noise and then disappeared."

"Made a lot of noise?"

"You bombed the old Synthetic Neuroscience Institute of Technology."

"So they say."

"You planted the bomb right where your father's office was."

"Did I?"

"You did," he said confidently, having reviewed every report available on the incident, and several that even he should not have been able to access. He'd studied it from every angle. Everything discernible from evidence—but not the emotion behind the actions. "I want to ask you about that. There's so much I want to ask you, I have so many questions…"

He trailed off, a thousand questions jockeying for position in his mind, creating such a cacophony he couldn't select a single thought. He stared at Ruth, attempting to focus, but the more he looked at her the blurrier everything got. It really did seem as if he'd conjured her into being.

"You feel as if you conjured me?"

Derek took a step back, startled. He never believed in psychic phenomena, always wrote it off before and after the Singularity as quack science, but he made another Mental Note to take a vested interest in it. Starting immediately. And also to research whether or not psychedelics done half-heartedly decades ago could still swim around synthetic systems.

"Because I should remind you," she said, sidling up to him, leaning in closer and closer, so close he could smell her; her scent was woodsy-sweet, like early autumn. "I am not here because you summoned me. You are here because *I* summoned *you*."

And just like that, she gave him a hard shove, knocking him off balance. Before he knew it she had twisted a thick rope around his wrists, binding his hands behind his back.

"What do you want?" Derek asked, quickly recalculating his circumstances.

"First, swear you'll stay in the privacy modality."

"Private mode." He automatically corrected her, then realized how stupid that was. She had the upper hand. His were—well—tied. "And what if I don't?"

She gave a sharp tug of his bound wrists, and he whimpered.

"We each have our own strengths. Is yours a high threshold for pain, Dr. Abelson?"

"No," Derek said, panting, already drenched in panicky flop-sweat. Shit. This was going terribly. "No. I just—all right. I'll stay in private mode. Is this… is this about your father?"

"Not everything is about my father," she growled, tugging again at his restraints.

Derek winced. "Then… what?"

"I understand that you like to keep a low profile," she said.

"That's right."

"You let Hess take the spotlight. But without you, there would be no synthetic society."

"Without your *father*—"

She leaped forward, slamming her hand over his mouth and shoving him against a wall. Her voice was a low growl through gritted teeth.

"Mention my father one more time and you'll regret it."

He already regretted it.

From behind her hand, he nodded, yes, he understood, no more mentioning her father. He nodded so hard that his head knocked into the wall behind him. She released him as quickly as she had grabbed him, putting distance between them again. He stared at her, terrified, fascinated, and for the first time in years—really, truly interested in what might come next.

"Now," said his captor, unsheathing her knife. "Let's start talking."

CHAPTER 50: FELIX

SOMETHING WAS UP WITH ABELSON. It was not unusual for the horny little hermit to disappear for days on end, but when Monday morning came and Derek did not show up for their sole and only mandatory weekly appointment, Hess knew something was wrong.

He sent Derek a message. No response. He sent one marked urgent. Still nothing. No response for two days now. No one jerks off *that* much. So Hess pulled Abelson's files to check his memory logs for the past two days. Nothing out of the ordinary; some long stretches of time spent in private mode, as per usual; time spent in the lab, time preparing meals, poring over reports, strolling in the park. But something seemed off.

Hess went back to one of the logged memories: Derek in the lab, checking the results on a skin growing-and-grafting project. Hess checked the time stamp: *Sunday, 6:03:11 PM.*

Double checking his own memory log, Hess pulled up a file from the same time code.

Sunday, 6:03:11 PM.

He, Felix Hess, had been in the lab at six o'clock on Sunday evening, and Derek Abelson had been nowhere in sight. Somehow, the perv had uploaded a manufactured memory. The grudging admiration Hess felt at the innovation was swiftly swallowed up by a wave of suspicious rage.

Where the hell is that bastard, and what is he doing?

CHAPTER 51: RUTH

AFTER TWO DAYS TOGETHER, Ruth had learned a lot about Derek Abelson. She also learned a lot *from* Derek Abelson. To her incredible relief, the man had proven to be the most willing captive-informant in the history of the universe. He didn't like pain. But mostly, as it turned out, he didn't like Felix Hess.

Over the past two days, Ruth had gone from captor to confessor as Derek shared more and more information about the synthetic world. It was as if he had been waiting to pour out his soul to one who might absolve him of his many sins—or, as he wryly joked, his many Syns.

She learned that Derek was quite young when he began working with her father and Hess. He was as smart as they had been. But he never shared their drive. He could complete any task they gave him, but he had no appetite for fame, power, or competition. So almost against his own will he was dragged along into the new world, a barely-willing accomplice in its creation.

He underwent his own augmentation reluctantly, fearing something might go wrong, and fearing almost as much that nothing would and his life would stretch out before him—a life he might not want. Which was exactly the life he wound up with: endless, pointless, but less frightening than any alternative option.

Ruth's travel bag had been crammed with enough salvaged canned goods for several days, a large bottle of triple-boiled water, a small pot for boiling more, and the yellow legal pad Helena had procured. Two days in, the food was running low, the water supply had been replenished, and the pad was full of notes. The first few pages of transcription were in Ruth's scrawling hand. But in an unusual move, after one long day of watching Ruth's painstaking penmanship, her prisoner politely offered to take notes for her as he talked.

"I won't try anything," he said. "I promise. But please, you've gotta let me take over the writing. It'll be easier on both of us."

He was a gentler man than Ruth had expected. Everyone in her life had let go of gentleness, foregone softness. Even sweet-natured Rachel spoke abruptly and moved decisively. Derek chose his words carefully, moved deliberately, and had no armor. His voice was unhurried and smooth, his hands even smoother. Ruth had never seen such clean, clipped fingernails. She had to keep reminding herself that he was her prisoner, and that although he required her attention, she should not pay him the wrong kind of attention. She should not be honing in so much on the details of him. His smooth hands. His sandy straight hair, always falling in his eyes. The way he brushed the hair off his delicate glasses, a practiced move.

She forced herself to look from his straw-like hair to the nape of his neck, where the cold metal port sat. The solid little reminder that he was on the other side of the fence. He was a Syn.

A powerfully-positioned one, if not a power-hungry one. He'd worked with her damned father. He was her enemy. Focusing on the port helped her clarify her mission, and also made her ask aloud:

"Do you need to be—plugged in, at some point?"

Derek rubbed at the negligible amount of scruff on his chin, an almost embarrassing lack of growth after nearly three days without a razor.

"We mostly 'plug in' to share information, so it's to your advantage that I not plug in. But yes, at some point, I need to recharge—whether through securing my port to an access point, or firing up my portable charger."

He patted his pocket.

Stupid, Ruth!

How had she not patted him down, seized anything on his person? It'd been years since she watched a cop show on television. She'd never held anyone hostage before. A rookie mistake—and yet a mistake that somehow hadn't cost her. He had not yet used this charger-device, and now was disclosing it. Still, she should have known better.

"What does re-charging entail?"

He shrugged. "It's like any old electronic device—cell phone, radio. Our synthetic components hold a certain amount of energy, for a certain amount of time, with variation depending on our model, how much organic energy we create or expend... Recharging just refreshes the 'battery' part of our synthetic systems."

"And if you go too long without charging? You run down your battery, basically?"

"Yes. Our synthetic system starts to shut down."

"How long can you last without it?"

"We've run tests. It varies. I think we're already more reliant on our components than we should be. Hess wants to see us go full-robot." Derek wrote that down on the legal pad. *Full robot.* He underlined it and started doodling a boxy little cartoon of a robot.

"How long?"

"How long before Hess starts taking people full-robot?"

"I meant how long before you will begin feeling the effects of not recharging. But I'd like both questions answered."

"Hess is already working on getting us closer to being more machine than man. There are programs underway that will allow solar recharging, installing illumination systems so that in the event of a blackout or whatever we can basically *be* flashlights, automatic system alerts so if we have a systems failure or we're off the radar too long, tracking devices will be triggered to alert Heaven to our exact location and needs—don't worry, we're not quite there yet. The tracking systems, we have, but they're not automatically triggered yet. I've disabled my internal GPS. No one will know where I am unless I want them to. And Ruth—I don't want them to."

He looked up from his doodle, his gaze intense. He wanted to stay with her. He wanted—

No. Stop it.

"How long before you will feel the effects?" She asked coldly, clinging fast to her rapidly dissolving resolve.

"I'm feeling some of them. Headache. Moving a little slower, since some of my organic energy is being used to keep the synthetic stuff firing. Nothing terrible. Another day or two, well. I might start showing my age."

She had forgotten that she was two decades younger than him, by natural accounting. He had shared already that he was synched at thirty-two, making him appear younger than she. But that was years ago. He was over fifty, in actual-years. But he appeared younger than she, without a wrinkle or a streak of gray. That should lessen her attraction to him.

It didn't.

"Then I think it is time I presented you with a choice," Ruth said.

"A choice?"

"Yes." She took the legal pad from him, tucking it into her pack. "I've collected as much information as I can safely get from you before search teams find us, or you need to recharge, or my people fear that I am dead... and so I'm supposed to present you with two options."

He paled. "Is one of them death?"

Her mouth twitched. "All right. Three options."

"Oh. Cool. Let's hear the first two," Derek said, swallowing a nervous smile.

"You can either be held hostage, for ransom, and we will see what your people are willing to yield to us to recover you," Ruth said. "Or you can be freed, and become an informant for us. Go back to your world, your laboratories, and send information our way through secured transmissions and set appointments for sensitive in-person conveyance."

"Option A, hostage," he mused, weighing the options. "Option B, rat. Lab rat, really. Like, literally, ratting out the other guys in the lab...I mean, the poetry alone makes Option B more appealing, now, doesn't it?"

"Well, it's not exactly—"

"Option B," he said, without hesitation or further jokes. "I choose to be a rat. But only if it means that you'll be the one I meet up with when it's time for the info-exchange. And only if you'll tell me more of your story."

"I... all right," she nodded, managing to stay her tongue from expressing her gladness at this choice, and the caveats that came with it. Then an older, wiser side of her took over again: "But how do I know that I—we can trust you? Our only piece of insurance is, of course, all of this information—written in your own hand, remember—which our other informants can easily slip to your authorities."

"Yeah, that wouldn't go well for me," Derek said, almost amiably. Then his eyes narrowed. "But you can also trust me because there is no one I hate more than Dr. Felix Hess. Look, I'm not confrontational. Live and let live, right? But if I have the chance to make his life harder, to maybe even someday dismantle everything he got us all to help him build—I'm in, Ruth. I hate him. I hate him as much as... as much as you hate your father. More, even. I hate the world he made me help him build. I want out. Ruth, I swear, I am your willing accomplice, and whatever you want me to do—"

As he talked Ruth's resolve was wavering, and then it was gone. Heart stammering, she dropped her pack and kissed Derek Abelson, hard, on the mouth.

CHAPTER 52: DEREK

DEREK OPENED HIS EYES, slowly re-orienting himself. He couldn't remember the last time he slept so well—not plugged in, not in a bed, and yet resting more deeply than he had in years. His past few days had been unexpected, terrifying, exhilarating, life-changing. Probably not how most abductees or prisoners of war or whatever he was would describe their experience.

He looked down at the infamous Ruth Fell, lying in his arms and looking nothing at all like a hardened and dangerous rebel. Her eyes were closed, and her pixie-small head rested comfortably on his slim, bare chest. She shivered slightly; the floor of the cottage was cold, and they had no blankets. He held her tighter, wanting to warm her, wanting to keep her. He also knew there was one more thing he had to tell her, before she returned to her people and he returned to his world to start spying on behalf of the Originals. If he didn't tell her now, she would not forgive him later.

"Mmm," she murmured, nuzzling further into him, still asleep. She was so much softer and more vulnerable this way, with her defenses down and the gentleness of her so evident. Though he has only known her for a handful of days, he knew she wouldn't like being seen in this light. This was not the cultivated image of a warrior woman she had honed and hardened. He was privy to something special, something rarely beheld. Ruth, at rest.

He didn't want this sweet moment to end, but he knew what he had to do. One final confession.

"Ruth, wake up," he said. "I'm sorry, but there's something—there's something I have to tell you."

"What…" Her eyes opened slowly, then closed, and for a moment she was still. Then they snapped open with electric speed. Taking in her surroundings—his body, the floor, the lack of clothes—her eyes widened in a sudden panic. She pulled away from him, grabbing for her clothes, hastily re-dressing, sheathing her knife, putting distance between them as he began talking

"Ruth, it's all right! It's all right, it's okay—it was better than okay—but listen. I know you have to return to your camp, I have to go back to the Synt before I'm discovered, and I'm going to have to come up with a hell of a story… maybe something about fugue states, start a study… anyway, I'm sorry, I'm stalling. Listen. Just listen a minute, all right? There's something I have to tell you. Something you need to know, before we…"

She was fully dressed, and he was still on the floor, shirtless, vulnerable. He wanted to tell her a thousand things, but he had shattered their sweet brief scene together and everything was already going to hell. She stood apart from him, looking at him with suspicion, and—he hated seeing this in her expression—regret.

"What do I 'need to know'?"

"You told me that you did not want me to mention your father," he said, watching her stiffen at the mention of him. "And I shared with you everything that I could, without bringing him up. But you won't understand how the core of Heaven works, you won't know how the Syn world really came to be and continues to operate, if I don't tell you the truth about your father. About what really happened to Nathan Fell."

Her voice was a flat sheet of ice. "What about him."

"You were told that he died, when his synch failed. That he was brain-dead. But that was a lie. There were only two people who knew that after his procedure, he did not experience brain death. Just Hess and me—"

"Three people," she said, unexpectedly interrupting him. Something passes across her face. "I… I remember a doctor, when I was very young, who said that he might not have died in his procedure. That she could not confirm his brain death—"

"Kansal," Derek said, verifying the name. He stood, grabbed his shirt, began buttoning it as he talked. "Yes. Yes, she wasn't in there the whole time but she came in at the end, so you're right, she might know something too. She's definitely a loose end that Hess is still trying to tie up, but she didn't have all the information, she only knew that he didn't die right then. She didn't know what happened next."

Ruth looked at him, a new emotion on her face. Fear. He took a step toward her, and she didn't retreat. He spoke as quickly as possible, his words tumbling out like an avalanche of rocks, crushing them both:

"It was all on rails after that procedure. Everyone believed the reports of your father's death, there was the right paperwork, an obituary, we named some buildings after him. But he didn't die, Ruth. His brain didn't die. It started… it started working overtime. It was like the procedure shut down his body, but jump-started his already amazing mind. He was still alive, and his brain lit up all the monitors like it was Christmas. Hess swore me to secrecy, kept everyone else in the dark as we figured out how to do it, but he figured it out. *We* figured it out. How to use his brain, which was not dead but alive and functioning at an entirely new level. We figured out how to use him to keep building the world he wanted. Ruth, he is how it all works. How we all became what we are. Nathan Fell's brain is what powers the core of Heav—"

And then, like the flipping of a switch, Derek Abelson's eyes flickered, and he dropped dead at Ruth's feet.

B ACK WHEN HESS HAD PLACED a failsafe in Derek Abelson's brain—a little code he'd quietly embedded during a routine systems check—he didn't know what it would look like when the failsafe alerted him to its use. After all, it would be a one-time thing.

In the old world, Hess believed in insurance. Life insurance, health insurance, car insurance, homeowner's insurance. He was devoted to precautions, in general. What he could not insure through external means, he insured in other ways. Copying every important file. Minimizing risk by expecting it, and working around it. Derek Abelson was an obvious risk.

He was the only one who knew that Patient X was Nathan Fell. That all of Heaven relied on the brain of the cyborganics master architect. Hess knew that this level of information meant a zero level of blind trust. He needed insurance. And so Hess designed the failsafe.

It was a simple but lethal program, quietly embedded deep within Derek, hidden behind a million other files and folders and applications in his brain. It was an autonomous and silent system, not reliant on the Heaven network, operable even without a full charge, no need for Hess or anyone else to push a proverbial red button to deploy it. It was a bomb set to detonate automatically if the code to set it off was detected. If ever Abelson spoke aloud these words, within seconds of each other, the failsafe would be alerted:

Nathan Fell / Alive / Heaven / Core / Brain / Power

A simple enough set of words to avoid placing too closely together, if one knew that their utterance was a death sentence.

This failsafe overrode privacy settings. It overrode internal revival systems. It overrode *everything*. It had only one function, but that function was hard-wired. It would work only once. It would be needed only once—or, hopefully, not ever. Abelson was useful, and Hess didn't necessarily *want* him dead.

But if ever he shared that information, spoke those words, no matter where he was or how offline he seemed to be, his fate was sealed.

It would appear to be an aneurysm. Like an aneurysm, it would be an unseen, unknown predator lurking in his brain. Waiting to attack. And like the worst of aneurysms, it would cause an immediate hemorrhage in his brain, killing him instantly. Even with no knowledge of the bomb in his brain that might be triggered by loose lips, Derek was smart enough to know not to ever mention anything about Nathan Fell's true fate. The cold war he and Hess waged went on without active battle.

In the years since Hess installed the insurance program, it lay
dormant. Hess, however, was not a believer in loyalty or liability.
Every time Derek went in for examinations and augmentations,
Hess quietly slipped into the room for the procedure, taking a
glance for himself, ensuring his little insurance policy was still in
place. It always was; still pristine. Unused.

Until that morning, when Hess received a small alert.

It was an automatic message, containing very little information, nothing that would make sense or convey meaning to anyone
but Hess. It was triple-encrypted nonetheless:

> FAILSAFE DEPLOYED
> STATUS: SUCCESSFUL
> RECORDED TRIGGER STATEMENTS
> [ATTACHMENT]

Heaven and Hell. The bastard finally did it.

Without a moment of mourning for Abelson, Felix downloaded the audio file and listened to the words that triggered the deto-
nation. Capturing what Derek had said in the end was important,
obviously; it would inform Felix as to how much was let slip before the bomb went off in his brain, and perhaps even yield clues
as to who was now in possession of the information.

Felix replayed Derek Abelson's final, damning words, caught
mid-sentence and ending mid-sentence as the program predicted
the final word and sprang into action:

> *"...his brain, which was not dead but alive and func-
> tioning at an entirely new level. We figured out how to
> use him to keep building the world he wanted. Ruth, he
> is how it all works. How we all became what we are.
> Nathan Fell's brain is what powers the core of Heav—"*

Hess listened to it again and again, growing numb. He had to hear it several times to confirm, though the revelation was evident in the very first listening. The recording was clear, uncorrupted.

Derek Abelson had shared this information with someone named Ruth.

Surely not Ruth Fell. Surely not...

If that girl was still alive, and now knew the truth about her father, Hess might have a real problem on his hands.

LIMBO 2045

CHAPTER 54: JORGE

"ABELSON IS DEAD," Hess announced matter-of-factly to his assistants.

Kennedy let out a sharp cry, like a kicked kitten. Jorge kept his expression neutral, though his heart thudded in his chest. A small internal warning went off, alerting him to elevated blood pressure. He quickly dismissed the notification.

"The Originals assassinated him," Hess said, and Jorge knew he was lying.

"Originals?" Kennedy gaped, stupid, terrified. "How...?"

"He went willingly," Hess said, eyes darting back and forth as he reviewed an internal file. "His captor was someone he met, decades ago. Ruth Fell."

Jorge's stomach clenched, especially when Hess immediately appeared to regret sharing that actual sliver of truth. Ruth Fell was still alive. So the resistance was still ongoing.

Thank God.

"I thought she was dead," Kennedy said, distraught. "Ruth Fell. Jesus. Do you think she... I mean, should valuable staff be worried that we might be, er, at risk?"

Valuable? You? Fat chance, asshole.

Even as he dismissed Kennedy's fear, Jorge realized he couldn't write it off. Hess and his close associates were obvious targets. Jorge himself might be a target. He imagined being taken by Original rebels, forced to betray the Synthetic world, finally being free from Hess...

Maybe I should paint a giant target on my back.

"I'm going to meet with the Council," Hess said. "You'll meet with the media team. Keep it simple. 'Unfortunate circumstance. No security breach. Taken hostage when off-site—'"

"Do we know that's all true?" Jorge interrupted.

"Yes," Hess snapped.

"How?" Jorge knew he was pissing off his boss, but he could not will himself to care.

"I'm sorry, Jorge, were you suddenly given level-seven security clearance? No? Then all you need to know, and all the media needs to hear, is there's no cause for panic. But I do want you to mention that the primary suspect is Ruth Fell."

"Should we say anything... nice?" Kennedy chimed in, meekly. "About Derek?"

Hess blinked, uncomprehending. "What?"

"Some mention of how he helped pioneer our technology, and—"

"Derek wasn't a pioneer," Hess spat. "He held on to coattails, and then died like an idiot in the woods. Don't waste time memorializing him—" Then he stopped short, and added: "You should mention that he was senior Synt staff. A pillar of the community. Assassinated by rebel maniac Ruth Fell. But don't paint him out to be more than what he was. Understood?"

When Kennedy nodded, Hess shot a warning look toward Jorge, then left.

"Shit," Kennedy exhaled. He looked at Jorge, evidently hoping for at least a moment of camaraderie. "I mean, *shit*, right?"

"Let's get the brief over with," was all Jorge replied, ignoring Kennedy's crestfallen face.

Jorge sent a message to the media team, requesting an emergency meeting in half an hour in the Nathan Fell Memorial Conference Room. He received an instant reply. It was too quick—no one on the media team could have reviewed and responded instantaneously.

Seeing the note float before his eyes, invisible to his co-worker, Jorge realized it was a new thread. Unrelated to the media message, although overlapping. Triple-encrypted; as soon as he deciphered it, it disappeared. But the words, even when erased, jumped up and down in his mind:

> *Do you like your job, Jorge?*
> *Do you like your boss?*
> *Your warden?*
> *If not, we should meet. Second message to follow.*

It took everything he had to keep his breath even, his heartbeat steady. Was this a message from some Originals, gambling that Hess's peons might not be his biggest fans? How the hell would anyone—*anyone*—know he thought of Hess as his warden? He waited with bated breath, staring at nothing, living for the promised second message.

"Jorge? We have to go to the media meeting," Kennedy said.

Jorge sat through the media meeting, delivering the prescribed lies tonelessly. After the meeting, Jorge plugged into Heaven, checking and re-checking before doing so to make sure his public logs were clean, free from any trace of the first message. He felt obsessive-compulsive, scrubbing and scrubbing his mind like dirty fingernails, washing and rinsing and washing and rinsing and still fearing an unseen but incriminating speck he somehow missed.

By nighttime, there was still no second message.

He plugged in, hoping an alert might jolt him from the dreamless non-sleep of his overnight charge, but none did.

He set out at five for his morning run around the Synt. No message.

It was while he was in the shower, rinsing off the sweat from his seven miles before sunrise, that the promised second message finally arrived.

He slipped on the wet ceramic floor of the tub, narrowly avoiding cracking his head open in his excitement. Soap still clinging to him, water streaming down his back, he hastily grabbed a towel as he decrypted the missive.

> *Today. Noon. Lunch at cafeteria. Sit at the third table from the east wall.*
> *An end seat. Face the food bar.*

As soon as he untangled the code enough to reveal the message, it was gone.

His morning dragged, each minute between him and noon dawdling painfully. Kennedy seemed to slow the time down further with his dumb questions and intermittent lamentations about Abelson, who he'd barely known. Jorge kept his head down, showing no additional emotion in his golden eyes, quietly counting the seconds.

At ten to noon, he left for lunch. He took the staff elevator to the basement level, the only remaining cafeteria operating in the building. There used to be seven full-service cafeterias, back when all staff lived on-site. These days, very few staff members elected to eat in the windowless basement cafeteria. Hess still ate there, because it was conveniently located, and also because his wife would never be caught dead there. But he ate at odd, irregular intervals. The likelihood of him being there at noon was low. It was a brilliant meetup, feeding in the belly of the beast. Hiding in plain sight. Strategic, but still bold.

Jorge shifted into private mode, not an unusual move over lunch. He made his way through the nearly-empty line. It was Southern Supper day, and while he rolled his eyes at the stupid theme, he immediately began filling his tray with collard greens, macaroni and cheese, and a golden-brown chicken leg that all looked delicious. Then he slid into an end seat at the third table from the eastern wall. There was no one else at his table, or any nearby table. As directed, Jorge faced the food bar. As each person went through the line, he wondered: *Is it him?*

The man with the braided silver beard, old for having synched— feeling trapped in this age of preserved youth? Or, there—the younger man, strong, muscular, training for combat? Most Syns aren't so aggressively fit…

"Don't turn around."

Jorge froze, muscles tensing, organs vibrating. He was almost embarrassed that he was surprised at the voice of the person behind him. The distinctly *female* voice.

"Southern Supper day," she chuckled. She was seated at the table behind him, back-to-back, nearly touching. So close he could hear her soft inhalation of breath between words. "I want to hate it, but I love the damn specials. Greens, fried chicken, and Lord, this macaroni and cheese. Just like home. I also love it when the music kicks in. Eats up all the sound, so anything said in private mode also won't be overheard. And me talking to you just looks like me singing along. Isn't that convenient?"

Jorge had not even heard the music, but as he tuned in, there it was—Loretta Lynn singing about being a coal miner's daughter. Old world Southern music piping through the cafeteria, protecting them.

"Now listen, Mr. Marquez. Us meeting like this is a one-time deal, and the offer I'm about to make you expires as soon as it's made. You're in a very interesting position, ground zero for everything the director is doing. I also think you have a lot of reason to resent the director. So tell me: Do you hate your job? One word answers. We can't both be singing."

Jorge tried to move his mouth as little as possible, exhaling: "Yes."

"Good. Take a bite of this chicken. Looks better for the camera. And it's really damn delicious. Good. Good. Keep eating, talking with your mouth full makes it harder to see when you're talking. Here's my offer—fair warning, the risk will be high, the pay's literally nothing, but if we do this thing right, we're gonna destroy this whole world."

Here she paused. She slurped her sweet tea, dragging it through the straw mercilessly. Then she began to sway. He could feel the movement. She practically sang her final question.

"So. Are you in?"

His answer was immediate: "Yes."

"Good," she said. He heard her pick up her tray. "Pleasure lunching with you, Mr. Marquez. You're about to start hearing from me frequently. Keep your head down, now. Join the clean plate club. And don't try to get a glimpse of me. Safer for both of us if you never do."

And with that, she hummed herself away, and was gone.

CHAPTER 55: RUTH

R UTH BARELY MADE IT BACK to the basecamp, sobbing like a child as she hiked through the woods, clutching her pack, sometimes stopping to vomit. Though she had pulled no trigger, taken no steps to harm him, she knew the man had died because of her. The man who had been willing to help them, who could have made a difference. She mourned the loss of him as an individual, and as an asset to the cause.

She knew she should be more upset about the big-picture impact than her own stupid infatuation. She barely knew him. And yet, she had connected with him more quickly than with anyone she'd ever met. There was something about him. Something that felt like destiny.

She tripped, twice, on her return to her people. This never happened to the sure-footed Ruth. She hated the weakness and disorientation she felt, the shame, and the absolute lack of clarity, moral and otherwise. When she managed to rip her thoughts away from one recollection of Derek Abelson, his smooth hands and nervous charm, her thoughts pinballed into another dark corner, where he was trying to tell her about her father, right before his life ended.

Something about her father still being alive. Being central to the whole Syn enterprise. She wished she knew what he was talking about; she felt certain that what Derek told her about her father was more important than anything else scrawled onto the glaring yellow legal pad.

When she finally reached the old office building in Connecticut, bedraggled and exhausted, she was spotted by Helena Garrison, the night's appointed lookout. Catching sight of Ruth, Helena hurried to her side. As soon as her tribeswoman's arms were around her, Ruth's legs gave out. She collapsed heavily on the older woman. Ruth's ankle, twisted in her second fall, was swollen and screaming. Her throat was dry, her whole being hollow.

"Sweet girl," Helena said, kissing her cheek, half-dragging her toward the building. Ruth was grateful for her old neighbor and friend. She had a stupid and infantile desire to crawl into Helena's lap, tell her everything, cry and cry until she felt something other than loss. But instead, it was Helena's sad duty to inform Ruth that while she was away, while her own tragedy had transpired, tragedy had also struck their little band of survivors.

Sophie Fell had passed away.

Too tired and broken to care about seeming weak, Ruth began trembling. She opened her mouth, and at first no sound came out, but then a wail rose from her and filled the darkened sky. Her keening summoned everyone, and they flocked to her, hugging and sobbing.

When Howard emerged, very last of all, he looked so old and weak that Ruth nearly did not recognize him. The tall man was suddenly gaunt, and looked so lost—not lost in a wave of dementia, but lost because his own beloved compass had been taken. His true north was gone. Ruth clung to her uncle, fierce love and rage and guilt coursing through her. She would never forgive herself for being gone when her aunt slipped away from them.

The next morning, Helena gathered everyone for the funeral. Always an accomplished pianist, Helena had once aspired to be a composer. With little access to instruments, save a flute carved for her by Howard Fell, music was less and less a part of Helena's life. But that bleak morning, she stood before her people and gave a brief prelude to the service:

"I think… it is important, it is a sacred obligation, for us to recall our loved ones. Each loss is a loss felt in our hearts and worldwide. I have written a song… a song that will be rewritten, over and over, as the lyrics are adjusted for each life the song honors."

And with that, she sang the first of the story-songs; an elegy for Sophie Eisen Fell.

The story-song began with the words of the Song of the Original Resistance, then lifted and soared, plunged and rose again as it became something new and old and sacred:

> Standing here, I almost see
> The girl I was, the crone I'll be
> Blessing of age, the passing of time
> Teaching us all, profane and sublime
> We will never relent, we will never rely
> Thus we will live. And thus we will die.

> Thus Sophie Fell lived.
> Thus Sophie Fell died.

Sophie Fell was born Sofia Eisen
She never met a stranger
We were all potential friends
This trait truly defined her
Until the very end.

She married her beloved Howie
And their children numbered eight
Six she bore, two more she claimed.

The door to her home was always open
Her heart, too, was always open
To anyone in need
To all eight of her children
To her beloved Howard.

Without her, the world is quieter
There is less laughter now,
and what once was open...

There may have been more words intended for this story-song, but Helena's voice gave out. She sobbed. Everyone joined her in the sobs, and humming, repeated the tune. Memorizing it. Committing to it. Knowing that each of them, in turn, would have a story-song sung for them.

They laid Sophie to rest behind the office building, souls cracking afresh as each knew that her grave would go unvisited, as soon as they fled this place.

Four months after Sophie went into the earth, Ruth still inhabited a world of ghosts. She was haunted by day, and tortured most of all by night. She saw visions of Sophie, of Derek, and most chillingly of her father. While the other ghosts were heartbreakingly sweet and swift in their visits, her father was a lingering monster stalking her nightmares. He would appear from the abyss. He would smile at her, but in place of his teeth were needles; syringes, dripping chemicals. He moved toward her, slowly, to pierce her with the pinpricks of his teeth and draw her into his world. She wanted to flee, but her feet were rooted to the spot and he came slowly, so slowly, but relentlessly and inevitably, his teeth gleaming and sharp—

She would wake screaming, sweating, fiercely determined. But determined to do what? She didn't know. She only knew that her hatred for her father had been stoked. It went from a slow-burning ember to a raging wildfire within her. Until she destroyed the world he created, she would not rest. She would not know peace.

"Shh, Ruthie," came a gentle voice at her side. Rachel. Yet another ghost—but this one still breathing. She placed a cool hand on Ruth's hot forehead. "It's all right."

"It's not," Ruth gasped. "It's not."

Rachel traveled her hand from Ruth's forehead, to her forearm, and then, achingly gently, to Ruth's taut stomach.

"It was the man who died, wasn't it? Your hostage? Derek?"

Stubborn tears filled Ruth's eyes, spilling out against her will. She was unable to hide anything anymore. Not her emotions. And not her pregnancy. She nodded, wondering how long her twin had known, and kept quiet out of respect.

"I've known for a month or two," Rachel said, answering the unasked but obvious question. "Probably almost as long as you've known. I was hoping you'd tell me. Ruthie, everyone else will know soon. You're showing. And this is something wonderful. It will bring hope. Look at how everyone adores my Cal."

"Adores him," Ruth whispered, "and mourns for him."

"Adores him," Rachel said firmly. "As your son or daughter will be adored."

"This should never have happened," Ruth said, trembling. "The chemicals in the water. My age. All the trouble you had. And just once, just once, with that man—who—who died—"

She collapsed into her sister's arms, crying for everything that had been, that was, that would be. Even as the new life grew within her, Ruth's guilt and grief relentlessly reminded her that death was all around.

Nearly nine months after her night with Derek Abelson, Ruth Fell gave birth to their son. He was born in a field, without the assistance of medical technology. He was born against all odds, emerging with a triumphant scream. He looked like his father, and sounded like his mother.

She named him Ere, for her love of all that was. All that she wished she could give him.

A wandering tribal life would be all her son knew of existence. He would have no home, attend no school. But he would have a village that adored him. Rachel was right—the entire tribe was buoyed by the spindly baby boy. Howard's eyes found a new light, and he recovered a bit of his former charisma. Cal was the most enamored of the new arrival. The massive toddler told anyone and everyone that it was his job to keep his baby cousin safe.

Ruth enlisted Howard's help in educating the boys. His memory for things long past was far better than his memory of what he ate for breakfast, and teaching the boys seemed to invigorate him. Howard wanted to inspire them, teach them that they had the ability to make things better; Ruth disagreed, not wanting to feed them false hope. Howard, Rachel, and Ruth were united in their decision to keep Ere and Cal in the dark about their grandfather, Nathan Fell. Who he was. And what he might have become—a terrifying question mark that still loomed over them all.

To her own surprise, Ruth found moments of joy in motherhood. She loved her boy with a ferocity unlike anything she had ever known. She would fight for him, she would kill for him, but as the years went on she sometimes even found herself doing something more extraordinary: she found that she could hope for him.

She also sang to him.

She converted the old war ballad, the Song of the Original Resistance, into a lullaby. She always kept her rough voice low, softening and sweetening it by never singing above a whisper. She infused the lyrics with her love for him, her pain for him, the Original pride they shared:

> *Standing here, I almost see*
>
> *The girl I was, the crone I'll be*
>
> *The blessing of age, the passing of time*
>
> *Teaching us all, profane and sublime*
>
> *We will never relent, we will never rely*
>
> *Thus we will live. And thus we will die.*

THE SYNT
2062

MAKING IT ALL THE WAY from the wilderness into the Syn girl's bedroom was an exercise in luck, skill, and bizarre happenstance. Especially once Cal made it to Central City. After exiting the tree-clearing ship on which he had stowed away, he navigated the strange, scentless metal passageways from the adjacent hangar and into the main complex of the Synt.

Once inside the main compound, Cal was acutely aware of just how much he stood out. Knowing the importance of blending in to his surroundings, he did his best to disappear and found he could not. Eyes flicked in his direction; he knew that soon he would attract overt attention rather than subtle interest. He also noted that the fast-moving Syns teeming from passageway to passageway all had access to some sort of coded system, blinking or swiping or pressing panels to gain entry.

Human-machines blinking at other machines. Freaks.

He didn't know how these systems worked, but he knew what mattered: he wasn't part of it. He couldn't fake it, couldn't blend the way he might melt into a forest while hunting. In nature, he could find a way—but not in this synthetic landscape. From the stale air to the unnaturally cold temperatures to the Syn methods of communication through silent exchange of electricity rather than words, it was all impenetrable, inhuman—outside his wheelhouse.

But for some reason, though she had spent the past nearly-two decades shitting on him, Lady Luck was in his corner that night. He backed up against a wall in a corridor, contemplating his next move, and heard a soft click as the wall gave way behind him. He had inadvertently found an unsecured exit door, marked SERVICE EXIT, and managed to open it. Not knowing what would happen next, he slipped outside.

Cal greedily sucked in a deep breath of actual outdoor air and assessed his situation. It was dark outside now, and that was an advantage; one cheerful little pro bobbing along in a sea of cons. Eying the structure and determining that this must be where Ever lived, Cal knew he had to get in. Going through security and navigating the interior would be impossible. Scaling the exterior wall and hoping that, in the dark, he would not be immediately spotted by monitors—well, it wasn't the best plan ever, but it was all he had.

And thus the next leg of this journey began, with a flying leap toward the building, aiming for as high a point on the wall as possible, and specifically for a small shadow that looked like it might provide something firm to grasp. Cal's tired body smacked hard against the unforgiving steel wall, rattling his teeth and setting off an unpleasant ringing in his ears, but his right fingers did wrap around something solid, while his left fingernails dug near-uselessly against the wall. Still, the object in his right hand was a better grip point than he had anticipated. Swinging himself into a slightly better position, he squinted in the darkness, trying to make out to what exactly he was clinging. It was black, hard, but had a clear round panel on one side. The clear round panel was made of glass. He looked at it, cocking his head. A small red light clicked on, startling Cal and nearly making him lose his hold on the object.

A weapon.

Instinct took over as battle-ready Cal's left hand sailed swiftly away from the wall. He slammed his thumb into the round glass eye of the weapon, shattering it. There was a small beep, and the red light clicked off.

Easily subdued, he thought, with no small amount of self-satisfaction. Craning his neck up, he saw that this shattered eye was not alone. Its brethren rested above him, one every meter or so; as he watched, the nearest one made a small beep, a red light clicked on—and the eye pointed itself toward Cal.

Eliminate the enemy was Cal's first thought.

Use the little metal bastards' carcasses was his second.

He hurtled toward the wall, catapulting himself upward, grabbing for the next red light. He caught it. Smashed it. Heard the next one click on. And kept climbing, little metal-bastard carcass by little metal-bastard carcass.

Cal glanced around quickly. He was several stories up now—high enough that were he to fall, broken bones were inevitable and fatal injury quite likely. But at this level, the sheer wall was no longer steel alone. There were intermittent panes of glass. Windows.

And just a short distance above him and to his right, a light teased from one of the window. Like a beacon, beckoning him. Lady Luck—and maybe another lady—urged him on.

Cal took another flying leap, and another, aiming on this last jump not for the metal-bastard straight above him, but for the window up and to the right. And before he knew it, he was pressed against the glass, and there she was.

Ever.

Her brow was furrowed, face troubled, but she was made no less beautiful by the cloudy expression. She was a lake after rain. She was a silver sky. And oh, God, that tiny silky little dress, showing off her petite body—

Cal flushed hot, and tapped at her window, as gently as he could. He did not want to frighten her. He needed her to let him in. The girl scrambled to her feet, drew the silken garment she wore tighter around her. When she saw him, her eyes went wide, but she did not scream or retreat. She walked toward him without fear, and when she spoke, her voice was commanding.

"Identify yourself," she said.

He'd hoped against hope that she would know him, but did not allow his spirits to sink. He kept his voice steady, calm. He spoke slowly, focusing on his words almost as much as he had to focus on not plunging to his death if he lost hold of the window-sill. "You may not remember me, Ever. We met only briefly, when you and Ere–"

Her eyes went wide. "Who's Ere?"

Cal startled. He was about to ask if her question was some sort of joke, but she looked genuinely inquisitive and somewhat uneasy.

Who's Ere?

What the hell does she mean by that?

He knew this was the same Syn woman, the one his cousin had loved and lied about and betrayed his people for—and yet somehow she had no knowledge of Ere at all.

Is it faulty wiring? Some sort of mechanical glitch, messing with her memory?

Cal didn't like those implications. He resented being reminded of her synthetic status.

Then the breeze outside kicked up; his left foot shifted and he nearly swayed away from the building. Clutching at the sill and picturing broken bones on one side of this equation and Ever on the other, he forced his stupid skinny cousin from his mind and hoped Ever would continue to do the same. Maybe she had some sort of totally normal human memory loss, maybe she'd never been as interested in him as he had been in her... whatever the reason, Cal wasn't going to second guess this unexpected turn of events. He decided to see it as a stroke of luck.

"He doesn't matter. He's just—nobody. He's not why I'm here."

"Why are you here?" Ever demanded.

She wasn't just pretty. She was fierce. Forceful.

Cal liked that.

"I'm here for you, Ever," he said honestly.

It must have been the right thing to say. She came to the window, pressed a button, and the pane slid aside. He heaved himself forward, wanting to ensure he landed in her room and not on the unforgiving pavement hundreds of feet below.

"Who are you?" she asked, looking up at him.

"My name is Cal," he said, mesmerized by her.

"Cal," she said, and gave a little skin-exposing shoulder shrug that nearly made him pass out. "Why don't you tell me a little bit about yourself?"

"Oh," Cal said, unprepared for this most basic of inquiries.

She laughed, fortunately amused at his idiocy.

"Well, let's start with… I mean, how the hell did you get here?"

How did I get here?

The question had been echoing in his own mind for so long. But that was then. This is now. He is here. In this moment. With this girl. And his only path is full steam ahead.

"It's a long story," he says, and smiles at her.

She smiles back. Takes a step toward him.

And then a dozen helmeted black-clad Syns burst through her door, throwing Cal to the ground. When he fights back, one of

them jams a sizzling weapon into his spine and he begins convuls-
ing, electric agony coursing through his entire body.

"No!" Cal dimly hears Ever screaming. "Stop!"

Her screams fade to a buzzing and to silence, as his world goes
from searing white-hot pain to a black expanse of nothingness.

ACKNOWLEDGMENTS

I spent a lot of ink on acknowledgments for the first book in this series... and will use at least as much when the final installment goes to print. In fact, I'm already working on the long and emotional essay of gratitude that will accompany the end of *Original Syn*.

For now I just want to thank you for continuing along this journey with me.

See you on the other side.

SYN & SALVATION

THE EPIC FINALE - COMING AUTUMN 2020

C AL WAKES WITH A START.

He is lying flat, restrained at his neck, wrists, and ankles. He struggles against the restraints for a moment, testing them without exhausting himself. They're solid. He doesn't cry out, since he knows he has no allies here. He instead goes still, conserving energy, and not wanting to give any further alert to whomever or whatever might be monitoring him.

He surveys the room as best he can. It is walled entirely in glass, which increases Cal's unease. He is on display. He can't turn his head enough to see what might be on the floor, nor to see past the glass walls. He also can't see where any door might be. He hears a sound behind him; his hands curl into fists and his whole body tightens, ready to fight.

Someone approaches the bed.

A man.

A Syn.

The man is slight, narrow of shoulder and chin, the sort of man Cal could easily dominate in a fair fight. He wears the same dark, sleek garb all Syns wear; his face is thin, his nose beaklike. When he sees Cal staring at him, his small green eyes go wide.

"You're awake," the Syn says, his voice somewhere between excited and fearful.

"Where am I?" Cal growls.

"The Synt," the man says, before giving a sort of irritated pout. He must have realized he was giving answers instead of procuring them, because he snipes quickly: "What is your name?"

Cal's initial instinct is to either keep his mouth shut or lie, but he's not sure what good it would do. A better strategy might be to provide a truthful answer to an innocuous question like this one and save the real resistance for down the road.

"Cal."

"Cal what?"

"Cal… Harper," Cal says, unaccustomed to including his surname in an introduction.

"Cal Harper," repeats the Syn, his gaze sliding oddly off to one side. "There is no record of any Original with that name who would be anywhere near your age. No close variant. It does not appear that you exist, Cal Harper."

"And yet here I am. What's your name, Syn?"

"You're supposed to be the one answering questions," says the thin Syn, his tone almost whiny. And then he relents: "Kennedy." He shakes his head, as if correcting himself, *stupid stupid*. He tries to regain conversational control. Cal clocks his insecurity, catalogs each weakness revealed. "Why are you here, Mr. Harper?"

"I don't know," Cal says, relatively honestly.

He was here to see Ever, yes. But why did she have to be a Syn? Why did his infatuation lead him into enemy territory? Why was he imprisoned in a glass box of a room? Why was he here in the existential sense?

"That's a lie—"

"I don't know," Cal repeats in a much louder bark, and the Syn flinches.

An easy scare. Good to know.

"Fine, if you won't tell me, we have other means of—" Kennedy abruptly cuts off mid-sentence, eyes going funny again. He mutters something; Cal can't quite make it out, but he's pretty sure he catches the word "prick" somewhere in there. Then the Syn turns on his heel and exits the glass box room.

Cal thrashes once, yells out: "Hey! HEY! Where the hell are you—"

Swish.

"Cal Harper."

Cal freezes. Someone else is in the room, not yet in his line of sight. Someone new. Someone Cal can already tell is far more dangerous; a true predator, not an easily startled little scavenger like the Syn called Kennedy.

"Let's make you a little more comfortable, what say?"

Cal tenses, preparing for the words of comfort to be a sly predecessor to some sort of assault or injection. Instead, the restraints at his neck, arms, and ankles snap back, releasing him. Rubbing his wrists, Cal sits bolt upright and turns to see his captor—though unbound, Cal is very aware that he is still caged.

The man is shorter than Cal would have predicted, but not as slight as Kennedy. He exudes a quiet power, his movements conveying lean muscle and sharp brain. Cal knows not to underestimate him. Releasing Cal, so casually and with such little fanfare, was a potent warning: *I am in control, and unafraid of losing my grip.*

The Syn and the Original study one another.

Cal takes a swift inventory of his captor's face: Fixed, sharp eyes; sallow olive skin; hair graying at the temples, indicating an older age than the average Syn without revealing any meaningful hint as to his actual number of years on earth.

"Allow me to introduce myself," the man says at last, in his own time, on his own terms. "My name is Felix Hess, and I am the Director here. But I believe you're less familiar with my work, and more familiar with my daughter Ever. Not *too* familiar, I hope."

Heaven and hell.

This man was Ever's father?

"Exactly how do you know my daughter, Mr. Harper?"

No one had ever called Cal "Mr. Harper" before. He was always simply *Cal,* or *cousin* or *nephew.* Hearing this formal, detached moniker makes Cal's mouth go dry. He tries to swallow before croaking a hoarse reply: "I don't… I don't really know her."

"And yet you were in her room. One doesn't accidentally scale several stories of any building, Mr. Harper, and certainly not this one. Who are you working with?"

"I am not… there was no one else with me. I came alone," Cal says honestly.

"We have gotten off on the wrong foot, Mr. Harper," Hess says abruptly, with an unnatural smile. "You, breaking into my building; me locking you in a holding room. Not exactly a warm introduction on either of our parts. Let's start over."

"Let's—what?" Cal asks, confused, trying to keep up.

"I am, first and foremost, a scientist," declares Felix Hess—which strikes Cal as an odd thing for a father to say. "We have fewer and fewer Originals in the incorporated sectors. You are much younger than the average Original. That intrigues me. I'd like to invite you to stay here at the Synthetic Neuroscience Institute of Technology for a time. As my guest. What do you say?"

"Guest."

Cal repeats the word flatly. He knows that no matter what, despite fake smiles and offers of hospitality, he is not a guest. He is this man's prisoner.

"Yes," Hess purrs. "I'd run a few tests while you're enjoying our accommodations. I can assure you, nothing too invasive—blood work here, bone scan there. Contribute to our working knowledge and some ongoing projects."

"And if I refuse?"

"Oh, Mr. Harper," says Hess, unapologetically. "That would be unfortunate. I'm really only offering you two options: Be my guest, or stay in this room, where Kennedy will check on you every few days. I highly recommend the route of invited guest rather than neglected animal."

Cal's mind races. The odds of him escaping from this room are low; security is tight and he has no idea how many more guards, alarms, or barriers stand between him and the outside world. And even if he escaped, what then? His aunt is dead, his traitor cousin fled, and all that remains of his once-proud tribe is a handful of elders shuffling toward their graves.

He came here to find Ever. Ever is still here. And Ever is still the goal.

"Guest," Cal growls.

"Excellent choice," Hess says, smiling a broad and empty grin. "I'll have one of my assistants take you to your new room. And just so we're clear—you will have many rules to abide by here, but one above all: Stay away from my daughter."

WL HOUSE BOOKS, an imprint of Homebound Publications, specializes in genre fiction: science fiction, fantasy, mystery, and thriller. Myth and mystery have haunted and shaped us since the dawn of language, giving wing and fleshy form to the archetypes of our imagination. As our past was spent around the fire listening to myths and the sounds of the night, so were our childhoods spent getting lost in the tangled branches of fables. Through our titles, we hope to return to these storytelling roots.

WWW.OWLHOUSEBOOKS.COM